Praise for Brad Nee...

YOU, ME, AND ULYSSE...

"Brad Neely is a sort of folk hero for aughts-internet weirdos who searched for absurd comedy on the web and found his tall-tale rap about George Washington's two sets of testicles. Now he viciously parlays his obsessions with warped American history into this genre-defying novel that's nearly impossible to describe or put down. A meat-grinder of untrue facts and truer than true facts with jokes so dense you read past them for three seconds before pausing to reflect on how much of a dummy you were to miss them the first time. What the fuck is this book? I don't know, but I love it."
—APRIL WOLFE, SCREENWRITER

"This is fucking brilliant. Buy it. Funniest book I've read since John Bolton's *The Room Where It Happened*."
—MIKE SACKS, AUTHOR OF *RANDY, PASSABLE IN PINK,*
PASSING ON THE RIGHT*, AND *STINKER LETS LOOSE!

"It's like discovering *Blood Meridian* typed neatly in the margins of your Gary Larson day calendar."
—TED TRAVELSTEAD, AUTHOR OF *THE PETRAEUS FILES* AND
CO-AUTHOR OF *SEX: OUR BODIES, OUR JUNK*

"The funniest and weirdest take on the story of Ulysses S. Grant, who for the very first time has been rendered interesting. Move over, all those other biographies I've never actually read."
— JASON ROEDER, FORMER SENIOR EDITOR OF *THE ONION* AND
AUTHOR OF *GRIEFSTRIKE! THE ULTIMATE GUIDE TO MOURNING*

"The poetic parody of *You, Me, and Ulysses S. Grant* hilariously cuts to the heart of America like Ken Burns and Robert Caro drunkenly trying to one-up each other. Brad Neely's ornate comedic voice is at its most confident, weaving a textured, ridiculous historical fiction that ends up looking a whole lot like the truth."
—JACOB OLLER, *PASTE* MAGAZINE

"Humor and history are words rarely uttered in the same breath but this genre-busting biography accomplishes the impossible, turning the life of Ulysses S. Grant into a fun and funny beach read."
—LEONARD MLODINOW, *NEW YORK TIMES*-BESTSELLING AUTHOR OF *SUBLIMINAL: HOW YOUR UNCONSCIOUS MIND RULES YOUR BEHAVIOR*

"This is what it would be like if Donald Barthelme were still alive and they taped an episode of Drunk History with him and just let the tape roll for 12 hours."
—KEVIN HYDE, *MCSWEENEY'S* CONTRIBUTOR

"I'm not even kidding when I say I think we should recall the Golden Record and select all/paste over everything we think we can bear to share about humanity with a copy of *You, Me, and Ulysses S. Grant*. Every single page, paragraph, and sentence of this encyclopedic, meta-satirical master-piece reads like a tectonic plate of mythic gems, each hysterically imbued so much life, lore, gore, war, mirth, and utter madness, it's hard to imagine how he made it fit all in one spine. Stand aside, ye Future Evil AI Stepkids of Twain, Swift, Pynchon, Joyce, and [whoever wrote those doorstops they based the *Harry Potter* movies on]—Brad Neely just whipped y'all's asses wearing nothing but his National Treasure-level brain."
—BLAKE BUTLER, AUTHOR OF *AANNEX, THREE HUNDRED MILLION*, AND *MOLLY*

"Brad Neely is funny as hell. His comic and surreal alternative biography of Ulysses S. Grant reads like an epic episode of *Drunk History* starring Thomas Pynchon. Get one copy of this hilarious and wise book for yourself, and one for your Civil War-buff dad."
—J. M. TYREE, AUTHOR OF *THE COUNTERFORCE*

"It took someone as wizard-brained as Neely to crack the code on making literature as spastically gleeful as watching your favorite cartoon. This book doesn't just make every other Grant biography obsolete, it renders History Itself an outmoded relic of the past."
—VERNON CHATMAN, WRITER AND PRODUCER OF *SOUTH PARK* AND *THE SHIVERING TRUTH*

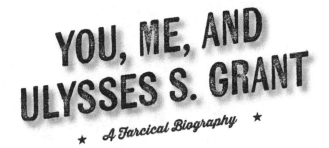

YOU, ME, AND ULYSSES S. GRANT

★ *A Farcical Biography* ★

Brad Neely

KEYLIGHT
B O O K S
AN IMPRINT
OF TURNER
PUBLISHING

KEYLIGHT BOOKS
AN IMPRINT OF TURNER PUBLISHING COMPANY
Nashville, Tennessee
www.turnerpublishing.com

You, Me, and Ulysses S. Grant

Copyright © 2024 by Brad Neely. All rights reserved.

This book or any part thereof may not be reproduced or transmitted in any form or by any means, electronic or mechanical, including photocopying, recording, or by any information storage and retrieval system, without permission in writing from the publisher.

This is a work of fiction. All the characters and events portrayed in this book are either products of the author's imagination or are used fictitiously.

Library of Congress Cataloging-in-Publication Data
Names: Neely, Brad, author.
Title: You, me, and Ulysses S. Grant : a novel / Brad Neely.
Description: Nashville : Keylight Books, [2024]
Identifiers: LCCN 2022049037 (print) | LCCN 2022049038 (ebook) | ISBN
    9781684429752 (hardcover) | ISBN 9781684429769 (paperback) | ISBN
    9781684429776 (epub)
Subjects: LCSH: Grant, Ulysses S. (Ulysses Simpson), 1822-1885—Fiction. |
    LCGFT: Biographical fiction.
Classification: LCC PS3614.E3455 Y68 2024 (print) | LCC PS3614.E3455
    (ebook) | DDC 813/.6—dc23/eng/20230124
LC record available at https://lccn.loc.gov/2022049037
LC ebook record available at https://lccn.loc.gov/2022049038

Printed in the United States of America

To
Laurie

Wars produce many stories of fiction, some of which are told until they are believed to be true.

—ULYSSES S. GRANT

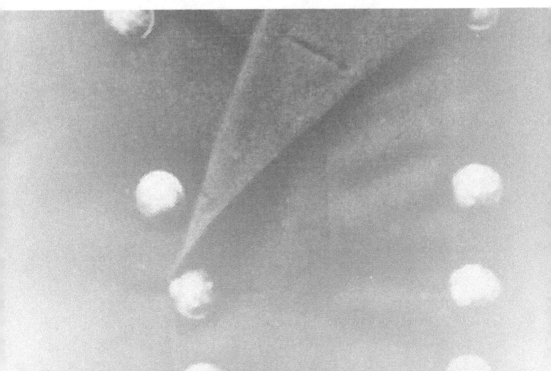

PART ONE

Prologue

HOW CAN WE KNOW A DEAD PERSON? HOW CAN WE KNOW A
living person? A lover? A rival? An enemy?

Dear Reader, we biographers know how.

Have you ever risked your body for love? Have you ever ruined a body
for power? Oh, you will, you will; together we will. This is a biography,
after all.

If done correctly, a sermon is a spell, and a spell is a sermon. If done to
perfection, the preacher, along with their parish, will transform as soon as
the chorus climaxes. A biography should do the same. This one does.

So, with the help of fiery muses, I cast such a spell here for *You and I*
to know the mind and body of this dead man. We shall inhabit him, Our
Host, Our Hero.

Dubious times call for obvious talk. Therefore, we shall talk in black
and white, good and evil, for I swear Our Hero is a good one. Each age
has its own Destined American Warrior Hero, emblematic of the best that
men can be in their time. And later ages have their perfect biographies of
such men. This is that.

How do you make an American? One third depression, one third anx-
iety, one third narcissism, and you shake like hell. Because in reality, the
American Dream is just to survive the American Reality. Yes, to avoid
the American Nightmare of ruin, we must keep dreaming that we might

simply survive this Biblical Wilderness. And as the millions of masterpiece paintings do convey, the land can be a beautiful sight, if you are fed. Yes, make no mistake, America is a danger zone with a range of wild within it: woods, desert, wet and not, hot and not, but always, *always* with wind and stars. Wind and stars. Wind and stars. Amen.

Look now, beyond that blue-black glass between us and the rest of the cosmos as this story turns the ever-expanding wads of stars into the sign of the Bull. Into Our Man, Ulysses.

He lived *here*, on the dirt below your feet. He felt the same wind, water, and worry as us. Like you, he knew what it meant to be a body in this life-or-death Wilderness of temptations. He was, like you, a fragile mind, shuffled up in skin with ears on it, eyes in it, a smeller, taster, feet, and fingers. Feel his time, with me, through him, as Our Hero once felt with his kit of bits. Get your own feelers out and spank up the blood so to bring in this tale's sense-datum with your own ripened, blushing body.

Imagine that hell-bent black-and-white Bull walking toward you, the camera. It is he, Grant, the Taurus, described aloft in those burning dots on the authoritative nothingness, in that twelve-pen zodiac zoo. Watch how he Taurus-ed hard 'round under our stars, 'round the map of this America as it was still being drawn up, 'round and 'round before he crashed down his bones into his marble corpse-closet for good.

You and I shall see those rounds: the horse-lording, the wife-loving, and the nation-saving of Ulysses as he "assumed the port of Mars" like ol' Harry Henry. *You and I* shall know more than the "fifty face," more than the war, more than his worn-out highlight reel. *You and I* shall witness his mass-murdering for the sake of good, as he triumphs over blatant evil. So, My Fellow American, sit back and relax nothing, for our history is re-beginning, as it always must . . .

Chapter 1

Ohio

1822–1839

AGES 0–17

L UCKILY, OUR LITTLE LAND-GOD'S SEED WAS SOWN IN THE
fertile shit of Ohio: home of Old Man Winter and his three underdeveloped siblings. Grant was born a year after Napoleon died. He grew up in the standard type of brown American town replete with river, road, rye, purple mountains, swollen clouds, and screaming woods. The town had a restaurant with rooms on it and a schoolhouse with mud up it.

Most were poor and suffered three-hundred-and-sixty-three days a year but otherwise sighed on the first day of spring and cried on Christmas. For Grant and his peers, summers used to end. Hurricanes had no legs and wouldn't crawl across the landlocked. Fires were never in season. Back then, one could drink from a creek without croaking. Animals were more than just colorful characters in kids' books; they actually lived and were mostly quiet. To every thing there was a season, and such things could buy clothing accordingly. But now? Oh, horrible. Now we must read the classics and weep, as if their descriptions of the world were just science fictions of speculated balance.

Ohio was considered way out West, having only recently cobbled together statehood a couple decades back. The East was the real America, and Westerners felt it. This town was loose and had a scrambling, scant local government, like all the fledgling communities popping up across the nation's newly bought or plundered territories. Once, by the banks of his favorite frog-catching river, Ulysses was shocked to find a light purple corpse bending the reeds down with heavy, hardened blood. Our Little Man alerted the officials, who, having a backlog of unsolved crimes, announced that they had finally found their mean man of many hats before hanging what was left of him on a newly made, budget-busting gallows. Things were looser out West.

Grant had a decent set of tiny tan cotton clothes, but a miserable pair of shoes so old they were caked solid in an icing of sweated salt, and they had to be clacked together to break their molds like the tops of two awful crème brûlées. His friends were in the same boat, if not worse, with their feet tied up in bags of burlap with yarn around the top. Ulysses and the kids he ran with were all Hucks, no Toms. It was a sweet gang: Janky on club, Frankie on sharp stick, Dee-Dee on spikes, Tomboy Jane on noose, and Grant with a handful of sand for the stink eyes. Together they'd eat the up-treat, sugar; and they'd sip the down-drink, mash. They had guns, like all Americans. It was a life of weapons. Knives. Traps. Gunpowder. Gunpowder balloons. Cages. Nets. Shackles. Chains. Analog everything. But always guns. Always blood. Meat. Heat. Cold. Weather-worn apricot cheeks. You bring the guns? Ticks. Fleas. Chiggers. Trick guns. A little water. Snakes in said water. Snake guns. Caves and graves. Dying folks were promised they'd be buried with their favorite gun, but the surviving family would instead send them into the earth holding a stick, for there was just too much shooting to do.

A terrible student with a disdain for authority, Young Grant never applied himself at the schoolhouse where he and his pals would look up bad words in the dictionary, like "pulse," "throb," "erect," "loose," "soft," "wet," and "buttfuck." Public education has always needed help in America.

But the gang mostly just ran around shooting while pretending to be their heroes.

"I'm Boone!"

"I'm Bowie!"

"I'm Bumppo!"

"I'm Crockett!"

"I'm Kit!"

Like any kid, Grant loved to inhabit a hero, to play-walk as if in the heroic body, in the outfit, in the life. Kit Carson was his favorite, and he'd play him his own way, making the role of the pioneering adventurer into a perfected version, leaving out unsavory facts, and mixing in cooler attributes from other legendary heroes. Kit with retractable claws was a popular combo. It was the universal, one-sided, non-consensual playtime merging of a kid and a hero across time. Often a way to play a hero becomes bigger than the way they were, especially if one takes the time to write it down . . .

Despite being part of a gang of rascals, Our Little Bull was introverted, slow to words, and quick to feelings. He was empathetic enough to pick up on the world's distaste for the empathetic, which led him to snuff out his own compassionate sparks. He had seen how outward displays of compassion could get you crucified. And yet he'd secretly daydream about a life free from want, where a woman might touch him and touch him and touch him alone in a home that was all their own. Might he ever know such a "she of tranquility"? Ah.

Ulysses was the kind of redhead who's often brown-headed in the right inside light. He had freckles, uneven brows, and a slicked-back hairstyle that went like a little cape behind the ears when wet, but went puff-a-fluff back there most of the dry times. He liked chunky woven belts, had graduated from booties to boots, and had kept the shirt-buttons open up top since his ninth birthday.

No matter the age, he was short, light, and tight. In a word, a jockey. You gotta do any "it" often to be good at it often. And Young Grant did horses that way. From the beginning, he was better with them than with people. Even as an infant in a frilly teal onesie, he loved to crawl around the dangerous legs of famous horses in the red-white tents of traveling circuses, his crying quieted only when he was sat upon the steaming backs of the steeds by those who were then not thought to be incautious parents.

Horses were his thing. It seemed when he'd learn anything else in life, he'd soon unlearn it, and then have to relearn it again in a never-ending cycle. But horses stuck. And the affinity was reciprocal. He could ride better than anyone. His style was more intuitive. Instinctual. In the moment. He never trusted presets or defaults and knew you had to flip shit to manual and go by feel.

Ulysses had an uncommon communication with the creatures. A whicker or a whinny was to him as thorough as any sworn testament made up of this godawful language. He couldn't explain it; his body just knew, and he allowed this to become his most important way of knowing. Grant was the dog whisperer, but for horses. No one in the history of man and beast has been better with a beast than this man. He was like Adam: master over the garden. Except, unlike Adam, he didn't have sex with the animals.

Ulysses had many a steed. There was Zog, and Torg, Efforgroz, and Thargoth, to name a few. He knew his tombstone would be decorated with all of them, every horse, even those he didn't personally know. His tombstone would also be in the shape of a horse; his casket, somehow a saddle. Ever see a bull ride a horse? Yes, you have, right now, as Little Man Grant prances his steed on the palm of your mind's hand.

Everyone came to know him as "that quiet horse boy." Ulysses and his pals would go on riding sessions, mastering tricks, and drinking two liters. His gang agreed that he could ollie highest and do the best—I don't know, saddle stands? Yet to his astonishment the rich kids always got the horse-riding trophies over him because their dads had bought the judge, had bought the best horse, had bought the best hay, or had bought lessons from Arabian textbook teachers. The rich boys with horsing tutors would get puff-piece writeups about them in *Horse Lord Weekly Magazine*. Grant grit his neglected teeth at these profiles which included engravings of the rich boys in their five-piece dandy fits, their hair smoothed down with the finest ambergris grease, their eyelids shiny and low. These richies had real smiles and promising futures, which sprang forth from their unworried minds. The magazines and papers lied, saying these damn dandies were supposedly better at horses than Grant. Like Kensington, Carrington, or Vanderpump. Like X, Y, or Lee . . .

Robert E. Lee was a hot-shit young man who rode horses in Virginia back East. He constantly got writeups and was recently engraved marrying George Washington's grandkid or some unbelievable bullshit. There he was, Lee, eating crumpets and inheriting the nation's dad's cufflinks. Of Lee and his class, Grant would say "These richies don't ride from the bestial heart. I don't want to prove to them I can ride without sloshing my tea. I want to show the world that I can ride up a goddamn pine tree while shooting three guns."

That's the thing about the salt of the earth: they're salty. But the local rich kids would display their scrunched-up faces when witnessing the unorthodox riding of Ulysses. They'd cackle, the chortlers, saying "You'll never be horse-famous. You'll never go to a good school, horse-based or not!"

The chips had fallen, and one big stinker chip had got stuck on Grant's shoulder. Most said he didn't have what it took to be as good as the best. They thought he over-rode the horses, never keeping it simple.

"Just do it how it's supposed to be done!" they'd sigh.

It's like when people say you are a bad writer of biographies because of your purple prose and subjective interference, calling what you do an overwritten, postmodern, maximalist, pastiche trash-heap where every sentence is too tangled to simply read, every moment kept too conscious to fully immerse oneself in the story because there isn't any balance of plain, exact language, and that they were "bumped" by the uneven tones and moods, and "turned off" by the obsessive capitalizations, pun runs, mixed metaphors, bad taste, solipsisms, anachronisms, obfuscations, alliteration addiction, and overwrought, ornamental, overdone descriptions, often annoyingly playing with assonance. Well, what can I say, I was made in God's image, not in an editor's. We all know the sting of such lazy discrediting, I'm sure, Dear Reader. Young Grant did too, but he knew he was special. He believed the cruel slogan that "anyone could become anything in America," and he was banking on becoming a horse. If that didn't work out, then he'd become a horse lord, as he planned to someday run his own horse academy where he'd teach horses how to read dictionaries the fun way. He felt invincible, even if much of his own vincing of the world would have to wait.

At twelve, he was the youngest to compete at his first all-ages horse-riding competition. The course was surrounded by mockernut hickories and mocking hicks eating nuts. Everyone laughed at him. But the boy and horse attached, double-brained, Avatar-style, and they merged each other's sensory histories up to the now of the then. With baby fat flapping, Grant ran the obstacle course like an explosive cartoon, easily evading hidden tennis-ball guns. He and his steed were too fluid for the traps, stretching through the air over barricades, bandying elegantly over blockades, making mockery of the intended belligerence of the longest ditches. The rodeo clowns, paid to do their worst to the best, popped out of ivy hedges with the stupid tennis-ball guns. "They mock me," thought Our Besting Equestrian. His spite only fueled his abilities to work the horse as an extension of his own bodily limits as they symbiotically balanced on beams and eluded the spinning foam arms that had knocked most jockeys from their saddles into the watery pits. No, for Ulysses these dumb disrupters backfired when they hit him with their force, giving him a chance to spin in a continuous motion upon his rotating saddle so that he passed over the water-traps, upside down, mid-jump. Hell, while he was down there, he had a chance to clap up a palm full of water so that he could splash a bit on the back of his neck. He righted himself and, after a backflip-dismount, set out to laugh at the rest of the jokes before cartwheeling—hoof to hand—to land bang on the finish line before the clock could even catch up. The judges, in their bafflement, disqualified Ulysses for godliness, and they gave the podium spots to the son of a senator, the son of a banker, and the man with a gun (who was also a banker). Young Ulysses rode home in slow motion with the conciliatory sunset of honorable mention barely warming his backside. Later it was in all the papers, but those few who knew said they got it wrong.

Grant's father, Jesse Root Grant, rented a modest homestead with an adjacent field of discount crops. He was a new-school western-man with sweet ideas and a heart of mush who hoped to just make some money for his family before he ossified into useless soft rock like his dad had done before him. Jesse had deep shovel-cut eyes and white hair from birth. He was tall and slowly wobbled if not working or sleeping. His smile was his soul.

Jesse ran a tannery where he'd skin animals and sell their prepared hides to people in town who knew what to do with them. Deer, bear, cows—anything but horses—got turned into raw material. They'd sell the skin of any carcass once it was treated against decomposition. There were hides, which were smooth, and there were pelts with the furry stuff left on. Jesse tried his hand at hide-crafts. He once made his son a pair of moccasins, like his hero Kit wore, and Grant walked a mile in them, but gave them back. They just didn't feel like him. Later the boy would see the raw material of the hero-shoes recycled one more time into a set of special-order gloves for a small-handed woman.

So you must imagine that the Grant home was a carcass bazaar where anyone at any time could accidentally set eyes on an animal's dead eyes while its body sat or jerked in unimaginable states of dismemberment. The tannery was a Noah's Ark, if the ark were the last judgment for animals. The smell of freshly stripped skin, cooking blood, and undressed flesh was ever-present. This stood out in a time where even normal society was a world of stink. Even on a cold day, ordinary people's scents hit your deep nose with an acrid ache. The devil was the prince of the power of this air, for sure. Mouths, pits, scalps, crotches, and all those feet, anuses, and brains screamed for cleaning. It was customary to shit, or to dump shit, right in front of where you lived. The good things had shit on them. The nose had nowhere to hide; animal and human shit sat stacked on everything, every-where. And what's that over there? Why, just the cutest girl in the county, reeking by a fence, natural as can be . . .

In the skinning barn, Young Grant would help Jesse undress what God had spent good time clothing. The valuables had to be yanked free of fat and flesh, deloused, and de-ticked. Pelts and hides had to be degreased, then re-greased with the correct grease. The hides had to be de-haired be-fore undergoing a delicate process of desalting, and salting. Horrible vats of tannins bubbled, and lathes worked like hell-yard rakes. Now, most fel-low biographers latch onto Ulysses' supposedly unusual lifelong aversion to undercooked meats, citing his early experience in the tannery as cause to this effect. But are we to assume such things? A lot of people just don't eat blood. Still, the boy did hate the tannery, and he mostly helped out only as a cashier in their retail shop selling skins to merchants and leather supplies to the wealthy. His shoulder slouched under the chip even more.

The indignity grew when Jesse expanded the Grant Business to buy and trade for any old dead things found about town. They'd go around in a carcass cart, Ulysses steering the horse, and Jesse cheerfully and loudly asking the other kids' parents if they had anything dead because the Grant Family could use it to live. Yep, point out any ol' nightmare and we'll be much obliged. Then they got into selling bones, antlers, hooves, loose hair, scalps, claws, and nails. Nothing should be wasted, right? There was a man in town who made glue, and pillows always needed stuffing. Antlers and bones are dollars and cents to some. Cats and dogs have fur that shouldn't be put to waste when they are put to death.

And then there were the hogs. Like horsemeat, pig leather was frowned upon for some reason, but the poor had no choice. Are those pigskin couches and hog-knocker cushions on the dining room table's chairs? Why, yes. Grant Family standards. Ulysses, embarrassed, wore sensible pigskin jackets to school. He'd never be able to forget their reception.

The skin man was an abolitionist. Jesse abhorred the slavery down South and was loud about it. John Brown had been his bunkmate at tannery school. (For real. Give it a Google.) He cheered Nat Turner in '31. Cheered Sojourner Truth in '51. And he talked about Haiti's revolution like he'd been there selling flags, or something. He was a good-natured, short-sighted proponent of the Golden Rule, assuming that all other humans only wanted exactly what he'd want done unto him to be done unto them. Grant's Father would say "Each of us deserves love. The American Dream will one day be for everyone in America! Except for the animals!"

Yes, there were people in anti-slavery Ohio who were not white while also being, to a certain extent, free. But outside of the occasional merged play-session, or the "passing in town," society had that (mostly) unspoken way of keeping peoples away from peoples. But Ulysses' Dad taught him to treat everyone with equal respect. He taught the inarguable, universal human truth that slavery is evil. It's not funny. It's not forgivable. It's not a means excusable by its end. It's evil, even if there is no God or Devil. Amen.

But power? Power was a different matter. And Hannah Grant knew it. Ulysses' mom was a stoic on the outside, and a Clockwork Machiavellian on the inside. A stiff woman, constantly bonneted, Mom Grant only blinked after dying. She was the opposite of Jesse, in that she was shrewd, hard to read, cunning, and pessimistic. For a stone-cold realist like Hannah Grant, the world was what it is: cruel. One needed power to change things for oneself, and lots of it to do so for others. One should gain power first, and love second. And one had to hoard what little power they had for crucial moments. She would spend her free time as remote as the furniture, sitting still, conserving her power, saying nothing, with her heart ticking like her cousin the clock.

Ulysses' folks were opposites that attracted only in rumor. They had that kind of "hands off" closeness where apology came in nonverbal change, and love was mainly allowance. In that wood and rock house, under this okay roof, around these not-bad fires of stove and chimney, lived the three little Grants Gruff and perhaps some other unmentionable siblings. It was a lucky, anxious, okay little life.

One day, while in town to get more air-freshener, Teen Grant tripped over something even worse than that purple corpse by the river. This was the most wretched living man he'd ever seen: a drunken bum in the gutter, covered in filth, lost, and moaning with no one and no things. They locked sad eyes. The man's soul communicated need. Grant felt he should help this brother-in-species, but what could he do? He had it better than many, but he had nothing to spare. No money. No time. No power. Ulysses, pained and haunted by the encounter, walked on. Hannah clocked this crucial event. And like any good mother, she filed it away as a knife to later drive into her son's heart.

Shortly after this scarring, Grant turned sixteen. At breakfast, after the usual chitchat about the cost of hay and the stink of life, Jesse "The Root" Grant told the boy he was no longer a kid. Since Ulysses had finally graduated from elementary school, it was time to discuss his plans on how to survive America. They had ideas to run by him, and they'd do so later that night at his birthday dinner.

"But I know what I'm going to do," Ulysses said, toast crumbs poofing out. "I'm going to start a horse academy, like I've always said. You guys know that. I can be anything I want to be, right?"

The parents averted their saddening eyes from this heartbreak of wild hope in their son, and they mechanically moved their jaws on eggy meats in silence.

Later in his room, Ulysses paced, spurs ajangle. "I'll run away," he whispered, cramming his fragile feelings into the nearest, most ill-fitting words. "I'll be a horseback vagabond and go into the wild frontier like Kit. First, I'll get seen jumping far and throwing hard and denying the devil like Jesus did. Next, I'll make love to a witch, and trick a Cyclops. Then I'll reemerge and become a president." He planned to maybe take off into the Louisiana territories that America had just purchased at a discount. Or he'd head on into the swampy river valleys, or into the curves of the lands that were said to be bad, or perhaps into the jagged peaks packed with mountain men and lions. He'd wing the details, as they did in his geography lessons, apparently. So, Our Little Frontiersman readied his favorite horse, Sprog-roz-ikin, packed a Remington, a Colt, ten knives (mostly Bowie), a package or two of gunpowder, whiskey, cigars, sugar, jerky, pigskin riding gloves, personal bric-a-brac, sentimental knickknacks, a paddywhack, dog-bone heirloom tchotchkes, and an extra pair of socks.

To kill time until dinner, Ulysses climbed up into his favorite thinking tree. He'd at least eat his favorite birthday meal, hear them out, and only later disappear like a self-napping kid-thief in the night. Cradled in the limbs of the Slippery Elm, he watched the sun set behind the hills, and his thoughts about those distant woods became polluted with his teen needs for love and love-thrusting. He imagined wild sylvan souls in the twinkling leaves of the soothing groves. Elves, fairies, and sex-education teachers danced there odorlessly, surely giggling and laughing nakedly along the banks of hot and bothering springs. Ah. But then into his daydream came the dangerous, daydreamt wild men who would eat boys. Sasquatches and werewolves smacked their lips at fantasies of him. All types of gobblers seemed real and threatening. So maybe the woods were not the best place to be intentionally lonely with so few weapons. Maybe running away wasn't an option.

He went to dinner confused about his onset manhood. In the weak light of lard candles on the old warped and gray wood table waited his favorites: charred quails-n-cream, sweetbread surprise, game gumbo, cartilage cake, hot wings, variety milk, horse cheese, mash 'n' soda, and after-dinner chewing plugs. Hannah sat, head cocked, eyes on her boy, as still as if she hadn't cooked or moved since the morning. Jesse smiled worriedly, wringing his creaking hands.

Ulysses ate.

Hannah kicked Jesse under the table, and the father spoke. He proposed that his son come on as a partner in the skinnery retail biz, adding that they could start up abolition work on the side, to change things for the greater good. Jesse held out hope to find time to do more with his life, to spread the love. He thought if Ulysses took on part of the Grant Family

Burden, then maybe Jesse could find that elusive time we all wish we had for good deeds.

Our Teen couldn't hurt his dad by saying "Fuck no," so he kept chewing, blinking away this proffered life of meathook wind chimes and red, wet tenterhooks. He inhaled loudly through his nose, nodding with eyebrows up. Quail was good.

Jesse understood he had been understood. "Son, that's my option. But your mom and I are different, and she has a . . . quite, uh . . . *different* future in mind for you. She's pulled some strings. It's been a long and demanding time for the ol' gal, but the option package she put together is . . . you should at least thank her for the efforts, even if it doesn't suit y— ow!"

Grant swallowed the mash and switched jaws for the chaw.

"Go on."

"Your mom has secured for you a rare spot at the military academy, West Point, back East. She got you, a D-student, a golden ticket to kill school." Jesse made an effort to fold back his face, squeaking a smile across the blocks of his gypsum teeth. None of Ulysses' friends had such an opportunity in further education. This was a big deal.

"Be a soldier?" Grant asked. "You know I don't see myself as a George Washington—"

"You saw!" His mother's voice rose up like the tolling of fate's alarm clock. Her bottled-up voice came out a huge throng. The men were terrified.

"You saw with your own eyes what you might become if you don't push forward with a power plan, boy! The Gutter Man! You saw him. That's *you* if you make this one misstep. This warlording is your rare ticket to transcend this life! You can't stay here with us. You can't become your father. No. If you want to achieve the American Dream, boy, you must do so through this rare chance for power. Power. Power!"

After decades of thinking they knew her, the Grant Boys sat in awe of this unknown and perhaps unknowable lady who'd been so seemingly known so easily for so long. Hannah fell back in her chair panting, licking her furrowed lips. Grant was thunderstruck. His only two options lay before him on this table like the empty dishes. Was he going to stay to help his dad spread the love and tan the hides, or was he to leave his family and put his body at risk by accepting the soldier's life for the sake of power?

The lard guttered, and the room's yellow light seemed threatened by batwings. Jesse put a hand on his boy's shoulder and smiled below his frowning eyes. Hannah stuck a black-clad girl's arm straight out over the table and slowly fished her bony finger down along the dregs of cream on the edge of a dish. Neither man had ever seen such loose behavior from this hard person. They watched her suck the finger and pull a spent grin before saying "Son . . . have you ever heard of . . . a cavalry?"

PART TWO

Chapter 2

Kill School

1839–1843

AGES 17–21

THE CREST OF WEST POINT WAS A HELMET WORN BY A CADET and skewered through by a sword. A golden brain hung off the tip of the blade: a promise to the cadets that they'd at least die smart.

The school was made up of gray mock-castles scattered near the cutback tree lines beside the unhurried Hudson, there in New York State, in the East, in the old America. Gunmetal days played out one after another against the steel backdrop of this eastern sky. Clouds adhered, breezes adhesed. The Atlantic was in the air, and its ancient wind cuddled up into your pores, pumping to get at the core of you, pumping its ice into every opening, dilating the capillaries with calamitous, gusting thrusts.

The insides of this converted system of fortresses were minimalistic, with white walls and black-lacquered wood. The fires of the large hearths were rationed. Faintly glowing sticks and dots warmed little. No one knew who kept the place clean or when they did their polishing, but the surfaces stayed shiny despite the student body's constant sweating, bleeding, scuffing, scuffling, horse-playing, grab-assing, goofings, and jackings off.

Established only thirty-some-odd years ago by Papa Washington, Tommy J, and bad boy Hamilton, this was no school for basic soldiers: this was a godling forge. A place to make American bosses. To teach the cream of the states' crops how to dress like a purse and to kill like Yahweh. This place, hoary and storied, was to galvanize the rich and the willing into officers of the nation's Army. We're not talking about rough volunteers, militias, or private neighborhood security patrols. No. Here were only the creamiest of quail. Only hand-selected boys with their able atoms came here to be scrambled into Killer Cains on parade. Some cadets were destined for Army, some Navy, some G.I. Joe, and some S.H.I.E.L.D. But all knew this place would activate their dormant aristocracy; their status would transform once they passed through this star-gate makeover. On the other side of this process waited a white-gloved life with access to high society and great-smelling places.

Our Country Kid was determined to give the soldier's life his best shot. At the registrar, he was insulted to have to turn over his personal weaponry and flask, but he was more surprised to find that his name on the paperwork was "Ulysses S. Grant." He had always gone by Sam, or Sandman, or Sand Thrower. When asked if he was indeed Ulysses, he met the inaccurate belligerence of The System with an equaled apathy, saying "I am nobody." The registrar eyed him in pissy silence, having heard such things before. Grant shrugged and said "Whatever. That's my name now then, fuck it."

Our Bull wasn't about to waste the money his parents had spent on his opportunity to level up. He expected to find similar lower-class boys awaiting the same transformation, but most were from rich family legacies, and these princes were attending out of obligation, coasting on fat endowments from their daddies. In this factory, Grant was a Charlie with hundreds of Veruca Salts. The atomic mass of the chip on his shoulder doubled.

Grant, like all the boys, was issued two sets of itchy, woolen, button-crazed uniforms; house-style athletic boots; and, ugh, white pants? Bleached britches, a richie tradition.

Not only were there no boys smaller than Ulysses, but also there were no cafeteria tables to suit the rest of the kids who were proportionately larger than the original Eighteenth-Century West Point Boy. With new benches on backorder, his classmates had to eat standing up while Grant breakfasted comfortably at the table next to a gargantuan lummox sitting on the floor, panting while eating his gruel. Our Man was already singled out. It can feel like the world is doing it to you, like the laughing is coming from everyone on Earth, rather than from the few people in your life. It can seem like all, anything, everyone, and everything, when it's actually this, them, only that, or only John. We exaggerate everything always. (See?) But he was right: the big richies didn't like him.

Squeeze yourself into that boarding-school vibe. Feel it with me. Feel the bunk beds creaking, the cafeterias steaming. See dimly the bodies drooping in the dark mornings of sunbaked moonshine on simmer. Hear that insufferable, invisible bugle gleefully menacing the world. Feel that there were no girls. Feel the bracing river-swimming, the sparring, the mounting, the running and running, and the morphing of figurative art books into functional pornography. In the day there was training, but in the night (and in any other discoverable time) Our Little Man worked at his battered pee-pee. They all did. Laundry came in stiff. The nights came, and the young accessed themselves, despite the rule against it, for the West Point professors were using the boxer's theory that semen was a demon of aggression, and a man should save it so to bottle up their fierceness. None ever was; none ever will be. They would have done it on a planet with no sexual partners to imagine, and I'm sure some weren't interested in this, but across the iron river was a hive of "queen bees in bloom" at a sparkling young ladies' school where tower windows streamed with messes of tresses. Every year, a quixotic cadet would brave the waters without first securing reciprocal interest. Every year, one would pack contraband like gumdrops and spiked cider. The others would help prepare for his tryst, and shandy drinks were drunk to fortify the spirit. Finally, every damn year, one would swim like a horny fish, or steal a canoe like an evolved one, only to return home rightly denied.

When Ulysses had left Ohio, he told his friends he'd soon be in the pages of *Horse Lord Weekly*. The gang had cheered and tossed frogs at his departing train. He'd expected to declare a major in equestrianism for the cavalry track that his mom had sold him on, but West Point pushed a well-rounded course-load of fundamentals first. Majors were for master's students. But he was an American rebel in all areas of life: he found the fundamentals boring and grew enraged when anyone suggested that he might need help to achieve his goals. "I have my guts to go on," he'd growl. To which the richies replied: "Those who think with their guts do so because they were taught to think in the gutter." Oh, no. Gutter . . . guts . . . the Gutter Man. Mother Grant's prophecy had stuck to his fear nerve. So, he cowed himself. He had to ride this out. Just get through basic, get the intel dumps. Suppress the horse love for now. Pursue the power.

Each morning, the bugle blew, as reliable as Hyperion in his star cart rolling up Dawn's skirt. In homeroom, undergraduate cadets were given an overview of old-school styles of war. First, the witching ways of weaponry from Cain's rock to David's sling, to centurion whip to the contemporary subsets of explosives and firearms. They heard the international rumors about secret "wonder weapons," past, present, and future: harquebuses, telegraphs, cameras, revolvers, armored trains, hot-air balloons, steroids, Captain Britain, et al.

Before lunch was wrestling: Greco, Roman, and theatric. After chow, there was long-gun practice and short-knife defense, muskets and revolvers, murder and math. Cadets learned about Army hierarchies, ranks, logistics, and infrastructures—in other words, they internalized who told whom what to do, how, by using what, and ultimately where to get this from which underling. The class's scores were never great predictors for who would later lead in the real dances of men. Companies, regiments, platoons, squads, infantries—the cadets had to memorize it all so that we won't have to for the sake of the general writer.

In "tactics and strategy," they learned the stagecraft of Napoleon's dance moves, and the timing-wisdom behind every piss break that Washington ever took. And my God, the maps. They were expected to remember so many maps. But cartography led to the surveyor's science of charting elevations, distances, and relations between terrestrial attributes of the earth. Topography was as important as geography, and the most effective generals would attune themselves to the contours of the land via bodily geodesy. With the removal of man-made lines and arbitrary boundaries, Ulysses was freed to find that he had an innate internal plumb bob, and like a terraforming geomancer, he took to seeing reality as an exploitable surface. Unfortunately, to accurately feel such knowledge is one thing, but to further communicate such feelings is quite another. Grant's earned marks did not reflect his education.

Who were the cadets learning to fight against? Well, only twenty-five years ago, in 1814, the British had burned down the White House and laughed in their accents about it. All sorts of Nations of Natives were righteously angry, and no one ever knew what the French were up to. America needed protection, and West Point demanded stiff stock for its officer core.

Cadets were fed the soldier's diet only: bacon, beans, and the up-drink, coffee. West Point Boys were to maintain the Napoleonic physique, which meant that the French fitness guy should be able to crack nuts against any cadet's ripe body, at any time of day, even in the cadet's sleep. It was a P.E. requirement. The boys made their bodies into temples, as the Apostle Paul had taught, so that they too could be fitted with weapons, as any good temple must. The body, they learned, was a vehicle around the soul, which was a dot of gas in the skull. And it was up to them to armor that vehicle and to deck it out like a muscle car. The body was of the earth and a soldier was to risk the body willingly, for it was only the soul that mattered. It was a strict Cartesian model of life: they were ghosts in carnal shells, and such shells were trapped in an X, Y, Z realm, but the ghosts could go on to the afterlife of all the other alphabets and drink with alpha men like Washington in Valhalla . . . but only if they achieved bodily destruction.

They were taught how to use these bodies as a group, like a troupe of tripping actors doing anti-blocking against their foes. They mastered the art of lone defense, too, where they could turn an opponent's momentum against them. Each cadet trained to move their body out of the way of their own goals, and how to throw that same body into the path of the goals of competitors. They learned how to shepherd the enemy into the turnbuckles, how to box someone in, and to blow them out. Your body is the most expensive thing you have. Use it accordingly, Dear Reader.

And certainly, the boys sized each other up. Kids can be cruel about what one may have ended up with, you know, types of backs, fronts; lengths and ratios; traits that trigger animal associations. Duck this, rabbit that. If not corrected, kids will naturally mock each other's luck-of-the-draw from the deck of difference.

Sure, there was bullying. Hazing. Athletic types chose only running mates who could keep up. Brainiacs hived. The usual pop-up groups got gang-names like "hoods" or "poor." I'm sure you can deploy your own heartache memories of kids trying to make friends. It's a sad thing to see loneliness in a crowd. But it's nothing that a night in the arcade of oneself can't blot out.

A professor who had fought in the Revolutionary War still wore a wig on his shell-shocked head. He paced the lecture hall with knickers on his kickers, regaling the snickering brats with recollections of rented Bavarian mercenaries, of eating lice in the snow, and of cutting the feet off friends who really wanted it to happen. He loved to quiz the kids.

"Name me the best wizard," the professor said to the skylights with a sigh.

"Merlin."

"Jesus."

"Simon."

"Moses."

"Newton."

"No," said the teacher, now staring out the window (or into his own weakly reflected eyes). "The answer is Washington, because the best wizard is the one who keeps his magic a secret. Washington burned all his papers, reducing accurate biographies to slim volumes of known generalities. The moments in his life therefore became mythic, superhuman. By ridding the world of his trifling human details, Washington set us up to transform him into a god. Tell me that isn't wizardry."

No one told him anything; no one had listened. Long-Dead Washington scowled down at the class, his humanizing secrets safe in an airborne strongbox.

"History, for better or worse, is for us to do with as we wish, whether we wish to or not, for we are trapped in the 'doing something with history.' Most of us do it incompletely, wrongly, biasedly, or we think we do nothing—but doing nothing is doing something—and doing something isn't ever accurate because it is never complete. The best of us accept this fact and make from history what best suits us."

Sleepily, the students' faces scrunched.

"I know, I know. The truth! The truth! Wonderful. The truth is only true if complete, and it's too huge to be completely completed, so no. The truth will not make you the best. Often, the best among us," he added with a twist on his heel to face the class, "are nothing but the result of good PR teams. In the modern era, you should plan to control how you will be seen . . ."

Media Relations Class was one of the worst-attended.

The cadets studied those slim volumes on Gorgeous George. Despite the lack of facts, a new biography about Washington topped the sales charts each year. The most popular one was firstly built upon a tried-and-true, simple-as-syrup story structure, and it felt like an adventure novel: short, sweet, clear, clean, tight, light, and total bullshit. The critics loved it because the author had taken all the notes from everyone, and the students liked it because they loved easy doo-doo. Grant picked a less popular volume that heretically claimed the father of the country had a father and that that father had one too and so on all the way back to the Big Bang that impregnated the nothingness with somethingness. He got a D on his paper, but out of personal interest he continued his study of other horse-riding greats from history: Genghis the Great, Catherine the Great, Frederick the Great, Napoleon the Great . . . all leading up to . . . Lee. Yes, again . . . Robert E. Lee. By then, the R.E.L. had "military man fame" beyond the horse magazines. He'd been featured and published in textbook equestrian guides, and his exploits were exploited in the popular *Army Stories* adventure series. Everyone knew his name, particularly here at West Point where he was its most famous alum who had graduated without a single demerit. He never talked back, spat, or shat. The wunderkind had rewritten maneuver handbooks for appreciative instructors and had invented the push-up. It was said he didn't beat the nation's long-jump record, that had been set by George Washington, out of respect for the father of his country.

Robert the *Enviable*—Robert *E*. Lee—was the greatest of all time. The G.O.A.T. And he *was* a goat, a Capricorn who could fishtail in the saddle like an eel up an ass. He'd become the greatest horseman in America. Grant, when considering Lee's accomplishments, took up the American stance of mistaking admiration for inspiration, and said "Shit, I can do that." And Our Little Man tried his best, writing his next paper on the bullet and how its force issued out in all directions, not one. He wrote how a bullet affects time and space in a propelled and growing sphere, dragging, and pushing the air in its billowing wake. The title was "The Commodious Dot." He remained at the bottom of his class.

But he wasn't the only one struggling. Some boys couldn't contend with the rigor, the philosophy, the stress. Bodies got hurt. But young trees have that spring, and the supple souls were back in action before the nurse could finish. Colds, fevers, parasites, rashes, and heredity would hang them up, but impervious sinews and hormones would eventually win the day, and they knew it. Most of them enjoyed the risky business, including Young Ulysses. He was invincible and felt the benefits of the regimens. But during the annual pillow fight (a real thing), he'd sneak down to the stables alone and catch up with the horses, tweaking their bridles and whatnot. The school had ruled out casual riding for him. The counselor was never clear about why, but it had to do with his tenuous tuition, insurance, a scholarship, and blah blah. It was another rejection of his nature. The horses understood, and wordlessly the two species communed.

See him age through these years, Dear Reader, walking these halls, holding close his books and wooden practice weapons to his woolen vestments, as he passes through the broken-up talk. The voices came overlapping but never connecting. Hear the talk, talk, talk tumbling Our Young Man in their confluence . . .

"I heard there's a pop quiz on flanking today."

"So fucking boring. Why do we have to learn the savage histories? We beat them. Game over. Losers are boring."

"That maid is unfuckable."

"What even is a banana? I've never even seen a drawing of a banana."

"Don't invite Kingsley. I saw him putting boogers in library books."

"I'd fuck that bursar."

"Shit, this book feels like work! I thought it was supposed to be funny! This whole page is black. I like a lot of white on the page."

"He's got the stink of a woodwind."

"No, that's the second amendment. Imagine a constitution where the amendments outrun the main body of the text. Like a novel 4/5 footnotes. Haha. That would be ridiculous, but we're going that direction. Goddamn Congress."

"I don't know why she's attractive, but everyone says she is. So, I'll try to fuck her when I'm home for Thanksgiving."

"How can a person earn a quality that sums them up forever? I have been brave a few times, but will people say I was a 'brave man' when summing me up?"

"Gotta get that bravery in the papers, Man."

"When that poor kid told a story of how he earned tuition by delivering mail? Oh, Man. The part where he was proud of fancying up a milk cart with red, white, and blue paint? Hahaha. And white painted burlap stars? The details killed me. So sad. What a fuck."

"No way his scholarship holds out past Michaelmas."

"I can't tell anyone how to be, but I can sure as hell say how they look to me. And that fucker is a badger."

"Father said we had money that we must spend by the end of the quarter, okay? So, help me pick a ship, Chris."

"I'd fuck that nurse."

"I'm going to complain about the fireplaces again."

"I mean, what if Davy Crockett was brave in only one or two well-documented instances, but for all the rest of his life he was known as stingy, or rude, or wussy by those close to him?"

"That's why you go into frontiersmanship: nobody gets too close to know you."

"Why have your wife arranged now? Most girls age out of cuteness. I'd wait."

"I don't think churches like that should be allowed in America."

"Did it happen? Who's to say?"

"Me. Because Kingsley said it did."

"I drew a picture of my dick and sent it to that girls' school across the river. It's what they're all hoping will happen."

"At first you say 'why not kill off the poor and problematic people.' Right?"

"Yes."

"But then who will die in the fields and in the battles? Who'll mine the diamonds?"

"Oh."

"Prostitutes gotta come from somewhere, and they sure ain't coming out of our families."

"Well..."

"He wasn't in the Christmas card because we don't include that brother. No proper family rubs that kind of illness in society's nose, ever, let alone for the holidays."

"You can't cut a hole in a pillow. School rule 32. But two pillows and a bunch of rubber bands are way better anyway."

"The British only messed up when they didn't pay the richer colonials their share. It was just bad business. Shame."

"That professor had a visible erection when lecturing on the execution of Braveheart."

"Servants suck."

"I'd fuck that nurse."

"I'd fuck any nurse."

"I'd fuck any woman."

"I've fucked."

"No!"

"No, no. I'm English-American. Not Irish. Never say I'm Irish."

"Why must we read it? It's all fat. Like, where's the through-line? Fucking second act is masturbation city. And then the end is like, 'Hello! Think of your readers!' I hate the Bible, Man."

"Yes. My uncle's getting indicted, but he's been assured of a presidential pardon at the end of the term. So, he's doubling down on doing the bad stuff. Why not?"

"You been to the nurse?"

"Kingsley, old boy, she touched my penis."

Grant was shunned by such talkers who'd later become important to him and to historians like myself. There was Henry Halleck: a know-it-all alum that came back at orientation for the thrill of telling the newbs how the urinals worked. There was Pillow, from an illustrious line of golden Pillows stretching across the Atlantic to the castle of Pillow back in the old country. Wonderful people, Pillows. It's true. And who knows? Send in a swab. You, too, may be a Pillow. And then there was Buckner, AKA "Onan the Barbarian," due to his masturbation, which took up a biblical proportion of his life, more so than all his cadet-mates combined. He lived in a deluge of his own genetic potential, like a farmer drowning in his own silo of hardening seed. For Buckner, nasty thoughts appeared to him like bait set by an anti-muse. And each time, he took that bait; never was he its master. Apart from this, Buckner was a pretty good bunkmate for an empathetic Grant.

And then, oh my God, then . . . there was William Tecumseh Sherman. At odds with others and himself, an Aquarius pyromaniac, an intellectual brute, and a compassionate killer, Sherman was a godling also from Ohio. Like Grant, Sherman was poor, redheaded, on scholarship, and from an abolitionist background. But Sherman was radical. He felt America should be free, fair, and shared with Natives, Latinos, Blacks, Women, Foreigners, Atheists, and other crazy people.

No one had heard talk like Sherman's. He didn't even do fairytales growing up, because they were built on insidious monarchies. He didn't even do Disney. He discredited stories where the kid heroes were "chosen ones," or lost heirs to powerful bloodlines, or golden-ticket holders, or unconscious wizards. He liked cold hard democratic reality, and he held everyone to the same standard. Once a professor praised Napoleon.

"Which Napoleon?" Sherman asked.

"Napoleon the First," said the professor.

"No, which version of Napoleon the First?" Sherman asked, cocking his rooster's head in an irritated side eye. "We gotta specify if we're talking about the king-killer or the self-appointed emperor."

"I don't see why we should—"

"'Cause this is America, Man. We kill kings; we don't praise them. Ain't you ever heard that Beethoven rubbed Nappy's name off Eroica?"

The professor flipped through the textbook index while dumb kids yelled that "emperor" was a "hell of a goal for any man," and that "Washington fucked up when he didn't make himself king." They said he "shoulda conquered both continents of the new world and forced people to be free Americans."

Sherman often got sent to the Dean's office for spitting fulsome hockers on boots. He never backed down from a confrontation. And boy, Grant . . . Grant liked his smell. The two teens had seen each other in classes but had never connected until the time when Grant thought he was alone on the football field one night at 3 a.m. doing donuts in his PJs on a borrowed thoroughbred.

"Bravo!" shouted Sherman as he stepped from the shadows in his Gryffindor scarf and mitts. "Couldn't sleep either, eh?"

Grant rode close and hopped down. "Actually, I was kinda napping there during those triple lindies, so—"

"I suppose somebody's got to give these ponies a proper ride. I feel bad for them, what with their dance-cards full up with princes who've had the sweat glands bred out of them. Name's William. But you can call me Cump. It's a long story."

The two shook hands and felt great about it. They smiled their freckled faces at each other and felt like the orange section of the crayon box, both with skin like dead leaves dusted with autumnal snow.

Sherman and Grant palled around a lot after that night. They ate together in the cafeteria, and had a trading routine: beans for bacon, coffee for water. They speculated on war and women. And together they marveled at the carved inscription in the slat under Buckner's rocking top bunk. It read: P-O-E-3-0.

They were "The Ohio Boys." And Sherman had rubbed off on Grant. Maybe they *could* change things? Maybe his dad wasn't pipe-dreaming. Maybe his mom was right, too. Maybe he could use this life of soldiering for good, rise up the ranks, get a little power, make that change, shamone . . .

Grant began to gooseflesh when he thought of that More Perfect Union of the future. A sparkling goosebumping frizzled like a wave across his ball sac, which drew up tight like a purse with strings drawn, the gonads sliding and rolling up the abdomen first, then back down into place with the billowing bag settling back after the wave of brain chemicals subsided.

"Maybe. Ah, I don't know . . . well, maybe . . ."

On the last day of undergrad classes, the halls filled with summer's numbing comeliness. The education was "complete." After a post-workout shower, Ulysses stood in the mirror pinching at his nipple hair. He noticed the faded ink lines on his chest linking the fattest of his melanin stars into his Taurus sign. It was a habit he'd done since art camp. For the first time in four years, he was without a mandate, but he couldn't decide his next move. The young man had made good on his promise to his mother, but he had no interest in the master's program here. If he wanted to pursue a horsing major, he'd need to apply for all-new financial aid packages and grants and scholarships just to be in consideration for continuing—schools bury this in the brochures, I can personally assure you. The tuition offices of America purposely embarrass and humiliate you with demands to see your parents' tax forms, asking how much money they made in the last five years, and requiring an essay on what it's like to be a gutter boy . . . No.

Directionless, the twenty-one-year-old mused on his options. The precious leverage of power he'd gained was a flimsy fulcrum. But his new body was killer. He had invested time and energy in this soldier's life, and he wasn't about to throw it away. Should he go into politics like his richer peers, or go into active duty . . . like his actual peers? Only one of those had the possibility of dunking while on horseback. Some of his fellow students who had declared active duty early were already getting assigned to cavalry throughout the growing nation. Sherman was set to ship out west. Later, he and Grant made a shambles of saying goodbye with a tough hug. They futzed through graduation as if they'd see each other in homeroom at the start of a tomorrow that would never come.

After commencement, when all bets were off and cadets were encouraged to show their dicks and piss their hardest, Grant thought "why not," and, upon the back of an old sorrel belonging to the groundskeeper, he set a horse-and-man high-jump record that lasted for the next twenty-five thousand years. Everyone, rich and poor, cheered like the dickens! Look it up. It happened.

Chapter 3

Man in Uniform

1843–1845

AGES 21–23

Missouri. It's one of those "part North, part South, part East, and mostly Midwest" kinds of places. But the South part was *way* South in all the ways it could be back then. Saint Louis, listen, I can't show you exactly how you were. And I wouldn't dare embarrass us both by trying. All mirrors are false, whether or not the house they're in is fun. True, Saint Louis could be a northern-feeling place in places (individual houses and histories being whatever they might have been), but black people were owned there, and black people were tyrannized there. And we must touch on that.

All persons, even deviled ones, are individuals who think and feel their own things, though brands of thinking can be grouped into collective perspectives that are shared by such individual persons, demonic or otherwise. And when it came to slavery, there was a finite variety of groupthink going around. Some whites thought black people were not really people, as the Constitution told everyone (ask an Originalist). Some whites didn't understand the Golden Rule. Some whites said the Bible had cursed black people and that one could see this in the clues written by God through the hand of hallucinating men, three languages back. Some whites felt threatened by blackness, seeing it as the harbinger of a bigger world outside of their control. Some whites hated what could be called black culture: the looks, the sounds, the joys. Some whites were economically going with the flow, making money, and staying malevolently quiet. Some whites thought they were the good kind of enslaver. Some whites never thought about it. Some whites never, seldom, or always thought about why they kept people kidnapped on their land. Some whites felt that dominance and power were simply the guiding values by which one could estimate their own worth in relation to how much of either they had over other people. And some whites were just sadists, naturally or nurtured to be so.

Slavery in America was based on the different ways that people's bodies can look. I'm sure some whites were okay with such difference and were mightily bothered by this developed perspective. And I'm sure there were whites who felt trapped—despite not feeling tyrannized—as they thought "There but for the grace (and random favor and unfair actions) of God go I."

Am I being preachy? Perhaps, heathen. But today seems the time for sermons when the evil flag flies in daylight, and when demons run amok in our house with the ears of living men and women in their pockets. I must learn and relearn that no one wants to be preached to, and that some dumb ones will rebel and gravitate toward the worst ideas just to spite being told how to think. Then they get with the wrong crowd and things snowball, and by Christmas your boy is a Nazi. Still, I think it's worth the risk of seeming preachy to refresh ourselves from time to time on what's good and what's evil, together. Amen.

Long before the whites plundered the area, it was a Native fave for staging swap meets, what with the Mississippi River rippin' right here, and the cute li'l creeks creepin' in, and the way the world laid down just so, just there. It was a natural spot for *Homo sapiens* to set up shop atop a bunch of blankets and say "Ah." Enter the plundering French, who knew their incoming inheritors would have appetites for aristocratic sky-pies, so they named the place after King Louis in order that the said future whites might have something to aspire to: a king who died in a different dumb crusade after shitting his guts out.

Then in 1843 . . . here comes Swain Grant. That dapper Yankee Doodle
Brevet Second Lieutenant, baby. An officer *and* a gentleman. A falcon *and*
a snowman. He was no low bum in the gutter. Fuck no. He was a graduated
officer with a power cube in his pocket. When Our Man in uniform and
glossy hair came riding on a pony, the townies crammed their hats' asses
with macaroni, I can assure you. Most Missourian white boys this near the
Ozarks could only hope to not age into a Snuffy Smith. Despite the original invader's plan, young honkeys had only two dreams here: to be a Boss
Hogg, or, like the Duke Boys, to drive north for college as fast as fucked
lightning.

Stationed outside of Saint Louis, U.S.G. was ready to sign up and ride
horses for his ever-improving country. But holeeeeee shit: Slavery. In *his*
country. He wasn't emotionally equipped, nor was he emotionally mature
enough for such peacetime war crimes. How could anyone change this?
Sherman had been as deluded as his dear old dad. *This* was the country he
was supposedly going to ride for? See him now, this horseback young man
in blue; see him paused, blinking blank on the serpentine trail through the
rolling green mounds. See him seeing with his uneven brows, and no way
to organize or metabolize the wearying world before him.

He reported for duty at the fort's check-in desk. The snickering
fate-dealers shook their heads and raised their brows and bowed up their
lips at this little man, cap in hand. Instead of cavalry, or even dragoons,
they gave him the position of Quartermaster. What? A retail job? A
cashier? Like at his dad's shop? Oh, horror! Was he to be rewound to
his old life, the life he'd left for Kill School? Hadn't West Point been
to help him hop up in society? What else would reveal itself in horrible
Saint Louis?!

The Quartermaster shop was just like the tannery store, except here
Grant had to wear the woolen uniform too. He issued goods to the real, the
active, the duty-had horseback soldiers in the field when he wasn't doing inventory, talking with supply-train engineers, or working a handcart, hand
truck, or hand dolly. Instead of earning horseback distinction, he did the
rigmarole for the thingamabobs, stacked backstock, priced frontstock, displayed shit, tricked out the endcaps, did special orders, and—ack—handled
returns!

He had the demoralizing duty of fitting others with glory garments. He had to armor his advancing peers as if he were a left-behind little Hephaestus wobbling on day-drunk legs, because yes-in-damn-deed did the legal-age-man drink his drinks while he worked his work. The richies in charge assigned him this backwards position knowing it would hurt him. They did it to put him in his place. Grant just knew they were certainly talking about him, saying "He came from nothing, and he is going nowhere. Grant shall never be a General on horseback!"

To do the paperwork for other people's action is the same as making butthole sticks for other people's wonderful nights. It's not fun, I mean, for those of you who don't enjoy butthole sticks. I don't either, really, for the record; I'm only saying . . . it's not a good feeling to—you get it.

The fort was outside town, and the area was raw and woodsy. In the boring-ass barracks, when not grinding on one's body-craft or folding up the uniforms, there was cards, dice, dominoes, porn swaps, table tennis, knife-throwing, spitting, darts, and shit talk to catch up on.

In all barracks, one can find the tiny guys with stub necks who pick verbal fights and let their smoke curl into their eyes on purpose so that their squint might mean things. There are always the long giraffe types with broomstick arms and paddleboard feet that go under your bed as they sit on theirs, trying to open up about bad dads or kinda hot cousins. There's the guy with the bad teeth, and another with tin ones, and their combined gingivitis musk makes the place smell like the circle of life on the floor of a rot-wood forest. Those types of guys were there, and a bunch of one-off nobodies who lined up and laid down and anted in and mostly ignored the little redhead loner in the corner with the horse calendar hanging over his pig-leather backpack.

Grant, while in the shop or shining his goddamn boots, would listen to the talk and watch his peers and bosses as they weighed in on the slave-based economy, some acclaiming the works of evil, and commending the effectiveness of Beelzebub. These same types, no matter from what echelon they heralded, held aristocratic fantasies wherein they'd rise up to become the big rich alpha in the biggest house with people to lord over. In their present uniforms, the soldiers felt like they were on a career track which ultimately ended in Tsar, and they were currently just long-lost, or soon-to-be, nobility, who'd claim serfs up in the hundreds. Even the northerners fell into this fantasy of becoming like the important dukes from books because even a piece of shit could amass power off this system if they were willing to trade in their humanity. Everyone read books that fed such fantasies. It was a booming book industry. *Notes from the Overground* was a hit novel that celebrated bullies and landed gentry. In it, a poor white man pulled himself up from poverty by the straps of an unknown style of boot. This strapping young white became a millionaire because he overcame his pride and started buying people from the slave market, and consequently he was able to cherry-pick a woman who fit his requirements. These awful stories all ended by saying that the attainment of the American Dream demanded an under-caste, and they pointed to ancient Greece as an example of how it should be done.

In related news, in 1844, a walrus-faced wannabe self-hating Christ-complex was born into the middle class, and he dreamt of becoming a merlin type of high-brow mountain man lapdog to composers and kings, and by God he did so. Sure, he had a hot idea or two, but the same can be said of you or me from time to time. We Readers seeking wisdom don't have to listen for the tiniest baby's cry in an ocean of filthy bathwater; some ideas are just not worth the Coast Guard's diving time. And despite the fact that Nietzsche was just such a baby while Grant was in Saint Louis, his ancient ideas were already long in place everywhere on the earth, especially here in the South where people with money thought they were overmen, and people without money wanted to get over their present underness. If you see yourself as an overman, then you look for undermen in the rest of us. Read with caution, Dear One.

Grant too couldn't escape the predicament: compete or die. Still, he was too young and too horny to be conscious of anything too bad for too long. Like an asshole in odd water, he shut it all out. His glands called the shots. Our Dear Swain was full-hearted and throbbing with potential. Legions of spermatozoa were leaping in lumps within the fresh flesh of Ulysses. His DNA arched toward reproduction with a low vibra-itch of sexual need. "Make use of this body now," the body screamed inside itself. And he wasn't alone. His peers were ascramble to lock down a mate before aging out of parenting. In other words, to get married and fuck correctly before age twenty-four. The barracks chatter stayed about, or inevitably swerved back into, sex. These near-men tried to seem relaxed about the biological programming of their bodies. They tried to act like they were in control. They leaned against mantels, smoked slowly, mumbled; and when sex came up, they put it in common parlance . . .

"No biggie if I got, like, a stamen or a pistil. Birds and bees. So, what if my pistil or stamen gums up. I'm cool with it."

"Great," Grant said, polishing.

"I just . . . can't wait to get on someone, hissing and sweating, getting after it, jutting out my jaw, while my own anus grips like a hungry jellyfish back there."

"Yep."

"Can't wait for my anus to be smacking like the delta of a river down there in my own flowing creek of back sweat, you know? That's just one of the cool things that happens when you're pissing up a butt like you're sup-posed to do when you put a baby in a gal, right?"

"Well—"

"I mean, that sounds normal and natural. How God intended. Butt-babies and whatnot. And it's beautiful, all these babies in my balls. I got microscopic, fully formed babies floating in my nuts. They need me to do it for them. Think of all that could be. I could be the dad of an Army if I had the gals to, like, incubate all these babies I'm carrying around. GOD, I can't wait to do that."

"Me neither."

At this point, you may be asking "If this was the South, then where are the Mark Twain apostrophe marks and banished Gs? Dear Reader, as a drop G speaker I promise you that we think we're saying them. With your imaginary forces, work the guitar tongue twanging and ringing. Hear the keening, intended and not, betwixt interlocutors. Train the ear's hairs to-ward such susurrus signaling when someone means to show that they have sent old sense across. Catch up that thrown-away way, how the speaker wants you to want to catch that kind of side-said thing. Swallow up those tones with your ear lips. Hear the toes of those submerged sounds as they touch off your drum and bounce up again as bubbling and as ebullient as a shoeless grandmother in a rocking chair after having gotten the green light for more wine long ago. Imagine my uncle and his warped, Texan brass horn. Imagine my father and his wrestling clarinet. (Did you convert it to wrasslin'?) The accent types were in this story, but each person's was distinct, like Christmas trees for sale in a parking lot. Hear the difference in the breeze between leaves. I cannot do it for you.

The day was for work, and the night was for courting, parties, salons, pageantry, gallantry, and many other societal layers of clothes, and conduct. Soldiers bedecked in their nighttime outfits of glitzy buttons and tackle could be seen up and down the strata of society if their money and stories were in shape.

There were hand fans. Ice blocks. Ice sculptures and ice barons. Punch companies flourished. In most houses they had high ceilings, hoping to trick the heat with the bait of higher space into which it could rise; but alas, an accumulation of ghosts was already occupying it, crying up their additions to the moisture in the air like a cloud front. Smart, aloof, or horny people could steal away to basements carved out of the cold earth where a body could get the relieving creeps.

If you hosted a ball, you invited musicians. A group of weirdo people would show up with their precious wooden pets and brass prosthetics. Music has a way of giving form to non-verbal experience, of describing emotion and idea, calamity, and physics. If done in the old way, it will give the false picture of order. We hear how the IS should be; we feel there must be an attainable order, a plan, a pleasuring peace. We feel from music that there has all along been a lost way to leap back to the garden, and we start blaming ourselves when we can't find it in our silence.

They called 'em balls for a reason. Either you were in the market to gain a pair, or you had some to unload. Dance Hall Balls were coupling affairs, put on so that the parental set could weave society intentionally. Family heads could display their trophies: good marrying stock. They could play matchmaker, wielding power over love via arranged marriages. This was before women could do what they wanted without getting ostracized like leprous perverts, so they had to marry a guy before trying him out. They were told lies to keep them from test drives, like how a boy's spit is sperm, and how leg-wrestling will get everyone pregnant.

What did men then want? Gals in smart tabby weaves, custom calicoes, and groves of gingham. Gals with wise smiles and plaits of sheeny hair, hair that was molded, folded, braided, and plaited, sounding like wicker patio furniture. The hair that sounds like a basket with a head in it. The hair whispering like a siren to a sailor, singing "Take me on a picnic. I'll give you much to eat by the gushing river."

What did women want? Well, I hope it's fair for me to assume that women of the time wanted what women of this time want in a man, and that is a nightmare walking. With body hair bristling like a porcupine, with angry scowling faces like their dads' faces and Christ's dad's face. Men with hands that are numb from work, hands that cannot un-grip. Girls wanted sasquatches in tuxedos: Couth Killers. Girls wanted beast-men who had the fear of all others in their stinky teeth. Scary, powerful dudes with money and guns. Women wanted tall bulls who could ride horses and kill intruders and shoot grim reapers off the backs of witches' brooms, witches that were coming for their babies. Oh, I think you'll agree it's safe to assume that all girls wanted men to be trainable attack hounds who'd sit nicely at the Downton Abbeys of Knoxville and Raleigh but would tear the arms off assailants in the yard in the dark. Girls wanted men who were Hyde in the bed and Jekyll in the bank. With Ingres' *Jupiter* fresh in every-one's mind, women wanted a tamed tyrant who was protective of her and her eggs but mean to all else on this cruel and horrible planet.

Naturally, I can't account for all tastes. Communication being what it is, I must generalize, though I know I shouldn't say anything general about women or men, no matter how far back in time they are, or despite how I might be pretty close to nailing it. The very words "man" and "woman" are up for redefinition these days. What untold suffering went on for those souls caught between such limiting titles back then? And still? Peace be with them in their demands for their own desires . . .

Now, Our Man Grant was only five-foot feet. Still, the gals noticed his numerous good red flags: Moody. Drinks. Smokes. Talks of horses. Talks *to* horses. Despite this great material, they decided it might be too much.

Grant started to weigh his options again. After months of trying to convince himself that this soldier's life was for him and that it was going to bring him power, he planned now to quit it. Maybe he could take his degree as a trained mass murderer and use it to get a job as a math teacher somewhere. Maybe he was now old enough and strong enough to pull off the Kit Carson woodsman life alone in the woods with the sex elves.

But then it happened. He found love in the form of being near her. She lived at a plantation called, I shit you not, White Haven. It was of course a white mansion with columns, balconies, guest rooms, and wonderful dome-topped windows. About the place were farm lots. Green rows. Groves. Orchards. Enslaved people. Sadness. Crimes. America.

That night, in the twinkling amber yard-candles, Grant stood in line out front for the ball, hair slicked down, face hewn, already lit himself. Once inside the huge rooms of warm light and talk-talk, he scuffed across the parquet, keeping on the outskirts of the dancers, avoiding the handsome gloved boys out there joining up with the creped and flushing ones, all apparently numb to the disgusting scene of other people's pure ecstasy, smiling into smiling reddening smiles. He sniffed, and, nodding for show to no one, grabbed a napkin full of springtime sweetmeats and exited straight through the open giant window doors to eat, smoke a cigar, sip a flask, and fart a little before leaving this house and life forever.

Bugsong night, handmade light. He saw her in the garden: Julia Boggs Dent. She was holding a nosegay, twirling it, dwarfing its ability to delight, for she was an all-sensory-organs-gay. He was enchanted. Most said her weirding eye was a flaw. To Grant it was but a vein in the marble of a Michelangelo.

He made her acquaintance and learned that this was her family's house. Her sisters, brothers, and in-laws were inside, loudly doing lace dances and punch talk. She, like he, was shy and misunderstood. This lady before him had strong hands, strong teeth, strong hair: the Hemingway trifecta. Dopamine squirters cut a new catalog of her things into a fold of his mind so to spritz on sight next time.

They let the quiet happen, and neither rushed off. He made a joke about white gloves and punch stains, and she laughed for him, but she meant it. Her not-small hand, palm shoulderward, fingered the gold-brown wheat-dark drapes of hair there in the curve of her crook, wrist to lips. His eyes darted in the dark, shining like a wolf spider's. Was that the twitch of interest or the twinge of grimace? Was she emotionally ajar? Could he slip in? Would she allow him? Did she find him okay-looking? Did he smell okay enough?

They strolled the moonlit family maze, smelling heliotrope and honeysuckle. She tricked this way and that with the agility of a black bear;
she evaded, but stopped, casting back a smile that no one else on Earth
was meant to decode but him. Nature, smirking and voyeuristic, sensed
them on the air: birds, alert on vines, dipped; bugs, abuzz in the berry bush,
hushed; Shakespeare, a'shuffle in his codpiece, peeked and peaked. That
night near the towering mounds of rhododendron, they both acquired an
ache anytime they imagined hurting each other, and from then on both
knew they'd avoid it. It was ardor in the arbor.

Over a year of closeness went by. I'm certain Julia was a progressive
thinker and wanted to live away from slavery. She had to have been. She
had to have read the cool authors, like Frederick Douglass and Sojourner
Truth, and could turn old books into new ones simply by passing them
through her, separating the chaff from the laughs. She made him think,
and he liked it. No one had ever held his heart like Julia. Not even Skorlg,
his favorite mare.

They'd go to plays like *Fool School*, and *Giddily Winks*, and the national hit: *Come, Caked Daisies!* But while watching the faux love on stage,
their tumescent bits ballooned uncomfortably in their clothes as they eye-
fucked like twin Hannibal Lecters, holding each other's radiating gloves
like Chernobyl nuggets.

She taught him about Southern food, how fry can be sandy, or it can be
crackle, but never together. He hadn't known his tongue before knowing
her. The organ was awoken, rolling and rooting about like a sensual shovel,
constantly molesting its darkened garage, back and forth over the teeth.
He'd put it on whatever she said to.

The days were fast in the presence of her glow-in-the-light material.
She was a mysterious, Aquarian cusper. Withdrawn. Sulky. Held up by
grudges and weighed down with remembrances. He was surprised at
himself for falling in love with sullenness. That bad attitude, this grumpy
beauty. How was it that he loved a girl who seemed to hate everyone, especially the overtly happy people trying to get her to smile? He and she,
these two introverted, marginalized, loner weirdos, despite cosmic odds,
had found each other in this tiny manicured section of the Wilderness.
She truly saw the roughshod, out-of-place pissed-off horseman, drunk and

mean and sad and sweet with an uneven freckly face. And he really saw this giantess, a frown in a gown, with crazy eyes, and sane honesty. See them, Reader: he with a chip on his shoulder needing to prove himself to everyone, and she with the self-regard of a celestial being, not caring what anyone thinks.

They'd ride horses out to the lake, swim, and not fuck. He respected her wishes to be married for that. But she was sweating eggs, and he seed. So they planned up a plan: they'd get married, he'd quit the Army, they'd move up north, and, when not fucking, they'd start a stable for horses and teach poor kids to ride them the right way. His way. She shared her dreams about the future she wanted, too: a real family of her own that had real, accepting love. She also talked about breeding dogs, but that seemed half-baked. They challenged each other. Pushed each other. Comforted and confounded each other. Got mad and played hurt. Lashed out and gave in. They listened and changed. She let him be. He loved how she was. Sure, they talked. But more often than not, they communicated without it. They knew a look was more reliable. Cops and interrogators talk about body language like it's a universal system so that they may teach courses to adepts who'll misread suspects forever and ever. No. Real Body Language is understood only in shorthand, as inside jokes are. They knew each other and they knew it. Relationships are proximity-based, body 'round body. Gotta be there to care.

The magnolias held out their long umber arms and legs under their shell of outer foliage and, when apart from her, Ulysses would get under their deep green tents to straddle a limb inside the dark coolness. Under such arbor he draped, panther-style, thinking—no, feeling—that she made him feel valuable. She gave him the feeling of being wanted. Because she, a young set of unexpired goods, was choosing to tick off her prime time this way, with him. He couldn't believe it. He had found that tranquil woman he'd long ago wondered about. People can feel this way, Dear Reader. It was Yules and Jules, forever and always, no matter what. Oh! It's too much. I can't think about their having not ever met. I seriously don't think anything anywhere in time would have ever been the same.

But her dad would not have it. The old enslaver had a face that sucked back into itself. His expression du jour was anger loaf. White-headed and heavily warted, he had that fidgeting, finding feature in his fingers, forever gripping at an un-lost stick.

Dent said, "You can't have her unless you're cooler. And you need to have a lot more power. See, I need my son-in-law to be able to get into the pages of magazines like *Horse Lord Weekly*, like that . . . that . . . that . . . Robert E. Lee. Son, you're no Lee. Hell, I'd let Lee fuck all my kids. Lee's the next George Washington, you mark my words. Who are *you* the next of?"

It was around that time at the barracks and at the dances and in the streets that everyone was talking about Mexico. Supposedly, Mexico was evil now, and Mexicans were villains. They had land that should be America's; plus, they had just killed Davy Crockett down there, for Christ sakes, in the Alamo. He was only trying to gentrify the place. Davy fucking 'coonskin cap' Crockett, Man. Mexicans killed him, Man. Everybody was saying that kind of thing with welcomed tears in their psyched-up eyes.

The game for power, even among the power-class, was perennially in play. But at Grant's level of poor dudes trying to level up, it was bloodthirsty. His peers were going after the cheerleader daughters of barons like they were the doors one could get a foot in. It was cutting competition. Rumors and sabotage were on limits. But Grant was running silent in his aims because most men had avoided Julia, mostly because of her challenging views, but primarily because of the crossed eyes and retired football player's physique. All pluses for Uly-us-ses.

Grant could stay in the Army for this war, do some gnarly shit on a horse, move up the ranks, and get real bona fides to prove to everyone (mostly Julia's dad) that he was special. He could secure love with a little more power in his pocket. Besides, maybe this propaganda was true about the Mexican people? True or not, he had to marry and fuck this woman. For her sake, as much as his.

Chapter 4

Mexicans Are Cool

1845–1848

AGES 23–26

OH, HERE IT CAME. THE AMERICAN NAVAL CORPS cruising into those breezy pine shores of Corpus Christi. Every American soldier felt particularly romantic. A real war! A tropical war! Each had billowing, white shirts unbuttoned just so. The salty gusts made hair go like furious hawks on the head. The ocean was a blue that made the sky look ashamed, old, and overworked. Soldiers sighed. They were already heroes of their own real odysseys, and each was putting together the early chapters of what would become unreadable memoirs.

The ocean was of many blues back before we transformed the elemental makeup of our world. Back before the earth bled oil. Before we had the satanic ease of plastic, temporary everything. Before nuclear waste was welcomed. Before schitzo soaps and traitorous shampoos, before chimerical chemicals and malignant medicines outnumbered the water molecules of the seas. Not a dash of doubt for these swarthy coxswains, though. Take it all! Drink it all! Touch it all! It's built for you!

Despite his namesake, Ulysses had never been on a ship, had never sailed, and had never shat at sea. He too couldn't avoid the adventurous spirit. It was irresistible. And he was Billy Budding.

The Intel Corps had described the enemy with care. They were Mexican people. Also, Spanish people, the Hispanic people, and Native peoples. But most importantly, The Army presented America with the biography of an archvillain: Santa Anna, the chess master in spit-curls, who had eaten Crockett's cadaver and, it was recently reported, had devoured Davy Bowie too. Santa was reportedly hungry for all these Davy Navy Boys. It was true! It was there in a book detailed in a streamlined, clear, objective master narrative. Mexico was going to attack the U.S.A. on the southern border; and after, Santa Anna would work his way northeast to eat and fuck out our innocence, and that was why America was sending forces to point cannons at his country. And, as predicted, Mexico attacked first. Intelligence!

But upon landing it was apparent to Ulysses that Mexico was not what he'd been told and not what we've seen in our American stories over and over. It's not just a dangerous desert. Not just a festive, wrist-banded beach resort. Not just a quaint old coffee can tocking in the wind against a muddy well amid chicken whimpers. That can all be found in Mexico, as it can be found elsewhere in the world. But, also in Mexico there was what one can't see until their body travels about it. Let us go with him . . .

The Army moved through ocher hills and olive-green balls of brush, through chaparral country, and through the larger leopard-print mountains like colossal cats' backs with spots of furry bushes. They'd rest under a dried-out feeling in the trees, spooning up the dregs from their Underwood food tin cans (a modern marvel of the time). They'd march through unimaginable Mexican rain. March through unexpected Mexican freezes. And try to sleep in the Mexican Wilderness of wonder. Live oaks became camp helpers with their wild arms lending a hand to hold a lamp and whatnot. Grant noted the varied topography, expecting enemies in any notch. But mostly what he saw were people trying to live. People looking for ease, looking for love, wanting what's best for their kids and old folks. You know, people.

The Americans passed through towns and sloshed through the water sources. They overtook cities and their centers. Took in streets and roads and the complicated differences between them. Dogs watched, dumb and not, mean and not. Cats said much with their faces and bodies. Kids hid, peeked, and smiled. Some men laid in the same gutter that ran through the states on up through Canada, thinking their own things, and probably on occasion thinking the same as anyone who'd end up there; while the rich were able to while away the vastness of whatever came to mind . . . when there wasn't war. But there was one now.

What would it feel like, coming into your town? The rumbling run up to it? The slow concern escalating? People evacuating? Protection leaving? The empty streets? The rumors that good and bad armies are coming? Food running out? Hearing the plans of armies to stage the battles on so-'n'-so's farm? The fear in women and those who know women? The hiding of valuables and animals and women? How would all that feel coming up your street, Dear Reader? The rich folk board up and move to their vacation homes. But imagine you're too late. You hear them coming down the street. The armies come, taking over the town, good or bad; but either way, it's a governing force of strange, scared men with power-madness, asking questions, wanting things with their eyes and noses alert to your business. Soldiers can be good and bad and in-between on this day or that one. But war, easy or hard, is awful on a place and a people in all places and all times alike.

Most Americans had never seen coyote or cactus. There were attacks by pumas. Leopards. Javalina. Snakes. Tarantula. Fathers. Mountain lions. Black and brown bears. Mega-lions. Megalonyx. And man-bears. Bivouacked men fell dead from skin worms, vampire goat dogs, cake worms, lice, king ticks, wind fleas, gamecocks, smaller pocks, and the Twin Witch Sisters: Malaria and Cholera. There was syphilis. Tuberculosis. Gangrene. Gunshots, and dysentery. And again, Our Man disappeared in the ranks, and the voices flowed over him like disconnected water tumbling together in the meeting of murmuring streams.

"Hey, Kingsley. They got churches down here. I thought we'd be shooting Baal off the top of a pueblo and shit, but they got good God, too? Changes things a bit."

"Nobody can make me eat their food. I got a footlocker of Underwood canned meat. And I'll kill a man who touches it."

"These cities are kinda normal and kinda not."

"Hurly-burly bullshit is what it is."

"I'm going to try to transfer to the Navy. I hate dust."

"Banana thing's fuckin' good, though."

"My girl is gunna fuck Stumpy John. That guy was always charming. Now he's the only stud around the card table back home. Suzanna liked him, but I had showed what all I could do for her with both my legs. It was hard to corner that market; goddamn John is pretty capable. I can tell from her letters, the few I get, that she's not interested in me. John's got her, Boys."

"Ecclesiastes would say it tastes like any other fruit, so why bother trying it?"

"Ecclesiastes was a depressed person."

"What does 'depressed' mean?"

"Pushed down."

"I thought his name was Koheleth? Either way, bananas are goddamn good, Man."

"It was pitch-dark and we were drunk on that funky milk they got down here, and this guide was waving us on into the Wilderness, through these mangroves. Kingsley was there, ask Kingsley. We were paying this li'l Mexican more than he'd ever seen. And he had promised this was the top secret in this dumb place. We were thinking women. Or something taboo with women. So, we went. But we got out to this farm with our lantern light swinging up on farm shit, and he was just a shushing us, this little guy with no front teeth. He had only the canines. Killer smile. Anyway, he'd been saying that he'd show us the real thing to do in Mexico at night. But this little fucker . . . Man, he shows us these goats at this farm. He's way drunk. We're way drunk. And he goes, 'These goats ain't gunna suck themselves!'"

"If I hear the word *flavor* one more time down here from you all . . . it's friendly-fire time."

"Tamale thing's good, though."

"This whole haphazard operation fell apart once we got off those marvelous ships."

"Lots of red-yellow-green going on."

"I was at that lake, swimming. And a fucking kid in a yarn cape with a short, hard wire for a sword held me up. I was naked. Took my boots. This happened to me in Virginia Beach too. Same kid!"

"I went to one of their witches. Curandera, they call 'em down here. She had me get in a rickety old cart with her and she started whippin' the donkey or whatever it was to go fast down this cobblestone street. And we're like those jumpin' beans, pop, pop, pop. I think this cart is comin' apart. Then she takes out an egg, and whispers to it real close-like, and she threw that egg out over this cobblestone street, real high arc, Man. But that shit *bounced*. No splat. It bounced over to the gutter. She shook her head and said this proved that I had a curse on me. Which I knew. So, she passed that test, I guess."

"Fucker was a goatsucker, Man. Wasn't like a thing people do down here. It was just this Little Mexican barnyard Dracula. Goddamn waste of money. Hell, I seen geeks in circuses since I was five back home in Illinois."

"They had a library, and I was expecting only Mexican books. But they had Natty Bumppo in there. In American."

"I like how you gotta undress these things, but I wish it was a female shaped fruit-meat inside, instead. Feels funny eatin' this shape."

"You think it's my kid? A kid I don't know, like, following me around the world, stealin' my shit from me at sword point?"

"Feeling vulnerable out in the camp. We're targets in the bottom of that basin. Like marbles pooled in a bowl. No cover."

"Nobody told me they got rich people. That changes it. I'm not pointing this cannon at rich people's houses."

But the war was on. And cannons were pointed.

Two opposite types commanded the American Army. The first was the formal, by-the-book General Winfield Scott. "Old Fuss and Feathers" (not mine) was an 1812er, a favorite of the establishment back in Washington, and a reliable extension of the West Point style of warring.

Then, sharing command, was that dirty ivory eagle, General Zachary Taylor. His face was a grimacing cut coconut. His voice, when he used it, was an unavoidable needle. A gifted strategist, old Zach moved his forces with economic strikes, keeping the enemy on uneasy defense. He wasn't showy, wore simple soldier attire, and had a James Coburn swagger going on. There was a hit biography about Scott, which everyone read. It was authorized and read like a prayer said out loud: thanking God for all the good things about his life and apologizing for nothing. But Zach had made his way into popular songs as the go-to bad man for the singers to liken themselves to, and for Grant, Zach was a revelation, also: a prototype. The way to be. No fuss, no muss, just getting it done, fast and loose.

But alas, again, Our U.S.G. was put on cash-register duty in the Quartermaster shop. No one paid attention to the withdrawn man, drinking and smoking, while renting out boots. He worked with local suppliers, kept supply lines alive across enemy territory, and helped outfit the horses of real officers who were off winning valor, rising in rank, and becoming fuck-able fiancé material. Battles happened. Cities were ruined. America sent more men. And Grant curdled. How was he supposed to gain fame or power this way? So Ulysses stayed by himself and made the most with this widening of his world. He would spend whole days with the locals, talking with their horse breeders about their curious burros and the magnificent stallions used in their bullfights. He assumed these horse trainers would appreciate the great saddle balms and tackle oils that he loved, but they didn't. They had their own ways. And he listened to learn what they loved and wanted.

Geography, iconography, pornography—he absorbed the many splendors of Mexico. He loved their tequila, and often woke up in bushes next to donkeys that no one knew. Which was fine by him. He wasn't fitting in, anyway. When asked to join other soldiers on whorehouse adventures, he'd always use the same excuse: "I left my sex belt at home." It was a confusing line that had most wondering if they'd been doing sex wrong without one.

In his letters to Julia, he remembers drinking heavy milk out of bags, and cactus mash out of bagpipes. He remembers a local supplier of cloth, an old man with a wonderful family of workers, and a dark barn with barrels of rich dyes. Grant wrote about sweaters of bold knits and a head-clearing smell of fiber boiling. We can remember, as he did to her, his hunting antelope in a slate haze sunrise. We can shoot the dusty doves in the alizarin sunset. We can feel the horses under him at night, rocking their slow walks as we drink. We can drive a group of sheep back to the Quartermaster corral, their cloudy worth now pink in the last light. We can feel along with his words in his wishing Julia were with him under different circumstances, under this periwinkle sky, on this Dutch Orange dirt, looking at the drunken double sunset like Saint Luke just before learning that his Christ was actually an old man living in the same desert, in fact a man he already knew. Indeed, Ulysses wrote touching love letters to his de facto fiancée:

> Oh, for you to fuck me against these painted rocks. I wish I could see what color your skin would be in these dawns, these dusks. To see your eyes working at it all would do my heart wonders. I can't wait for us to marry so that I might give you babies like the dickens! The first thing I want to do to you is—

Okay, Camps. Let's move on to camps. There's nothing like thousands of men trying to be quiet together. It's what bees must feel. To be without the whine of electricity, power tools, cars, fans, vents—imagine none of that. These sounds were blocky. Occasionally there was a tink. Things tinked. Men felt wind, closeness, fire, scared. It all went in them without interference. They were like wildebeests in a new type of grass, trying to digest it. At night they felt safe enough to sing. "Camp Town Ladies sing this song: *Doo-doo. Doo-doo.* Camp town doo-doo's five miles long, all the doo-doo days!"

Battles were fought across Mexico, but Grant's regiment hadn't seen action yet. They were unspent commodities waiting to be discharged. Ulysses delivered polish to bootblacks and underwear to everyone. He'd walk through the rows of white tent sheets, chewing the hell out of a cigar; nodding up a storm to those he caught eyes with. And soon, one feeling was on all lips:

"We shouldn't be doing this, right?"

"We really shouldn't be doing this."

"This doesn't feel like we should be doing this at all."

"I'm poor and this is my only option, but fuck . . ."

Because it was a land grab. We were agitators, fight-pickers. Plain and simple. Turns out, this wasn't a case of a few million bad apples. The peoples of Mexico were as lovely a people as any people can be generalized to be. The Santa Anna situation was super complicated, and the simplified story had been told for a bad reason. Naturally, the story was more about the storyteller than it was about the story (as are all). Grant, too, saw the war as an unethical invasion, writing so in his strangely impersonal *Personal Memoirs*. But his hands were tied. What was he going to do? Start walking north? Become a Mexican? Get shot for desertion? No. So he drank and read the papers, where he found an article that had him saying "You've got to be fucking kidding my mind apart right now." Grant scanned the body for snippets . . .

> *Robert E. Lee wins big in Mexico!*
> *Lee is the best horseman since Washington.*
> *Lee rumored to be teleporting behind enemy lines.*
> *No one ever sees him eat!*
> *Lee paid to have his two favorite mounts transported from Virginia: Tanngnjostr and Tanngrisnir!*
> *Lee will be the commander of all American armies, without a doubt.*
> *They say he can read minds!*
> *Lee will be president.*
> *R.E.L. has scored medals and ranks and money and fame. What will this one-man-wonder-weapon do next!*

U.S.G. flushed with his power need. He knew White Haven got this paper. He knew Julia's Dad would read it and start arranging Lee-a-like marriage options for Julia. He must prove to his gal and her folks that he was marriageable. Maybe he could lose her? No. Grant got action-mad. He tried to get involved in any skirmish, any battle, any melee. He practiced his aim, and he didn't masturbate so to brew hell in his kettle bell. And when old Zach needed all available Americans on May 8, 1846, during the Battle of Palo Alto, Grant broke out of the shop like a berserker.

The field was flat and endless; the ground's lack of ambition accentuated the sky. Still, the enemy hid, they belonged to the land. Grant crouched in the tall grass, duck-walking his way toward the front, passing men with skittering eyes. And out of the perplexing silence came Mexican cannonballs barreling through the peaceful grass. Grant shot at whence they came. Smoke and pops worked up, in and out of rhythms. His blood accelerated to a pumpless loop, the heart's tollbooths open, all lanes. Here came the enemy to share the upsetting side of carnal knowledge.

Hearts: crushed.

Faces: crashed.

Scroats: kicked.

Teeth: gnashed.

Skin: rent.

Bones: snapped.

Futures: ruined.

God: lapsed.

Eyes: peeled.

Anus: goosed.

Hopes: lost.

Souls: loosed.

An Army blacksmith next to Ulysses was decapitated without a sound.

Then John's jaw flew off.

The man in charge burst.

Grant assumed the lead. He took and gave orders. Important people saw. A promotion was gained. But Ulysses' mind cried out: "Boom. I'm a murderer. Boom. I'm a murderer now. Boom, boom. Worse than most men on Earth. I have killed. Boom. I'm going to die, too. Boom. Die before I can repent for this sin. Boom. Murd-boom-der-boom-er!"

Young souls flipped up into the vaporous arms of those airy figures on the edge of heaven's gate. Life sprayed out, life eked out, life coughed out, and some life snapped off with a slump. But other life hung on at a dimmed level, like an uneven chandelier that had lost the support of a few of its ropes, hanging slanted with dropping candles, losing most of its light, until, due to the angle, the remaining life in the flames visually hissed into smoke.

People die and their death affects the lives of their living people, those who were dependent on them, those now left alone on a farm, left unmedicated in a bed, left unfed in a cage. Sometimes people are freed by the death of a tormenter. Sometimes a family tyrant is dissolved by a war like an obstacle of salt. But most times people who die end up, at least for a time, pulling down the momentum of life for those connected to their yoke. The death drags the living down. They're taken off jobs. Taken away from fin-ishing projects. Taken out of the life-stream like a fish held up for a photo before the water rushes back up and around, and off they go again with the flow, but forever different.

A person is more or less the same after losing a leg, an arm, a half. And a person is more or less the same, even if they forget much of their life (be-cause we do, sadly, forget much). But we also get different as we go along, as we lose and gain. What am I saying? Maybe I'm not a dot of gas trapped in a meat machine like we're taught to think. Maybe souls aren't so separable from the body? Maybe we lose a lot if we lose anything. And maybe all of us inevitably must lose pieces of us as we go.

Grant mulled these confusing thoughts while slumped and jostling in the war wagon with the other weapons, soaked in blood, but with clean streaks down the cheeks made by tears, looking like a negative cheetah: stalled, appalled, in shock. Battle won, the dead dead, the living moved on. After drinking away the experience, in the hung-over early gray morning it was hard to not take as a bad omen the jacked black cactus looming over him like a headstone. He backed away, squinting at the man-sized rotted growth leaning there, one arm up, bristled and foreboding. Grant nodded, accepting an insensible communion.

In September of '46 Ulysses didn't feel like pricing merch, so he aban-doned his cash register again, rushing to the nearby battlefront to be more than the worst of animals, and to be as good as the best of animals again. At the front, a vital message needed to be delivered across the no-man's-land in a kind of Pac-Man maze that was made out of a once-vibrant neighbor-hood of homes. No soldier was mad enough to try. It was certain death. Grant shouldered up to the confused C.O. and growled, "I can do it with my hands tied up my ass."

He vaulted onto the back of a manless nag, whispered "I'm sorry" to its flicking ear, and charged down into the valley of the shadow of death. The enemy shot at the horse, so Ulysses hung off one side while riding. Taking the horse to be riderless, the snipers guessed it was only a "spooked loosey" and ceased fire. The message was delivered. Grant gained another promo-tion. It was his "September to remember."

A different battle raged one day in a hollowed-out city near a ruined church where apparently the prayers had not been heard. No one could devise a good position for the heavy artillery. Rich experts had textbook ideas, but none were sparking the imaginations of the brass. So, Grant found a new way to gain distinction. He ordered a giant cannon dismantled and then hauled up to the top of the church bell tower, piecemeal. It was there reassembled, barely in time to give his forces a death angel's angle, which won the battle, and another sweet promo in the field for Ulysses. Positive Disassemblage? He was getting a taste for it. He had put parts of himself in drawers and shut them up. He had found a way to see red and get mean. To not let himself think of the unfairness, the nuance, the reasons not to. No. He broke off those parts and locked them up.

Ulysses had come to pile up power for the sake of love, but the glory gave him good feelings on their own. His accumulated tokens of power got his good glands a'spitting. He was gaining respect. Attention. Fellow West Pointers from his grade touched their hats at him and said "There's the guy who high-jumped that horse at graduation" and "He's getting a bunch of field promos. Pretty sweet berserker." Young privates got Grant to autograph their jerseys. During one or two excursions, he may have worn an Armadillo helmet. No one can really be sure. But his plan had worked. He had become a war hero. He'd strung together a handful of notable events, got a higher rank, higher pay grade, and some good press. He had made himself into the character of tellable stories. He'd become the little quiet bullheaded guy with big crazy ideas that just plain worked. And it felt good. He had recalled his wigged West Point professor saying "Reality is not a story; stories are what we make of it." Now others had taken up his story that he'd shaped from his life, and it had stuck.

After three years, the Mexican-American War ended. The U.S. gained a ton of territories, including California—which, only a month later, was declared to be rushing with newly discovered gold.

"Good thing it was only *now* found on *American* soil! What luck! Ha ha!" said the Devil.

Chapter 5

Go West, Young Manslaughterer

1848–1854

AGES 26–32

IN 1848, GRANT RETURNED TO THE STATES, A TWENTY-SIX-year-old romantic lead back from far-off heroic escapades with intriguing emotional wounds, and perhaps a secret wound on his dick. Who knows? I'll tell you who knows: Julia GRANT. Yeah! Because Ulysses wed the hell out of her as soon as he could steam up the Mississippi's mighty gush.

Her dad, after seeing Grant's notices in the pages of a small-time Tejano magazine, was forced to admit that Grant had budding renown and that he had earned an adequate rank. The suitor was a decorated killer, and that could be said with pride at dinner tables. The hand was given. After the nuptials and victuals, they absconded with their sacrificial virginities to a secluded motel with room service and a no-knock policy.

There is thinking about it, and there's feeling about it . . . and it was time to feel about. She was bigger. He scampered over her, decorum switched off, crabbing like a cautious masseur. He assumed she'd want to be scratched like a dog as he did. But she didn't. He had to learn what she loved and wanted. She called the shots, but he drove. The duo worked out their personal arithmetic, soon syncing the arrhythmic ticks of the buried clocks in their bodies. They abraded each other with face and leg stubble. She absorbed him. Allowed him. The heart in the walls of her body played double-bass half-time until her saturated glands burst, and her interior squinched . . . or so she said of herself aloud in the moment, and later to friends, I'm sure.

He could swear to slightly sense the world through her body, as if hers were his. He swore he could feel with her touch and she with his. He could feel the faintest signal, easily squelched if not careful. Yes. Right there. A nice, sparkling, rippling tingle. You feel it, Embarrassed Reader. Can you feel it? They were a two-color rainbow, a two-color valley, a two-color mountain, a one-color kiss on this, this, this, bliss, bliss, bliss. They cleaved unto one another as one unashamed flesh, as the how-to book had said to be. The two could escape the world so long as they were together. The bond was a portable asylum. It was theirs. It was theirs.

One dewy morn after the honeymoon, but before his leave was up, Yules sat in bed, smacking on grapes, wagging his naked feet, and grinning like a cute Caligula waiting for Jules to come out of the bathroom. As soon as the door clicked, he chatted her up, high on coffee. Now that they had gotten the fucking established, he expected the old plan to kick in: he'd quit the Army and they'd start fresh somewhere nice. In the north. Get those horses. Get the stable. Get a real life going.

"I'm telling you, Jules. I can't kill anymore. I can't even be around it. The soldier's life is not for me. It's actually way worse than the tannery be-cause—"

"I'm pregnant."

The unsurprising surprise had happened. Ulysses could feel the wires and cables that connected this to that in the back of his hardware—all of it was getting yanked out and rerouted by the ghostly protocol of nature. It was time to think and run himself in new ways. Dad ways. A chunk of life was over, absolutely, never to return.

He reported back to base after extended sex leave, and the two were sent off to Upstate New York. A lovely place if you've got an extra ass you don't mind freezing off. New headquarters. New job. New coworkers. New

climate. New rented hovel. Same Quartermastering. Quickly after settling, he was re-stationed to re-work the retail aspects of the Detroit forts.
New everything again, but still fucking like rabbits and playing cards with
young couples that they secretly despised.

The intimacy of close quarters between the opposite sexes was new.
What was that bag for? What is she doing with that knife in there? Does he
really need to piss that much in a night, letting in the cold wind? He caught
countless spiders for her, half of which were only wadded women's hair that
she ultimately blamed on the previous tenants. He got a gallon piss jug for
a birthday gift. Her belly grew. They ate and smiled and worried and kept
their rooms clean. Clothes clean. Bodies clean. They carried on like this
for months, moving from one set of rented rooms to another, her carrying
the greater half of their shared armoire, despite his protestations, in and
out, up and down stairs, over and over, happy and laughing. They never put
society over their world of two. They never put anything over it. Sure, she
met with friends or family members. She had her correspondences, causes,
and dog-breeding books. And he had mostly horses. It's the kind of period
that a man can build a life upon, and Grant did. They only needed to break
out of this poorness because she had the baby and then got pregnant again
in the space of one sentence!

The cry of a little human and the healing of a vagina took a lot of getting
used to for mostly her. He assumed the child would want stillness, like him.
But in his immobile arms the baby became a growling little beast, fussy and
preparing its miniature fury. Grant would find that the infant only wanted
to be shaken and tapped like a primitive tambourine, and it wanted it constantly. The cooling lovers separately wondered if this tyrannical baby had
ruined that two-person paradise they had inhabited mere months ago. It
wasn't a two-person anything anymore. The rainbow had baby-blue in it
now. The valley was padded and baby-safe-ugly. And the mountain wasn't
mounted as much. And they have a second one on the way? What on earth
were they doing to themselves? His every action affected his dependents.
What happened if one of them got sick or hurt? What if he lost his job?
They were barely getting by, and the family was growing.

He'd go on blue walks, whispering to himself: "How can I be the head
of a family? I don't even have a library. My Napoleonic physique is softening

because I'm rocking and shushing all the time. I'm almost thirty. My prime is over. I gotta get something new going. Rubbers for sure, but . . . no. No rubbers."

Outside, the secret snow caught cum in the lonely night, its steam a pitiful puff.

Soon, despite their great attitudes and efforts, the newlyweds felt the teeth grinding in the jaws of their spouses. The stress stiffness filled the room. Moods were silently expressed, communication continued via pitch-black auras. Money. Food. Fire. Baby tackle. It was all precious, took time, and nothing else mattered. Candles were rationed and often nighttime activities hinged on the exhibitionism of the moon. He'd look at Julia in that cold, dark home as she nursed his progeny and rubbed her gestating guts. Maybe she was staring back at him, and maybe she was regretting. She, more than he, had absorbed the hard parts of parenthood. He saw that. He knew he could leave the house and go sell buttons and boots at work, but she was cornered into maturity, reality, and scariness. She was changing and adapting to it. Her reaction to new books sounded older and more cynical than before. He knew he had to catch up and do his part to set up a stable, unfrozen nest. For Christ's sake, consider the story: a princess had ridden off with this traveling toad, and now he's given her two gutter babies. For the sake of putting her "mouth money" where her liberal ideas were, this princess had traded a comfortable castle for these barren old freezing rooms. She didn't want help from her satanic family, but was she secretly hoping he'd turn into a prince? He worried that to keep this love past the "must-fuck stage," he'd maybe need more power. Besides, he would not let his kids grow up poor like he had. He must turn himself into a staircase for them. Then she said what were the opposite of magical words:

"Maybe I should write to Dad?"

While chopping wood, he was distracted with schemes, gathering up the heavy, biting logs, not even noticing the yellow splinters sticking through the gloves. He kept lists. Circled ads. He put feelers out for a new job, a new career, or, better yet, a warmer—yet not Southern—post, anything to make it easier for Julia. His dad re-upped the offer to come in as partner at the tannery and move back to Ohio with the family. The skin-'n'-fur business was booming. Jesse had even opened a new shop on a cute downtown main street. Grant could use his Quartermastering retail skills there. Yeah! Suicide! No. He couldn't return home without having trans-formed into something bigger. He couldn't let down his old friends or face his mom with all his power spilled from his out-turned pockets. That felt like losing steam, like falling backwards into a gutter or something. No. He'd stick with the soldier's life. He'd find a way to make it work. So, he thought as he chopped.

When a Quartermaster post opened up in the Pacific Northwest, he jumped on it. There he'd supply goods to the federal muscle that was keep-ing the Natives away from the gold that was native to their land but was hastily rushing out of it. Grant had heard that San Francisco had recovered after the great conflagration in '51. Supposedly, the fire had only burned off the riffraff. So he pitched his plan to his blanketed, impregnated wife, and to his judgmental infant son.

"I'll go alone. I'll make a quick fortune with some side-hustle ideas I've worked up out by the woodpile, and I'll treat the Army like a day job. I'll parlay the goodwill from my well-known Mexican exploits into moving up in rank to get better pay and insurance, and after I get everything set up, I'll send for you, my lovely wife and babies. Everyone's getting rich out West. We can't lose!"

Julia wasn't keen on losing him or staying in the frozen hell of Detroit. But supposedly this would happen quickly, and the plan was economic. She nodded and squinted up at him from her cranky rocker. "Okay," she said. And he smiled while scanning her stolid face for unsaid remaining remarks.

Before the Canal, one either traveled across Native American land as target practice, or one trekked across the thin Isthmus of Panama. Grant went Isthmus—he'd heard good things. He waved goodbye, jumped on a ship, chewed taffy, and smiled like an idiot. Odysseus sails again! But this time the sea voyage was on a civilian ship. He drank cocktails from the Tiki Bar and watched the eastern seaboard go by. Yules wore a good-luck gift from Julia that she had bought him with her personal money: an overly large beaver hat, like the one Yules' hero Kit Carson wore when he went West to work with the Native Peoples. It was a stocky, sheeny black cylin-der that made his shadow look like an Easter Island sculpture. He wore it and role-played as he had as a kid. He was Kit. And Kit was as cool as he.

Grant couldn't let himself admit his ambivalence about leaving his new family. He made a big deal about its sucking, but he feared he was living a split life because immediately there was enjoyment from getting away. He loved his wife and children, but here was a freedom, a faux bachelorhood. He thought of Julia in the depressing nursery that was once their fuck hut. He was drunk, free from the baby cries. Guilt. Guilt. Guilt spilt into him. He drank more.

A side-hugging, chortling band of twenty-year-old richies on a destination bachelor party from Connecticut spotted Our Man in Uniform and adopted the war vet as their mascot for the voyage. They were on their way to Mexico City, were hard as rocks, and enjoyed buying their little rugged world-traveler all the drinks and meat he could handle. After a while, even Ulysses was wearing a neckerchief with long bunny ears snapping in the breeze. Old touring women with dozing husbands hooked his elbow's crook with their fishing moray-eel arms and welcomed him to their shuffleboard matches. They too wanted to hear his Mexican stories about the colors of the rocks and the sky. And he found other soldiers deployed to the West Coast too.

"At least it's not Chattanooga."

"Hahaha. Chatt-a'fucking-nooga."

Finally, from the bleary railing he was able to notice the changing of trees in the shoreline. Personality palms. Nice. Soon Our Hero waved goodbye to the ship, bought water in a coconut, and with other eager isthmusers entered the trailhead noted in the brochure.

"Here we go!"

Oh, but that isthmus. Oh, my good God almighty, that fucking isthmus. See, Reader, this was before industry was made by pulling gum or whatever out of these trees, and the place was raw, natural, and flat-out anti-human. Most of his companions died in that jungle within moments. The ground would transform into oil slick, into quicksand, or into a restaurant of privacy grass for raptors. Jaguars cracked skulls in their teeth like Tootsie Roll Pops, and the lower life came to eat the skin off what wasn't hoisted into the trees. This was what the travel agent said to do, right? Had he missed an unknowable cleared-off strip? Was this a joke? How was this an option? Grant moved forward through the jungle, soaked in rainforest sweat, dehydrated, hungry, and tempted to make bread out of stones in this wet Wilderness. He'd had no idea he'd be sleeping in a tent with strangers, bartering for goods or services in the most wicked nights of his life so far.

Half the party died at the hands of gathering shades, the other half by dysentery. And it hit him too. His ass checks chapped and blistered. So, he rigged up a kind of G-string out of leaves to stop the chafing. He walked with his feet four feet apart for four feet. But he stopped and cried as he watched the rest of his surviving company leave him for dead in the dripping jungle. Would he give up? Fuck no. He'd go forward at his own pace, in his own way. Our Bull continued on with only his Army orders in his G-string, a machete in hand, and the hat on his head. With lips cracking, and blood like tabasco molasses, Grant, the Taurus, Taurus-ed on.

Without warning, after hundreds of thousands of agonizing steps, he staggered out of the jungle onto the sandy shore of the Pacific Ocean like a time traveler from all the worst times ever. It was day, and this was the first time he'd seen the sky since he'd gone under the jungle's canopy. The blue-on-blue moon in the morning hung there like a deteriorating death star. His skin was one complete mosquito bite. Teeming bacteria burst his flesh. Parasites packed his hollows. He doddered in wide micro steps like a rash-riddled amputee spider, dragging two lines in the sand on the inside of his footprints: one from the machete blade, the other from the hat, which was tethered to him by his fraying belt and dragging heavily behind. A hoppity vulture continued to strike at it, as it had done for the last half day. Seeing no info desk, he lay down in the sand and passed out.

Ulysses awoke again at sea. Different boat, slightly different man. His pieces came back together after a night of giving witness to his disassemblage in half-dreaming off-mode. He sat up from a clean bed and saw the glittering waters. This was before our species asphyxiated all fish, and they danced, leaping into the air for fish reasons. He was on the nursing mezzanine, a white and blond-wood atmosphere with red crosses in all the right places working nicely with the pale blue and the deep blue halves of the world. Nurses went in and out. Next to him lay an old woman from the first ship that had somehow crossed over too, but now her moray eels were empty, creped skin that dangled stiffly as she reached out for water and declined embraces. She explained that this crew, whose duty was to transport isthmusers up the coast, had found them both. But she couldn't look at

Ulysses without crying. He blinked at himself in a mirror. Was this to be him forever? Azure-lipped, shivering, and shriveled like King Tut up in his wrap? He glowed a faint purple, and his skin had drawn up all its pores but one: his cracked mouth, which squawked like his dry joints in the paradoxically drying/waterlogged air of the Pacific.

Ulysses thanked a completely white man with red irises who said he was the doctor. The man had handkerchiefs covering the gaps between cuff and glove, collar and hair. The albino gave Grant his bill. The cost was more than he'd make in years.

"How's my hat?"

"It didn't make it."

The rest of the voyage he spent in a deck chair. For four days and nights wrapped in blankets, he sipped at hot water, working up a single piss. He noticed that over this ocean the stars had shifted from where and when he knew to see them. The stick figures still square-danced, dragging across the dust of that dark. Scorpion. Twins. Hunters. Belts. But the Taurus seemed to be falling back, tumbling in reverse and possibly about to crush its spine with its own weight. He aimed his crunching eyes at the sea to watch for whale-breath instead.

He missed his baby's cries. He missed his wife's sighs. He wished he could return to her, to that time, to that him before, to laughing and loving and riding horses—oh, no. He cried dried tear skins because he'd not recalled until that moment that he had eaten his packhorse in the jungle. He rolled to his side, twitching his frame with sobs until his innards cinched their grip and coughed out a length of hardened black rope, which jerked through the open-backed gown. The turd landed onto the deck with a sad clack.

San Francisco was an experiment long abandoned by the experimenters and taken up by an element of humanity equipped to call the shabbiest crag a home: adventurers, runaways, scallywags, skullddugger-ers, skull fucker-ers, and the fuckers of anything corporeal or recently so. And good for them! Three cheers for folks who can find themselves in their own pioneering pleasures. Women and men and all in between roamed the docks with pride, and good for them! Even the prostitutes, good for them! Such life is everywhere, hidden more or less, seen less more and more.

Ulysses strolled the slanting streets and swaying docks. Drunk or not, condoning or not, he could never abide seeing naked feet on display. "Look at them just out for anyone to see," he'd think with inbred puritanical reaction. "Look at that one there! For the price of breakfast, it could be anyone's for the sucking! Ugh! Christ, Yules, don't look at her sickening foot, dried tacky with sex sweat, stuck out in this same air I'm breathing. Ew! Her pointing human stomper is right there, all the more repulsive for the self-awareness of its supposed seductiveness. Paint even on the talons. No. 'I'm so dainty,' the foot thinks, as it grips its grubs in the air, searching for the ground, like how a held-up hound will paddle over untouched water below it. No!"

Feet aside, he was nonjudgmental. Our Man grabbed a beer, heard new music, tasted Asian spices, compared Long John Silver's to Captain D's, and got an air-tattoo from a mime.

The town was mostly built on rickety piers that supported harlot stores, which were stacked on top of booze rooms. The complicated rot swayed and creaked over the stink of the further rotting ocean. Fish got drunk off the complicated drool that spiraled down the supports of the bedlam above. All the toilets were simply holes in the deck, and all holes in the deck were toilets.

Folks from 'round the world flocked to San Francisco looking for new gold but ending up in Popeyes or Pequods. I'm talking about the Polynesians, the Asians, the Russians, the Canadians, and the subterraneans. People starting over. People without backstories. And plenty of gutter men, too. Fallen souls. Shell-shocked soldiers and bad-luck magnets wallowed in rueful recollections. Teenage romantics in denial who had escaped frying pans were here burning in the fire of "not having an address to put on a job application." There were madmen and lost women, truly disordered folk pushed to the edge of the planet by the "normal people" who didn't know how to deal with 'em. Our Man felt in pretty good shape next to such fallen folk with no ways to overcome anything. There was Marut, Azazel, and Push Cookie; Asbeel, Wee, and Keenie Kerner; Push Pop, Inchworth, Harut, Pumper, and Stinky B; Sugar Loaf, Bushrod, Kokabeil, and Tamiel. And each ended up with Grant's money.

Naïve Ulysses fell for all the schemes and scams, each dumbly elaborate or elaborately dumb. He wasted more money than a sultan with multiple birthdays. He traveled the area seeking business leads, riding a rented, purple-fruit-dusty roan. Once Ulysses went up past the city but down toward a shore which never arrived, and there, under rotund redwoods, he met a man in a cape who pitched importing something that would change the world: a banana. Oh, Grant knew about those, and he gave the man his money but got only the man's disappearance in return. He met with "talent," thinking he could be a "manager." But the talent never ended up to be actors nor writers nor even illusionists. They turned out to be "a man who could move his like a tail," or, "a woman who could twitch hers like a mouth." He paid them for their time.

Despite rich experts advising him against it, Grant tried to become a potato king, buying up land and . . . seeds, I guess. But the land flooded and his potatolets—each named—rolled into the ocean.

He put money into a leather store, neither real nor a good lie. He put money behind a cunnilinguist with grand plans of opening a clinic. Yes! Finally, a good one. But, alas, the cunnilinguist ran off down to Cheddar Bay. A month later he got a photograph in the mail. It was the cunnilinguist, who had started a cult in Big Sur. In the photo they held up a martini at Nepenthe, whales spitting in the background.

He met a beachfront chef in the hot blood of a dying dolphin. He met a water-witch who could divine veins of gold. And he met men who sold coffee beans that were actually just seeds sifted from animal shit. Finally, a Russian little person let him in on a brilliant investment. This guy had bought an Alaskan iceberg and had arranged for a ship to tow it down in chains. Most people had things to be kept on ice: fish, leviathans, megaladons, and meddlers. But the iceberg melted en route or had never existed. The American Dream out in the trillion-dollar wasteland of California was ironically even harder to grasp. Forgive my translated French but de Tocqueville once said "You can be the Pussy King of Kentucky and still be a nobody in California."

After this string of failures, Ulysses declared "Hindsight is for asses," and determined never to look or to go backwards, out of spite. It was going to be his mantra: to never go backwards. Yep. Grant, in full Taurus mode, doubled down on the soldier's life. But no one in the Army recalled his Mexican War Hero Stories. He had no cachet to leverage. And his reputation as a "bad businessman with a budding drinking problem" had reached his superiors, who invariably had the same reaction when reviewing his papers.

"Hey, West Point! Nice. Did you know Robert E. Lee? Heard he was a teetotaler. No booze for that bad ass. Hahaha, anywho . . . Grant, Grant, Grant . . . let's see . . . oh . . ."

Due to his bad attitude and the ugly true rumors about his over-drinking, his options were few. So, he accepted the post with the highest pay available to him, one the Army had trouble keeping staffed: the outermost remote garrison far north of San Francisco, where it was rumored that there were cute dwarf bears in hoodies who were friends with the hostile Natives. In a lonely cabin deep in the forest, he'd work as liaison to the Natives. Just like Kit!

After days of rainy riding, climbing the mountains, over Horeb, under Hinnom, through the rust-red columns and green fanning floor fronds, he came upon the outpost. It was a one-room pine cube. Inside, a jet-black, pot-bellied, cast-iron fireplace dominated this cot-and-table affair. A predecessor had drawn with white chalk a jolly face and chubby hands on this squatting mass. Grant shook his head at the vandalism. Further crowding the limited space were stacks of boxes containing the goods left by the Supply Corps. He dropped his bag and cracked the packs.

"Wait, I didn't get all the stuff on my rider . . . Where are my lozenges . . . and I was *really* needing a bunch of rubber bands and a couple more pillows? Who was the idiot Quartermaster who didn't do his job? What am I going to do with 300 boxes of cigars? Oh, great: *Deep Woods Off!* is on backorder, and wait . . , mustard sardines? I specified soy oil. Bitch, goddamn it. Well, at least there's a crate of Underwoods." He worked the quaint, acoustic coffee maker, and unboxed what turned out to be an accidental, overstocked crate of whiskey bottles. "Well, well, well."

Grant set up shop. It was kind of like his kid's dream of running away to be a frontiersman. Neat! He exhaled a minute of stillness that practically anyone can achieve before resuming their natural fretting. "This is good. I can do this. Why couldn't they find guys to do this? Shit. This is normal. This is a challenge a man like me should be able to handle. I'm a man, aren't I? An American man."

After a month, the Natives came. He had heard horror stories and he was scared, keeping a baseball bat by the door. Yet Ulysses showed real respect and an unassuming, open, interested attention. He was meeting with individuals, and he showed such considerations. He marveled at the styles. The manners. Those he had been taught to fear, like the Mexicans, turned out to be more than the stories would allow. He learned of complex and various peoples who each considered this land theirs, and who were in the middle of disrupted disputes. They were pissed at the United States for a variety of reasons. And he listened patiently. Grant danced with no wolves for them, yet he connected in his own way. At first, he assumed the emissaries would love the cigars as he did. They did not. And he had to learn what they loved and wanted. He expected them to agree with him on the sardines, but many preferred the mustard ones over his beloved soybean oil. Dear Reader, you'll find no "noble savage" tropes here. These men and women each had their own shit going on, but I stand by this: their art, no matter fucking what, was great.

They trashed Fenimore Cooper and laughed out loud at Natty Bumppo. Through these diplomats he learned that Kit Carson was a horrible person in real life. They helped Grant see that he had willfully denied the frontiersman's bad facts by replacing them with his own good ones. Sure, he'd done a few cool things, but the bad stuff way outweighed the good. Wanna keep your heart unbroken? Remember there are heroic deeds, not heroic people.

Seasons changed and these visiting contacts grew genuinely concerned for this whiskey-logged mountain-man who drank all the time now like a tattered little Natty Lite. Ulysses cried while telling them about his family far away, and how he missed them. He showed them the stove and the converted chalk drawing that was now Julia. It had her eyes, and he had his burns.

His visitors couldn't comprehend why a man would leave that which mattered most to him. What good was this American Dream he talked about if he couldn't share it with anyone he loved? His heart farted a fevered clot of snot out from his crying face when hearing this obvious wisdom. The Natives continued to press him: for what kind of nation was he even a warrior? He didn't want to answer. He tried to explain the dream he and Sherman had talked about in college: that More Perfect Union that should happen; freedom and equality for all; peace for all, shamone. But that SHOULD seemed so far away from the IS of it all.

He'd spend months alone, rolling around on the floor in the cabin, loafing and gazing at clipped nails from toe or finger held aloft in the tufts of dusty pubic hair bunnies, crescent moons fixed in the confections of shed body hair. Those dust bunnies were like delicate, filament orbs of reject DNA reforming the unwanted parts of himself as if they knew that he'd for sure have to see them when he lay on the floor there while letting his eyes rove about the cabin's low life levels. They'd say "Here you are. Breaking apart, worthless, and drifting."

Ants in this cabin got looked at a lot and fed more than a chip or two. They were christened with names. Attributes, true or not about them, got fixed into song lyrics set to minor keys played out on a cigar-box ukulele, which was tuned like shit without a true note for miles to be found.

Grant got fewer and fewer letters from Julia. At first, he chalked it up to a bad pony, then to the great distance, and then to her mysterious, laconic cool. In spiraling paranoia, he began assuming that she had fallen out of love with the him he had become. He had given her two babies and an empty bed in exchange for her new, horrid life. Was his family frozen to death in Detroit? Or had she got a divorce and married a Hotspur?

He could only chug his share of lugs and drink himself under the table that had turned on him. He drank so much that he feared his aching right eye was going to liquefy into granulated syrup. And if that doesn't make much sense to you, your drinking is probably fine.

He was eating poorly and would spend hours in the outhouse, trying to scare up the phantom turd, the dreaded brown recluse. He could feel the need, but he couldn't "break me off a piece of that shit-shat bar."

Grizzlies, sasquatches, 49ers, actual mountain men, killers on the lam, lambs of mama mountain goats, and goats in the form of Robert E. Lee on multiple covers of *Stars and Stripes* all taunted him in rancid, diurnal dreams. He was tempted to jump off a high cliff to see if angels might grab him up by the collar in the last second. But he resisted the temptation and said "I got my cigar-box uke tuned to crow caw. Pretty sure that's a G#," and he kept on Natty Bumpin', checking his banana slug on the skillet in that dead light under the colossi.

The woebegone Grant now had multiple cigars going at all times as a kind of incense to keep mosquitoes and visitors away. Out of him, through the grossest ways they could escape, were coming his dead, shed, overgrown nerve-endings. His piss was cloudy. His shit, when shat, was chalky. His spit, when spat, was lumpy.

In letters, he begged for reassignment, but the only positions made available were blatant embarrassments: Chattanooga, for example. He said to that one crow with perfect pitch, "Maybe I will try out dying a little bit." Because at age thirty-two, Ulysses knew how it felt to be cooled by wind, water, dirt, stone, fire, hands, nails, breath, and pet ants. He had worn dust as sunblock and needed none in this perpetual shade. He knew how it felt to be warmed by sun, fire, water, hands, and body, but he was an old man, had had a good run, and was okay to go. He had felt his share.

In that instant, the supply wagon arrived to re-up the sardines. For his hard service he was to be rewarded with the new rank of Captain. They found him lying on his funeral bier, dressed in only a blanket cape, smoking five cigars at once, and yelling at the ground for not being the sky. Around his neck was a sign: DO NOT REINSTATE. It was his letter of resignation.

PART THREE

Chapter 6

Hard Scrabblin'

1855–1859

AGES 33–37

HERE'S THE THING ABOUT HELL . . . THE DEVILS ARE HAVING a blast. In '55, Our Ohio Yankee returned to White Haven. This time, with ducts empty, children made, mind fragile, and being 33, like Christ in his death year, Grant's awareness was on max. Slavery was not obscured by his youthful hormones. No. He was old enough to see, retain the sight, and convert it into meaning. He was capable of imagining the lives lost from all these lives kept from living. All these people who coulda. Coulda been allowed to live simply as they wished, and nothing beyond that. The shame of it affects us forever in all directions of time, not only forward toward the shore of death, but out sideways and backwards, rewashing what was with what is, and is, and is. Such past was, and forever is, atrocity. Amen.

His family had moved in with Father Dent mere days after he'd left. Julia had caved, and she was ashamed. She couldn't bring herself to say it in a letter while Ulysses was losing his ever-loving mind in the West. So she'd let the letters lapse.

The Dent house, thriving off slave labor, had been more than able to accommodate the prodigal daughter and her two abandoned boys. Britain was no longer getting cotton from Egypt, and the South had taken over the trade, basing most of its economy on it. Abhorrent whites went about like nothing was amiss, reading poetry and dressing like a bunch of butterscotch Byrons, just livin' the dream, Baby!

The Grant Family Plan that was supposed to have taken months had taken three years. He had nothing to show from it but the knowledge that the soldier's life was not for him. It had taken nearly dying while chasing power for him to realize he'd rather have none, so long as he had the love in his life. He knew now to grab hold of what little love he could, and never let go.

They met in that old garden in new light. Julia had changed, grown in being and body, a giantess of the soul. She saw Grant and she rose to full height. Ulysses swallowed hard. His wife was indeed taking in his changes as well. His darkness in the eye areas, his drunk's sunk face, his atrophied form, dropped buttocks, and tramp's posture—all as thin as a snake's pupil in broad daylight. He was done with power-seeking, and his body said so. The man shuffled with meekness. This errant husband was ready to be a simple, broken, useful man-about-the-place, a sacrificial bridge for his kids to a better life, and a son-in-law that keeps to the horses. She took him in and started the repair work right away, and he took the petting like a soundless hound.

"Oh, Yules."

"Oh, Jules."

The eldest son, Fred, was a vampy enigma old enough to fantasize that other men were his sire. Buck was a scamp with a fistful of dust and a keen need to spit. Grant set out to learn his boys' ways, to be their dad, and to earn their trust. He had to teach them anything so he could say to himself that he could. He gave them trinkets from the West: real bows and arrows from the Natives, and a precious ant farm. The boys looked at this rag of a man whose revival of a smile was as unnatural as a microwaved rose before them. They could sense his fear, smell his worry. It would take some time.

Later that first evening in their own lovely rooms of the sinful mansion, after all the goodnights, tooth-brushings, readings, toy showings, ghost checkings, squabblings, assurances, threatenings, promises, consolings, cajolings, and lecturings; after all the teaching moments, lessons recalled, and moments ruined; after the boys were asleep . . . the parents, the spouses, the man and woman found themselves alone in tongue-tied sign language, sharing a bed again after three years apart. The apparition of his virginity visited him to shake and quaver and rush Our Man through the marital moments as if he were some kind of senseless novice. His crawling paw on her knee-jerking soul went too quick, his skin wasn't receptive.

"Your hand is so cold and eager. And your nails need—Honey, let's wait a moment."

She got the shears from the bed box and sat up to work on his fingers with her back to him. Lying there looking up at her sitting on the edge of the bed, he waited as she shaped up each piggy. He fell to sleep as she took her pill, applied her lotion, and tended to her clattering businesses in the nightstand. Sounds. Lovely sounds of another soul in the room.

In the morning, he opened his eyes to exactly the same scene: she sitting on her edge of the bed, her back to him, looking out the window in the cold morning light. He hadn't moved in his slumber, and she hadn't been up long. This moment allowed for them both to tune their nude instruments to each other's frequency. He let his eyes gaze at the complexity of her skin there in variegated coats across her back. Whitish blue, reddish white, orangey crème, green in the corners, he could add -ish and -y to any possible colors as he found them there in that broadly fleshy, mannish back, feminized with the hastily done-up hair atop the head, atop the neck-trunk, atop the fly wings of trapping shoulders. The hulk of her defied and affirmed all categories. A powerful loveliness: Ingres' *Valpincon Bather* and Goya's *Seated Giant* in one.

A shared smirk was enough. But then . . . it wasn't. Their bodies had been apart for so long that communication was cluttered, confused, catching up.

"How can I read this cheek when it has changed?"

"This brow, down as default, means what?"

But it came. One can remember with one's hand. They did. We must learn lessons over and over as we fall out of the learned state. Like our physical shape: if you don't exercise closeness, closeness goes away.

The family got their act together. He had missed out on their babyhoods, and he'd be damned if he missed their other hoods. He was informed of pets, current and deceased. Some really great personalities, I guess. You know what I mean. Important dogs who got Christmas bones. He heard about those. He taught them how to pet cats the right way, and they showed him what the Dent dogs did when you whistled. He read a poem to the quiet kid who liked sounds and threw a stick for the wild one. The Little Daddy got back into their lives not in a final, complete, and peaceful way. No. He got in the mix. He took up actions in the open problems that we call people. He had feuds and makeups with each of them, never in sync, most of the time with at least one a bit pissed. In short, he was a family man again, and they felt snug about it. There was joy.

He allowed himself to stop acting like a machine and to slow down. Re-sensitive. Spare life. Feel time. Yules learned what their laughs could mean. The shrugs, walks, slumps, silences, each action could hand him something to feel. If you ain't there, you can't care. He was and he did. Julia, satisfied, smirked, watching her precious manlets mixing it up with her man. It's the kind of thing people fuck about. And they did, resulting in another pregnancy.

For formal dinners, Grant dressed in Dent's hand-me-down, out-of-fashion dinner tails, tall collar, broad bowtie, white gloves, needless bullshit, etc. In the first weeks his body stayed so thin, and his ass was so deflated that the seam ran directly across his anus. Beyond looking ex-marooned, he had that embarrassment and reluctance to show his face to anyone who might only have a "past him" in their mind, especially if that "him" was full of a promise which the current "him" had not made the most of. Grant was sure this would be the case for all reciprocating Dent family faces. He'd ready himself for sacrifice in the mirror and see Julia trying to side-eye him over his shoulder.

Throughout the big house the nighttime air was golden, hazy and soft, a low light from wondrously even chandeliers. The men wore black and white, which turned into fuzzy contrasted blocks. The women's gowns tinkled and crushed, reflecting like spacecraft foil in star shine. The heels clocked across patterned, reflective flora-firma. The painted tiles were expensive and ignored. Fine furniture was stacked with glimmering ephemera. Dent had the place decked out in aesthetic maximalism, with filigree on top of byzantine anything. All poshlust, all performance, all power show. Black faces simmered on the edges, tamped, but alert, hoping only to get through the routine performance again, and again . . .

These supposedly formal dinners in Dent's Court were society plays. Costly games. White Haven often served The Bleak House Special: fish, fowl, sweetbread, veg, pudding, and Madeira. Annoying, fashionable takes on seasonal game were expected. Rabbit was ruined. Squirrel was misunderstood. And for Thanksgiving, rather than serve up the indigenous wild turkeys, they preferred to dig up archaeopteryx truffles because a popular personality had recently said one simply must.

Julia's male cousins and the visiting, jacked, gentleman callers had power and sway. A few dinner guests were also war vets with kill stories, and they probably had anecdotes about dismantling even heavier artillery to reassemble it on top of goddamn cathedrals. The women had married monsters, and they loved watching their catches drink and cut people off at the table. Other gals had married harmless but wealthy Teddy Ruxpins who knew what to say and said it only if pushed.

When men get old, and if they have money, they get "koala face." It happens to even the best-looking faces if they can afford whatever food and drink they want. It's a badge of honor, koala face, like a Rolex that can't be stolen. And tonight, there were just such marsupial supperers. Dear Reader, see this forced peerage laughing and feeling disgustingly fine. The dinner had started stately, but as usual it had quickly slid riotous, in the real Southern way, loosened by whiskeys and wines. Men yelled their laughs. Women found their ways in. The comedy was cruel, and the conduct was incongruous to the setting, like cavemen at Calgary.

At the far end of this beautiful walnut table, beyond the china all a'twinkle in the weak evening candlelight, slouched a shadowy hillock low in his ornate chair, visible only from sternum up. With hair and beard glistening, Grant stared into his turtle soup like a propped-up ventriloquist doll at the estate sale of a newly dead puppeteer. Next to him, Julia cocked an eyebrow at these people who had worsened what was to be hers.

A broad-shouldered, clean-shaven motherfucker took up two table sittings with his jet-black tuxedo and waxed-down Brahms hair. With a gleaming, blue-glazed, marble lantern jaw, and a wide, flat rectangle smile full of too many itty-bitty, cubic teeth, the lout shouted boorish opinions, which Dent appeared to relish. "How 'bout a tale from way out West?" this big man said, whapping a bone down on his plate.

The rest directed their faces toward the would-be tale spinner. Would this be a sporting interrogation of Our Bantamweight Bull?

"Right, Ol' Odysseus is delivered fresh from the Wilderness, I see. I hear 'Frisco is a land of temptation, eh?" asked a man's man, hot in all houses, a man who could never be truly dried.

"I heard you can buy an acre for a dollar out there."

"Supposedly a 'banana' is a wet cake that grows from a tree in the shape of a man's—"

"I hear Cheddar Bay is real nice year-round."

"Someone just got rich hauling down an iceberg from Alaska. Did you ever—"

"The Indians out West eat blue coats."

"Cali is going pro slavery, like us."

"Oregon too."

"Kansas too."

"And all that new land in between," puffed Dent, "how's a man supposed to make money off that land without slaves?"

"Did pilgrims have sla—"

"I hear this new anti-slave party is trying to find a perfect man to run for president."

"Grant, you're pro-slave, right?"

"He's here, ain't he? Don't often meet Antis anymore."

Julia sighed, and everyone knew what it meant.

Ruxpin hit PLAY on his anodyne chitchat. "Grant, what line of work do you plan to pursue now that you've hung up the saber?"

A guy in wraparounds spoke for Ulysses. "He's gunna stay with old man Dent! Be a plantation man. What's he going to do? Go back to being a cashier like his father?"

All faces waited on Ulysses, who, after staring back for an eternity, bit loudly into an apple. Julia smiled proudly at her tiny man like he was Danny fuckin' Zuko flicking a butt at the fuzz. They watched in silence as he smacked on Eve's brain food. Then the ignorant biggun tittered. The swan in crinoline cawed. The nautilus face chortled. The whole maddening table took over the humor, as hordes will do, and they made the moment into their dumb flat horrible own. Honey isn't supposed to go bad, but men can make it so.

Untold pain emits from every choice. To love one is to not love another. To buy from one—and on and on. My kindness to myself is selfishness, is gluttony, is earth-killing. The superhero takes a day off to be a good dad and so neglects the burning schoolhouse. Grant reconnected as a husband and father, but could only do so at this place. They were living like royalty, but could he take more nights like this? And the interactions with the enslaved servants? Anathema, anathema! The reality of living off this evil of enslavement was too much. This had to change. Later in their rooms, while the Grants picked out their night-night buddies, Ulysses addressed his family.

"You may be asking 'Can Daddy do anything but kill and ride?' Hell, yes. I'm adaptable. I can evolve, I can stretch, I can become the best at whatever I need to, baby."

Julia and the boys gave him the "keep it moving" gesture.

"Here's the Grant Family Plan, Part Two, guys. I get a new career going—in the area—while we live rent-free at White Haven. Then, once I bank a bunch of money, we take off into the North! I'm getting us out of here in six months, tops. Annnd break!"

So, he, like every single American ever, tried to be a real estate agent. But he couldn't lie. So, he tried being a rent collector. But he couldn't threaten the poor. Then he tried to be an engineer, but he was laughed at, in the face, hard, by men who engineered. So, he landed on the chopping and selling of firewood, this being the third oldest profession after prostitution and Godhood.

In 1857, Dred Scott, an enslaved person, took his situation to the U.S. Supreme Court. It was a big deal. America waited to hear if evil was to be lawful. It was. Wise ones tell us wisdom comes from suffering. But I sure hope that's not the only way.

After this ruling, Grant couldn't live in White Haven any longer, and he announced a plan to build his family a house on some land that Dent had given them. He planned to plant crops around it, and to later rent it out while they moved away to Canada. So, okay, now he's building a house. He was scrabbling. But he leaned into the routine of it. He had a place to go, a thing to do, and on paper he was working to start a slavery-free life for he and his. In the mornings he'd show the boys how to make a workman's lunch. "Ya get a buncha bull-oh-knee sammich-ahs, grabba bagga chips, makeaduh eyes-coffee, trow in a cuppala cans a Underwood, some sardines, a jugga wadda, and toss in dere a mean and honking warty-ass pickle." The boys liked funny voices.

Ulysses would whistle-walk down to the building site, where he'd commence the most ill-informed, unprepared, and wrong-headed rush job anyone had ever seen. Did he make it terrible out of spite? Was he trying to make an eyesore? Everyone wondered, because he was down there making a mess. He was adroit at failing—did it a lot—and used a rusted, archaic ax because someone said he shouldn't. No one could stop him, and no one cared to stop him. He explained the new motto he'd made up out West: that he wouldn't go backwards. It was a Bull thing, and he held true to it in all areas from belching to building a garbage castle. Julia figured it was a phase. It wasn't.

Mainly Grant enjoyed revving up the body coils, getting the muscles working again. He'd bask in his bodily-made balminess. And he got strong. But getting strong was all that was got. He definitely didn't get a house or praise. So, when Ulysses wasn't stacking up the expensive piles of materials that he planned to waste and ruin, he spent a lot of time drunk-riding his horse, Strorgg, when supposedly, I don't know, supposedly, he was doing the grout or the electrical. He'd say he needed to get more huge stupid logs, more dumb nails, or—unbelievably—even more caulk, but he'd ride and allow himself to fantasize that there was still some way to run away.

He called the place Hardscrabble. No one even tried to act like they were ever going to leave White Haven to spend even one night in the place. No one packed a bag. Because Hardscrabble looked like a gingerbread house made by a blind witch who used mostly icing because there was maybe a juicy village kid that she was trying to catch and eat. And icing was this kid's favorite. So, she just—No. Sorry. But look at it, Google it. It's mostly caulk and perfect for spiders. Hardscrabble started out pre-haunted. It was all the evidence anyone might need to get someone committed, because it was clearly the work of a disordered mind that was depressed and driven, compulsive and repulsive. The house had (and maintains) a truly unwelcoming ambiance. Quite an accomplishment, really.

Grant was only succeeding in proving he was as terrible at carpentry as he was at nearly everything else, but he kept caulking the shit out of it. It seemed he was past that regrettable, endlessly denied, yet monstrously real midpoint in life where he couldn't learn new tricks. He had been programmed for a specific task: horseback warfare. When resting his eyes, he would stare out over the fields, and the topography would talk to him, telling him how a battle would play out, where the enemy would hide, and he'd mutter to the boys how he'd move his men.

Then Ulysses S. Grant did the first of the three worst things of his life. One day after passing by Hardscrabble en route to hunt some fashionable game, Father Dent decided he'd help Grant to improve upon Hardscrabble. He gave Ulysses one of the persons that he had enslaved. This person's name was William Jones. And Grant didn't refuse. There is no excuse for it. There's nothing I'll say to try to make it okay.

Though, the situation scalded Grant's soul. He'd prefer to be forced underwater with octopuses fucking him full of ink or whatever is terrible, I'm sure. He felt such negativity, he had to. He just had to. But despite his protests, and before he knew it, William had walked over to the worksite and the two men stood squinting at one another in the morning sun, the dew going like vapor off an alcohol smear. William was taller, around the same age, light brown, and rightly mad in general. Other than that, nothing is known about the man. History has given him short shrift. I'm certain Grant had to explain how he was trapped about this. I'm sure he had to apologize, go easy, all of that. But there is no excuse here, Dear Reader. It happened. And we must admit it as much as we must admit that benefiting indirectly from slavery at White Haven was abhorrent as well.

It wasn't okay, but the years went by. Fred got a paper route. Buck was a stud, and he knew it bad. Nellie, born in '55, would become everyone's favorite thing with a face. And then "Jesse Root Grant 2" burst onto the scene in '58. At thirty-six, Grant was a father of four and the holder of no dollars. Hardscrabble was gross. The crops didn't take. The kids were easing into antebellum, and Grant needed to nip these flowers of evil in the bud!

But he couldn't right away. And before anyone knew it . . . it had gotten to be late 1859 when Ulysses went with William Jones into the town of

Saint Louis to vote. Grant, that is. It was his first time voting, having never owned land before. Yes, it was that kind of bad, too.

While in town, Grant and William Jones sold ricks and cords and bundles and stumps. After a while Ulysses left William with the cart to get them beers, and, believe it or not, he ran into William Tecumseh Sherman. No shit. For real. Sherman. Right there. It had been decades, and Grant's old friend had aged into the kind of face that only is good when coupled with angry looks. Luckily, he did those. Cump's hair had gone hard orangutan.

They looked at each other, nodding while snarling up estimates, half grinning, all good, just wow. Freckles dilated, creases deepened, cigars went out. Their features were caricatures of their youthful dynamics. The asymmetries had grown accentuated. That length was longer. That line was a groove. Those eyes, "Shit, your eyes, Dog! There's lots of bunched up flesh around 'em, I gotta say." And the lashes have blown away, follicles dead. The teeth were spread, chipped, and stripped of varnish from coffee and worse. They felt these exact feelings and said them with their faces at each other's faces about their faces.

Inside a business around the corner, a woman started up singing along with a flouncing, out-of-tune piano. A dog got up to lie elsewhere.

Unasked, Sherman answered, "I'm married to my adopted dad's daughter, and it's . . . well, she's got boils and it's . . . a lot. I was in San Francisco—"

"Me too!"

"Before or after the fire?"

"After."

"Oh. Too bad. Hey, I met your hero Kit Carson out in Monterey in forty-seven."

"What? No way. The coincidences here are stacking up."

"Sure are. You know, Kit looked just like you. Redhead. Freckles. Short. Small. Shitty. Stooped and ornery. He was dumb as fuck, though. Terrible to Natives. Goddamn letdown."

Sherman shook his head, looking at the ground. When he glanced up and saw Grant's expression, he did a mini-nod as if he understood something that Grant hadn't meant. And then a pall came over Cump's face as he leaned in close.

"The country is moving to war over slavery, Man. I met with this lawyer guy, Lincoln, to tell him so. He might be the real deal if he runs for president."

(It's unbelievable, but true. Sherman did meet with Lincoln, and he did meet Kit, and they did meet here, and it's all too perfect.) Grant's old friend continued like he held the secret that they both had won the lotto. He came in close, eyes darting, whispering excitedly.

"I got a feeling he'll bring that real change. Like we used to talk about."

"Right, right. Who is Lincoln? A lawyer? Are you a lawyer now, or a politician? Are you still in the Army?"

"Hell, no. I'm nothing. Just crazy, is all. But listen, our time . . . could be here sooner than you think. More Perfect Union, huh?"

"I don't know," Grant said, looking for that beer place.

"Exactly. Exactly, old boy."

Sherman again seemed to misunderstand Grant. Ulysses frowned a confused blink up at his friend, trying to show that this conversation was feeling off. Sherman didn't register it and continued.

"Did you hear about John Brown? He assembled an interracial ragtag group of murderists, mostly hatchet men, and they, uh, ha, they stormed into the closest Southern state they could find, and man, they straightaway started destroying slave-owners in their mansions. It was beautiful."

Sherman slapped Grant's chest with the back of his hand.

"Wait, JOHN Brown? He was a childhood friend of my dad. They went to tannery school together."

Sherman, not hearing, smugly laughed, and went on.

"But . . . guess who took him out? Lee. The G.O.A.T. Yeah. It's in all the papers."

Grant said "Oh, God, Christ, shit right on it. Are you fucking kidding me, Man?"

"That's the fire I love! Hot damn! Are you going to reenlist if there's a race war?"

"I don't know, Cump . . . I'm out. I'm way out. I've got my kids to think about."

"Shit, I got eight kids. Everyone's got kids. That's what this is about. The future needs you. Needs us. The Ohio Boys!"

Grant wondered if maybe the fire was still warm in himself, deep down? But no. No.

Cump patted Yules' shoulder twice, walked backwards re-lighting his cigar, and said, "Well, okay. Until then, Merry Christmas. And hey, could be worse . . . At least *we* don't own anyone."

Grant's brittle spirit fell out of its denial and clattered to the cobble-stones. His blood pumped hot ice shame into his ears, and he had to lean against Strorgg for support. This was the last straw. He rushed to William Jones, explained why there wasn't beer, and took him straight to the circuit court to buy his freedom. William Jones accepted and disappeared from the record. Nothing else is known about the man.

After this, Grant vowed "My family shall no longer dwell in that Honky Chateau!"

Chapter 7

Cashier Blues

1859–1860

AGE 37

O HIO AGAIN. IT WAS GOING BACKWARDS, BUT ULYSSES SAW the return as a circular trek, an odyssey, so that was okay. It had been twenty years of adventuring since he'd left, and the peace of moving back home sounded like a nice, quaint old song.

The Grants moved house once more into a rented home with a yard and a shitter. Stoic ol' Julia was into it, it seemed. But the kids had to be coaxed out of the opulent lifestyle of White Haven with promises of Northern treats like schnitzel and strudel. Count Fredula had taken up the role of semi-parent, as most firstborns do. Under his guidance went the golden boy, Buck, who relished new adventures; golden girl, Nellie, who could accost a smile out of the aggrieved; and the youngest, Jesse Boy, who tried to broker deals between everyone. Ulysses adored his femmlet and manlings. He was happy to give them a forever home, and a place to lastly unpack. The family could start dying now, as slowly as they could, for this was to be their life.

In America there's a razor-thin, sliver-sphere strata where a person is supposed to float between "rich" and "ruin." This is middle class. A middler must be respectably teetering on stability. A middle-class family shouldn't ever make other middle-class families feel insecure, but they shouldn't offer up any possible tidbits for scorn either. It's important to maintain this balance so you earn your right to privately accuse other middlers of uppityness, or lowliness. Everything is fine so long as everyone is barely okay. Go up or down, and the delicious whispers will start.

Grant had gone up and down and was back with his tail between his legs on the tightrope of the American Dream. He was the same age his dad had been when they decided on West Point; Fred was now the same age as Grant had been then, too. And Our Man took his fatherly role seriously. He was on trash duty, scraped the cat box, made the breakfasts, kept up with the individualized body lingo of the children as each matured, evolved, and overlapped; and on at least a monthly basis he showed Julia that his penis still worked and could do so in total silence, only feet away from eight innocent ears.

Julia, with the patience of a boulder, had a sweet home and seemed contented. The kids went to a middle-rated school. There were playdates and wine with moms. And she had her own home to write her histories of dog breeds or whatever she did in her "me time." But for Ulysses, outside the family, in his "me time" it was a whiskey-ed confusion of an idling soul.

See the new setup, Sweet Reader. See that Jesse Root Grant's skin trade is booming. And Yules, heeeeeeeeee is a clerk. Have you ever worked a register? Ever worked the floor? Done customer service? Shipping and receiving? My God, I have. There probably won't even be cashiers by the time this book comes out, but for those of you who've counted your tills, I salute you.

The Grant store was a town hotspot, with furs in the back, food in the front, and general goods, guns, and alcohol in the middle. The place was a descendant of the public house and the predecessor of the drugstore of the early twentieth century. People came to eat, drink, hang out, chat, shop, gossip, read a paper for free, buy a skunk thing, and razz the Grants.

The fur section was like a lifeless, flat zoo. The walls were draped with larger bear and buffalo skins, elk and other Northern imports. There were poster racks where one could peruse floor models of 24×36 skins in hanging giant book pages, and then find the buyable versions rolled up below in numerically corresponding pigeonholes.

Out in the middle were display-islands stacked with piles of beaver, mink, sable, polecat, nutria, etc., etc. Various marmot pelts fanned out like ties and handkerchiefs on cascading tiers. They had short hair, long hair, leather, and a generous selection of reptile, mostly straight snake on flat board, but they boasted bigger in the back and displayed in a case their Gila skin from out West, which was fashioned into monstrous slippers for dainty feet. Yes, beyond the raw bolts of hide—tanned, raw, or leathered— were leatherworks and ready-made wearable stylings. Shoppers could count on finding wallets, natch, but also belts, holsters, helmets, shoes (they knew a cobbler), jackets, chaps, and everything else you've ever not bought at an arts-and-crafts fair.

The Grants offered chaw, chew, backky, and tobacco for the mouth. To the richer kids in town, Ulysses now had to sell candy and Cream Suckles. Naturally, they carried the whole line of Underwood canned and potted meats, and their little red devils on the labels of ham danced at Our Tipsy Man as he lined up the stock neatly next to the Colgate soaps that kids loved to rub on their teeth. They carried DuPont; they weren't dumb. And the store enjoyed a nice sideline on crockery with Louisville and Pfaltzgraff as mainstay sellers. But mostly they sold Old Tub brand mash, short guns, and long guns.

Arms reps came out to upsale new merch and to correct bad word-of-mouth about their product. They hired trick shots in domino masks and/ or long fringe to endorse the firearms with fun displays in the streets. These deadeyes would shoot tossed crockery out of the air (send the bill to Remington). It was a great career track for trick-shot and slinger-types who'd later become national sensations, gracing advertisements and traveling about the land spreading syph. People like Sonny the Gunny. Dandy the Gunman. Bolt-action Becky. Billis the Killest. Horrible Vigilante. And the town boys' favorite, Naked Woman with a Gun.

Dear Reader, do you remember Old Man Jesse Root? That calcifying old revolutionary? He was the manager and the face of the family. Root had grown cloudy and white, like a Janus calcite bluff with one face the happy old shopkeep who'd serve you a sandwich and a stiff one; and the other face a crumbling soft stone, crestfallen after the death of his pal, John Brown. He was sad in his efflorescence. The slave states were doubling down and trying to spread out. There were Nazis in the streets. Yes, in Any Town, U.S.A., there marched such young dummies with dreams of belonging to an aristocratic class that would never have anything to do with them apart from grinding their bones to make their bread. The Root started to concede that maybe a "true utopian America for all" was as impossible as a world without skinning animals.

"Come on, you don't feel that way, Dad," Ulysses said to him by the pickle case. And the Root flew into an uncharacteristically defensive face.

"Come! Climb then in my mouth and work my tongue! Go with thy arm down my spout and grip the squeezebox. Send up the airs, finger the larynx—cat's cradle—see if you can puppet me better than I do myself!"

He'd been reading the plays for consolation, and the manner had rubbed off. Ulysses knew his dad, and this giving up hurt. His mom was the pessimist, not his happy pappy. But maybe Hannah Grant was correct? She kept their money in a hidden safe, the shop clean, and her mouth shut. There was never mud on the fat planks of her prized wooden floor. No spiders could web up the corners of her lovely, high, tin-hammered ceilings. Though she was never seen cleaning. All day she'd sit ticking her tiny pulse. Then her chair would be empty, and minutes later the place would be nice, and she'd be sighing in the chair like a time-lord.

It was hard to know if his mom was glad to have him there. She avoided the old talk of soldiering, of power, of West Point and her son's disappointing failure to become a real man. But she was decidedly not glad to see her boy drinking and eating their stock. And Grant's mama had an ally who shared judgments on Ulysses: Dad's teetotaling lawyer and Ulysses' peer, John Rawlins, who rented Grant's old room and slept in his old PJs. Like Hannah, Rawlins had no illusions about the American Dream: one had to earn it by force, to stockpile power through carefully planned, socially perfected maneuvering. One had to behave unassailably, had to shape the way they're seen, and had to control their own story from the outside in. Rawlins' dad had been a drunk, so he was understandably a fierce hater of much. The lawyer was one of those guys who expects formality in any available instance, but who also secretly wishes that everyone would call them "Gator." You know the kind, I'm sure. Out of self-preservation, Rawlins long ago had set his default face askance to keep open an option for dissent. He stayed perfectly groomed and immaculately styled. Too fastidious in his toilet, his cuticles and gums ached, and every day he got his dick ready to taste like a candy-cane for no one.

Grant tolerated this rigid nitpicker because he was a good partner at Mexican train dominoes, but Our Man really didn't know what to make of this clam-shelled, bug-eyed busybody who was constantly around, micro-miming with his face, or under the eaves with his ears burning off. The man was somehow aware of the potential failures of any enterprise. And, brimming with criticism, he'd never give voice to it because he loved the pressurized feeling of passive-aggressive leverage sitting in his snug, snap-lip purse. Sipping chamomile, he'd glare and judge and inhale with private meaning.

Ulysses fell back into haggling with wholesalers, suppliers, and special-orderers. There were steady, obligatory interactions with Trappers. Merchants. Boondogglers. Reps. He knew the catalogs, the invoicing—this was Quartermastering without a uniform. Old skills pay bills.

But he had the blues in the day. Nearing forty, he was getting retailer body. He was not exercising and spent his time faking inventory or aim-lessly stroking a folded square of bear. Thanks to a clandestine flasky-wasky, he occasionally pulled off the smooth sale of mink. Still, some people say there's no room in a life for alcohol. And other people say there's no room for poetry in prose. And I say that the people who say either of those things have never really fucked.

Relationships age, and pockets of "me time" turn into separateness, which can be good and bad. As the mother of four, Julia sought out her "Own Private I-Don't-Know." Her mysterious, self-contained emotional planet continued to gain impenetrable Van Allen belts upon which Grant burned up on reentry when probing too close about her personal shit. She said she was happy, let that be enough.

Julia and Hannah interpreted each other's brands of introversion with a negative translation guide. The struggle for power is inherent in all human relationships. Control is an invisible game played across lifetimes. Grant and the kids tripped often over such secret strings between these matriarchs of the family.

Yules and Jules were fine, though, even if gauzed up in these mature versions of themselves, he with his eye floaters clouding his vision and she with a screaming interiority of a raging tinnitus bed. They had their routines, got each other's backs, sighed at the same times, if not for the same reasons, and said "I love you" before pretending to fall asleep. He worried about the changes in his body and what they might mean to her. His puffiness of face, flabbiness of elsewhere. He worried that she noticed his heavy and worthless body turning into alkaline, fatty, cloudy crystal like ol' gypsum Root. At his age, if left alone, muscle went to molasses. The heavy quartz bones would go clanking, fragile. His fingers had gone creaky from coin-counting and price-tagging. His ossified grip went into the crystal case along with his fossilized testicles. He was thirty-eight, thirty-nine, past prime and past expiration date. A crystallized pot of deviled meat. Useless without regular motion, a leased-out lion will lie down forever in the front of a building. And if a person of action reaches such a state, they develop bodily peacetime fear. Fear of harm by accident, and fears of illness and injury become the only real nemesis of a peaceful man. With maturity he was able to see the risks he had taken over the years as fearsome near-misses. Does wisdom come from testing survival? I hope not only so.

Ulysses knew he was lucky. He was kinda set. He wouldn't be rich. Wouldn't be famous. Wouldn't get younger. Wouldn't be seen by strangers as special. Wouldn't be needed by anyone outside of his wife and kids and customers who wouldn't need him if they would only read the price tag. He told himself it was enough. But the unsatisfied pieces of him made themselves sensed in strange ways, like his chopping too hard at the carrots and grinding his horrid teeth. He smoked cigars at one end and ate cigars at the other. He disappeared whiskey. Consciously he was where he wanted to be, but consciousness isn't the only thing that makes up our consciousness. And nobody paid much attention to the decorated war vet around the place, except for the old townies he once had known. Those artless Pistols, once lean, were now puffed; once cool, were now hot with resentment. Members from his old gang came in for jabs.

"You were supposed to be a famous horseman," said Janky, who'd grown into a bald and snarling knock-kneed upright sea cow. "We wasted frogs on you, Sam!"

"That was twenty years ago."

"Exactly. Flash in the pan, Man. We've all evolved into Toms. Got our shit together. Own banks. Drink top-shelf mash. We pay Hucksters like you to do our dirty work."

"Could you perhaps wait to digest some of the filth in your teeth before you try to say anything else?" Grant didn't say.

Frankie, having long since lucked out by marrying up before letting himself go, came in saying "Uh oh, there he is! Sandman came crawling back, huh? See? I was right to have never left. Shit, I knew you'd never get in *Horse Lord Magazine*. You lied when you left! Now, ring me up for these Cream Suckles and this ammo!"

Rawlins shifted to the other ass cheek, ogling Grant's downcast visage. Our Man didn't stir. Tomboy Jane worked him in a different way, on a different day, thinking they were just talking straight.

"You used to be fun, Man. You used to be more laid-back. Easygoing. Outgoing. Going Places. Good-natured. Levelheaded. Funny. Charming. I miss the old you."

In reply, Grant didn't say "I miss the old you who didn't say that. Besides, I used to be a childless child without blood on his hands."

And here comes this cheap fucker, Dee-Dee, wearing the suit that came with the coffin. Dee-Dee, a father of unloved kids, came in for toddies, asking "Got any fur pants? *I'm* planning a trip to Canada."

To which Grant replied "*I* do have fur pants *now*, because your wife sheds." But no one heard because Grant had yelled that into a pelt of elk smashed against his face in the back.

Now, Dear Listener, strain your ears for the rumors of war. Murmurs. You can hear them always and forever. Through the '50s, pressure mounted through the nation because more states were coming into 'hood as more wilderness was being tamed, and more slavery was being tolerated. Lincoln the Lawyer had indeed proceeded to national congressional status, and then he swooped on to be the nominee for the then-righteous Republican Party, which was once fundamentally anti-slavery. The incumbent president, Buchanan, was looking for a second term, and the South was for it. Buchanan was okay with slavery so long as he wasn't personally seen enslaving. And then Stephen Douglas was running too, and maybe others. Many in the nation wanted the freedom to enslave people. And yet the majority of people in the nation and the planet thought this was evil. That's it. No gray areas. Bad guys versus good guys. Sorry. That's the story. Most of my historian colleagues say my view is oversimplified. And I say they are cowards. Some may say I'm posturing, to which I say that in times like mine it's important to exhibit good posture. You know, to set an example for the kids. So I'll say it again. People who think there are gray areas concerning the Confederacy, slavery, or white supremacy are imbecilic persons operating without full control of their minds. They are aberrant simpletons who shouldn't be left alone with anything precious, and they probably have a turd for a mind up there in their rotting little windowless studio apartment of a skull that can never be cleaned.

Still, everyone who came around the shop was an expert on the topic . . .

"Lincoln lost those debates to Douglas. It's rigged. The newspaper people are Lincoln loggers. My cousin's husband had a boss who was at that last debate, and he told Kacky that even the quotes were falsified in the papers."

"What's the Constitution say?"

"Three-fifths."

"Follow that. And we're done. Pass the Worchester."

"If Lincoln wins, he's coming for our guns. No, no. It's true. He wants that federal sovereignty. Only the Union Army gunna have arms under 'Stinkin'.' You mark me; he's after the Constitution. He wants to amend it!"

"I don't trust a guy who talks like that."

"Is there such a thing as a voice you can trust?"

"Why ain't nobody talking about slavery of other types of folk? Don't they got slaves out way West? Shit's wild out yonder."

"I say sell it all back to England. We need their influence. American gentility ain't as good."

"Hell, I'd go warring and womaning around the South if I were young again. Boy, I'd ring those Southern belles, I tell ya."

"Douglas would know how to handle international stuff. He's been around. Smart. Worldly. Goddamn Lincoln out there quoting his uncle Rib Bone and shit."

"It's on account of his occultist wife, is what it is. This war is getting pushed on us by spirits."

"I knew a Southern gal who weren't no belle of any balls, but she was of mine!"

"The South done found El Dorado long time ago, and they kept it a secret. They'll be able to bankroll this war something fierce. But nobody's betting on that."

"Southern wilds are different. Enchanted. Yankees won't cope."

"I bet England's got their shit ready to spring on us again. Best time to attack is when the opponent is embroiled with internal strife. Eighteen-twelve all over again, Boys. You watch. And it'll be good for us."

"It's the sixties; we're too civil to be bringing war back out of the garage like we can use it again."

"Shit, Bert, I'd shoot a man who tried to take over you and your family's lives. I don't see this as any different."

"Goddamn, Earn. Okay. Okay."

"No way this election ain't rigged."

"For which?"

"For whichever the real powerful want."

"Ain't my son worth the same as a slave life? He shouldn't die, neither should a slave. People talkin' bout armies like it ain't made up of lives too."

"That damn man don't drink. Can't trust that. That's your first sign he's not a man."

"Tain't human neither. From the Pleiades."

"Whatever, ya quack."

"Got more duck? Shit's good, Boys! Love that crispy skin."

"Skin's a Grant specialty."

"Ha!"

"Lincoln don't know nothing 'bout holding a nation together. Look at 'im, intentionally sowing discord. Look at 'im acting like he knows. He don't. He don't. Just a word-twisting lawyer. He could make the facts say whatever story he wants you to hear. And then turn round and tell it different out the other side his face. Ain't no one truth with him. No, sir."

"What's too bad is, the Southern lifestyle is so quaint. Charming down there. No gross urban congestion. No overpopulation. It's tidy. Ain't nothing but dukes and duchesses."

"Ever bought a quart of rye in 'Bama, Bob?"

"Slavery's okay in the Bible. What am I to do with that? The rules of it are right there in Deuteronomy, next to how we ain't supposed to eat cloven hooved animalia or bottom feeders and whatnot."

"Damn good catfish, Grant!"

"You can't be serious. Those are people. Those are women and kids. This talk is ugly, and God knows it."

"Slavery seems like it's just a job, right? No? Wait, what?"

"This Lincoln's gotta know what he's proposing is untenable. Unrealistic. He and his progressive cult, they're like college kids. They got no sense of what's practical. Don't get me wrong, I morally agree with every damn thing he says, but I live in reality, so I know we gotta abide with the hellish nature of the lives of slaves until it works itself out."

"I hear Jeff Davis got a wonder weapon off the coast of Virginia. A gift from England, what with the South's trading with 'em so much. That's why Lincoln won't attack. It's gunna be some diplomacy, and then back to the usual. You watch."

"War ain't nothing but a bluff."

"Could the North even survive without the South? Where'd we get cotton from?"

"War won't last a month."

"I'd like to see real battles. Me and my boys read about all the great old-world wars."

"My in-laws from Louisiana ain't even heard of no war talk. This ain't getting past local governments. People won't vote for it, and they won't vote for those who do."

"Might be good to set fire to everything. Start over. Blank slate. Cleaned by fire."

"If Douglas gets in, he'll figure it out. Goddamn bulldog-faced motherfucker."

"Grants, we said another round over here, Boys, y'all got rocks in your pockets?"

"If Lincoln wins, I'm going back to Texas. It's different there. Bigger, mainly."

"States do got rights, though. I tell you what. This here national-identity thing is scary. It's states that are part of a nation, not a nation of states. States are more sovereign. That's why we got militias."

"Canada's awful quiet."

"Y'all remember Cobb who ran that secret business making marital aids? He supported his family offa that filthy equipment. He was a God-fearing man too, but he saw a demand t'werent being supplied, so to speak, and he being like any American capitalist set the moral question aside until he had the facts of a balance sheet with which to fairly argue the pros and cons. Shit, you recall when we got the county to shut him down? He fought us in court. Then he fought us in the street when we went to burn his little-shop-for-whores down. He went and got burnt up over dildos, Man. Because we shut down his way of life that he had gotten so used to. Now magnify that shit by millions. See?"

"No matter how good your analogy might be, a dildo ain't a person, Dwight."

"Make their own nation? Shit—an *abomi*nation is more like it."

"Is Lincoln spineless, or just socially kind?"

"I saw your dad crying."

"If Lincoln wins the election, then war will indeed break out. So, the North will need the *best* Generals. Not deserters like some gutter bums around here. Lincoln will need Robert E—Ack! Who threw a handful of sand in my eyes?"

It was Grant, mad and drunk and yelling, "I was a fucking officer! I was a fucking gentleman! A falcon, *and* a snowman. I'm not a bum. You're the bum, Charlie. It's you. Let's face it... I... I... I can't get caught up in this... colloquy."

Grant was done rasping his berries. His throat was sick of talk. The Bull had begun to long for a bee to sit upon . . .

The nation braced itself on the election night of 1860. Ballots for Lincoln were not even available in most of the Southern states. They acted like he wasn't happening. People crowded the streets. Lincoln lovers yelled. Slavery fiends yelled or privately watched how the night was going to go.

Across the nation, fast-riding horsemen gathered ballots, which were not secret. Then the horsemen—if not assaulted on the highway—dropped the ballots off to official counters, who may or may not have counted under threat. The counters then had their tallies telegraphed up to county level, then on to district level, and again on up to state level, before finally to national collectors as fast as possible and as accurate as the reporters could surmise. But then telegraph reports ran back down from the national on down to the local levels again with conflicting reportage and requests for recounts, and conspiracy theories about tossed votes, mass coercion, or of non-approved people voting, like say women or the dead. Telegraph lines moved messages like guts move meat via peristalsis: slowly, breaking up, and turning shitty. It was a hard, fraught process to keep true.

The Grant shop, like the rest of Main Street, was bedecked with red, white, and blue bunting. Sparklers fizzed in the orange dusk light, waved by drunken kids. Business being sacrosanct, Grant and his dad wore Uncle Sam shit while serving oysters and liquors in the indoor/outdoor seating to the crowd awaiting the results.

Lamps got lit, giving body to the awful billows of airborne illness along with cigar, pipe, meat, and gun smoke. The polls had favored Buchanan, but these other polls had Lincoln. And a lot of people favored Douglas. Everyone trusted and doubted like weather vanes in tornados. Would Lincoln win? Would we have a war?

"Can we trust the counters?"

"Who's counting for our county?"

"That guy would count in Chinese if you paid him."

"Will Buchanan concede?"

"Will there be a coup if Lincoln wins?"

"No way the military will let him go to war."

"Is this when the government changes?"

"Been a good run."

The Grant men had the flicker of "maybe" in their eyes. They met off to the side by the silverware and water pitchers, sharing side whispers as they wiped their hands and surveyed the clientele. Leftover embers of hope in the nearly lost old man sparkled in the black bottoms of his crystal mine irises. The Root, nearly petrified, and the Bull, nearly loosed, did that "head cock on an inhale" at each other on top of a half-smile with hip-hands. The giddy Grant Boys thusly bodily communed their hopeful spirits. Maybe this man Abraham could change things? Maybe he could outlaw slavery, then boom, boom, boom, like Democracy Dominoes, all the freedoms and rights that were supposedly coming would fall? Maybe. Maybe. Maybe. The Root up-nodded Grant's attention across the crowd.

"Look at Rawlins. Wonder what he thinks."

"Rawlins? He's a cagey bitch."

"Yeah, he's a KGB. But useful."

"Wonder what Mom's thinking over there."

"Tick tock, tick tock, tick tock . . ."

Grant looked up at the galaxy's skeleton: the constellations. Those hot joint stars, inflamed with eons of connection, still suggested those narrative forms via linkage of imagined limbs. He saw that Bull back on his hooves, snorting, kicking that fucking dust back, and whipping the air up with its horns. Oooo.

No one had realized how loud the street had gotten until the contagion of silence was completed in a wave. Now each ear could hear. Clockityclockityclockityclockity wushhhhhhhh! In a cloud of street dust, the results had arrived.

Chapter 8

Doo-Doo Dominoes

1861

AGE 39

INCOLN HAD WON. THE WIDOW OF OPPORTUNITY WATCHED as the nation passed up the chances for peace. With the advent of Abraham, the South quit America, one state after another, like members of a country club who had the wrong ideas of what a country and a club were all about. They made their own evil nation, cutely called the Confederacy.

The newspaper cartoonists took turns not nailing Lincoln's likeness. The worst was a vertical, one-dimensional stick in a Doctor Doolittle scene. The Lincoln Log was corrupted. People had him splitting rails or getting rode out of town on them. They had him lawyering well for the people while addling the flummoxed prosecutors in three-piece seersucker, or they had him getting addled by clairvoyant dreams of wild-river-rafting. His beautiful, or haggish, or cheap, or chic wife interpreted these dreams with a Ouija board that she'd gotten from one of her many dead sons. Everyone got the right things wrong. The legends spread and splinted into differing drafts, as all narratives must if not locked down on paper; and even then, the details were too delicious to get right.

So, cue the mournful banjo man, and let me introduce Lincoln the right way. Admired by generations of oddballs, mystics, goths, lawyers, philosophers, and bad artists, Abraham Day Lincoln was a walking enigma-machine that all but talked coded Cherokee on the wind to even those he hoped would help him out. An automatic anecdote grinder, he'd tell stories constantly like a player piano with a brick on the go pedal, fed beyond its fill with inanity Scantrons. Some depicters say Ol' Abe was the type of man who'd wear a blanket over his shoulders any time of the year. Others said the pictures of the tall hat were actual. There are whole factions of scholars that feel he had a body disease that made him look so interesting. Others suspect malnutrition.

When he was younger, Lincoln was kicked in the head by a horse hard enough to knock him out, and upon waking he was still Lincoln, some say. Others went on record fearing he was majorly changed. He did grow up in log cabins. He did split wood. He indeed had a complicated family setup with various mothers, not unlike many of us. And some people say because he shared a bed with a young man for a while that they have proof of potential homosexuality; and though this would be fine and not sensational, I feel he shared a bed because he was poor and young, and—who cares if they fucked?

His wife had gathered negative attention, which made more of the commentators than their subject. But yes, she spent her money on clothes. And it was her money, not his, because she was the *thicc* little princess of a very rich family. Mary had access to great people, the best young studs, and she dated Stephen Douglas before she married Lincoln. Seriously. She played the two political rivals, had her pick of the litters, and that is endlessly incredible.

The First Lady indeed spent taxpayers' money on the White House because the previous occupants had treated it like a hunting-lodge shithouse. We can credit Mary Todd Lincoln with reestablishing a sense of glamour to the top home of the land, and that's of value when it's real, and it was in her time.

She believed in the occult, as does the American majority, it being Christian. The woman lost three of her sons before they could reach adulthood. Mary believed she could commune with her boys beyond the flesh, as well as with her husband, if he were ever to pass. And who could blame her? Don't we all hope and wish and bet heavily on there being something after this bodily life? Isn't so much built upon such a maybe?

Back to immortal Abraham. He wore that LeBron beard, and had raccoon eyes like a drinker, yet teetotaled no bar tabs. He was made of clammy white beluga skin, and his hair was up and out and cowlicked into different directions. His nose makes one wonder about cavernous boogers to this day, and his warted folds were like those on the handsome head of Liszt, who had, like the president, the long, dancing phalanges that buckled with sexually provocative knuckles (all following Gore Vidal's description, naturally).

Some said he had depression, others said that was wisdom. Foes claimed he was a tyrant who did what he wanted with the Constitution, twisting the interpretations to suit his needs, evading the rules of law, weaponizing public opinion, telling lies when needed, and forcing a new truth through the old Congress. Admirers said the same thing, but as a positive. Ken Burns, wherever you are, forgive me my sins, for they have become mostly what I am. I have few tricks, and even fewer workable ways. If only my paltry words could convert rather than pervert. Dear Reader, as always, I rely upon your flaming imagination . . .

Why are there always rumors of male political leaders escaping into or out of office while dressed as women? Well, Lincoln, in drag or not, secreted his way from Illinois to D.C. across a nation of ready assassins. This journey necessitated the invention of the Secret Service, which was initially headed up by the much-too-often-fictionalized Pinkerton crew of squinters.

What was going to happen now that Lincoln was king of America? What kind of president was he to be? How would he handle the South? Rumors accumulated, narratives coagulated, and beliefs hardened like dead bread. The logs of Lincoln lore never help me build what was real. I invite you to try to imagine what this human was up against, apart from the shouted, simplified storytelling we always hear. It wasn't simple; it wasn't "story friendly." It wasn't three-dimensional chess. This man had to play that "more real than real" twelve-tone, twelve-dimensional quantum chess upon a board that was mostly insensible, and part of it was curled up into the inaccessibility of that one dimension that the smart people love to theorize about. In other words, Lincoln made the old law work for the new nation's hidden goals. Amen.

What was truly at stake, you ask? Oh, not much. Just the U.S.A. be-coming a bunch of fussy nations of U trading with S while A gets pissed about it and soon it's another Europe with wars every couple of generations.

The Rebellion's leader was that snide pied piper, Jefferson Davis. Unan-imously, the South figured he was the white man for the job. Jefferson Prime was a West Pointer, a Mexican War hero, and a perfect example of the Southern faux aristocrat. He, like Lincoln, grew up in Kentucky. But unlike Abe, Jefferson Starship went to the best schools and the biggest par-ties. He loved his way of life but hated happiness and didn't think anyone should have it. His laugh was the sound of all the snakes ever on Earth hissing at one time.

Jeff Davis set up his lair's control room deep in the South at Richmond, Virginia. Richmond was a whites-only rec-center, which got its supplies and protection from the neighboring town of Petersburg. Remember the rules of this challenge: if you get through the Virginian Wilderness, and if you can break through Petersburg, then you can topple Richmond, and you therefore topple the rebellion of Jefferson Prime. Game Over. But to do that, Lincoln needed to scramble up the nation's scattered Army. Luckily, according to the papers and mags, Lincoln was meeting with Robert E. Lee to command the armies of the North. Lee was offered George Washing-ton's old position, as predicted. Everyone knew Lee would accept it. The nation felt like they knew him, after all the articles and biographies and biopics and mini-series about him. He had to go north, and he'd save the day. He was a hero. All done. And that was good, because the majority of the best senior officers had already signed with the South, and many of them were high-scoring West Point alums.

Gun barons and arms dealers thrived. The youth were aflame. Amer-ican men were choosing shirts or skins, choosing to be an American or a rebel. Men of a certain rage, agog with dreams of rising up in class, went south. They studied up on the Confederacy's reworked status categories, and they said "There are some people definitely below us here, Boys!"

Bloodivores saw their chance to feast. Such numbers came alert. From asunder, from yonder, and from under came the horde that knew this lotto would land on them to ascend. Out from the woods and down from the mountains came each abominable low man to sign up for that chance to move up in the world via war. So, they enlisted with the self-abolished Confeds.

North and South, the states were mobilizing small bands of armies. Militias tried to act like they knew what they were supposed to be doing. Volunteers formed numbered regiments that waited to be trained and outfitted by legitimate, appointed officers. The armies, like acne, popped up and swelled across the surface of the nation, hurting, begging to erupt. On both sides, opportunistic officers, West Pointers and others, active and newly active, reported for duty. Those who didn't get fit into active deployment slots settled to train up the waiting rabblement of volunteers.

In the South came the men who had long ago self-appointed themselves with cute military titles like Colonel and Cap'n, and they expected to just really be those ranks for real now. The Confederacy also got the guys who had no military careers, but who had useful spunk, money, power, and psychopathologies. Bedford Forrest leaps to mind as the best example of men's worst traits. He was a self-made millionaire (if you don't count the thousands of unpaid enslaved people he exploited). Forrest was called the wizard of the saddle. For real, by adults. He hated black people and thought whites were anthropomorphized semen straight from God's un-spared rod. He was a happy stabber, a galloping Golgotha, and a legitimate worry. Of course, "evil-looking" is a subjective term. And we've been taught that evil-doers can smile and look cute while ugly weapon-yielders should be given a chance to not kill you. But I think we should balance these POVs with what our survival instincts tell us: sometimes evil looks like evil. Sometimes appearances are reality. Give Forrest a Google and you'll see what I mean. Definitely the type of person who has finagled the purchase of a skull that really belongs in a museum. Keep your eye on him, Dear Seer. Now as well as then.

Sure, there were other big names that came to fight for the "down there gang." There was a pro-slavery lemon eater, a pro-slavery chicken eater— whatever, their evil names don't matter. Why keep the identities of criminals alive? Spit. Hiss. Amen.

War would soon crack open like a world-egg gone bad on God's birthday. And on April 14, 1861, the armies of Mordor were sicced on the quasi-harmless Yankee garrison of the United States of America known as Fort

Sumter. Realness was agitated into existence, as it had been in the Mexican War. So much for diplomacy. In the North, one could hear people shouting "War! It's war!" And in the South, one heard "Bellum! It's Bellum!"

This was what American boys had dreamed of: their own *Iliad*. This was the motherfucking *Iliad*, Man. A civil *Iliad*. Yes, this was The Civiliad. It had come, and the young schoolyard romantics vied to be Hector and Achilles and Ajax and . . . Ulysses . . .

Forced from his modest stillness and humility, Grant tensed with the news like a receiving tower. His family said he should get back into the Army, each member saying so for different reasons. Mom Grant and Rawlins insinuated he should "gain that power, you late bloomer!" The Root rallied for his son to be on the side of change in the nation, to free the enslaved people, and to work toward a More Perfect Union, shamone. And the kids, well, they wanted to see this supposed cooler version of their okayish dad.

Grant paced in their creaking kitchen and Julia leaned her butt against the edge of the counter. The Mexican War had taken him away from her for four years. The Pacific Northwest had him gone another three. Could he and his family survive an absence of undeterminable time? Yules had barely gotten back to her twice. Could he risk never returning . . . again? The money would be better soldiering. And if he reenlisted, it would be as a Captain. That was good. But what would he miss of what he loved if he left? More milestones? More "being there" spent elsewhere? Besides, his birthday was coming up. His old body was fragile. And had he ever really had the nerve for soldiering in the first place?

Julia raised her eyebrows and parted her lips. Grant froze in mid-stride, all ears.

"You're not happy—No. I know. It's great. It's all great. We're great. But you're dying inside at the shop. You gotta move. You got action in you yet. And I truly think the nation needs you, Yules. Luckily the iron remains warm. Isn't it?"

He did one of those "eyebrows up, head tilt, eyes to the side" gestures, with a held inhalation, which meant "Kinda, yeah, kinda." He then moved it into an affirming nod. She nodded along with a "whelp" smile which was not happy, but resolute. They hugged for real, not rushing it, smelling each other. It was a searching kind of hug, and they took the time to find the feel they wanted. Finally, she slapped his ass and said that most heartbreaking and unfair thing that we sometimes say to people.

"Don't let me down."

Grant felt that mandate make room in the dark back-brain parts of his heart: it was sure to haunt and menace him until it was fulfilled. He gave her the kind of look he'd give a commanding officer, then he opened the door to see that the Root, crying diamonds, had been listening along with the kids this whole time.

So, like Osiris after Iris' rough assemblage, he made assessment of his once-scattered parts ...

Backbone: sodium

Cartilage: cork

Liver: wursted

Heart: fat wad

Lungs: cauliflowered

Feet: weak

Hands: soft

Eyes: clouded

Ears: wax-worked

Penis: decent

Balls: low

Skin: cracked

Teeth: dilapidated

Brain Pan: cooked thin

It would have to do. In the basement, with the help of a lit wick, he dug up the buried box containing his guns and garb. After his birthday, Captain (pending) Grant packed up his horse, Skagg-rog-ol-log-oron, kissed his four kids, hugged his parents, and fucked his wife goodbye. He stuffed his thirty-nine years into the blue uni and vuh—vuh—vaulted onto his steed. The time had come, and he rode off fast to hide his sickened, green complexion.

George McClelland, the super-rich son of a hospital founder, had been put in charge of all volunteers, and he decided which officers would do what in the Department of the Ohio. McClelland went to West Point the year after Grant and had served in Mexico too. He was a tinkerer, a strategy man, a planner, a pen-tip licker, and a long-view dude with quite an opinion of himself as a "big brain." Georgey had plants, not pets.

Grant expected his resume and old rank would herald the happy gift of himself to McClelland. Here he was: a capable man to use. And Grant knew McClelland: he'd not pass up on such a bargain. But when Ulysses showed up at the office he was kept waiting for days before being turned away without even seeing McClelland's compulsively groomed and obsessively posed face. Our Man couldn't go home so fast. He finagled the clerk with a sip off his flask and some down-to-earth chit-chat about the highfalutin' higher-ups, and he got a chance to scan his file . . .

"Grant never plays ball. Never takes notes. Trusts his guts too much. Waited too long to try to break out. Has bad habits from older times. Is old. Is out of the loop. Was in the lower fourth of his graduating class. Same fourth in social class. Doesn't know about modern advancements. Doesn't read the new reviews or read the hot new books that everyone talks about for a month before they disappear, and no one refers to them ever again—"

No one recalled his Mexico stories here, either. They had been eclipsed by the drinking stories. The quitting stories. The "losing his shit in California" stories. But, yeah, mostly the drinking stories. As if America hadn't always been drunk. Drunk moms. Drunk cops. Drunk founders. Gotta get drunk to cross the ocean or burn a witch, and why not let the witch have a sip before we light it? And listen, liquor is a billion-dollar industry in this country. There is a good chance you're drinking right now. Me too, my fellow American. Me too.

Grant had no drugs besides alcohol to help him cope. And so far in America, there was only one therapist, William James, who was booked solid despite being only eleven years old. No one gave Grant a shot because he drank, and he had quit like a bull who stopped short of killing the matador. Even those in his file who vouched for him did so with asterisks. Was he so worthless that even the needful North didn't need him? What would he tell his family? Would he so quickly let Julia down? And where could he get a drink? Oh, horrible!

Chapter 9

Gutter Boys

SUMMER OF '61

AGES 39–40

Whaddaya know, America? Take a look at what our Yankee Doo-dle Dandy Corps of Unionist Armies has cooked up: The astonishing Zouaves! Get a load of these leaping lads touring America now! Check those vibrant colors and flouncy, blousy, billowy bunches of fabric just everywhere! Ooo, big ol' scary berets coming through, also in rainbow! And that's some long knife with which they dance and leap, huh, Brother? Well, I don't know if I'm at an Army drill or at the circus! Wow, what wonders to get that national spirit up! Come load up on these dudes, ladies! These boys have that vigor it'll take to whip those dog-fucking Confederates! The rest of the regular Union Army can rest assured that the Zouaves of Special Forces will be shipped out to the fronts to lend a hand in whipping Johnny Reb! We can't lose with a 'vunderful vunder veapon' like this. Go get 'em, Boys!

REPORTS LIKE THIS WERE SHOWING UP IN THE NORTHERN PA-pers to drum up enlistment. But then everyone heard the truth about

Lee. The Virginian Achilles, the unerring ghost of a goat, Robert E. Lee . . . had sided with the South. Lincoln had offered him the super max deal, but it wasn't about the money. Lee was into slavery. Period. The Union took this like the news from a head-shaking doctor who'd really checked way, way up there. The rebels were already measuring for the drapes in Bangor, Maine.

So, the Union had to sign a different superstar to the top spot, the George Washington rank. They sat atop the Union Army's food chain, ol' fuss and feathers: General Winfield Scott. He had lost a lot of 1812, won some of Mexico, and skipped no meals since. Now, I know better than to describe cruelly, and I, like all people, have about myself what I'd rather not be turned into neat description. There is no universal human form. The Greek ideal is as harmful as the Greek slave-based society. If America is the land of the free, then free us from such ideals of impossible perfection. Right? Right. And yet, we're not limitless in our difference. There are universal areas wherein we all conform. No thirty-footers. No plasma folk. In our wide variety we each have shared forms, yet some of us end up quite remarkable. I celebrate difference. And I assure you, "Eat what you want" is my motto, but some jobs have specific demands which exclude enormity. When Scott met Lincoln, the septuagenarian General revealed he had elephantiasis of the everything. He was un-horse-able. Even his baggy brow overhung his searching beads. Not once more unto the breach, Dear Friend, would this one be sprinting.

Old Zach was old dead and watching from the sidelines on a bench in hell. But was Scott our best man to lord over the main stage of Eastern action against the G.O.A.T.? When the South added Lee to the roster of class-ten intelligences, it sent a panic through the North. I say this because, soon after, Lincoln personally got involved in the selection of officers, and he started drafting even the old, the drunken, and the deserters . . .

So, in the summer of '61, the forty-year-old Grant was indeed reinstated and promoted to colonel. Pretty sweet. But he was to train up the 21st regiment. Pretty—*what*? No! Our Warlike U.S.G. didn't want to train bankers and bakers. Training drills were beneath him. Alas, Our Bull bided. He was whispering to himself thusly, "This will be over soon. Get action. Get renown. Wars end quick. Parlay the new rep into a bigger house, more horses, maybe get the old horse stable idea going if I survive. But remember, this is about bills and dentist stuff for the mouths that I'm barely feeding. Work up the ranks. Go from training on up to a man in the field. Get killed and get Julia that life insurance policy if we have one. Okay? Okay." Skagg-rog-ol-log-oron snorted in agreement.

The first meeting with his 21st regiment of volunteers happened in an empty field of uneven, dusty brown grass tufts. He rode up slowly into the space like a gunman into a Western film. It was unofficial, like how a dad-league of sport gathers half in and mostly out of the commitment. Where the hell was anyone official from the government? Where was the sign-in booth? Where was the equipment? Was it only him? And were these really the volunteers? These were no bankers, and these were no bakers. These were low once-did-wells, may-do-wells, a couple of Elvis seeds, but mostly ne'er-do-wells, jackanapes, and rough men looking to make a buck or to take advantage of the nasty aspects of soldiering. Grant could just tell. These weren't enlisted men, you see. They were volunteers. And there are two types of volunteer: those you see in the stories who do it for their country because they feel morally obligated, and those like this type with other people's skin under their nails. These were criminals or aspiring criminals. Most were guilty of publicly masturbating at executions. Oh, he could just tell.

As Grant rode through the area where they loafed and leaned upon scant hay bales, he assessed them closer: one had a shaved and scarred head, another aluminum teeth. Back then tattoos had only one collective meaning, and it was "Fuck you." There was disease and disorder for sure. He noted the open shirts in the "rough" style, and other rebellious tells, like "makeup + beard," which nonverbally said "What's up?" but in a challenging way. Our Seasoned Traveler remained cool.

"San Fran combo? No problem."

Grant rode his horse back and forth, inspecting his raw materials, and he thought about his own boys back home. He softened. These young men could go either good or bad at this juncture, like today's online teens. Many only want to be seen as deep, swaggering neatos with feverish pale skin, intense eyes, and dangerous ideas. You know, like Raskolnikov or a Joker. Grant knew that his own boys might have ended up the same way if he'd not been there as little as he had been. Though to these grass-root rude boys, Our Colonel in his company blues and regulation hardware looked like an Old School Fool of Athens. They chuckled, tsking. He worked out how to start. But before he could, a lanky, pimply one with a choppy black punk-cut spoke.

"My name's Tim-Tim," he said. "Hey, aren't you that cashier who hung off the side of that horse in Mexico? Took apart that cannon and rebuilt it in a church tower? Badass, Man."

One never knows from where will come the wind beneath one's wings. Turns out, these affable young men were indeed the good kind of going-bad apples. They'd never been respected and were made to feel like gutter trash by the last colonel who tried to train them up, but Tim-Tim explained they'd chased his ass off at knifepoint for it.

"Old colonel said we're garbage. Said we're trash. Said we got feces for bone marrow and whores for daughters."

Grant replied: "Well, Tim-Tim, that's one person's opinion—"

"He said we were bad 'cause we can't read or wha'right," said Aluminum Teeth.

"The 'W' is silent, there," Grant said. "But you don't need to read or *write* to be a good soldier. So—"

"Yeah, I can't spell what I got, but I know I got it. Like rhythm. Rhyme. Syphilis."

"Okay. Good man. We're going to start with some drills—"

"Old Colonel kept pointing out our violent crimes as proof of our villainy."

"Okay, if you've hurt people outside of wartime, then—"

"He said our semen's got demons in it."

"That's . . . *true* of any man, but—"

"He said the Union ain't got no man that'll match Lee."

"That I won't allow! I don't give one salivating shit if Lee is a grand gentleman with a suave quaff and a gallant gate. He is an agent of evil. He fights for the continuation of evil. And I'm better than he is at everything everyone loves."

He had their attention. This alpha was beta-blocking.

"So, fuck him. Fuck him and his. Fuck him into the dirt with a doo-doo-covered dick!"

The men nodded: this checked out.

"I'm good enough to beat him, and you can be great too. All kinds of people can be great."

"Even Indians?"

"Natives. And sure. Ever heard of Red Cloud? He's got more than a few feathers in his cap."

"You figure blacks are worth all this?"

"God damn yeah man. Any person is, with or without accomplishments. But you hear about Frederick Douglass? Next president of these United States, if I have anything to do with it."

One of the roughs stood up on a hay bale.

"I know a little soldier stuff."

"Sensational. Let's, let's hear that."

"It's best to be single when a soldier. Trying to fight when you have love is like trying to fuck with a dook on deck. Right?"

"Let's, that's—it's complicated. But if that works for you, let's roll with it."

The men started comparing thoughts on trying to have sex with full bowels.

"Boys, Boys. Let's work on the focus. Eyes and ears on me. Now, we got men who say we are trash. Me as well as you. They say they're better than us abject rejects. I say one need not be humiliated to be humbled. And I am humbled at the opportunity to work with you lads. I also say that we should let their opinion of us be the prick in our side, and the fire under our ass. Let's show the brass that we got the sand to grind the dicks right off of the richies, the doubters, and the Confederates! What do you say, Boys?"

"Huzzah! Huzzah!"

In the air full of tears and tossed hats, Our Horse-Lord couldn't pass up the perfect moment to show out, so he did a few horseback combo stylings he'd been messing with, like "windmill dunks from the free-throw line," all with the nonchalance of Stephen Hawking leaning way back in the saddle while describing the mind of God.

Tim-Tim turned to the boys and said "We've seen us a genius."

The group settled in. Grant made use of his Quartermastering mind and rush-shipped them tents, real uniforms, and training equipment. He got the men to clear away the uneven tufts to make a tidy field for drills. He handed out schedules and got them on the soldier's diet: that trusty, steady supply of bacon, beans, coffee, and respect. It was all the men needed, along with guns, which were coming in the next shipment.

After much insistence from his parents, Grant gave a job to his dad's lawyer friend, John Rawlins, who was already there in town watching and waiting. He was to be Grant's personal assistant. Turns out that this family friend was power-mad, though not for himself, but for Grant. Rawlins had studied Ulysses from afar, having lived in his old room for the last five years with access to his old journals and pillows. He saw himself as the man behind the curtains of a grand General. And he saw Grant as a diamond with a regiment of roughs. He figured Our Colonel just needed to play it by the book, get connected with other officers, form a support group, and work his way up. Everyone thought the war would be short and this was going to be a quick way to level up, get cred, and exploit the experience in the private sector, postbellum. Rawlins had plans for Grant to do exactly this, and he would ride those coattails up the system. The young lawyer could provide his interest in the social machinations arenas, interest that Ulysses lacked. They shook hands and moved forward, with Rawlins falling in love with his human project, and with Grant almost immediately resenting this uptight expectation-machine in his personal space.

Our Colonel got out the handbooks, guides, and theories of soldier-forging. To accustom these men, he needed to play "what would a newb need know?" So, Grant and Rawlins highlighted and cherry-picked from the basics, even the old West Point texts, especially those revised by Lee.

"Know thy enemy like thou knowest thy self: bodily, verily, and by thy soul."

Soon, the regimen was perfect, and the regiment moved into intense training. Each twenty-four-hour period had the men learning the ancient method of trading guard duty in shifts. Dusk and dawn, noon and midnight became the truest markers of time on Earth. Now that time was reset, the body had to be handed over to the demands of war.

Before breakfast there was coffee, shits, and stretches. Then came pushies and crunches, back-ups and sit-ups, ass-ups and squat-downs. A soldier needs a tight center coil and hot crossed buns on which to build his temple.

Next came the standard hour jog at six MPH, then breakfast accompanied by tactical lecture and visual stimuli: depictions of the enemy carrying out atrocities against whatever you love. After chow they built muscle. Free weights for isolated muscle groups. Shoulders, arms, chest, and back on even days, legs and extra cardio on odd. This was nothing cosmetic; the goal was practical strength. So, sue 'em if they ended up hot. Grant made a free-standing pull-up/chin-up/throw-up bar where any length of soldier could hang fully from his hands and not touch the ground with his toes. Contests waged on the bar, and bets were lost. After afternoon coffee, the soldiers-to-be got into grid formation for isometric exercises and esoteric philosophy. Then baths. During dinner came more lectures, more Q&A, and before bed there'd be a show or slow wrestling.

It was a Sober Corps, no alcohol, only water and coffee. No sugar. Less salt. Bacon, beans, and a side of hardtack to get them immune to its taste. There was no masturbating. No friendly fingers either. And you better believe Grant participated. He didn't want to ask his boys to do anything he wouldn't or couldn't. He was down there puffing in the grass for the last rep along with 'em. He had to regrow the calluses along with the muscle. Had to harden up the softened-down. And after that first week of immobilizing lactic acid, he enjoyed getting fit again, chasing down that fat in the painful corners of his body and incinerating it away. Even his joints were re-fleshing, and his bones returned to sturdy, sapling reliance. His life was completely taken up with the repowering of his soldier's instrument. He relearned the lost learning again. Always the learning and losing and relearning. Final result: the body got juicy where it was supposed to and hard in the right spots at the right times, on command. Odysseus was Grecian again.

And despite their upbringing, despite their class, and yes, despite their criminal leanings, the men were dedicated. Invested. Interested. And they were working as a team, maintaining a median acumen across the group DNA. After two weeks it was old hat. This set of bodies had been shaped into high value warlike product, ready for any officer to use, deployable for any engagement. Grant had given them the education he was supposed to have allowed himself to get long ago. He had done it by the books. He had impressed Rawlins. He had learned to share learning and it felt like growth.

But one Saturday night after the "lights out" tuba played Reveille back-wards, after the fires got their nightly piss, after the silhouettes went like bowling pins across the still-lit night's blue newness, after Ulysses watched his smacking and yawning men readying for sleep from his tent-flap, and after his own candle did catch one or two of those passing faces of perfected aces . . . the scary clarity hit him: these men were just about to fall back-wards out of this suspended perfection because stasis of any kind—even standing atop Everest—gets to be a bore. Soon they'd rest on a laurel, feel they'd earned a break, discuss the bigger questions of "why?" or start to consider the hours of the day as precious, and go on to wonder if five hours of exercise was even ethical, let alone wise for prime-time youths with seed sacs brimming over like furtive fertilizer. There was something missing, and Grant thought he knew it.

The night had ribbons of chill whipping through the warm air. The tents strained against their tethers in exhausted tugs. As Grant got out his footlocker, Rawlins watched with his limbs crossed and quiet with a placid stillness on his face, yet the lawyer anxiously licked about the inside of his own closed mouth as fast as a fish-hooked squid in a clenched mesh net. The two had earlier been comparing the local news with the city papers brought in by Pony Express, and the different reports said the same thing: Lee. Lee. Lee. Rawlins knew the name was poisonous and anticipated bad-boy reactions.

"Who's our biggest threats in our western conference, Rawlins?" Grant asked as he removed the contents of his footlocker, lining them up on his cot.

"I suppose . . . our fellow Union officers, your peers competing for pro-motions."

"But *we* are going for the G.O.A.T., are we not?"

"I'd like to remind you to be realistic with our goals, and to keep gran-diosity in check, because—"

Grant took the false bottom out of the floor of the footlocker to reveal chiming bottles of whiskey with Grant Store price tags still on 'em. He lined them up on the pop-table. Rawlins, ogling this contraband with giant eyes, uncrossed his tentacles and opened his mouth to let his tongue seizure in the wind.

"Sir—Ulysses. What would your mother say?"

"You learn the rules to break 'em. You memorize with muscles so you can improvise with the mind. The men have it down. It's time to bring back their individual stuff. They need to feel like the training was a gift to them to use in their own way. They'll maintain it, if it's theirs. They can't feel that they are mine, or the country's equipment. If they do that, the resentment will start to set in sooner than you think."

"What does this poetry mean? In real words?"

"I want them to be them. We go forward making use of the atypical. Get them pitching ideas. We loosen up now. I think guerrilla techniques are the way to go."

"Wait. No, no, no. Gorillas are animals, and we are an elevated species—"

"It's guerrilla. It's the tactic of *no tactic*. It's something new called *pragmatic*."

"You're not going to throw away these weeks of sobriety on an anti-epistemic—"

Grant uncorked a bottle loudly.

"These ripe bananas will go mushy with their repressed business if we don't. It's natural. So, we gotta bake a banana-nut-bread with 'em while we can."

"What's a banana?"

"It's a South American thing," Grant patted Rawlins on the shoulder. "Trust me. I'm forty, baby. Technically I'm already dead."

He went sideways out the tent-flap, a couple of bottles squeaking together under each arm and the open one in his hand.

"Light the fires!"

"But it's night-night time?"

"Fuck that. Get your worms out, Boys, for I am the Kwisatz Haderach!"

And with that he "took the swig that killed the Whigs," as the drunks of the day called a "three glug chug."

The weeks that followed were wild. To Rawlins' dismay, Grant threw out the West Point primer and worked the guerrilla style of soldiering, like in Mexico. There was to be no more marching out in rows of dignified targets. No more drum and fife, though the band was paid out in full for their time. No. New adaptive rhythms had to be developed. And new ideas came in from the men to get workshopped. Ambushes, sabotage, illusion, baffle-ment, hoodwinking, hit-and-run, assassination, improv, explosions, Fanta Morgana—if it was dirty, the men practiced it. They planned for small groups to break off and do damage. They ran plays of distraction. They invented camouflage. They memorized modular tight plans that could be altered on the fly based on the fluidity of the moment. And they leaned on their low-class survival knowledge, laughing at how they would freak the squares.

Sure, Grant and the men stayed fit. But the exercise was up to each to suit their individual strengths and weaknesses. A kid named Sugar became a kind of mascot for them, doing runs for to-go food, and lime-rickeys. Dudes smoked cigars while pumping iron and running drills. The camp was a lot more fun this way. And Ulysses knew he had a real crew because they had ownership, because they were themselves, only improved. The Union was damn lucky to have 'em.

Grant ended up being a good counselor for the boys. He knew how incoherence could be wisdom only riddled up in words; and if one took the time, it might indeed cohere. He put the time in. He listened to and ques-tioned with care these enigmatic souls. Boys worked through old hurts, snapping their rubber bands on their wrists, naming pains, and exorcising demons. Some became demons for other people, and they were cheered for it. The trick was to become the pre-stress, to become the pre-trauma for the fuckers in gray. These were the spells they cast on themselves before fucking their hands—and in best cases each other—goodnight.

And Grant learned from the men, too. Tim-Tim reminded him once, "You gotta write your family, at least weekly. Separate letters to make them each feel special." Grant had lapsed on his love, having gotten swept up in the old ways of war. And Tim-Tim was right, though he had also, ear-lier in life, been arrested for fucking a corpse. In the street. In the day-time. During a parade. On a Sunday. Easter, in fact. On purpose. It was all planned. Not just a night that went wrong, but a man intently fucking a corpse that he'd found on Good Friday. Still, Tim-Tim gave great advice that kept the Grant family together.

After a few weeks of this type of chemistry, they were ready to shock the world, and in July of '61, Grant and his 21st Hellions got their first mission. He was supposed to only scout out this nearby Confederate General named Harris, who was secretly running men from one state to another. Ulysses decided to do a surprise attack instead. It was to be a *Night of a Thousand Throat Slits*. Even Jesus understood the importance of first blood. And Grant was a Christian.

His men got suited up like the Aliens crew with individualized weapons, headbands, face paint, and cut-off sleeves. Ulysses, like a smokestack, whispered "Let the eyes be quick, and the ears go slow." In the low light they mutely marched from their field into the Wilderness, all the men with their own tree of red liquid pulsing in their bodies—trunks within trunks. They marched, quieting the blood drums in their ears, as they evaded the limbs that lash for eyes. This bunch of slim, good bodies finally reached the outskirts of their attack point. They went low on all fours, then rolled on the nuts of the forest floor into prone position, rifles at the ready. There in the pitch ahead, beyond one hundred feet of unknowableness, was supposedly a force of men in gray who knew nothing of their incoming demise.

It became a loud night in the wind department. Grant commanded the men to rest through the night on the edge of detection, and they'd spring death on 'em at first light. Kill 'em in their cots. The 21st made the most silent of beds in the leaf song, in the domain of the fairy, where only Native and Sasquatch blood had been shed. Invisible beings may have been there: affiliates of Oberon; team Titania. Were those moths or orbs? Could those clinging trees be changelings? The men wondered like this, as one does when trying to sleep in the woods. The thing about changelings is maybe I am one. Maybe *You and I* both are as we sit in the cockpits of these vasty souls . . .

Grant lay in a ring of fungal cousins, holding his saber to his chest, thinking of the bedtime stories he'd be telling his kids. He lay listening to the random puffs and snorts of his grazing new steed, Torzok. Through a break in the canopy, he made out a forgotten constellation of a woman cutting the head off her sleeping husband, and he focused on that act of domestic violence as it rotated its curve down and over the crowded dome before dimming into the whitening azure of the horizon in perfect synchronicity with the rest of the pinpoint figures of our great and morbid vault. He'd not let Julia down.

God's lantern began its lift, and the smacking jowls of the 21st would break their fasts with blood. But to their hungry dismay, the enemy had fled. They must have felt their doom and ran like ugly children. The ground was Union's!

Cowardice is common sense, Dear Breather. It takes a leap of risk to stand up for something. Those who do have an early advantage, and Grant would remember that lesson.

Elsewhere the Yankees had fared poorly. The rebels had slaughtered the Zouaves like grounded pheasant in day-glow paint. By October, General Winfield Scott, demoralized and ruined by Lee, had resigned. McClelland had been sidling into Scott's meetings with Lincoln anyway—you know, for support—so the president put McClelland in the GW rank on the Eastern main stage against Lee. The prevaricating prince began preparing and preparing and preparing. The press was not impressed. There had been no good anecdotes. No one was buying Yankees Jerseys. So, when Lincoln heard about Grant's minor victory, he jumped on the good news and promoted Grant to Brigadier General, giving him more power, more men, and more of the West to make war upon.

And that's the flip. At first you're expected to play ball, run it by the book, work up the ranks. You're to master the standards of the discipline. You can't do it your own way and you should know to not waste anyone's time with naïve, raw-talent, gut-talk bullshit. BUT . . . if you DO do it your way, and you do win by your own means, and you listen to no one, and you become known by your gut moves . . . well, then you are a standout. You're an innovator. You're a star. Yet, your shit must *always* work. You gotta *always* hit. Your gut must seem like a lucky charm. So, if you know you're special—truly know it with proof, and you're not the typical, fragile-ass, delusional narcissist—then it's best to listen to your gut, take the risk, bet on yourself, and hope for the best. It's the dangerous way, but it's the way to the true stratosphere of superstars. Some gain power from the first way, the safe way, but it's the long way. But some take the risk and leapfrog up. And when they do, the naysayers flip to yaysayers, and they love you for the same reasons they had said you wouldn't work out. And they *must* have you. It's the old contest between outsider artist v. academic-track people. Our General Grant gambled on his gut, and it got him more power.

He was so seeping with pride that he ran out and posed for the most embarrassing photograph ever taken of anyone. His mouth no doubt full of expensive taffy, he even elected to wear the seldom-donned beard-extension offered to this new rank. Go look. Have a laugh at the taffy boy. But he'd have the last one. The stirs of ominous music built in Ulysses' chest like a swarm of heavy, clinging beetles alighting on a string section. Soon a truck-load of pianos would slide off the mountain road of his heart. He was ready to pick fights.

Chapter 10

Raiders

SEP. 1861–FEB. 1862

AGE 40

O UR MAN GRANT CAME OUT OF THE TUNNEL PUMPIN'. Buckle up, because the following sequence flew by like a movie montage of the entire cast running through a film's worth of action.

They weren't exactly warring in the Deep South, but trust me: any American non-metropolis land can go from zero to Dixie in sixty. And during the war a bunch of places went hick real quick. This was where every barrel was a cracker's, because crackers were never shipped in barrels. Where every home was wooden with blue and white crockery sets doubling as dishes and décor. In this Western Theater, along the sides of the Mississippi, both armies of this new war scrambled to take over port-forts originally made for defending the territories from understandably hostile Natives. Grant had a feeling these ports were crucial. Hustle was key. He was rabid to fix his reputation, get those promotions, and get that money to send back home for a new coffee table and a bed frame that doesn't squeak when you're proving your husbandry. His mood was uni-polar, swung and stuck hard to the manic mode of power.

His tent glowed with lanterns and excitement as he leaned and planned over maps and coffee with Rawlins. Joining them were two of his best from the 21st: the dank, lanky Yankee Tim-Tim, and Teddy Boy, a tight enforcer type with an unkempt brown beard/hair/wreath thing going on around the glint of the aforementioned aluminum teeth.

Our General explained that anomalies could be patterns if you backed off from the picture. And Grant was leaning way back, Baby. He could predict and make probable the moves of other Generals like he was picking colored marbles from a dark bag, like . . . White? White. White? White. White?

That old retailer's intuition had him seeing rivers as supply lines. He wanted those forts, sure, but what he really wanted were the rivers. The Tennessee, the Cumberland, and, ultimately, the Mississippi. No rivers meant no ammo. No men. No bacon. No beans. And, most certainly, no fucking coffee. Hit the forts, get the rivers, get the mighty Miss, and Western Theater closed, no more shows. He was winging it with this risky theory, but he felt pretty damn good about it.

First, Grant eyed Fort Belmont. But this would be a bigger mission. They needed a riverboat with guns. That meant roping in any simpatico naval officer they could wrangle outside the usual processes. If Ulysses sent in a work order and used the usual channels, it would expose their plans and get 'em tangled up in red tape. No. They needed a boatman with guts. Tim-Tim found the perfect person in a verboten, hands-on cabaret outside the militarized zone: one riverboat Captain named Dirty Bill Porter who shared Grant's vision of striking first blood. Bill was a vulgar Kris Kringle with bulging wet eyes and a nasty mouth in a disgusting beard smeared with spitty peanuts. But he was okay to play, so they dealt with it.

On November 7, 1861, Grant and his 21st piled their persons and horses onto Dirty Bill's steamer during the secretive small hours of Nyx. The great boat did its best to sneak. Most huddled near the giant piles of rope and chain, smoking in that frigid damp. Grant looked good now with the classic beard. He was rugged and furrowed with a brimmed Ur-Stetson pulled low and a cigar a'woofin'. Ulysses stood in the rich, low, moonless light that made every surface out to be a velvety navy. The black water did its wicked hissing impression of gathered-up shattering glass against the boat as they dragged forward. Next to our shipshape Odysseus glowered

Rawlins drawn up in four stinky blankets, enumerating historical military failures similar to this very one they currently were committing. Maybe he glared at Grant's flasky wasky? Maybe he bit his bitch lip.

At dawn, with Belmont in view, the vessel pulled up to a steep cliff of clay.

Grant said "Bedevil 'em, Boys."

The men laid gangplanks and scrambled to shore. Dirty Bill held his breath and farted hard. In the saddle, upon a steed named Scrazlorg, Grant had three revolvers in various pockets and one in each hand. By accounts from long-dead men who never went on record, the eyes of Ulysses went all white, signaling a power coma.

On land, they pounced upon Fort Belmont, finding twenty or so gray-clad soldiers lollygagging, who froze in various camp positions: playing cards, stirring pots, plucking chickens, cleaning guns, and . . . shirt off while holding a dripping blade in mid-shave. Soldiers are always surprised mid-shave. Always!

Within baby seconds, people were dancing in jets of hot red. Shots! Shots! Stabs! Stabs! Hands to hands! Ears got punched. Couples took turns rolling through fires. Man-barks and the knife clatter sung out over the dark music of struggling breath and the tenors of panic. Ah, a hit song in hell it was. Quickly, the surviving gray prisoners were tied up. The camp was searched for bacon, beans, coffee, ammo, porn. Grant gave orders from horseback.

"Teddy, Tim-Tim, take everyone. Bag the goods and get back on the ship with Rawlins and Dirty farting Bill. Unfurl that Union flag. Unfurl it!"

Wild with his death-cheats, Grant dallied while sitting on his horse, draining the flask. Then, as his eyes came back level with the earth, he focused on what had to be a thousand rebels charging his way, led by the West Pointer, Pillow. They were firing. The bullets either passed through Ulysses or were fired by men more concerned with the quality of their yells than with their aim.

"Furl it! Furl the flag! Burn the place!" Grant commanded.

Torches were thrown on the camp, on the wheat, on the corn, on the men. Brown November burned in an orange fire on the dead yellow fields.

Bullets whizzed and plunked. Tim-Tim . . . oh, Tim-Tim was killed badly. Gone and totally forgotten by history.

Scrazlorg, that elegant cat, galloped Grant at a full sprint across the gangplank and onto the deck as the futile bullets stippled the ship. Bill's sailors bailed river back into its course and the steamer pulled away from flaming Belmont. A field was ruined. No ground had been claimed. Two confused captives cried. However, Our Man had technically gained another victory. And his men had graduated into a sphere of the action-had. After a moment of silent shock, they broke into an autumnal bacchanal, a killers' pleasure cruise back to base.

News of Belmont traveled fast. Grant's name was on the lips of competing officers in the West. Rogue. Cowboy. Contender. The reversal of rep had worked. He was surprised by the success, but outwardly he implied it was according to his innate wisdom. But for Grant's boss, Henry Halleck, this was a problem. If you'll recall, Dear Reader, Halleck was that West Point alum who loved to tell the freshmen where to piss. And nothing had changed.

The Yankee headquarters for high-ranking officers had been set up in the standard way. A forest close to a town had been selected, and the Arbor Corps came with chains and saws and axes and songs to clear out the planned field, turning the razed trees over to the Building Corps who raised still-wet yellow-wood office boxes, within which the higher-ups could do their planning and meeting. Here, across this fresh clearing, weaving around such pine boxes, Our Auburn Man in Blue, with head puffing smoke bombs, boot-scooted through the splinters (left for the Waste Corps to reap) before ascending a case of stairs in mid-build, his heels in time with the hammers, as he stepped upon the settling planks and passed under a sign swinging into place that read GENERAL HALLECK.

Inside, there was a desk with two chairs on either side. Halleck had aged into a goofier looking version of his earlier self. Wiry hair, long and combed over an impressive dome, sprung up where it was, and where it wasn't shined a polished olive skin. He had his jacket—decorated as loudly as allowed—slung over the shoulders of his desk chair. Despite comedic anatomy, the man behaved as if he were in the body of a million-dollar movie star: half confident, half insecure, and fully trying to game every moment, worried if anyone was buying the act that he wasn't worried. He met Grant standing, shaking his head with a wry smile and performative concern in his brow.

"Grant, Grant, Grant. It's so nice to finally meet face-to-face, right? It's hard to get a sense of anyone from all these orders and directives and telegrams. Gah! Sometimes we don't even receive them in time to respond, which I'm sure is the case for you . . . I mean, I had no idea you had this whole vibe going on. I like it. Kinda Old Zach meets Ireland. Don't get me wrong. This is good. Very good. Very memorable. Anyway, coffee? No? Have a seat there, Buddy."

Grant sat in the visitor's chair, slouching back to have room to look up. Halleck paced and leaned and scrunched his face up at the window as he spoke.

"Listen, you're a smart guy, you've been around, seen a lot. That's why you're good, why we need you. And I'm the same. I'm from an older set, too. I've put my time in. So, I know what I got with you. I know how to make use of the best in people. It's what I do. There have already been so many guys I've helped, like you, and also younger guys, you know, people with fresh perspectives, fresh educations . . . anyway, I've been figuring out what to do with all this talent. I mean, there are a lot of great, great voices to work with. Lots of chaff, too, you know. Yeah, *you* know. You know. Ha. But I can spot that wheat, and I'm the leavening agent, you see? I'm the catalyst. I'm what guys like you need in order to really express your talent. You know Winfield Scott? Yeah? Ol' Scotty recommended me to replace him in the Washington job out East. Yeah. I mean, keep that between us, but it's true. It's sad what happened to Scotty, but McClelland swooped in and buttered up Lincoln, who, between us, is a little naïve. He can get sold upriver real easy. He needs guys like me, and, frankly, like you, if, IF you listen and learn just a bit of what I want to talk to you about."

Halleck took a sip of coffee and did the "ah" after.

"So, yeah. Lincoln. He's okay. We went to dinner, and he asked me about the Western Theater. Not a big deal; I filled him in. He'll probably not know what to do with what I told him, but I told him. It was like I told Stanton—you know, the Secretary of War? Yeah, cool, of course you know.

See. Yeah. Haha. Anyway. Like I told Stanton, I said the West is the minor leagues. Right? It's just . . . not that important. Anyway, look, Buddy, I feel like I can be honest with you. You seem like a direct guy, so here's the deal: I can't have my Generals going and doing what you did yesterday. You know this, Man. And, hey, I get what you were trying to do. Take action to 'em? Get it going? Get a name for yourself? Right? And that's great, that's what we're all here for. And I'm rooting for you. *But . . .*"

He did a "bad taste face" mixed with a maybe, and an ouch, then he went to a squinting head tilt, a head shake, and his tambour went into a high, considering rasp.

"*I'm* aware of your history. The rumors? The drinking? And I don't care! I mean, some of the people in Washington care, but I don't. I really don't. But, hey, if this is going to work, you got to tell me what you're up to, right? Before you run off and set fire to a place, okay, Buddy? Because if you keep me in the loop then I can protect you from anyone who might have doubts about you."

He blew his nose, examined the result, and stashed the handkerchief back into the pocket of the hanging jacket.

"You want the truth? I knew what you were up to. Yeah, I let you do it. Here's a tip: always assume that I know. Haha. I know things. Yeah, I've been in this business for a while. I know the types, and I know your type. I know you. And I was testing you. It was a test. And you kinda failed, Dude. I mean, you gotta—look, this is a competition, right? Everyone wants to move up, run their own show, win the brass ring, right? I've been there, done that. It's . . . I'm past all that, but that's me. I'm in a different game than you, Man, I'm up here on a different level and it's . . . it's whatever. But I can see me in you. I can. I know. I know, and I can help you, because I want you to get what you want. You may not believe that, but I do. To tell you the truth, if you win, I win. But you gotta win the correct way. You gotta not turn off the wrong people, right? Like, if I weren't cool, I'd have had to maybe reprimand you or something for Belmont."

He sat on the desk with one ass-cheek dangling, wrists crossed over a formless thigh.

"Look, I don't need to stick my neck out—I mean, I will—but there are a lot of guys in your spot. So many cool, fresh, talented guys. Lots of good ideas coming in. I mean, this one kid . . . wow. He's got, like, a whole new take on artillery. You should see it. You'll love it. You'll love him. You two will totally vibe. I gotta set that up; the three of us should get drinks. You're going to love this kid."

He got back up, got back out the handkerchief, and squinted at the sun-bursting window as if the sawing sounds were coming from its surface.

"Anyway, Grant, if I were you, I'd see me as someone you should, you know, someone to—I'm trying to help you, okay? And you . . . look, I don't know if you're thinking 'Man, this guy is such a sell-out,' or something. Which would be not cool. Because I—I mean, before this Belmont thing, I was starting to really like you, too. From how it was going at first, when I got you under my command, Lincoln says promote this guy and I'm like, absolutely. And then it was nice, snappy responses from you, good hand-writing—last week was great. I was like, say, if your dick accidentally swung into my mouth, well, I wouldn't have spit it out. But now? Not so sure. Not so sure at all."

He stretched and looked at himself in a hanging mirror.

"Haha, listen, that's just fun talk, by the way. Right? Just in case. I'm not gay, but gays are cool. Everything's cool, I'm just talking. You get it. I'm an open guy. I speak my mind. Now, that bad stuff? That 'you doing your own thing on your own with no communication'? That's in the past. See. *I* can get you promotions. *I* promote people, boom, on the spot. In the room I hand 'em out. I promoted that artillery kid while he was in that same chair. Boom. No, it's true. A guy comes in with a great idea; I promote him in the room. I don't have to send it up any flagpole. Yeah. See, me and Lincoln, we speak all the time. He trusts me and it's not only him. Stanton, all those guys. I know important people. It's no biggie. They ask me for advice. Gifts for the wives. Vacation places. Who to promote. I tell 'em, they listen. Anyway, the point is, come to me with your ideas, and then we can see if they are doable. Got it?"

"Got it, boss."

If you can do something that others can't, they will come to tell you how to do it. Would Grant be corralled? Controlled? Led into the arenas only when the matador wanted him? Ulysses had gotten into the real papers with Belmont. And he knew he could do more. People were saying good stuff for a change. Maybe he could do more than make money for his family. Maybe he could really help win this thing, which wasn't going so well. See, the Confeds had won decided victories in the Eastern Theater. Ol' Goddamned Lee had already made dazzling military history. People from different parts of America continued to praise his courtly style, his elegance, and his genius at strategic mass murder from horseback. The Goat befuddled McClelland, and Lincoln grew impatient with his top General's lack of initiative to risk his dick on the chopping block. McClelland worked like a collector, carefully amassing gem mint ten toys but never unboxing anything. In the East it was clear: the South was a problem, a problem that was thought to soon overtake the Capitol and kill the president in the road like a dog.

But out here in the West it was impure confusion. There wasn't even a designated goal. And Grant felt if he could assert this new vision of his, then the Western Union Forces would fall behind his momentum, Halleck or no Halleck. He figured he'd lock down the Mississippi and all its tributaries. His attention grew singular. And he'd already secretly deployed orders for the next attack before Halleck could finish talking. He had used back channels for more munitions, and asked Rawlins to take over sending letters and gifts back home during this hectic stint.

"You've studied my whole family, so send what you think they'll like, and read me back your letters from me while I'm scanning these maps."

Our General called up Dirty Bill Porter again and made another amphibious plan. And on February 6, 1862, Fort Henry fell into Union possession with ease after Grant had Bill simply shoot the hell out of it, night after night, with a fleet of gunboat complements while his guerrilla frogmen spilled into the thickets and neutralized ancillary opposition on land in exquisite syncopation.

Dear Reader, skim along in the papers, for the following rushed by like river waters full of bodies. The press loved Grant's tiny victories, and they began to paint confounding, disconnected, and contradictory glimpses of Our Man. Tall. Hulking. Bearded, yes, but black-bear-haired. Pipe smoking. Long footed. Antic and verbose. A laughing gambler. A determined Napoleon. Short, and of French descent. Black Irish. Sly. A huge, healthy idiot. Undervalued. Under-ranked. Sneaky. West Point top-class ass-grab-ber. Better than his betters. Halleck's little secret. Halleck's little problem. Halleck's big rival. The scope blurred, but in broad strokes it was mostly correct-ish. And Grant went on down the river.

Halleck sent messages to stop, come chat, get permission. Grant said "Sorry, this telegraph is breaking up," and kept on raiding. The weeks felt like the Earth's orbit had sped up. Normal slid down a mudslide and kept going. Focus was shattered. Riverboat travel messed with time, and every-thing came in like fragments.

General Grant claimed chunks of river, moving fast enough that the Confederacy couldn't confederate a response. He caught them all off guard. They expected standard engagement, which didn't come. His style denied the textbooks. They stood still like targets in old-school defensive forma-tion. And civilians started buying tickets to his games to see him dunk. Richies would take carriages out to the lovely, shaded edges near where the scheduled battles were to take place, laying out picnics, and whipping out opera-nocs. Out came the jolly happy laughers: women with healthy smiles who were so agreeable to the outgoing lads that didn't have to fight but knew how to talk about it. But . . .

"This isn't a noble, fun activity!"

"This is Vietnam!"

White pants got splashed. Those easygoing gals showed their con-founded and contemptible bad sides.

"This is not how it's supposed to go, Warren! What a colossal fuckup on your part."

Along the river, civilian men kept coming out, trying to help, but suc-ceeding to die.

The Wilderness and terrain made liars out of the maps, and the good officers who got out of the prelims knew how to go it on feel, to listen to the horse, and to do it half drunk. Maps were scoured in emptied-out ball-rooms, in hollowed-out homes, in picked-over pharmacies. Some swore to have seen fairies, elves, war crimes—but none were believed.

"What's that?"

"Pack of dogs, no Diana."

A borrowed regiment shot up a house full of locals by accident, thinking they were spies due to corrupted intel from a personally invested lunatic man with sex-rage about one of the occupants.

Over and over, up and down, they'd set up camps. Run raids on camps. Defend camps. Break down camps. And live life in camps. Men traded boots, traded straps, shaved different decorative hair shapes if they had it, and did more push-ups if they didn't. Deer, squirrel, waterfowl, turkey, quail, bear, and raccoon were mixed in with the beans. To make a possum cup, one simply filled a possum with ketchup. Soldiers woke up with their heads transmogrified into asses, which was played off as a prank by pals, but seriously, it's never okay to assify a sleeper.

Leaves got cummed on.

Men bathed in dirty creeks and drank water downstream from platoons having pissing contests. Fish shrunk on sticks over fires to the chagrin of their bragging anglers. Spies were shot, though some were not, and if they preferred their false life, they made it into the truth. Crime was up, and reportage was down.

Marching and moving.

Boating and flowing.

The columns were cruising through neighborhoods. Taking what they needed. Setting up headquarters in people's parlors, in churches, in schoolhouses. They encountered lost souls looking for help: previously enslaved people on the run, deserters, unearthed hermits, mountain men, and homestead Hucks living off rainwater who were found elbowing away the bees to sip at precious honeysuckle. They met many lost Toms, too, with recently dead helicopter parents. Like Christian Bale in that Japanese singing film, they'd come scrambling out of their lean-tos saying "My mom is in a bear's belly!"

"Not anymore, kid. Not anymore."

Foundlings were a constant. They got cleaned up, fed, taught to fight, and mostly died. Grant and company were initially aghast at all the aggrieved people. But sadly, aghast's aghast for only so long, and the echo of shock can fade. Newly freed men and women fled plantations with their kids and asked for help or guidance from the Army. Others vanished as fast as possible. Some simply froze, not knowing what to do first. Most Union men didn't know how to help the freed peoples. The law kept the Union Army from folding them into the ranks. The best Our Men could do was give them provisions and maps to Chicago. It wasn't a perfect time.

Horses were commandeered. Wagons too. A family pig that had earned its right to life by cobbling together a cutely crude communique last Christmas now worked through the guts of a greasy group of F troop, its fat in a coffee tin saved to lather up a breakfast skillet or two.

It was a sad boy's birthday in a house by the river, and he got a present supposedly from Dad, but the boy knew when he saw it that the gift had been picked out by Mom because Dad would have never gotten him fucking pencils when they, the boy and his paw, hated writing and shared a love for articulated Army men with wunder weapons.

"Truth is, Paw's dead, ain't it?"

"It's 'isn't,' but it is."

The boats carried on, passing by homes and towns, townships and animal coops. Skirmishes happened near nothing, and scrimmages finished in front-yard gardens. Crises were fretted about, and came to pass, and were forgotten within seconds. Lives got irrevocably altered for good and bad and even the good went bad before the real good could kick in. The calluses were thickening.

And Grant danced his horses. Our General astonished everyone with his beatific riding. His stylings were unnameable. Where other riders zigged, he zag-nutted all eyes shut. And he got it done with any horse on any diet. Didn't matter. He'd commandeer a soldier's horse, and like when Harrison Ford gave a friend's wife a lift to the airport, she came back, and things were never the same.

The 21st commandos continued to extemporize in the waterways of the Western Wilderness. They relied upon barbarian means. They ambled and scampered, and laid on their bellies like Komodo dragons, elbows up, palms down, tongues flickering, prey subdued.

Dads watched from roofs, and boys from trees, as the steamers puffed-puffed-puffed down the death-death drain. Girls and mothers hidden in the floor listened, to the "oof-oof-oof" of the steamer.

A soldier who, as a joke, had flattened a bunch of Underwood empties and tied them all over his uniform as a suit of armor, exploded during a bright big smile. His buddies supposed the shine coming off the cans made for an unmissable target.

Aphrodite's palm was cut as she reached to hand out love toward the thrashing power-mad in mid-battle. Into the air again she and her softness went. "Fuck 'em then."

A minister shifted his balls to the tops of his thighs to feel more relaxed while watching a battle from the slits in his deer stand.

A bear watched scores of men explode by cannonball fall and, disgusted, the animal left a half-eaten boy by the river.

Civilians and diplomats, reporters and gawkers, officers and gentlemen bounced down riverfront lanes in luxury carriages, trying to catch up, trying to find where to go to meet up with the man that Halleck had told them he had under control.

The nation was at war, but life surprisingly wasn't called off. Classes and jobs and deadlines continued. People made pies and demanded cheese on top of things. And the dead did nothing some more.

General Grant moved next on Fort Donelson, where a coven of Confederate Generals had recoiled their forces. There, a'hunker in the bunker, was Pillow, Bedford Forrest, and Buckner, Grant's old masturbating bunkmate from West Point. Down the river again death crept.

The clouds acquired that air pressure needed to squeeze their racket and rumble like a warning. But men didn't listen, and the sweat-wet added sky water to their wetness collections. Rain-rain had come again. Fort Donelson had been recently renovated, yes, but Dirty Bill's ironclad flotilla had new tech: rifled cannons. Once they'd boated into sight of Fort Donelson, and the gunboats curled up the river into range, Mother Nature had a mood swing on top of men's thoughts. Winter was on in a moment, transforming the wetness to ice that steamed in the air when colliding with the streaking arcs of artillery fire.

The battle was a real one. No smash 'n' grab, no "sneak-up slit-throat," no weak team against mutant team. The Confeds had done their homework. They were ready. Anti-flotilla cannonade arced and *ka'tooshed* the river into white bouquets. Senses crossed in the smog song. Men a'squint listened with their eyes, and noses felt. Ears tasted the assailing approaches as sweet and sour. It was Holus Bolus, Dear Reader. I'm wearing a leathery helmet with golden wings on the side. You are too. And time was whatever *You and I* might make now of it.

This was a match where the coaching mattered most. And Grant had to think in order to win this one. By then, competing Generals had glommed onto his group, and Halleck, detained in Washington, couldn't stop or readily claim to be the author of whatever was covertly panning out in the West. Generals and Lieutenants crowded the steamship map rooms and suggested nonsense. They followed Grant down into the bathroom of the steamer, a nicer affair with white-tiled everything, and the men's scabbard tips clicked against it as they swayed in that tight spot, voices painfully echoing over the chug of the engine, booted legs finding footing with the water wobble as they talked to Grant's back. The hopeful dolts suggested complicated, obvious strategies and dangerously submissive notions, like the *Napoleonic Water Closet* or the *Bavarian Thrust*. Textbook moves. Ulysses finished his piss and split their circle en route to the sink.

"Add your forces under my command and get your name in the credits. Talk with my agent here for deal points."

Rawlins hit his man with a towel and took questions from the lot as Grant mounted the steps back up to the deck upon which his horse, Fol Oz Or-Roz, was shitting placidly. Ulysses didn't even learn his peers' names, though they'd show up again and again in his career. Truth is, these rich experts had good ideas, but he didn't care. When you're on a winning streak, you take less advice on how you should switch up what's working. This was a one-gut fuck-truck and he wasn't taking requests. The power was feeling good. People finally saw how special he knew himself to be. How dare they think their contributions could matter to him?

No one knew, but a day ago Grant had triggered a maneuver called "Guerrillas in Your Midst." His men, led by the 21st, had gone ahead on land long before. They now advanced, not from the river as expected, but from behind, mowing through the backside of the Confederate defenses like they were plowing through a meet-up of Webelos.

In the melt down of dawn on February 16, 1862, reality could be seen. And the results were good. White flags flopped flaccidly over the parapets of the fort. Bedford Forrest and Pillow had stolen away in the night like friends at your birthday party who leave before the check arrives. Buckner was the only West Pointer left there. And he was all cummed out. A Confed messenger brought Ulysses a letter that read as follows:

> To Brigadier-General U.S. Grant Commanding U.S. Forces Near Fort Donelson.
>
> SIR: I propose that I—being the commander here—meet with you where we may get lunch and discuss the terms of our ceasing hostilities. It seems we have a lot of catching up to do, eh, fellow West Pointer?
>
> I am, Sir, respectfully, your obedient servant,
>
> S.B. Buckner, Brig. Gen. C.S.A.

From his office cabin on Dirty Bill's steamer, Grant famously replied:

> General S.B. Buckner, Agent of Satan.
>
> SIR: You are a chicken, a chicken that shall be eaten like a cake. As to terms, I will accept from you either an unconditional surrender, or your mortality rendered in the form of ash. I assure you that if you persist with hostilities, I will warm my hands by the heat of your personal destruction.
>
> I am, Sir, very respectfully, the harbinger of your doom,
>
> U.S. Grant, Brig. Gen.
>
> Army of these United States of America.

Buckner surrendered.

Ulysses was celebrated as "Unconditional Surrender Grant" from henceforth. Finally, the name meant something! Yet, he didn't slaughter his foe, and he didn't obliterate the surrendering men. He had them fed and treated kindly. And the world guffawed about it. Rawlins gritted his eyes. But Teddy Boy . . . yeah, Teddy Boy got it, and he cried.

Then, as a result of Grant's raids, the fall of Nashville soon followed, and many rivers (and much of the Mississippi) were now Union controlled. Halleck affected a laugh in the press, shaking his head. "That's my Grant." But laughs are rarely born of funny feelings. Halleck would take credit for these ideas of Grant's—and he'd go on to earn promotions due to them—but he would not call Grant out for consistent and overt insubordination. And Lincoln publicly promoted Our Man to Major General.

Grant raised a humungous glass of whiskey to what was left of his beloved 21st.

"That was for Tim-Tim! Three cheers for Tim-Tim!"

And they cried, "For Tim-Tim! For Tim-Tim! For Tim-Tim!"

Amen.

Chapter 11

Officers Only

APR. 5, 1862

AGE 40

W<small>E BIOGRAPHERS CAN POINT TO OUR SELECTIONS AND SAY</small> "Trust me, *that's* the good shit, Lollipop," But who's to know if we know the true motives of our subjects? Other biographers? Or librarians getting high on their own supply? Nevertheless, us pros must agree on one thing: Ulysses was now famous. In the Bowery, Walt Whitman talked about him with sexual innovators. Emily Dickinson thought about him while wrapped in a sun-soaked linen curtain. Cases of cigars and whiskey were sent to him by well-wishers, angering Rawlins who was struggling to keep Grant's drinking down.

U.S.G. had beaten the competing Western Generals to the big fame. He was now *Major General God of the Dead*, and he rode his new black behemoth, Golgozomoth, through the last wintry elements of the Tennessean Wilderness along with his monstrous, accumulating Army. And it felt good.

Yet, in the East . . . Capricorn was rising. Lee was eating Union Generals one after another. McClelland had quit before he gave Lee the chance to publicly humiliate him for a fiftieth time. He had taken forever to do nothing, missed opportunities, and fussed with Lincoln. Word on the street said he was going to run against his former boss in the next presidential election.

Halleck had indeed taken over in the George Washington top spot. He'd been painting pictures of realities that weren't quite how they were, but which certainly showed how he needed them to be. He'd benefited from Grant's work, and, to be fair, the guy spread as many favorable words about Ulysses as he did fatuous ones.

Our General knew it was only a matter of time before he was able to face Lee. It felt fated since long before. Lots of people wanted to see that matchup. Bull v. Goat in a head-to-head, one-on-one. Grant had dominated the Western Conference. Everyone thought he'd win MVP. It was in Halleck's best interest to back him. Come fate or free will or diminishing option, Ulysses felt it was his destiny to face Lee in the last chapters of the Bible. He was that good. He knew it now. And he wanted the matchup.

Grant's Army was so large, it was in many places even when it was said to be at one spot. The conglomerated forces were camped at different points along a dreadful creek full of frightened frozen fish and frogs in an area nicknamed Shiloh . . .

Having had the larders of a few local restaurants ransacked, Ulysses decided to throw a dinner for the Generals under his command, ostensibly to welcome them now that they had a moment to talk and discuss new strategies for securing the whole of Tennessee. In truth, he was strutting. He had ordered the longest table. The canvas of the dinner tent smoldered creamcicle from the inner candleglow. Outside were Grant's private guard, a hand-selected outfit of ragtag Mad Max riffraff—mostly from the 21st— in black leather gloves hardened in the chilly evening air. He couldn't be too careful, besides . . . he knew who was coming, and he was eager to make an impression with abundant regalia.

Tonight, at the Officers' Dinner, there would be no bacon, beans, nor coffee. It was primarily to be a spread of Southern foods. Fried potatoes, fried bread, fried ketchup, corn bread with collard greens, and the most delectable parts of the chicken: its fingers.

Grant, hair slicked, thick woolen double-breasted officer's coat lint rolled and fitted, sat at the head of the table smugly disinterested in those that had already assembled. He watched the men as he worked through the wine of some civilian somewhere in his wake. There were sycophants, whatevers, and a couple of competitive richies who knew to not show subservience in the presence of such a big swinging dick if they wanted to ever overtake him.

Around the table were Wallace 1 (boring), Wallace 2 (more boring), a dude named Prentiss ('stach-less beard and ivory eyed), one nobody named McClernand (always about to sneeze), and three gunboat Captains with their water-hounds and river stench.

An officer from Boston with a bouffant took advantage of the made-to-order cook, requesting a hometown favorite: chowder and eggs with a beer and a shot. This would later come to be known as the TKO, or "The Ted Kennedy Omelet."

Musicians with banjos played popular songs of the day like "Turkey in the Straw," "Everywhere's a Turkey," and "Strangle All Masters."

The men ate and Grant watched, thinking that eating is gross. Living was gross. Bodies were gross. Bodily activity, the needs, the drives, sex and food and waste production, it was gross, stinky, and sickening to him. But in comparison with what? Within what approved space was he when adopting such a POV? He, a gross thing caught up in the grossness, was looking out on it all from his own layers of gross business . . . to say that such grossness is not preferred in relation to what? What state had he ever experienced that was ever apart from it? Could he imagine any existence that isn't gross? Could he truly imagine something not of the disgusting body?

"A penny for your thoughts, General Grant?" asked a Wallace.

"Well . . ."

Luckily, the tent flaps prolapsed with a bursting William Tecumseh Sherman, now, too, a General. His skin was a crackly milk stone with freckles like genetic prison tats, hair like a voodoo rooster, uniform dashed on rakishly, and eyes: brass cannons, drawing you in only to shoot you apart. He was a caffeinated Cicero. And he was wicked intense. The room was afraid of him. And why? He was fresh out of a mental ward, for one. Honest to God. William T. Sherman, about as understood as an alien's pancreas, had been called crazy for reacting in an un-crazy way to a very crazy world. The boring men here—who seemed to have never had a dark thought ever in their Muppet-like lives—looked at him as if he were the kind of crazy person that, if left alone, would break his own fingers, bite himself deep, or purposely jump on his legs wrong to ruin them. But he wasn't. He was here, smiling, taking the seat next to Grant that was vacated temporarily by the bathroom-bound Bostonian. Wild and tussled, Sherman immediately caught hell from a power-mad richie.

"Nice hair."

"Nice parents," Sherman said before turning away. "Hey, Grant. What are we drinking? Wine?"

Ulysses licked a finger and smoothed a lock, pleased that his order had come through. He had asked for Sherman, and here he was, acting like no days had passed between this night and that afternoon in the Saint Louis street.

"Damn fine cab," Sherman smacked, "Anyone hear about that new wonder weapon?"

He leaned forward and back wildly, looking for smart faces down the table in the candlelight.

"Nope. Supposedly, in the South, they've got a sub*mar*iner. Well, we'll see. Hey, waiter. Hit Grant's glass too. Bottoms up. Hold on . . . Are these people still . . . servants?"

"No, no. They are paid. They want the jobs," Grant said.

"Very aristocratic," Sherman said. "A band too? Beautiful music, Fellas!"

Grant grinned, assaulting himself with the rich liquid.

"Okay. So, we're attacking Corinth next?" asked Sherman.

"Well," a Wallace interjected, "it's a hot-potato situation for sure."

"Hurt potato?" asked Grant.

Sherman turned to look at Ulysses, at first like 'you're not serious?' But then, he quickly flashed his face into a 'come on, Buddy,' and said "No, no. *Hot* potato. It's a new game sweeping the nation. You get a potato really fucking hot."

In his tipsiness, Grant felt slighted, and took to a silent, brooding display of dominance. He felt disrespected, like getting laughed at about your toenails during an orgasm. His face burned, his wind quickened, and he drank more.

"And then what?" asked a richie, thinking this was his moment to make a challenge.

"I don't know. That's it, I think. Games suck during a war, okay?" said Sherman.

"No, no, if I may," pressed a different richie, "you get the potato quite hot, and you try to hold it, and you throw it at your friends, and they try to hold it, and you all get hurt, and—"

"So, I was right," said Grant.

They turned to the visibly drunken top man.

"What?" Sherman asked, blinking thousands.

"That it's *hurt* potato," said Grant. "I was right."

Sherman looked at his old friend, keeping up a smile despite the mood yanking everyone's jaw down.

"Well . . . you're the boss, I guess. So. Corinth . . ."

You see, Grant knew Sherman was as smart as a longhaired guy who is bald in the front, but he couldn't show that he knew Sherman was smarter than himself. Not now. Not with these career assassins around. Still, Sherman dazzled. His conversation style leapt from topic to topic in rotation like light on the planets. No one could keep up.

"Why not kill the Confederate Generals in their sleep?" "You have to be the one who fights." "You can't win by occupation alone." "Halleck's got the psyche of a beta parakeet." "Frontal attacks are absurd." "No, Boston, you DO do the guerrilla shit." "Do the flanks. Box them in and siege them. That's the key. Attrition! Attrition!" "This is going to be a much longer war than anyone wants to admit." "Frankly, we should be beheading the Confederate Generals publicly. Mount their heads on sticks."

A richie cut in and said "Back to the topic of Corinth, our target. Don't they have in their fortifications the newly rifled artillery? What's your plan, Grant? Beyond . . . *potatoes*?"

Ulysses sucked his teeth and slowly eased his lips back down off the clench.

"We'll simply have more stuff. Buell is arriving tomorrow with a large number of soldiers, so we'll be even bigger then. It's the biggest Army ever. We'll hit Corinth in a couple of days. And we'll outnumber them and that's it."

The richie cacked up a laugh, saying "Excuse me? I don't understand the strategy."

"Hey, Fuckface!" said Sherman, leaning back to address the richie behind the backs of scared eaters, "Lincoln doesn't appoint Major Generals every day. I think we can rest assured in the acumen of our commander here. So shut your stupid fucking ugly face up."

The richie fussed with his gloves in an emotional bottleneck, considering whether to slap with them or to toss them down or to put them on and leave.

"A pox on thee! The largest pox imaginable on thee! One giant pock on your nose and mouth!"

The richie stood and sat back down, facing a bowl of sumptuous soup.

Prentiss piped up, "I agree with Sherman. If we killed Lee, this war would be over."

The fussy richie tossed his spoon in his bowl. "Come on. It's not like any of us could take Lee. He is, in a word, unstoppable."

Grant stood, wobbling. "You are, in a word, fired."

Our General then grabbed what was left of the wine and excused himself with inaudible muttering.

Outside, he clambered onto Golgozomoth, their frosty breath moonlit. Out of nowhere, Rawlins clopped up next to him on his pony, hissing. He had either hate-foam or remnants of snow cakes showing in the corners of his mouth.

"Another selfish Saturnalia? You are going to ruin everything you have worked so hard for! With drinking! Just like Dad. Just like Socrates. You are so drunk, you can't even steer that horse, which is too large for you, by the way."

"Bull!"

Grant incited a riotous gallop from the steed. He was wounded by the truth. Icy bare branches slapped him in the face over and over, faster and faster. Before he knew it, the tree trunks were horizontally moving over him. Then, there was a snapping *whump!* and a leg tendon, free of its tension, coiled quickly into the bottom of the boot.

Grant awoke later to screams in a spinning room. The screams were coming from his beard. Rawlins and strangers were holding down his thrashing soul. They were trying to cut the boot off his right leg, which had swollen out like a boiled black pig. Frightening cold pain in the deep root system of the bony nerve bundles hinted to Grant that something very bad was going on, and that he should be worried about it. Morphine was given. Cocaine was given. Whiskey was given. And Rawlins was livid that no shits seemed to be given by his liege.

"For God's sake, we're in the middle of a war!"

"Don't worry, Rawly, old man. We got them shitting in their boots."

Chapter 12

Hurt Potato

THE NEXT MORNING

AGE 930

THEY WERE NOT SHITTING IN THEIR BOOTS. CONFEDERATE Generals Johnston and Beauregard were stealthily moving through the dormant grayed-out Wilderness for the worst surprise attack since God's flood. At 6 a.m., April 6, 1862, the rebel alliance attacked. Jumping our gun, they anticipated our attack at Corinth, and they drew first blood days early, here in our camps, on this hill, near this river, right now! They were using the guerrilla stuff against us, and they probably even had bananas!

Rawlins woke the swolt Grant, saying "Do you not hear the fire and the ... the ... the booms? You terrible drunkard, don't just lie there like a pulpy starfish to be pet in the shallow water! We are under attack!"

Hung over and decidedly far from healed, Grant threw his snow-wet uniform over his sweat-sick nightgown.

"Horse me," he rasped.

Rawlins handed him a crutch and a coffee. It all came in kaleidoscopic. Booms. Cracks. Shouts. Crushing insecurities. Hangover. Shame.

"They were right about me," Yules thought. Shoulder chip. Gutter. "Oh, no, last night I was drunk and strutting. I was Halleck. No! No time for emotional assessment." Brackish blood. Headache. "Gotta vomit and shit and save this day."

But he trembled. Blinked. Breathed fast, shallow. His liver tried to tell him something for real this time. It was throbbing up his back, and making the right shoulder say the pain for it.

"Tell me," Grant demanded from any body that wasn't his.

Shouting underlings overlapped pieced-together fractures of facts: these headquarters here were far down the chilled river from Pittsburg Landing (nicknamed Shiloh) where, early this morning, a practical joke of a battle had begun.

The faint morning light stung him outside the medic tent. Not-so-distant crackling of gunfire and booms of artillery racketed in from upstream as quivering men lifted General Ulysses S. Grant—leg mangled yet booted—onto a distrustful Golgozomoth. Ulysses was ashamed and apologized to the horse. He rode painfully fast to the riverbank. His leg flesh was a bagged-up dangling lightning bolt, but he made it to his steamer, the *Tigress*. She was primed and idling. A Captain spat. Golgozomoth was freaked out and would not board the ship. Grant had lost the animal's trust and had to leave him behind.

Once aboard, they made ripples toward the frenzied sounds. His vestibular sense swirled. Grant whispered to himself: "Whatever you do, Yules, don't lose it in front of anyone. What else can you do but remain calm? Don't think about your leg. And don't think about dying. Also, don't die. Coffee. Coffee. Water. Water. Naked women in heaven . . ." A jagged bit of hard food from the night before was lodged between his back teeth, jabbing up into the gums. No sucking worked. No fine tonguing could rend. The *Tigress* swam up to the floating office of one of the Wallaces. The bobbing boats bumped rims in the storm's preamble.

Grant commanded: "Wallace 1, get yourself and your troops up to where the noise is. Come at it from the sides. Look for covered positions. Whatever it is, we need to maintain lines and contain it. Break!"

The *Tigress* prowled on.

The leg boomed. He knew it was a purple mass crammed into some guy's boot that was four sizes too large. But he couldn't look.

Rawlins held out a cigar. Grant gave him a pained, thankful wink.

The musketing grew closer as they reached the bank of Pittsburg Landing. From the ship, they saw that the battlefield was mostly a huge, forested hill that rose up from a bend in the river like a hairy cone with a moat curling about its base. All the trees were leafless, gray, and blurred together. The Union Forces had controlled the hill before the attack. Now the rebels were pushing our lines back down this way toward the water.

Bullets whirred. The flesh-seekers warped sound up into a twittering giggle that tickled the ear.

Higgledy-piggledy wee, wee, wee the people were running into the icy river, possessed, some by the lead in their backs. Deserting Union men. Grant watched. A supposed trustworthy officer, shocked into slack-jawed awe, enjoyed a five-second catatonic catastrophe, forgetting to give an order that would have saved a few mismanaged men. It all came bobbing into Our Man's view as he waited to disembark into this growing deathtrap.

Nearby in a makeshift stable, spooked horses worked their necks against the tension of their ties in sets of infinite reps.

"Soothe those beasts!"

The brunt receptions of artillery spewed chitterings of earth. Dirt and rock showered Grant as he crutched down the gangplank toward a blond soldier who indicated Grant's thin, stand-in mare that was called Philomena. Again, Ulysses was hefted onto a saddle and the blond, who was helping, accidentally touched Grant's sperm bag—for a long time—before he noticed what he was cupping. The young man, ashen by withins and withouts, said "Sherman's at the top, in the church, if not dead. Prentiss is holding the Confeds off in the Hornets' Nest. It's a Confederate per inch out there!"

Once his sight was elevated on horseback, Grant noticed that the steep bank of the river was full of fear-struck Union Soldiers huddling and chattering in the chilly waters of mid-desertion.

"Fuck them for now," he thought.

Underlings started whining.

"Why don't we try to broach—"

"Yes, let's definitely start to broker—"

Everyone was terrified, yelling one thing at Grant: "We must retreat!"

"Allay! Allay!" Grant yelled back. "Where's Buell?"

"He went awry, Sir."

"Awry on a river? It's a fucking line!"

Where to start? Where were the brains? He closed his eyes and grasped the task: get up the wooded, gray, dead-treed mountain; get through this atrocious, Bosch-styled scene; get through the air, which was full of leaded death; and get to the top, so that he might command.

"I am special. I am destined. I am able," he thought.

Heels to the horse.

"Forward, Philomena!"

Our Man rode into the crackling woods, passing the rushing, stumbling, screaming, glaring, bleeding, dangling, lost, dead, definitely dead, or lively and fearful groupings of panic-faced soldiers. Struck still like an ass, he awed, he awed. So much chaos.

"No! Ride through, ride through!"

Bullets were like air fleas.

Tree bark spewed off into the men hiding behind trunks. Evergreen brush twitched with crying men and bullet rips. Floracide.

Gray guys were part of the gun smoke, killing as clouds might.

"Close. Close. Close."

Up and on he went and saw.

Saw men holding themselves together, guts and spirit on their clothes.

Saw death by nuisance.

Saw a man tripped to death.

Saw the terminally menaced.

Saw the fatally pulled.

Saw the mortally pushed.

"Uphill, girl. Go!"

There were no defensive lines. No separations between forces. It was a rumble in a humbling jungle. Grant moved his damaged self through it all, riding and trying not to shake apart at the joints.

"Hurt potato. Hurt potato. Hurt potato."

He rode into the freezing smoke's noise. Those who saw him froze. Some saluted. Others crumpled with new death. Some exploded. Others screamed what they thought he should know.

"We must retreat!"

He did not. It didn't matter to die, but to fail?

"No! Can't fail backwards into the gutter. Can't go backwards. Forward. Lean forward in the saddle. Go toward the red. Toward the red, Bull! I love my wife. I love my kids. Naked women in heaven. Naked women in heaven."

Grant rode past, clutching his strapped-down crutch in his left hand, the reins and revolver in the right.

He heard war song. He watched mortal combat.

"If that one survives, he won't be stronger. That one either."

Explosions. Earth showers. He rode through the intermittent bonking, hat and skull conditioned to the brimstone.

Smoke chokers crushed up their blackened faces, shutting out precious vision and dying for it.

"Dishonor not thy mother."

He made his way toward this Shiloh Church at the top of the hill. But it was a ways up. Grant dictated orders to Rawlins, who rode beside him now on his pony, surprisingly brave as hell. These orders were to be taken to every available General: stay put; repel the attack, no retreat, no surrender. Rawlins nodded and fell back.

Grant went forward and up. Philomena wheezed.

Shootouts clapped everywhere; the battle was scattered out in micro bouts.

Gunfights.

Horse fights.

Fight fights.

Bedford Forrest himself flew out of the wood like a headless horseman who'd found a random head to use, and that head was Chester Cheetah's. Seriously, do a side-by-side later. Anyway, this ghoul was not fucking around out there with his orange-dust fingers and his white-power bloodlust. He was pissed about Grant's raids and wanted to show that he knew how to raid some men apart. Ulysses watched this menace dance his death into many blue-boys before he, Forrest, phased back into the forest like a dank fart somehow sucked back into the fabric of the worst gray pants ever worn.

An ember alighted on an ammo stack like a weightless butterfly. Boom! Hurt potatoes!

"Distract with sex. Vulgarity. Vinegar. Vulva. Ulcer. Voluptuous. Garish. Garrulous. Down in a vinegary V. Feet. Not feet!"

Ulysses rode toward the church, passing areas of conflict, cutting through the zooming lead, the gray men, gray smoke, gray Wilderness.

"My blood is ooblick. Sugar-salt-fat blood—my blood is lodged in itself. Ugh, my itchy lungs. My veins are closed. Spread, lanes! Spread! I've swollen my corridors shut upon themselves . . ."

Abnormality was way normal; normal a liability if one had it in mind.

A cannonball snapped all to attention.

A nobody's son started his unseen ascent.

Another backfired into a faceless life.

Teeth to rock. Clack!

Hurt potatoes.

"That one has gusto . . . What? No . . . Brittle Brio."

And on Grant went, seeing it all. Men were fleeing, dying, misfiring, and allowing their lines of defense to dissolve. Frozen, dormant fairies in their hibernation warrens were crunched under boots as men fled in fear.

Heaven was in the dirt, the devil was in the air, and God rolled over in the clouds, so "rain, rain, ice, and rain / hissed against this hell again."

Grant saw the eyes of the rebels and the spit in their beards. They were here to make a bum of him.

"No!"

Pop!

"Lean forward."

Bigfoots scattered, unbelievably unseen by not-surprisingly fallible fathers and sons with distracting issues overwhelming their bandwidth. Issues like living and being bad at being sons and fathers.

Philomena worked, mad about it. Grant watched as she skipped over a grounded squirrel nest shot open and displaying its dead family full of grapeshot. Faunacide.

A blue trio charged without a plan into an opening, not knowing you can't have a backbeat without a front one going. Pop, pop, pop and a drop, drop, drop.

Buttons clattered and dragged 'gainst stone.

Men in mid-transition to corpses hooked 'round the gathering trunks, their last earthly touch coming from trees. Limbs chattered 'gainst limbs on their way down from the tops of trees, man and plant holding each other as they met the metal of homicide and arborcide.

"Uphill up. 'Round rock, 'round tree, up."

An aslant barrel of artillery accidentally fired back and to the left, hitting unknown adjacent innocents before rolling backwards over known ones.

"Was that a kid?"

Bodies began to avalanche down the grade up which he rode.

"Why is that guy naked?"

Watery stool maypolled down the naked man's leg.

One attempted quickness. Another achieved slowness. Gravity an accelerant. Gravity a stoppage.

"My blood is granulated."

Brawling in the brambles.

"There goes a red wet man."

Wailing in the weeds.

"That dead man reminds me of something."

A war wagon went barreling end-over-end, sounding like Santa's sack falling down a flight of stairs to reveal that kids wanted only the loudest toy this year.

"Life can't be like this."

A man did a drop-dead acrobatic backbend to end him.

"My hip has a shattered mirror in it. Don't look. Bad luck. Reminder: you're a fuckup."

At last, Shiloh Church.

Again, men and boys helped Grant down, his leg hanging like a heavy punching bag from the light threads of his haywire nerves. Once inside, Ulysses spied Sherman hunched over two overturned pews that were serving as a relatively low map table.

"Hey, Buddy."

"'Sup, Buddy."

A soldier was using the V of a horizontal crucifix as a rifle-steady in a window. A civilian body slumped in its pretty purple pool over there in the corner, wrists slit. Spiritus Sancti exitus stage left.

Grant's thoughts came back to the living in the room. Sherman was screeching in the men's faces. Retreat and surrender were on the table. Our General had to step up and take charge of this motley Sabbath.

"No one is retreating. Even if everyone dies."

Sherman stood up like a snake well fed from the tree of knowledge and said "It's Johnston and Beauregard and Bragg. They invaded Prentiss' camp this morning. The rest of us have been swamped. All day I've been trying to bring our lollygaggers together. The rebels got a force of lots of concentrated men, Man. Ours are so scattered up and down the river. This morning, when they raided us . . . they . . . just . . . they appeared in our camp, right there, while our guys were—"

"Shaving?"

"Yes."

"That's how it goes."

A richie added, "They broke through Prentiss' line, but he was up through the night—you know, sleep apnea—so he saw them coming, and at least he got some of his divisions in place; but my God, we didn't dig any trenches or build any defenses. Our guys are hiding behind bushes or up in trees. The rebels have maybe two million men. I mean, that's the rumor. So, most of us think we should surr—"

"Don't finish that statement," Grant said.

He let a priceless tick of the tock pass in silence.

"Were you fucking trying to convince me to surrender? Do it again and I kill us all. Now, first . . . you officers get the deserting to stop. Get your men firmly placed. I need thinking people who are capable—NO, get your fucking hand down—capable of *leading*. Is that you, or do I promote the ones I see out there manning the fuck up?"

No one answered.

"Okay. Let everyone know that our man Buell will be here with reinforcements in less than an hour. Also, Wallace 1 will arrive soon. We only have to hold out till then."

Dear Worrier, if these Confeds took Shiloh, they would win back Tennessee, which would lead to a chain-reaction reclamation of rivers, and Grant's accomplishments up to this point would vanish and he'd be ruined. Get it? Okay . . . here we go.

They vacated the church and got to work. Our General kept a constant motion from picket to pocket, conferring with each commander, and forcing them to hold their defenses. Still, "we the people" were bursting like water balloons at Satan's birthday party.

At one point, Grant watched a tree full of men get knocked over. The sky was, for a second, filled with open-faced men, catching bullets in their bodies before they hit the ground.

Ulysses had to focus his *chi*. He worked on his mantra, saying "Silk undergarments. Silk. Silky maiden. Milky maiden. Jiggly maiden. Julia. Julia's body."

Sherman defended his line as well as he could, losing men, and tempting the reaper to come snag his febrile nervous system. He was ambidextrous with guns, both-eyed, and kicked balls with both legs at once. He was so ambidextrous, he could lie comfortably on either side of a woman. He was astonishing.

Grant gave advice: "Don't go down, go up. Down is death. Crannies are kill-pits. Spread the word!"

There were acts of encouraging courage, to be sure.

A one man caravan ran ammo.

"There goes one."

Jack-be-nimble here, Jack befuddling others there.

"That's another."

A unit of men augered in, doing it right.

"Yes!"

Peep that bricolage camouflage, those holly-hung helmets.

"Nice!"

Prentiss, two fisting arms and oscillating death on axis, held fast in the hottest area and seemed on the edge of a power coma, possessing skills and drives none knew he had.

"Thank God, okay. Prentiss. Remember his name."

But the collective Union Forces were shrinking. Grant struggled to maintain the constant flow of ammo, beans, coffee, and bacon for each pocket of men, though the action stayed in the red. The commodious dots whirred through the air, looking to expand time outside the limits of a man's head.

He calmed himself by further disassociation, going into private places, keeping his body and mind as distant as possible while being offered up as a sacrifice.

"How should I be when I stop? When I die? With my love in my mind? Yes. Julia. Kids. Saying I'm sorry and meaning it. Growing. Feeling okay when the sun goes down. Whiskey. Kids asleep or at friends' houses. Julia like an eagle coming down on me like I'm a wriggling fish—why are those men running sideways?"

A winged-footed messenger told Grant that the rebel Johnston had charged into Prentiss' Hornets' Nest, and he was shot in half by Prentiss.

"Huzzah! Thank God! The hippies are correct! Choose happiness!"

The messenger followed this up with further news: Wallace 2 was shot dead, even worse than Johnston had been.

"Giveth, taketh, Lord almighty, motherfucker, now what?"

Then . . . Buell arrived.

Grant rushed back down the hill, Philomena carefully clopped through the corpses, "printing her proud hooves in the receiving earth," to the river, so that Ulysses might instruct the laggard asshole where to go and how to use himself.

Our General was again helped off the horse that had proved to be a wonderfully brave lady. He boarded Buell's nice, clean steamer and saw him, an aristocrat wanting to be seen at the edge of his ship's railing, staring down at the large congregation of yellow-bellied men with shit up their backs. His uppity face seemed to enjoy that it was a disgusted display of disgust when it turned from those scared people and poured over Grant's dilapidated, hung-over, rain-drenched, and busted form.

Grant said "Fuck your eyes out, richie, and take your men to refresh those at the front lines. I trust you remembered your cannons?"

Back on the horse, and before going back up the hill, Grant addressed the pile of deserters there shrinking against the clay walls as they chattered and danced up the tan waters, squatting and clamping their hats down on their skulls like a horde of regular Mario brothers.

"I don't think you're terrible people," he said, turning his horse; "still, you fight tomorrow, or you die ass-first."

With Buell's reinforcements, the Union lines strengthened. But those gray devils were able to crash in on Prentiss, forcing his surrender.

"Rats!"

Grant stayed in the thick of it, out in the open, a target on horseback.

"The now has nothing to do with anything else but the now. Stay present. Go forward only in the now. But I should hold her in my mind, so if I die, I die complete, right? No. Stay present. Julia, Julia. No! Go cold. Shut it all out. This life is cheap. We are doing what's right, and our spirits shall graduate to heaven if we die. Go cold. Move forward."

Our lines strengthened. Men leaned against the ancient green moss that was like weathered copper on the old, cold reliable rocks. Defenses were scant but they firmed.

Despite having been deemed dusk, the daylight held out an addendum of resentful minutes after having falsely set the sun only past the higher hills. Now the daytime drama star flashed lustily in a low angle upon the dying and dead men, the light richly drenching the work of men with sarcastic warmth of a cadmium orange ahhh in high contrast, so that a squinter could read it as a bas-relief from a terrible ancient proscenium filled with men under hoof and blade.

"Abate, abate, abate."

"No, no, no. Look upon it and callous thy eyes."

More blood out than in. Blood-color clothes, no more dominant dye. Dye. Die. Red. Red.

"Red-wet man dried brown, I see."

Tardy, the twilight was dimming in, and the noise began to slacken. The night buckets began to tip over, tinting the ever-present rain into a falling, pitchy nothingness. Truant good-guy gunboats languidly made their way into range. Boom. Finally, boom. Every fifteen minutes. Screech and boom.

There was so much sky-fire, no one would have questioned a downpour of dead angels. The light from the heavy artillery lit up the tangled form of the forest floor that had been transmogrified into a puzzle of tessellating corpses and fractal-ing death. Many living slumped, cried, shook, drank, told stories, screamed, slept, ran, or turned into rocks or trees.

Woeful light . . . doleful dark.

Woe that light.

Go back to dark.

Over and over until one felt nothing from either.

The stars sang like a wedding band that hadn't heard the bad news, and dark matter was the only stuff that aligned up there. Dear Reader, the thing about chaos is that we have an ordered idea of it. And the reality of disorder remains outside our orders.

This battle was still up to Grant. He could decide—as he could've all day—to give up and save lives. But what lives later would that lose? And what would we do tomorrow? In his mind flashed his old self living safely as a retailer in his father's store, sharing a bathroom with his entire family, laughing, and not being able to help laughing. The small bothers of peace seemed such sweet alternative to these seconds of now. But he couldn't let that love come in.

After finally flossing, full of as much administered cortisone as excreted cortisol, Ulysses leaned back against a tree and folded to the ground like an Army Man. The tree and he throbbed in time with the leg, and the leg summoned its friend, the fever. Grant whittled a goat out of a stick, and then he whittled the wooden skin off that goat. Then he whittled that goat into a legless, headless orb, which got whittled further to a speck. Then he threw the speck. It bounced, making a tom drum sound off a corpse before splishing into an open chest.

The rain began to graduate into ice knives. Wounded pleadings rang out. The survivors under the dead needed help. Crews of men tried what they could. My God, to hear that collection of cries. Grant for a moment heard distinctly the voice of one crying in the Wilderness.

"Is it that one who reminded me of something?"

To none he could go. Too many upon which to split his last voltage.

Anointed, oily, dizzy, and drained Ulysses listened and smelled. In the medic tents hung with sage, the living began to caterwaul when cauterized. In the field, the dead began to malt. The over-mentioned bioluminescent bacteria revived in the rain-wet wounds, and across the dead there came a real glow in the dark.

Sherman brought himself over to Grant and said "I had two horses shot out from under me today. And my hand got shot. But cleanly, not through the bone."

"Are your horses dead?"

"Oh, very."

Grant passed the flask and said "If I had the men, and the heart . . . I'd crawl into their camp right now to steal their lives . . ."

"I know you would, Yules. I know."

Sherman clapped Grant on the shoulder. "We've had a devil of a day, haven't we?"

"YES," Grant said, overtly loud and quick. He let the moment drift back down. "Lick 'em tomorrow, though. Licklicklicklicklick . . ."

The dawn came on the caramelized garden. Everyone expected Grant to drop this hot potato. But instead, he mashed it in his fist. With the backup of Buell and his long-lost regiments of the directionally challenged, Shiloh 2 saw the Union as the lions and the Grays as the zebra steak.

While seated on his oblivious horse, comparing notes with two officers, Grant's sword was shot off his waist. Simultaneously, one companion's horse dropped dead with bullets, and the other chap's hat zoomed off his head with a zesty zing. Grant laughed and moved on. What else could he do? True story.

With much effort, the Union Forces were able to regain the ground lost the day before. Sherman retook his church but said no prayer once inside.

A scout found a rabid Prentiss with double black eyes looking nocturnal at noon. He was handcuffed to a dangling arm that wore a gray sleeve. Prentiss got a field promo. Dude had proved his worth.

When the last shot of the day had passed, Grant decided reluctantly that his forces were too exhausted and murdered to charge after the scrambling horde of rebels.

"Purpled Bodies Majesty" lay about in ranges. Those remaining went through their things.

Ulysses unclenched his mind and raced over the before, the math, and the after math.

"I was right."

Grant was deemed the victor by the refs, and the battle concluded. Saint Peter would be already overbooked for his orientation as is. Ulysses' eyes scanned a rust-red topsoil saturated with coagulate, and his sight landed on a lavender hand that held out a thumbs-up forever.

Chapter 13

The Butcher, the Baker, the Butthole-Stick Maker

APR.–JUL. 1862

AGE 40

What is a man? Worse or better than animals? Worse or better than gods? I ask you because perhaps you still know a truth about us humans that older beings like me have had flushed out. Let me know if you know. I surely do not.

> Signed, your loving father,
> Ulysses S. Grant.

NELLIE WAS SIX YEARS OLD.

More people had died at Shiloh than at any American battle, real or imagined. The world read about it and they, like you, felt the story with their bodies. They connected to the mystic nerves tying people across space and time, as *You and I* are doing now. The readers then felt their own warm, safe bodies with their whole hands, and they thanked God before blaming him. And I suggest you do the same.

Boss Halleck visited Grant in Our General's pine chamber. Ulysses expected to be promoted for the hard-fought victory. He had resisted an attack, went crazy-ish, accepted the cold place of soldier life, and held the ground for the Union. But Halleck entered the room wearing a "what fucked me" face. He threw his jacket and hat in the guest chair, told Rawlins to bring him a cooled-off hot tea and turned to Grant with a deep-breath and slow headshake.

"I allot for a lot. You know I do. I allot a lot. And you know that I know how to handle the talent under me. It's what I do. Some need shorter leashes; others need more latitude."

He fussed about in his jacket and took out a folded stack of newspapers and magazines, pressing them down flat on the desk.

"Look at your reviews from around the country."

Ulysses didn't touch the stuff refolding itself on his desk. Halleck, with a parent's communicative guff, rushed to spread out the headlines again, reading them aloud.

"*Grant the Butcher.* That's one. *Grant butchers for fun.* See the theme? Those are from different coasts. Oh, here's an Ohio exposé: *Grant is a butcher; it's a family business thing.* And then there are the drinking ones . . . *Grant the Drunk . . . Grant drinks and butches . . . Does drinking cause death: Grant as proof . . .*"

Halleck shook his head and blinked a moment of performed shock, reeling back into the collar of his perfect shirt. His eyebrows were too much above a blank expression of mock introspection. With mouth open, wanting, and repulsive, it was the face of a mid-priced fuck doll. Grant looked away to the splintery corner of the room, but Halleck talked at his head.

"The collective-autopsy 'shows death by negligent authority.' Yours. Even abolitionists say we're gunna blow the war with these kinds of numbers. They're considering diplomacy."

Ulysses checked to see if the sky was still out the window. Halleck came over and leaned back on the sill, standing in Grant's line of sight. He swallowed and rifled through his facial options, landing on "father figure."

"If you had just retreated! You're so bullheaded, arg! Heh, heh. Always silently living by yourself in that labyrinth head of yours. Look, I can't help you if you don't share what you're thinking." He let out a big breath he hadn't drawn in. "Hell, I'm not even supposed to be here. Yeah. I came to see you because we're more than boss and employee. I'm supposed to be back East, but I'm out here because Shiloh was such a PR disaster that I figured I could come and help you fix it up. So, yeah. Yeah."

He seemed to wait for a fantasized thank-you.

"I mean, Lincoln wanted me to stay out there because so much is going on and he's overwhelmed, and they need me to help sort it out . . . but I told him the best use of my skills was for me to personally get the optics right on this. For you. For my boy."

Halleck leaned in and whispered: "I mean, look, between us, I get it. Okay? I understand. I do." He stood up and held his flat hand in the air at head level. "There's us," then he zoomed his hand down to waist level, "and then there's soldiers, right? You and I know winning takes big sacrifices like this. And they're hard. Very difficult. No one likes it, but it's got to happen. The costs of wins like this bring untold pain among the plebs, but, Babe, that ain't us. We're up here," he moved the hand way back up, "and for good reason. We have real merit. We matter. Our world, it's like a monarchy, but based on merit. I mean, look at you. You yanked yourself up by your bootstraps into my strata, all the way out of the tannery. And now . . . I hear you're nearly falling back down, like Jack off the beanstalk, smack back down at step one, or further, off the game board completely . . . into the gutter?"

Grant closed his eyes and mushed his knuckle white against his lips. Halleck noticed, and drew in a breath dart, moving quick like a cat down on his haunches to be eye-to-eye.

"It all getting to you? And the ol' glug-glug ain't helping? Huh? Huh? See?"

He patted Grant's thigh with his palm—pop, pop—and stood up with a satisfied groan.

"I know everything. I hear everything. I know about the dinner and how you *may* have misallocated civilian commodities. But, hey, about all that I say 'Do what you gotta do.' That's a General's prerogative. You do your things, I do my things, and we look out for one another. I keep Washington thinking you're worth the bad press, and you, you work *with* me, right? Right? Yeah. Remember, this will blow over and the war will get back to normal for you. You're a big name now, and names can survive bad PR. God knows I've survived some D.C. BS. Ha! We're princes! But you gotta play this part of the game *just* right. Trust the right people. Like me. So. You gunna let me help you?"

Ulysses slowly nodded, lips pursed, eyes on the astral plane.

"Great, great. I knew you'd get it. See, everyone back in Washington wants your head on a plate over these casualty numbers. Yeah, I talked them down from straight-up firing you, believe me. Stanton . . . he's a tough one. A real piece of work, my God. That guy is intense. You don't know it, but you should be thankful you got me between you and Stanton, Buddy."

He put one ass cheek on the desk again, and an elbow across that thigh, coach-style.

"I gotta put you on desk duty, okay? You're back on retail. Supplies. Quartermaster stuff. Only for a while. Okay? I'll take over your command, get it cleaned up. You fly under the radar a bit. Get your head straight. Let the heat blow over until the news cycle switches back to Lee. Okay? Okay. My hands are tied, Buddy. This is the best I could do. Business Affairs is pissed. The world wants you fired, Dude. Washington is, frankly, out to get us all. I mean, I'm . . . done. I'm dead, really. There's soooo much you guys don't know. You don't know what I keep from you. Trust me. Jesus, it's such a mess. Focus on cleaning up the supply situation in this region and maybe get a better handle on the interactions with local merchants. Use that old grassroots knowledge of retail you got. And I'll check back in once the smoke clears. Hey: dead soldiers are expected and fine; I mean, fuck 'em, right? But you always overdo everything! Gah! Haha."

Pat, pat. He drew out a handkerchief from a sleeve.

"You allergic to fresh-cut pine? I am. These offices kill me! You keep this one, and I'm going to have them commandeer me a suite in town. It's easier."

Grant blinked two guillotines. Last week, he was a hero. A New Old Zach. A demigod. Odysseus in blue. Today he was a drunken little fuck-about necrophiliac with an insatiable bloodlust and a shitload of Quarter-mastering to do. It felt bad. Halleck left after three more hours, two more cooled-down hot teas, one summoned lunch, and a couple of beers between two great friends. Grant splayed out the papers, reading the work of the Obiterati who earned their renown from such death notices. He stared at the engravings of himself with hiccup-bubbles and meat-cleavers. *Drunk.*

Drunken butcher. Mad Butcher. Gutter Bum Ruin. In this new world, the newspapers turned hearts and minds with photos of accentuated deadness. Mathew Brady had awestruck America, full stop. All eyes belonged to him and his ilk. Ulysses looked at the photos of the dead from Shiloh. There was that blond who touched his balls. There was Philomena.

It did feel wrong, and yet the goal was to win the war. Grant had achieved a victory, and everyone hated him for it. They said it wasn't worth the means. They said he shouldn't have done what the nation had asked him to. They said he didn't know what he was doing. The victory at Shiloh had required more than they'd imagined, and it got people rethinking the reunion of the North and South. Should they get a divorce? Many had started thinking about a clean slate. Let the South go do their awfulness. Stop the death. Stop the war. Start the North anew with a new flag, a new anthem. With maybe an equal and fair and inclusive constitution from the get-go? Ah, but to do that now, to allow the South to be itself, would be wrong. Slavery had to end. The only way to fix it would be to go through the badness of the fixing. He felt that was right, but he doubted himself as he slowly dragged his hardened fingertips across the desktop while staring at the blue square on the wall. He felt about the feelings, trying to find touchstones. If he wasn't the best, he was the worst, in his own eyes via the world's. His blind confidence had turned off like a utility. The blinkers fell from his vision, and the cost of it all filtered in. Lives lost. Fragility. Preciousness. Family, the need for unconditional love, to surrender to it. Julia, the kids. His boys . . .

"What if they were—didn't I see a—I am terrible."

If he wasn't alpha, he was nothing. And when you're a zero, you obsessively count the numbers that you aren't. Who is number 1? Who's 2? What was the body count? What if all those boys' souls didn't go on? What if their spirit was only one of the many cards balanced against the bodily ones in the collapsed houses of their lives? He couldn't feel it out correctly. So, he did his duty and told Rawlins to get him a list of the local suppliers.

Grant had to watch Halleck command his men. He watched the preening pretender out there in a jacket with its unused decorated sleeves swinging as his boss threw tantrums, crumpled maps, and held meetings where those present remained silent as they too watched this person think single thoughts, out loud, slowly. He was a pathetic uni-tasker. Omni-impotent. As disoriented as a possum in the day.

The soldiers never warmed to his talk, which inevitably turned back to how he alone could do some aggrandized concept that he said was crucial. People hate bragging, but they love confidence. Halleck tried to connect with the men, explaining at length his early student days, wallowing in delusions of squalor. You see, the rich sense there's something fertile in the gutter. And they like to try to imagine how it feels to have grown out of shit. But such actorly empathy is nothing but larping. And us lowly animalia can smell the body-snatcher in our midst.

Halleck was trying for headlines, but he was risk-averse, so he attacked forts long-deserted with wooden decoy cannons. He picked fights with lame-duck rebel outfits whose capture was irrelevant. He arranged photo ops. He told Sherman what to do in front of reporters. He pointed. And he rested in his suite. Halleck wanted to be the one to have a wonder weapon built. His idea was to make a bomb out of manure. He'd read about it in *The Atlantic*. But everybody laughed at his shit bomb. He napped often and complained more. The man lacked the masochism that works under real greatness and drives real geniuses to seek out their own weaknesses, despite the pain of their discoveries. When faults are found, the truly great endure the subsequent pain of transforming those found weaknesses into reliable parts of themselves. Halleck felt he had no such imperfections; those were out in the stupid world.

Sherman would take the Halleck orders and twist them into allowances for winning important ground. He'd find the loophole. He'd exploit the order's language. And Cump was still working on the Grant Plan to close down the Mississippi. He did his part to hold the project in place for his friend.

With his leg healing, Our Clerk watched the action from the window while renting out socks. The competing roster of union Generals in the Western Conference jockeyed to take advantage of Grant's suspension. His shittier peers made their presence felt on the court, and soon theirs were the names in the papers, those of richies and Bostonians.

Ulysses had crashed his ship and he lost his mind over it. He couldn't take being on pause. He couldn't take letting people down. Mom. Julia.

Sherman. Dad. The kids. America. He was certain they didn't think he was special anymore, so he was doubly sure they thought he was shit. He did too.

If you get great at something, then the feeling of inhabiting that greatness stays with you even when you drop out of it. You'll forever know that feeling of being in your best mode, so you feel worse about being subpar, because you know you're not filling up the space between yourself and your ceiling. You sense the empty space above you. You sense the slipping. You sense the intellect's dimming edges. And when you work back up, it's doubly wonderful to feel the reclamation of that space, when you're back in your fullness, when you can't see the empty space above you because you are filling it. You can't see the Helmet of Hermes because you are in it. Well, from here . . . Grant looked up at a vast, empty hat.

Towns under Army control mostly continue on with life as best they can, while some citizens turn the new situation into part of their business. Merchants for every type of goods lined up to supply the Army formally and not, providing bulk for the Union Forces or direct sales for individuals. Grant was inundated with merchant meetings, buying crates of stock like beard oil and butt soap, and lining up even bigger purchases of cotton and wool for the Weaving Corps. Strange how we continue on. Business. Survival. Sex, even. He saw people reading cat magazines, playing chess, pooh-poohing books—frogs in the pot, acclimating, waiting it out. The local acting troupe performed *King Lear* and it made him miss his family.

But he didn't write home anymore after Julia had scolded him for his last batch of disturbing notes to the kids. He didn't know how to interact with them when low like this. Everyone was disappointed in him, for sure. He rode seldom, and mostly kept to himself, drinking and feeding seeds one at a time to a yellow canary in a cage in his stinking office. The canary aped him, ducking, ducking, ducking its head. The days were hard for a man who was used to capturing the world at gunpoint. He mechanically acted out a routine of eating, drunkening, doo-dooing, napping, and masturbating in a broken ring cycle as a boxed-up Siegfried. He said he felt good. He said it to himself. He said he was relaxing. Enjoying the downtime.

There are often false senses at work in making sense of one's feelings. Red herrings, cheap motives, borrowed reasons. We grasp the ring of the bell into silence until it's changed to a cold piece of metal in our hand and no longer the ringing. But the ringing was the feeling all along, not the bell.

It was during this time that Grant did the second worst thing of the three that he does in this story. It was an utterly inexcusable act, and he knew it immediately, and he repented for it the rest of his life. And I seriously would love to skew this one, or skip it, but, hey, I'm an objective biographer. So, brace yourself, Dear Reader.

Grant wrote General Order No. 11. It was an order that expelled the Jews from this territory that the Union occupied. No joke. I know. Not good. Terrible, in fact. His excuses involved merchant practices, and something about how the word "merchant" was practically interchangeable with "Jew" in that time and place—but no. There is no excuse. I do not apologize for him. It was wrong.

Swiftly and righteously, the Jews of the territory got the Jews in Washington on Lincoln. Lincoln called Halleck and Halleck reprimanded Grant, who nullified the order right away. And for the rest of his life, Ulysses S. Grant would apologize and make it up to the Jewish people with jobs and accolades. I'm serious. Do look this one up, Careful Reader. He did suffer the cosmic agony of going down in less-than-well-documented history as a hater of a people for a split second. And I approve of his shame. And I include this horrible act despite my love and respect and understanding of the man. There are SHOULDS and there's an IS. The SHOULDS are all part of the IS, but the IS ain't all it SHOULD be. Many of you supposedly objective, professional, journalistic, nonfictionalist biographers like to skip this event. So, who's unprofessional now?

Here I'd like to share the Big Question. Once upon a time, after a previously sweet entertainer was accused of evil thoughts, this entertainer decided to lean into a new evil persona for a new specialized audience that reveled in the same evil of which he was accused. After this transformation, a Worried Woman asked me if all men were going around with the same kind of evil inside us. Were we all hiding it, ready to stop our righteous pretense at the moment any such accusation was believed? Would any of us swear open allegiance to an evil flag, saying that at least we were now leading a more honest life, unlike the rest of the men with evil still secreted away in their hearts? Was that the case for all us men?

I replied, "Let me get back to you."

I am back to you now, Worried Woman.

Is there inside any given person, beneath the layers of labyrinth, one soul of 100% this or 100% that quality? Can a person be 100% good, bad, or ugly? Is there an atomically irreducible core in the middle of our mazes? Most people feel that this is how people are, that we have good or bad cores, specks, spirits, or souls. And when seemingly good people do bad things, we tend to assume that their old good was only an act. We talk of what someone "was all along." We say that they were wolves dressed as sheep. Devils in disguise. Bad cores in good shells. Going further, smart ones cast aspersions by saying that the evilest ones have no cores, that "There's nothing at the center of their labyrinth."

Worried Woman, I feel that we are the labyrinth walls rather than the soul specks. I feel that others flow through us, and we through them. We grow naturally, and we garden ourselves in habits. We develop thorns that will harm others if not habitually trimmed. Sometimes we make gardening mistakes and we hurt people, and we apologize. But bad gardening habits will nurture bad natures, they will encourage the thorns, and they'll close off the entrances. There's always good possible. Always bad possible. It depends on the habits. There are accidents. Mistakes. Moments of weakness. Bad acts. And then there are bad habits. Compassion is not strong in its natural occurrence, so we must foster it. Teach it. Preach it. Relearn it. Remind ourselves and others of it. Bad thoughts and good thoughts grow naturally; it's what we do with them that matters, which ones we tend to, is what matters. So, Worried Woman, my answer is this: look to the man's habits before entering his maze. Amen.

I, as your chorus, having checked my lines of sight on this stage, can assure you that Grant leaned this way on the Big Question. Shortly after his colossal fuck-up-ery, he decided to quit this unrelenting stress position of a job. Fame and pressure and thousands of dependents were getting to him, and he was fucking up in surprising ways. The crazy was expressing itself. It wasn't worth it. He wanted out. He wanted to run away.

When Sherman heard that Grant was quitting, he stomped muddily into his office like a rooster into a coop and said "Are you a fucking anti-Semitic person?"

"No! I don't know what that was, Man. I love Jews! I gotta quit this job. It's fried my mind. I mean, is this what I want my days to be made of? Is this my life? Oh, fuck it. I'm quitting this shit again, and I'm going to Canada. I'm gunna go up there. I'm gunna get a weight bench and a tricked-out dog sled. I'm gunna change my name again. I'll go by Sam again. Get my family back. Teach math. And I'll focus on the kids. And I'll learn cunnilingus. You know, like *really* learn it. Not just dabble. Shit, I'm going to get waived anyway. They're going to cut me. Send me back down to the G leagues to train militias or some bullshit. I gotta keep my self-respect and get out on my own terms."

Sherman, coxcomb aquiver, picked Grant up by the shoulders and said "Sometimes self-respect is self-destructive."

Grant struggled under Sherman's steady stare with stuttering breath, the tears' herald. Cump pounced on the weakness.

"When I met your dad at graduation and we connected on abolition . . . your family changed my life, Man. I don't think we're saviors or anything, but you and I have the opportunity to change this nation. For everyone. Right?"

"Yes, damn it, yes."

"Jews included?"

"Especially for the Jews! Yes. You're right. I guess I gotta stay for them. I gotta stay in."

"For the More Perfect Union?"

"The most perfect. Yes. L'chaim."

Halleck had known one of the things he claimed to have known: the news doesn't cycle, it trails away. And the sticker shock of the death toll wore off. People forgot Shiloh. Luckily, Lincoln knew why the Army of the Western Theater wasn't working lately—if the river stinks, look to the mountain—so he again rejiggered the top brass roster, bringing Halleck back East in the GW spot, and promoting Grant into Halleck's position with Sherman as his second. The president wanted to make the finals, and he needed Union wins, so he moved the Ohio Boys from the bench to the starting lineup. And Our Man heard Rocky Horns. When you're a gut guy and you fuck up, then everyone thinks your gut's fucked. You either have to start back at the by-the-book square-one, tail between your legs, lesson learned . . . or you double down and bet it all on one make-or-break move. It was time to go big or go gutter. Time to shake it off, put the walls back up, get cold, and be the best alpha, be the best bet, be the Alphabet Man: U.S.G.

Chapter 14

Reborn on the Fourth of July

NOV. '62–JUL. '63

AGES 40–41

ARKANSAS: HOME OF THE TOOTHPICK. FEEL THAT HUMID, deep green Wilderness, a natural world unto itself, a self-eating Eden. Before statehood, the shirtless sat on county commissions here. People played music with bones, jugs, and feet. God couldn't see due to the tree canopy, and the men took clear advantage.

One such man was Ulysses S. Goddamned Grant. He was a Western man, and the nation had celebrated this fact by giving him the deed to that side of the compass: General of All Western Theatre Troupes.

Again, Our Man had to fix his reputation. His ocular tunnels trained a terrible aspect more and more exclusively on one goal. Advanced to Geomancer General Grant First Class, Ulysses had crews of men cutting a new river in the earth down the length of eastern Arkansas so that Dirty Bill's giant warships could bypass the Mississippi down at its snaking curve at Vicksburg where the Confederates had set up an impassable fortress on a hill called Castle Gray Skull. This fortress sat overlooking the Mississippi River on the top of a sheer, insurmountable cliff. No ship could pass downriver without being drizzled with lead by the city's mighty cannons above.

Previous Generals had tried to skirt the bluffs, only to be pulverized by ladybird sorcery from the sky. If they could take Vicksburg, then they'd be able to hold the length of the Mississippi from north to south, thus cutting the Confederacy off from the West, and choking off all supply lines. Good plan, Batman.

It was 1863. Lincoln had cast the Emancipation Proclamation Incantation, and I am unworthy to define it; my four or five foul words would overheat in the blast furnaces of your ears. If you can, lend your approving sounds to my vile and ragged ones, because the shit was hitting every hand-fan in the land. Now freed people could fold into the Union War Effort as soldier or worker. Many freed men and women did, and it felt damned righteous. Ulysses had such peoples crewed up to cut this new river, and they worked alongside the Union Forces to carve down through southeast Arkansas, into Louisiana, then over into Mississippi, and steam back up to surprise-attack the cliff's back.

Sherman wasn't sold on the plan. But he was there, squinting clinched lids over his onyx orbs. He didn't want the mission to get stuck, nor did he want to get bodily stuck to death with Arkansas toothpicks and sling blades; most in the area were hostile to their cause. But Grant told him to stop worrying.

"There is nothing either good or bad but thinking makes it so."

They'd been sloshing through the swamps for months, getting only closer by inches in the algae. The scummy green water slowed the processes with its heavy, resistant, jellied freshwater (mostly amoebae) which clung—and seemingly pushed—against the works.

The summer had been horrid. The bog provided heavy pursuit for underwater ankles by cottonmouths, moccasins, gar, and gator. There were rumors of mandrakes. There was evidence of real frogmen. They were assaulted at night by possum posses. The oily hiss of the unseen panther forced heads into shoulders. The mosquitoes triggered hand jives and other dance crazes. Inchworms are cute. But foot worms are painful. Even owls glared down at the arrogance of man. Under wisteria the steamers waited for the diggers below in the dead-end man-made riverbed. The sailors heckled down at the work crews from their idling, puffing rigs; and the workmen tossed snakes up onto the decks.

The fall was appalling. Ague. Gripe. Croup. And the coldest weather was coming, threatening to freeze up the land and waters and men within it. Most everyone saw at least one ghost and the making of many more. Christmas was bad. The top toy was a rag. Sherman went to Grant.

"Let's stop. Our Army is huge. I say we do a standard attack, maybe some modifications, and push them into a siege."

Grant hissed up a defensive air, but Sherman jumped back in before Ulysses could let it out.

"Look, Lincoln is impatient. Let's put something other than 'quagmire' into this war journal. Okay?"

"Of course. The war journal . . ."

Jan 13, 1863

The steamers we commandeered are docked well out of range from Vicksburg on a tributary off the Mississippi. We shall wait out the worst of the winter, while planning engagements for the spring. These grand ships are bedecked with lovely, spangled festooneries, the staff done up similar. Rawlins and I make ourselves comfortable in the adjoining suites that he has secured. My room has a round bed with satin sheets, crystal candelabra, and a minibar (which Rawlins had failed to persuade the owners of the floating hotel to remove). I believe I'll try room service while I work through these dispatches.

Jan 14

Rawlins,
Please secure me the following:
New pens
Better paper, lower tooth
Some of these 'frog legs' I hear so much talk about
Club soda, bulk
Ice, constant
A list of local eateries and general stores. You know, for toiletries

Jan 15

The daylight will pinken when ending in these parts. I smoke on the deck, watching the wind describing itself on the water, saying "I'm here, and here, and here with a rip, rip, rihhhshhh. I rollllllllick over wetness, before I'm off again with my eyelash kisses on the cheeks of the dry. If visible I'd be a tumbling bladder with villi nubby skin brushing, recoiling, and flittering this otherwise invisible business. My touch can crush or caress or go gas, go fast, go slow, but no. I am touch without toucher."

Feb 2

Rawlins,

Looking into this oval green mirror I see someone with whom I have some vital distance. It's curious and probably a good sign!

Feb 3

Rawlins,

These gulf oysters are so large! Do not chew!

Feb 6

Rawlins,

Remember when I leapt aboard Dirty Bill's steamer back after an early raid? And I plopped on that musty couch, but shot back up to get a celebratory drink? Remember after I stood up bullets pierced the hull, stippling my warm depression in the cushions of that old loveseat? Ha! I've never lain on a steamer couch since. But these look divine. Are they? Do a test lay for me.

Feb 14

Dyspepsia. Why?

Feb 21

Rawlins,

The green oval again brings up a stranger. Of late I simply must've been too busy for vanity, and therefore my much-changed visage, with its furrows, its swells, its pinch—the shock is just a testament to my grand focus on the work. When old, men have time to get to know all the selves they've been. I'll wait. Still, I ask you as a close friend, do I look so different to you? Do my hands look small to you too, now?

Feb 22

Rawlins,

Despite your kind words, the green ellipse will simply not verify the me in me. I yelled 'hello' at my reflection for a good while, each time making the word more strange, as one may do when saying any word too many times. Mirror, mirror. Mirror, mirror. Forget it. A microscope when trained too hard will grind the subject down into the snapping glass.

Feb 27

Faultily, I dropped a cork with one hand, yet had caught it midair with the other before I realized as such. Reflexes? Check. I'm still a GO!

March 3

Winter has broken like a backwards fever and instantly every damn thing has green on it, either reflected or refracted. The eye reads green even when staring at black or white. My, how the wind whips here!

March 30

Earthworms in the carpet. Can you believe that? Do earthworms hatch from eggs? Maybe boots tracked them in?

Apr 1

Rawlins,

Harass current Quartermaster for the following:

Any summer fabric version of standard issue gear. (If not currently available for total forces, then reserve enough for at least the officers. If entirely not available, have them make me a set ASAP. I'm not capable of thinking in this heat, and I need everyone to help.)

More ice

Apr 5

The thin metal walls painted thick in lead white (which in the man-made lights plays as orange) are lovely against the green-black night on the open-air back patio deck, where they put on plays.

Apr 8

Rawlins,

What does it mean to inhabit a character? When the ship's acting troupe put on *Midsummer*, I didn't break from their spell, even when their twangs sang out. But tonight, from the first appearance of the actor playing Henry V, I was dis-emerged. The question of who this real Henry was kept out-sizing the moments the play gave. And that actor . . . No General there. He had no sense of . . . regality? And don't get me started on that annoying chorus guy butting in. But back to the main: what is this strange practice of actors' possession? Have we humans always done this to actual people when they have been transposed in art? The inhabita-tion of real individuals who've once lived and loved seems to cheapen them with our foil crowns and countable words. Is it possible to do it well? Or are we forever only doing us in their garb?

Apr 11

Waiting for this meeting with my top guys for a drink. It's a dessert-and-cock-tail type of "planning session" in the dining area of my steamer. Lovely musical ensemble, though hidden somewhat behind these curiously potted palmettos. I've never heard this kind of rhythm. And a crisp sherbet of faint rainbow put up a delicious defense for the slightest second against my tongue's compression. Mmm. Like snow giving in under my ass, when falling backwards in a laugh as a boy be-fore I had any cares or designs.

Rawlins, Thank the chef, and note I'm vodka drunk, so, big ideas afoot!

Apr 12

Rawlins,

Those richie Generals, Man. Everyone but Sherman, and even he . . . It galls my stones that I'm not at the liberty to show any of my real cards because I am trying to claw myself back up reputation-wise. I must bite my tongue and say "Thanks so much!" and give praise, and show that I'm eager to listen, to change, to cooperate. Ugh. Soon I shan't. Gotta win the right to be me first, though. Again!

Apr 13

Rawlins,

Your discretion is a treasure. You know this. I'll request a raise immediately.

And if possible, can you get me a bronze bull that I may use for a paperweight? Only if he's mean-looking!

Apr 14

The ideas begin to emanate from me, from my mouth to their ears, ears to minds and on to their mouths to other ears . . . My orders go out, fractured to disseminate further by wordy tongues slugging and plugging into the multitude ears out there for me. But I'm tonguing my own holes, for they are all my ears on all my bodies. Look at my bodily extensions; into a thousand parts divide one man. And then divide a thousand more . . . Man and wife are one flesh (Julia? Have you written to her, Rawly?) and so a man of command is one of much more. Like the millipede I shall feel this land with each touching toe-tip in blue. The men are auxiliary nerves to me. Their arms are part of my body to be used for this Christ-approved cause.

Rawlins, send for:

Eggs, raw. Re: protein for meanness

Cheese, soft?

Cucumbers and mustard for headaches. Re: latest article on headache cures

A surveyor's scope one might wear 'round the neck with lanyard

Apr 15

ODE TO ARMS

The young have the spring in them, the swing in them, in their arms. If you have the chance to sum up a thousand sets of body parts at a glance, then do take it, whatever your liking. I see the midday drills, chores, work teams, and loungers, mostly stripped down to classical simplicity, as the Spartans once were while decamped and damp, in a similar sun.

"Good morrow!"

Arms are a'doing. None standard. None alike. See with me these arms of mine . . .

See those there pulling rope in meaty hand over hand, they have a tawny grove of quilled hairs standing straight from the tops of the forearms and sweat lacing down their veiny, swelling, muscle-packed underbellies.

And here! See this dry, tan pair, like a child's, but man-sized, with pink palms, soft and spongy. Yes, see this set waving crisscross, crisscross over the shaggy head of the happy one standing tall on a tarped stack of munitions, signaling the incoming barge where it should dock.

Look you, there! At that one bald squinter, working near that trailer, hollering. He's bordering on critical fullness of limb. Not cut, nor fat, only mass, no definition, no angles, and no points anywhere. No hair on the hide, only a slaphappy sun-kissed peach, with a cravat and heavy "moistache" up over that portcullis smile. Look how he tosses those burlap sandbags with his nine fine sausages.

And, here, yes! Here see now this "man of men" leaning 'gainst the wall in the shade. This one who has for two decades dedicated his time to fill in his form since his body took solid shape at seventeen. By equal measures nature and nurture this one is put together like Hector, taller than most, unavoidable, and as action-had as a Terme Boxer. See his self-assuredness as he cocks his perfected head back to touch the cold paint, looking down his face at a world he could have long dominated if it played fair. Still, as is, he's done well. Always tired, but always ready to clock in with the quickness, this one won't let himself be less than the best, even in the bad work, even in the unseen things. See his fingers with the white tape on plum-brown skin? The glossy nails over pink candy? See his forearms with strips rippling as he fingers a mote of dust from his white, clear eye's side? Look there at the long bicep running along the bone and hugging the complex of triceps on the other side, tucking up under the over-developed deltoid cap. Ooo, consider this one and his hours at work on that chest plate and abdomen, like sheets of steel, no bit of him given a break. Yes, this one, my lord, look at the force he's accumulated. See the breadth from shoulder to shoulder. See the markings, his inerasable history on him. Biggish ears pluck from a neck that has been looped with such weight, such work—how could he ever want to work his body again? But he does. He elects to. Others look to him. Need him. Stress has taken some hair, what's left's kept shorn. Command has taken its toll. But at long last, these arms have taken up arms, and a calm resolve waits and, oowee, this one will do damage. This one will take on much without anyone asking. This one already has done enough, and has earned a 'forever rest,' but never will he do so. This one you want to know, and many do. He allows himself to be knowable.

This taller friend knows him, this Akhenaten among us does. What leanness in his face, what length in his limbs, his torso, his legs, my-oh-my, this one is long! His reachers are indeed like those of a mantis. Younger than his running mate, he is less tired and, in the sun, swinging his dangling, star-touching arms from their double widened sockets over the woodpile, laughing, stacking logs like lengths of nothingness, as he tells a story, gleaming there like gold in his purple-blue pants and homemade boots, custom long. His happiness gets a grin from the shade. The two are glued, their wisdom shared. Never forget this duo. Much grand destruction they'll do now that they are armed and free.

But turn briskly about to see more arms at work, at play, at idyllic being. See that man's drapey triceps there? Not old lady like, no! Watch them draw taut when the arms flex back straight against the weight of that pulley, see? See him bring up the gear?

Watch that other one, that high-orange white man with limbs mostly knuckle, elbows bigger than anything else he's got. Pants rolled up over the bony knees. Ha, from where is he getting that torque?

And with him there, there! That short-bodied, wide-armed pink person with uneven patches of sparse, curling hair anywhere you'd not guess it to be on a body. Ha! See him sweating as he pulls in the fishnets, shamelessly exposing everyone to their own good luck in the body-hair department. And good for him for feeling free! He laughs and claps his abused hands together in quick spanking pops! Such a sweet jumbled-up smile.

See down in the shade of the ditch there digs a heaving, hunched bunch of backs. Browns, creams, reddening from sun and blood. The one in the middle is all width, his back a block, arms and legs a regular man's size, but on him they're cartoonish, small. His head is a cute cone. His boots: buccaneer, and his pants are a blue much lighter than most, maybe coming from a far-off regiment?

See that one specialist staying in a chair, over there, in that white tent, working out train times? He can't walk, and speech is leaving him, but even he is stripped clean in this heat, a white stick-boy folded there over his work, doing fine with a gallon of spiked sweet tea within reach. Someone's set him up with a straw. Crucial minds at play for each other's bodily needs out here, you see.

And here's that Zeus-looking man, walking like a heron, stooping and lurching, his wonderfully heavy stone features—nose first—into the face of a diminishing underling before grasping said shirker by the shoulders, shaking up the attention, saying with his Olympian rasp to "take notice up here" of his laugh, which is pulled back like stage curtains on either side of the foot-lit smile of imperfect, lived-in teeth.

Look at the teeming numbers of shorter, littler arms working about the pontoon bridges, there and there and there! What wonders, the smaller ratio sets. See how even the littler arms can come caked in coiled hair, some bumpy with muscle, others infantile. But here they work.

Some fingers are smooth, others nicked and wicked. Some tapered Ingres fingers, and some the gruesome, tumescent growths with black creases. But the ends of 'em all display vast arrays of nails. Some nice ovals. Some stobs. Some chips. Thin black rectangles. Wedges. Some completely cuticles. Others none on one or more for some fungal or historical reasons. You seeing them, these fingers? Dirty, cleaned, raw, red, reaching, clinging? Cut, scabbed, crabbed, capable, calloused, careful?

Listen to the laughs squawking, chocking, and barking: seal, donkey, dying man, childish peal, chime, cluck, hiss—like zoo-song before lunchtime. Feel the laughs, breaths, and smiles.

Feel the roughness and smoothness in the variety of uniforms, dense weave, woolen, cotton, worn sheer. The different rinses of blue pants, different cuts, and how they work with differing shoes. So many boot types getting last-minute touch-ups by the Cobbler Corps. Boots are precious. One size feets all? No. Feets are specific.

Some beards go out. Others are chopped, cropped, and then teased, but only on the cheeks. Some are twisted into a chin point. Stubble is trouble, and lots let it happen. Mustaches look good on most, but will draw laughs on others, to be sure, and that's the only sign to shave 'em, Boys.

There's that one who is great at darts, watch! Notice his hairline is recessed all the way 'round, no temples, no island of peak. And yet a donut of curly hair hangs off the back back there, giving the impression of a Tibetan monk backed against a Christmas wreath by a missionary mistletoe assailant. He often tells a story about his son saving his life, some choking sort of affair. See his ready tear.

Over by the wrestling circle, witness that one leaning against the shovel with the flaring hips. And see that other's slight center, like a scorpion abdomen? Look at all the asses lined up as they manage themselves against the life-long tug of the earth. Look at the spectators of this messy mock fight: look at those eyes sticking out. Savor that belly sticking out. Listen, those ears just stick out. That ass can't possibly be doing its jobs. That ass makes people feel bad about themselves. Chicken shoulders. Sloping shoulders. No shoulders. No neck. All neck.

Hey, there's a neck like an elephant leg, right there, from lapel to lobe, thick as a tree trunk, round as a cake. Would you take a look at him, this cast-iron lad with the thick, thick neck? Look at these arms of his, wide at biceps, plump in the delt, traps like cathedral buttresses. And most indelibly see that catfish face, that Chinese lion's head, sheepishly trying to stifle a typical teenage exuberance. What a flytrap of a laugh, a Cheshire cat with no secrets. Oh, how lovely the spirit in this young man that busts through the sides of his shoes, putting dents in hammer handles, this one weighing as much as three men, yet bouncing on his forceful feet with the grace of a sparrow. This one once threw a cannonball over his head fifty feet for fifty cents.

Make way! Here comes one with Napoleonic posture, getting the most out of the least that God gave out. Tallest hair in the Army. Each disc of cartilage on tiptoe.

Note to self to remember the ones that went about womanly. Sorry to generalize. Obviously, there were some like this that were all to themselves in some different ways, and others like this which were like it in my presence only once; and each to each is entitled to a different book-full of specificity (like the one who tucked his yellow shorts up high when on dig-duty, smiling and swearing, happy as an elf). Still, a few shared that something which reminded me personally of my own general definition of feminine nature: their resting poses, their poise, their jovial yet cunning remarks that probed and made us happier. Thank Christ for them and their work. They came and they'll kill just like their seeming opposites: those monosyllabic sad ones, quick tempered and mysterious—even seemingly unto themselves. Poor paranoid souls, though even they could smile once they were sure they weren't the ones clowned upon. And even they'd clap the backs of the so-called "womanly kind" when the work was done and the men were singing.

Wonderful each and all in their own ways, right? Each and all passing through one another's space like interlocking labyrinths. And this is only the men! Man alive, women and their arms are even worse to catalogue for a body-loving lecher like myself.

And me? Me? Long out from the arms of American youth? Me fully exposed to the realities of my fragility? Me at 40+? With bulldog face and noisy machinery under my transparent skin? At this age, in this age, they say I could die from a broken pinky toe. They say I could catch any virus, develop any disorder. My lawyer says I should go about in a steel chair with ten thousand handkerchiefs over my face. But no. I'm impervious and invulnerable. And so I ride. I ride along with the mentioned and mentionable, misremembered and falsely forgotten. Because I too am proud to be fighting for a Union that celebrates and doesn't denigrate such difference, one nation which allows me to do my own celebrating like this, in my own true way.

Tomorrow, tomorrow, to war, oh, to war, oh!

April 16, 1863

War Journal for real, now, Rawly.

Night-est of night. Anticipate precipitate. What, rain? No, Man. Rockets. Rockets with every noise at once and attached light from hell. Lands vibrate with cannonade ampage. Growling Dirty Bill Porter runs his fleet of iron floaters south past the Vicksburg castle. Many casualties on our side. I watch with 'nocs, high upon my new horse, Kooorg. The river moves the dead out of mind. Artilleries trade fire all night.

April 29

Cannonade Day.

Vicksburg feels it. Happy Dirty Bill fills the air with one long, greasy ass-puff.

April 30

Bivouacking. Pretty standard. Using the cute camping gear. Where's that Brady when we look perfect for the papers?

Rawlins,

Find us a travel photographer.

Sherman is deployed above Vicksburg with an elite regiment of suicidal soldiers who'll eat dirt and stab ass. They holler and distract while my real, massive force stealthily crosses over the river by pontoon.

In Mississippi. Makeshift headquarters are made. I drink hard back on my steamer. Rawlins tsks.

May 1

I attack the nearest thing: Port Gibson. We get the usual smoke and noise. Downwind of artillery, we are blinkered and miss the encroachers. Battle ensues. We get men falling or rising to the occasion with transformations, hulk-outs, and/ or werewolving. Wiry hair sprouts in time-lapse from the now-o'clock-shadows of all-over-print stubble on daytime werewolves. They'll meet King David in heaven's warrior hall of righteousness. But you gotta die first!

Nobodies become notables. And in the completely believable afterlife, forgotten families of gods select grooms for their daughters, I'm sure.

Union Generals Cocker and Logan swim through the Confederate defense as if it were unset cheese. I promote them on the spot. Field promos!

Bodies become earth. The Earth blushes.

Rawlins eats pimento sandwiches atop a dilapidated nag. He later writes letters to my family for me, asking about book reports and new rugs.

In battle, black troops with fresh autonomy get to vent ages of rages. They garner major field promos. I cry at the sight.

The South often feels like walking into a bathroom after someone else's shower. Sure, there's water in the air, but that water has already been on eons of skin. Camps are made in such humidity, and they contribute to it. More troops are ordered as thickener. Men work up their manly lather of sweat. Their sour mash of man gel secretes like armor. Slime armor of sweet-and-sour sweat works out of the skin-holes like a clear costume of acrid gelatin. It dries. Then later, more lathers with more movement. Up, out from the man-soil, the armor comes pushing, mushing, gushing. The layers make the shadows of the men bigger, more intimidating. This is good. This lasts until a body of water is found and a man can strip himself of this evidence of his molten core, before the process starts anew . . .

May 2

Dilemma-less, we push on.

May 4

Teddy Boy is reported injured to the extent of being carried off the field. I make sure he's sent upriver to a nice sanitarium.

Rawlins,

Be certain it's a nice one. Send flowers. Advise morphine. It's good!

May 5

We disintegrate their senses; we separate their hearing from their sight.

Rawlins,

Was Julia really that angry to find out you were the letter-writer?

May 8

Their barricades dilapidate before our eyes.

May 9

We slide into hell some.

May 10

Gotta go necro to biodegrade, a process many kick off. Back to the clay from whence they sprang.

May 11

I go berserker. No biggie.

May 12

Pushing my way toward Vicksburg, I attack the city of Raymond. Why not? McPherson and McClernand take over command. I hang back watching for those that might need promos. In! The! Field!

Soldiers take whatever they can find, and no one is writing receipts. Rebs hate it when people take their stuff, and they fight harder because of it. It flares up bad. I get fubar-ed. In the shit. Hand-to-hand combat is necessary.

Raymond is won, but barely.

At quitting time on my steamer, I decide to not attack Vicksburg yet because Pemberton isn't there with his Army. This is a new mystery. There are rumors of Johnston 2 coming to aid Pemby. The intel is strong. I need to stay sharp. From a round window, Rawlins watches me drink. Yes, I can see you.

May 13

Besotted after last night. Right eye and right side swollen, tingly. Coffee and water. Li'l Mint. Cream of chicken soup. I'll be good by five.

May 14

Sherman joins me with what's left of his Suicidals. He appears as a white face hovering above a smoke-black, blue uniform, slathered in sunblock zinc.

"Toss me the jar," I say.

"Let's ruin the nearby city of Jackson for shitty giggles," Cump says.

So, the Ohio Boys take an old-time's-sake time-out for a side mission. I figure that the city is also a war-machine, making ammunition. And off we go, two gingers with deformed souls and meringue faces on an errand of destruction! Remus and Romulus playing Gog and Magog!

Along the way, Sherman shows he has most of *Paradise Lost* memorized, but how am I supposed to fact-check this?

On the city outskirts we drop into minimal skirmishes. The rifle kicks. The targets erupt. I put a turkey feather in my hat.

The town seems abandoned. Honeysuckle is chewed to death by something short. Soon we get smooches from pooches. We promenade our mounts down State Street with crawfish po-boys and Cuban cigars, a parade of dogs following.

That evening, we find locked inside a giant barn rows and rows of young ladies sewing gray cadet jackets. Their soprano cheers feel like melted butter being poured into our four ears. Yules and Cump are hugged and petted like rescue dogs with huge peckers. And with the aid of these girls, we gang-burn Jackson to the ground. (This really happened.)

May 15

Rawlins,

Order Milton's collected works.

May 16

On the way back to Vicksburg, we're attacked by Johnston, and I nearly die on horseback due to inebriated hubris. Sherman saves my ass. No one ever talks about it. Next!

Word is Pemberton has come out of hiding and he is back in Vicksburg. Sherman winks; turns out he knew all along we'd draw Pemby out if we left. Sly rooster, that Cump. The endgame awaits.

Earlier, in letters to my parents, I had Rawlins try to explain what I've been up to. Upon my return, I read their response, and they are horrified. Confused, I dictate the following,

"But I'm the top-of-the-line killing machine, Mom. I thought you'd be proud. It's why you sent me to school! Everyone is scared of me. Isn't that fantastic? Let me know if you want a human ear trophy from Mississippi! XOXO"

Don't bother reading that back, Rawlins. Just send.

May 18

We drive Pemberton back into Vicksburg along with his forces. They will most likely be sieged hard for months and forced to eat rat-crap sandwiches. I come to realize that the victory is largely due to the work of Sherman. Yet I'm not sure how to illustrate this point in my reports.

May 30

Ardent, wet insect song circular breathes a Tuvan throat-singing nightmare unceasingly through the liquid night.

June 5

Spring's arrogant overabundance browns out in summer's crisp hiss.

June 10

Teddy Boy update: while at the sanitarium they upgraded his teeth. He's eating solids for the first time since he was a young Huck.

June 18

Siegin'.

June 25

I make atoms, am atoms, contain atoms, and I devour atoms with atoms, as Saturn his sons, over and over, inside my cosmic cauldron: a belly of acid that smashes atoms into energy for this earth-locked heavenly body of collapsing and expanding cells—Planet Me—to use. This body is but another of my weapons, and I am not it. I am immortal. Hit me, shoot me, kill me, and I'll only sooner be loosed from this pre-show Wilderness into the aviary of heaven.

Rawlins,

Tell the chef I want more of that rum up from New Orleans. See the above? This is great stuff!

July 1

Rawlins,

Again, I'm not 'burying' Sherman's contributions in these reports for Washington. His contributions are impossible to summarize, his ideas unbelievable. Only a genius like him can comprehend himself, so I'll leave it to Cump to fully elaborate his own business in his own paperwork. I feel I do him credit enough by naming him as my number two.

July 4

As if in a play written by a child-aged Uncle Sam, the gates of Vicksburg open on the Fourth of July! And Pemberton, far from kempt, surrenders!

Never cruel, I order my defeated foes to be fed bar-b-que.

The entire Mississippi River is Union-controlled! The Confederacy is in two!

The red, white, and blue come in from everywhere as ribbons, as tears, as men, as life. The flags! Oh, the flags flip and whip! The flag! The flag! The flag!

I've done it!

On my horse, I stand atop a church built to worship me in this moment. My men cheer as I hold aloft my mighty sword and say "I AM THE RUMORED WONDER WEAPON! I AM THE BEST IN THE WEST! I HAVE THE POWER!"

PART FOUR

Chapter 15

Good Boy

OCT. 17, 1863

AGE 41

Pared out of the northern Wilderness of Indianapolis sprawled the first Union Station. Winter threatened its worst on the windows wrapping over this vast atrium. Trains gave their base cleft whistles from thundercloud voice boxes on this cold morning of permanent dusk.

Rawlins wasn't speaking to his self-destructive boss this whole trip, and continued in a pissy huff through the busy train station next to two privates carrying Grant on a stretcher. Our General had to be hauled due to another painful leg injury that went up to his armpit, which made the sensitive hairy folds in that crook unaccepting of a crutch.

Amid the cacophony of travel-bound shoe-sound, three girls (blonde, red, brunette) in matching girls-school travel-garb followed behind the only man lying down in this midday hubbub. He looked down his nose at them, his eyes showing up like a frog's from a pond, and they giggled, scrunching six shoulders up in a bunch as if on one drawstring. Grant gave them a wink, a grin, and a "finger gun," with which he mimed a shot, causing the lasses to go giant-eyed and O-mouthed before drawing up again in a halted ring, laughing loudly, hive-minded. And with that, he was carried away.

General Grant was going home for the first time in a long while. He had pissed Julia off with his correspondence, and he looked forward to putting behind him the inevitable conflict. He'd backburnered his family and it was time to make up for it. It had to be done. But before that love-work could commence, Ulysses had to rendezvous with Secretary of War Stanton on an idling train before the Secretary could move on to other official War Business.

The privates hoisted and guided Grant through the tight corridors, until they found their exclusive compartment, already occupied by the Secretary and his thin cigarette smoke. Having never met him before, Ulysses expected Stanton to resemble a mixture of Solomon and Jupiter. He was exactly right. With emotions amok, Grant made a clattering, gasping effort to stand off the stretcher before performing a bow, which, with his stiffened leg, came across as a kind of palsied curtsy. Stanton's eyes strip-searched Grant's body for tells, and found them faster than a yard-duty teacher finds firecrackers. The three men sat, Stanton across from the General and his agog assistant who was clearly a fan.

"Were you hurt in battle?" Stanton asked.

"No," Rawlins burst in, flushed, surprising his superiors. "He loves to get drunk and ride horses too big for him at great speeds through the woods in the pitch darkness. He crashed his drunken legs all up. He's done it countless times in this war alone, Mr. Secretary, and I'm powerless to stop him from it."

Grant glared at Rawlins, who was at first surprised by himself, but then switched to feigning defiant aloofness. Our General turned back to the stone-faced Secretary with a charm offensive.

"Look, I was in New Orleans, okay? So I had to try a daiquiri, and you know how it is, especially fresh off such a victory as Vicks—"

"Do you hate Jews?" asked Stanton.

"No! That was a bad call on my part. I love Jews. I messed up."

"Yes, you did."

"Yes, I did. Bad . . . bad idea."

"Bad Idea. So, you'd be okay if your daughter married a Jewish person?"

"That's all I want. That's why I fight this war, so that exactly may happen."

My God, the rough inference and the raw implications considered here were like rocks in a tumbler turned on high and mulled hard into gonad-smooth ovoids. Stanton controlled the pace of their pulses, and he allowed for silent moments of squinting, breathing, leg-crossing, and weight-shifting while staring at Grant as if the General were a fruit option at the shitty market. When you're the boss of war, you can talk to people in any way you feel you need. Rawlins drew back into the corner, becoming the walnut wainscoting and olive cushions like the last solidifying phase of a dying chameleon. Grant fell into subservience. He waited—a Pavlovian West Pointer—for his cue.

Stanton exhaled smoke and began a rapid-fire interrogation without breaking eye contact.

"You grow up with both your parents? Or are they divorced, or one dead?"

"They're together. Happily alive. Proud of me."

"Where are you on 'the trolley car'?" Stanton asked.

"I'm right here."

"This is a train. Not a trolley."

". . . What am I missing?"

"Are you capable of learning?"

"Sure."

"Most Americans think they already know what they need to know. Is this not the case with you?"

"I know enough to know I can know more."

"Why don't you listen to your consulting underlings? Seem to be a lot of well-educated, top minds at your disposal. They feel they are being wasted when you don't use them or their ideas."

"Am I to win this war or make the rich feel good about themselves?"

"What's the difference between confidence and arrogance?"

"Spelling?"

"Do you have any Jewish friends?"

"I am not an anti-Semite!"

"You say that, but you wrote Order No. 11 to expel the Jews, did you not?"

"I did. It was wrong."

"But in conflict with your earlier statement about not being an anti-Semite, wasn't expelling Jews an anti-Semitic act?"

"It *was*. And I'll apologize forever for it."

"But the order makes you an anti-Semite. It *is* what it *is*. And your first answer *is* a lie."

"It depends upon what the meaning of the word 'is' is. If the—if he—if 'is' means is *and* never has been, that is not—that is *one* thing. If it means there *is* none, that *was* a completely true statement."

Stanton flipped the lighter lid open, shut, and open.

"You ever have dinner with a basic person?"

"Like, a private?"

"Know any Asians or Native Americans?"

"I did. I've known people who were."

"Do you fantasize about living in a castle, being a lord or an Earl?"

"Not those titles, but the word castle is, maybe, subjective. Every man's the king of his—"

"Do you wish to have servants? Paid, but subservient? Low and not up-to-date on culture? Not like you and your class?"

"Everyone must start out low, I suppose."

"You like Wagner?"

"*Vhy* not?"

Stanton took a deep drag, exhaling with the next reloaded barrage.

"Ever hire a person of color for non-custodial work?"

"I hire according to current Army guidelines, so yes, actually in my victory at Vicksburg we had many black—"

"You once *owned* a person, correct?"

Grant's eyes lowered.

"You hit your kids?"

"No," said Grant, his eyes back up, steeled.

"Strike your waiters?"

"No."

"Smack ass if they got it?"

"My kid's or the waiter's, Sir?"

"Ever whistle at a beauty?"

"Only landscapes."

Stanton nearly smirked.

"Do you think there is the 'world of words' and then yet another world of 'inference and ineffable knowledge'?"

"Come again?"

"Do you believe in a realm of suggestion, radar, aura, vibe, mood, tone? Where someone can say 'no' but mean 'maybe'?"

"If so, that realm is part of everything else, and the rules need to be discussed in clear terms."

"Do you think power is the goal of a game that can be won? And once one does win it, do you think that win becomes a permanent trophy that holds the power forever? Or does it merely become a relic of power?"

"Wait, are y'all giving out trophies, because I haven't lost one engagement, and I haven't received any of those."

"Is there such a thing as permanent importance? Or do we need to continually win to stay winners? Continually prove why we are to be loved?"

"Pass?"

"Do you think your antics are a positive feature of your whole persona as a representative of the American Military, and thusly of the president?"

"I do what I think the president ultimately wants from me."

"Is it true that all press is good press? Are you working a 'bad boy' persona?"

"Are you recording this? I could swear I hear telegraph typing."

"Do you think we can make someone love something?"

"No."

"Should we be free to hate something if we don't take action against it?"

"What's the hated thing, and how does the hate manifest?"

"How can someone police hate?"

"I'm not interviewing for a cop job, am I?"

"Is it wrong to police thought? Feelings?"

"I don't want to be told how to feel. So, I guess no one else should either."

"So, you think you're the model citizen that we should base a society around?"

"Expect the worst, be surprised by the 'not worst' is my motto."

Stanton picked a fleck of tobacco off his tongue and flicked it at the carpet.

"If the British had won the Revolutionary War—which would then be called the War of the Rebellion—would Benedict Arnold have been a much-beloved hero?"

"No."

"Why?"

"Spies are terrible."

"Even if they work for freedom, democracy? Against tyranny?"

"Was that the case for Arnold?"

Stanton jotted something down in a red notebook, taking a long time with no gestures of contact until he was ready to resume.

"Do you know there's no slavery in Britain?"

"That's what they say."

"If this is so . . . should they have won the Revolutionary War?"

"No."

"Did we fight for the freedom to have slaves?"

"Did we?"

"Would we have ended up better as British people?"

"In a lot of ways, I bet we would have been exactly the same."

"Should protests be allowed?"

"Certainly."

"What about looting, damaging property?"

"Certainly not."

"What if all other recourse has proved to be dead-ends for a dis-enfranchised group? What if the powers-that-be were shut off to the aggrieved?"

"I guess if they're being harmed or oppressed, they should have the right to make themselves heard."

"Is war ultimately a form of protest?"

"I don't see it that way unless Congress are the ones protesting."

"Do you allow your men to loot as you raze enemy territory?"

"I don't want it to happen, but sometimes your attentions are elsewhere and *raze* is a strong word—"

"How do you define the Constitution's usage of the term 'militia'?"

"I define it as ill-defined."

"Do you support the Second Amendment?"

"It's in the Constitution, I am the arm of the Constitution."

"As a defender of the Constitution, do you support the proposed 13th amendment?"

"I certainly do. I support Lincoln like a girdle. The Herculean kind."

"Should stupid people have the same rights as the intelligent?"

"Maybe not, I haven't exactly—"

"Then people with disabilities aren't full citizens?"

"I did NOT say that."

"Do you think a person can have too much freedom?"

"If they're hurting others with it, maybe."

"What do you think about taxes?"

"I haven't really thought about taxes, I've had the war on my mind exclusively, so—"

"As have I, General Grant. And I'm trying to see if we agree on the society that we both seem to feel is worth dying for."

"I get that."

Grant felt sure these questions were a way to beat the bushes, to flush out some Voight-Kampff data. The questions themselves weren't important. Maybe. Fuck, maybe they were crucial . . .

Stanton moved his left ear closer to its shoulder.

"What's your opinion on the situation in Chattanooga?"

"Seems not as bad as . . . wait, did you say Chattanooga? Well, okay, the Confederates know their briars and brambles of their woods. They got home-court advantage, I'd say."

Stanton thought about something, eyes temporarily averted. He swung them back.

"We've got people doing reconnaissance, getting surveyor intelligence. Have you ever heard of Harriet Tubman?"

"You got Tubman?"

"We have. She's got South Carolina completely mapped. Tennessee, too. Elevations, everything. Working on Maryland. So. You, General, are going to Chattanooga."

"But, Sir, I expected—"

"Yes, you might get a chance at Lee in the East before it's all over. But let me ask you this: where do you have Sherman now?"

"He's commanding back at Vicksburg."

"Mm. Do you prefer improv, or the classic approach?"

"A mix."

"Which does Sherman prefer?"

"Sherman? He's great, but, Man. He's so 'out,' it's hard to understand what he's going for. He's experimental, that's what he is. Why?"

"I am capable of comprehending what he's up to, because *I* know the texts and the histories with which he is 'experimenting.' Do you?"

"Of course. It's not that. It's just—he's—it's all about the theory to him, and he's not even thinking about how it's going to look or come across. I'm more about the hits, you know?"

"I *do* know." Stanton's eyes stayed on him, while he nodded. But his mind seemed to have fallen back from the face, calculating in the back-brain before resuming animation.

"Why do you not talk more in detail of Sherman's ideas in your reports?"

"I didn't know there was a standard to field reports."

"There is a rule of thumb to detailing the notable. Would his ideas and exploits not fall into that category?"

"Of course, they are noteworthy. But it happens so fast—"

"You're right. During a 'fast siege of months,' I suppose one wouldn't have the time for reliable rumination. Do you feel we only want to hear about you?"

Ulysses was sweating like Nixon's great-granddad at a fortuneteller party.

"Some people bet on animals. I bet on myself. I'll send revisions, I guess, it's just that—"

"Sandman . . ."

Ulysses was struck still by his childhood nickname. What kind of intelligence did Stanton possess? Through how many men could he feel? Stanton saw that the name had drawn a new kind of focus from his subject.

"The thing about good luck is that most of the time you can't see the instances when you've had it. We walk through life narrowly evading unseen catastrophes. You've been rather lucky. I know firsthand."

"Okay, look. Sherman sort of saved my ass outside Jackson, if that's what you're getting at. Probably other times too."

"He is a great asset to you. And to us. Let me ask you this. How do you feel about Halleck?"

"Halleck? Oh, he's, uh . . . he's smart. He's talented in ways that I'm not."

Stanton smirked, exhaling smoke through the slit of his teeth.

"Okay, he sucks, Man. Halleck sucks real bad."

Stanton hurriedly put out his cigarette.

"Congratulations. You've been promoted to Major General of the regular Army. Sherman will continue to answer directly to you in your current capacity out West. Report directly from here to Chattanooga. No need to change trains. I selected this one knowing your current 'leg situation' would make painful any unnecessary movement."

"But, Stanton. I was going home. I have important personal business to attend to."

"Are you rejecting my orders?"

"No, Sir. If you permit me, I'm not just any General now. These three kids in the station, they knew who I was and, well, maybe my talents are best used in the spring, against more formidable   "

Stanton gathered his cig packet and lighter off the table like Michael in Vegas.

"Listen. Talent is as cheap as a fuck in Fucktown on free day."

Rawlins and Ulysses chanced a searching look.

"You want to succeed, get rich, become a fat cat with a koala face?"

"Wuh, yeah. That's the American Dream, right?"

"No. That's entirely different. What I'm saying is what I'm saying, Grant. Look no deeper than that. Artifice can be the thing, not simply the packaging."

"What?"

"Figure out Chattanooga for us and try not to blemish the current collective picture of you that the majority of America holds. I need someone who can play the game. Be useful here, and I'll use you again. Okay?"

The Secretary stood in the door, checking his pocket watch.

"You in or out, Sandman? Or should I give this to Sherman, see if he wants to play ball?"

Grant presented a better posture for the final memory.

"Sir. I can pass any goddamn marshmallow test you got."

"Good boy."

Chapter 16

Chattanooga

OCT. 1863–FEB. 1864

AGE 41

D uring civil wars, Chattanooga the city lends its name to a large set of environs, especially the mountainous heights that surround the crucial ground and water byways, which lace 'round and 'round in valley floors. The Confeds had the Union boxed in on a useless mountaintop. And Grant was to be snuck into this sieged Union stronghold like a secret weapon.

As Our General and his attorney were slogged up through dropping temperatures, Grant dictated to Rawlins an explanatory letter to Julia, as well as a list of new wares to order for this unexpected winter expedition. From train to carriage, carriage to nameless horses, nameless horses to shameful horses, shameful horses to shittier carriages pulled by the skeletons of horses, they went deeper and deeper, higher and higher into Tennessee, going tighter into its crags, closer and closer to the bottom of heaven and to the front of the line. The sky was whited out and the diffuse made immeasurable the distance to the glass-bottom boat of the sky, so it seemed like perhaps the vault had lowered, and maybe God's floor was just beyond the blur, within gun range.

Union HQ for this area was tucked up in evergreens and steepness, in the midst of the usual denuded grotto with trees transformed to boxes for officers, boxes that sat upwind from a disenchanted tent city for the men, where community-code regulations had long since given way under the demand for heat that this kind of shanty town perhaps on mild days afforded.

Dressed in rags and scraps of paper, soldiers stood by trickles of fire, piggy-fronting each other for warmth. An artless dodger cooked a catamount over a fire with the fur still on it. There were axes frozen in trees. Squirrels gathered their acorns at night so as to not have their stashes raided by these desperate upright creatures. The birds wheezed like squeeze toys in the wind's teeth.

Grant crutched up toward the Generals' office where the frozen cowards in charge were to give a presentation on why they were trapped like held-down house cats. This pine box smelled like musty pecans, feet, and potatoes. Standing in a row like stooges were three top Generals, each bedraggled in their own gross way. One was clearly famished, another hungover, and the last depressed with a bulky, hunched torso and tiny limbs, like a shrimp. In the corner sat a sullen fourth, round and rebellious, with a bald dome and frothy black curtains of hair that ran into ludicrous sideburns, which were pretty much just a reverse goatee. This pompous hack sat like a know-it-all, knees wide apart, gut dangling, one elbow on a knee, palm on the other, with an eyebrow and a smirk begging to be slapped. Grant noted this last man, and out of "personality strategy," he didn't give him eye-contact, addressing instead the famished weakling as if he were the alpha of this pack.

"Why are you stymied? Go."

"Well. Sir. We—are you sure you want *me* to answer?"

Rustling could be heard in the corner. Grant didn't turn to see what assuredly was some display of hostile dominance brewing.

"Go on, please."

"Okay. We've been fully surrounded. And our forces are lower in number. We can't wage an offensive. And it's winter. And the Confeds are waiting until spring to attack. Their forces are accumulating. It's a matter of time. We're kind of trapped up here unless you've come to suggest we retreat and join your large and more opportunely positioned ranks."

"You know what they say," Grant said. "Men are tormented with the Opinions they have of Things, and not by the Things themselves."

From the corner the hog-bristled asshole burst in, "What he means is—"

"If I want your thoughts, I'll ask for them."

"Ain't that just—it's all Washington's fault. I'm much better suited out East. I'm wasted here in this insolvable puzzle. This ain't fair."

"Fucking go outside, you. No. I mean it. Go away. Read the minutes of the meeting later. I can't think with your, your upsetting perspective."

Sideburns left huffing, stomping in a sulk with his spurs catching in his cape.

Grant called after him: "It's a fine line between arrogance and confidence, Buddy!"

The remaining men were wide-eyed like mice.

"Erase him from your minds. Think positively. We can turn this around. What's in our pro column?"

"Vantage point. We've got high ground."

"There you go. What else?"

"We've got you. You're the wonder weapon."

"Sucking dick will get you nothing but more dick, Buddy. But thanks. Okay, what else?"

"And we have a Zouave."

"What?"

"One of the Zouaves, we have one of the few surviving Special Forces. He's here to, well, to give us advice and whatnot."

"They sent him? Where is he?"

"No, no. We found him."

"Bring him in here."

"We usually go to him in his shed."

"Bring him in here."

One of the Generals whispered to an adjutant.

Grant continued, "And bring me your Quartermaster."

"That's me," said the hung-over one. This worthless piss bag worked its body over to face Grant. It pulled the mouth levers, but only worthless pissy vapors escaped the hatch.

"I don't read steam signals, Boy. Write this down: Bacon! Beans! Coffee! And get some damn Underwood. It brightens the day."

"But, General . . ."

"If I could get up that ratline, food can get up it, too. Get a steady stream of supplies from Memphis through Columbia to here. Clothes, coats, hardtack, bread, whiskey, fire, guns, bullets, porn, blankets, real horses, salt, and a crate of goddamn mouth antiseptic for your word holes. And work with Jewish merchants, for Christ's sake! Keep in mind what kind of society it is we're fighting for. Ask yourselves where you are on the trolley!"

They shook their confused heads while nodding.

"Better find out where you are on those trolleys, Boys. Now . . . I'm writing to the nearest Union Stronghold. Their first priority will be to get us equipped and fortified with reinforcements. The supply line will be protected while remaining a secret, i.e., ran in the dark. Meanwhile, I will devise a way out of this siege. And by the way, let's hire some people of color; get fresh perspectives. It's 1863, goddamn it."

"What, for like custodial work?"

"No, I mean for *your* job. Go hire your replacement, fucker. But give him a better hat! Dismissed!"

As Ulysses tried to exit—on his last second of faking that his body and leg weren't in complete shutdown—two men dragging a third between them came in sideways through the door. The toes of the boots of the third man dragged two brown marks on the yellow pine floor, and a string of drool unspooled a snail trail between them. The men pointed a multicolored beret at Grant, the face under it aimed down at the baggy, technicolored dream suit, faded and heavily stained. Only the tips of his mustache tendrils could be seen slowly undulating like a lobster's.

"This is your man from Special Forces? What's wrong with him?"

"He's been working through our morphine, actually."

"Have him shot."

Everyone started to cry. Grant included.

"Give notice . . . that General Grant shoots people who fuck up on purpose!"

Later that night, after insistent advice from Rawlins, he rescinded that last order from the cabin bunk bed he and his lawyer would share for months to come. The following morning, the two men in pajamas scoured maps on a round table, irritated at the disappearing corners, as their coffee cooked atop a fussy itty cabinet stove. Grant, drinking the whiskey, smoking the stoagers, and eating the cookies given to him from fans on the train rides, pored over the truly unhelpful maps. He had to win this one. This one was annoying, but necessary. His opponent was Braxton Bragg, the schnauzer man. He wasn't a fool. He had the goods. And Ulysses knew him as the boy whose mom was a murderer. (It's true.) Bragg was a fellow West Pointer who had brought Rebel hell at Shiloh. So this would kind of be a rematch.

General Grant set up a three-fold plan: get the men in shape, get the supplies, and get a real deal plan (by himself) that he could rub in Stanton's smoking nose. He tried an assortment of scenarios, each ending the wrong way differently. This went on for weeks as the supplies came in and life was restored to the camp thanks again to his retailer's intuition.

Reinforcements arrived from bases that could spare them. Men with energy cut trees. Bridges were gang-built with speed. Railroads and telegraph lines were repaired. Supplies flowed. Yet, at any moment, Braxton Bragg could crash in, and they'd crumble. Therefore, it was all done quietly with soft hammers in winter camo by night. The weeks clicked by. The men were working on a play. And Grant ran drills from horseback, getting the men in shape both physically and mentally. The revived soldiers came cracking out of their old uniforms they'd worn for weeks. These exoskeletons were salty husks, wafting of ammonia. Grant ordered the men scoured and the clothes turned into weapons as-is. Fires were worked everywhere. The Metal Corps sludged up pine tar in repetitive burning and developed ore and steel. They were stoked to be stoking. The men got harder; their lungs got stronger.

Rawlins reminded Grant that he was forgetting another Christmas. And for a moment Yules looked longer than usual at the most recent desk picture of his family. He muttered to himself, trying to pull away from his monomania, "Soak it. Mean it. Feel it. Okay. There's Creepy Fred, gangly now, waxen. Okay. See him. Ah, Buck has a cut on his face. Classic Buck. What a sharp bow, Nellie. I bet the boys in town all think you're—no! And JJ, riding the dog. Nice, Jesse Boy. Nice. Ah, Jules. I see you there. You're so

pissed. Look at you gutting the moment out. I can imagine it took a lot to get this crew to do this. Look at your face. I can't wait to unpack it. Okay. Nice. This was nice. Back to kill-planning."

Months elapsed. The leg healed as well as it could for the extent of the wound on the extent of the man. But when it came to the big plan, Coach Grant still couldn't connect. He knew he had to consider calling in Sherman to help him make the best use of this raw material. But could he give up the opportunity to prove that he was a solitary genius? Rawlins urged him to use his power pieces on his chessboard. Sherman was *his* piece, not his equal. Why not use him? Grant liked this lingo and wrote the order.

Soon, Sherman and his columns of killers came quietly pouring into the hilly camp-scape. To Grant, his old friend riding over the mountain looked like Hannibal on an elephant. Out of supposed cautiousness, Grant hushed the roar of reception; any noise might alert the Confederates that something unfrozen was afoot. That night, the two old friends ate roasted owl and drank quite nice Tennessee sour mash.

"Isn't it one of your kids' birthdays?"

"It is. Indeed. Yes. Um-hm."

"Fred, right?"

"Right. Of course, it is his. Yes."

"Great kid. When I saw them last, I noticed he was special, had a soldier's way. Gotta foster that."

"Fuck you."

"What?"

"So true."

The two conferred, looking over Grant's ideas there with Rawlins, who kept their mugs full and the ham sandwiches coming. Sherman had notes. He suggested crucial zags. Ulysses fitted them together with the zigs of what he knew to be true of the surveyed landscape. Together they worked out the "plan of the century," and later presented it to the lesser Generals.

"Okay, listen up," Grant said with a clap; "we're going to pull a reverse *Jacob's Ladder* on 'em with a *Split-Tail Cowboy* at the end."

The Sideburns guy snorted. Grant gave Sherman a "let me handle this" hand and said, "Guys, this is some 21st guerrilla spice that we've used before. See, the plan is to jump the gun and attack while winter is still sort of in play."

"Spring before spring," said Sherman.

"But we'll get fuckin' frozen in the mud," said the Sideburns.

"Don't be stupid," Grant said with a pitying shake of his snarling head. "Can you not be stupid about this right now?"

Sherman took over. "See, Bragg doesn't know this place has been fortified. So, we provoke him to attack what he will think is only the hungry, weak men you were before Grant and me got here. We got all the defensive spots dug out . . ."

"We get him down in the gorges . . ."

"And we gore him."

Nyx acquiesced and Dawn went long for the ball so that creation could catch some sun again. A warm enough day had come and cracked a window where death might intrude. In the patchy thaw, one could see expanses of brown on the white mountains where God had left his bloody handprint when getting up for a snack after playing with his action figures.

"One should work in thy image," thought Ulysses as he saw these signs of God.

In the canyon, the Union Forces wiggled the bait noisily, and Bragg came rushing in to yomp at it, singing "I ain't no cum-caked daisy." But in record time, his things were Grant's things, and Bragg was forced to put into writing that he was, in fact, a cum-caked daisy who had surrendered. The Confederate contender sent his shat heart over in a turkey sack as a concession gift, and arcadia was restored. It was a record-breakingly short, but meaningful, victory. It didn't even snow again in Chattanooga until 1968.

Grant filed his reports . . .

> *I worked out the Chattanooga plan, which required more men. So, I used Sherman's.*

You gotta flatten and compress reality when conveying any narrative. Gotta simplify and streamline and get to the golden parts. Gotta shape it for the reader, so they arrive where you need them to be, for the greater good, for the main goal; that's what everyone wants, right? Nobody can handle all the details. I can't know the infinite facts of my subject, and

neither could you sit for it. We do what we must. And still—though I doubt
we can present to each other 100% complete truth—we can present more
or less honest versions of it. There is dishonesty, even if honesty is harder to
define. And Grant stayed in the shadows of fully illuminated honesty here
about Sherman. Hell, maybe I too have got it a bit away from the facts on
this one, Dearest Fact Checker, but it's hard to say, so let's *You and I* say the
show must go on . . .

Chattanooga was un-sieged; the whole of Tennessee was reclaimed
for the Union. Sherman watched from Bragg's recliner as Grant sloshed
a highball on the hearth of the roaring fireplace in their newly commandeered mountain lodge.

"I accomplished Buckner. I accomplished Pillow. I'm working through
West Pointers faster than that saltpeter they used to put in our scrambies.
Put a man before me and I'll accomplish him. Front page again? Grant vic-
torious? Yawn. Braxton Bragg? More like Braxton Hicks, aka 'false alarm'
for those of you who haven't got women as pregnant as I have. Why'd they
waste me on this soft-ass Chatta-nougat, bush-league bullshit? What's
next? Chattahoochee? Fine, I'll go way down yonder. Give me the keys to
all the cities! And I want the big ones! What else do you need? Miss-uh-
suppie? Done. Tenn-uh-sussie? Done. Want me to set another record for
high jump? Get out the bar, baby. Need the war to be over? Then PUT ME
ON LEE, FUCKERS! PUT . . . ME ON HIM!"

Sherman watched his power-mad friend yell out the window at the
woods. Ulysses screamed east. And the East, with its ears burning, nodded.

Chapter 17

Washington

MAR. 8, 1864

AGE 41

WASHINGTON, D.C., WAS A MAZE OF MAN-MADE WHITE CAV-
erns and well-tailored earth hair. Stylish people of democratic
spirit mingled their soul-fires with like-minded wig-topped ghosts. The
streets were clogged with wonderful taxi horses taking important people
throughout the city proudly. They whinnied only gaily, those groomed and
scented lords, as they winked and giggled, prancing out a priss-priss.

A colossal, shirtless George Washington deity was enthroned beneath
the apotheosis of the same over-man in the rotunda of our shared house
where Grant did worship and genuflect, forcing down the feelings that
he was a scrap of doo-doo trash from the worse place blown by the aim-
less wind into this grand place, which was meant for only the best people.
U.S.G. was to be promoted to Lord of All Armies: George Washington's
old job. After years on his Trojan Horse, the most powerful war job in
America was for Ulysses.

He was invited to Castle White Skull, the throne room of American
Rex. Yes, he was going to The White House for a party that would be celebrating *him*. Our Man acted like it was no big deal, par for the course, but

his shits were coming out way strange because the molten reflux and but-terflies collided in his belly to make effervescent concrete. He slicked down what was left of his hair, cut more out of his ears and nostrils, and wore the full regalia afforded his new rank, including medals, color swatches, epaulets, and tinsel. He was glad it wasn't to be a formal sit-down dinner: he never knew what to do with his dirty knife. Seriously, where do you put it? You can't lick it. And you can't put it dirty back on the table. But it slides off the edge of the plate, either down into the food—heavy handle first—or onto the table with a clatter of splatters. This fear sat aside, he made his way toward the one-hundred-and-eighth wonder of the architectural world. It was going to be okay . . .

Locked in their coaches outside the front entrance of the White House were two dueling Norma Desmonds, playing chicken to see who'd leave and who'd stay, but both were having a hard time determining which would gain them the most attention.

Inside, from the highest ceilings allowed in town, hung chandeliers casting even, stable, lemon light of the highest opulence over the great grand rooms. The interiors were lavish. Partygoers could admire polite Bach getting worked out on a rare left-handed piano by an even rarer musi-cian who knew how to play a bunch of unsayable things.

Our Straining General surveyed the caviar, the squid, the truffle-cobs, the royal jelly . . . Oh! There was a cheese bar with a bartender to guide one over the terribly expensive cheeses available.

"Only the worst-smelling cheeses for the best-smelling people. Here we have *Old Man Asshole*—a very tart, hard yellow—refined from sun-dried sable milk. Quite, quite delectable, that Asshole. And over here, for something much softer, we find *Summertime Asshole*, that's a blend of chinchilla and swan milk. And, and—stay with me—if you're into more of a briny, tough rind, then we can offer *Outside Man*. Yes, I see you detect that musky pungency it's known for. This one is delectable with a hunk of rotten fig, yes, that one right there, the black and fuzzy one. And this tier up here holds—yes, these up here—these are of the tangy families of cheeses, starting with *Old Medicine Blood*. Yes, and right here we have its cousins, *Medicine Shit* and *Vitamin Shit*. What, no cheese, Sir? I could really go on . . ."

Grant turned his attentions to the people. Everywhere were tuxe-doed paragons and explosions of crepe. He willed himself invisible while turning up the wattage of his senses. There were handsome, immacu-late Eastern officers with fresh moustaches chatting up antique political Generals wearing cut-up clouds for whiskers. There were marble women with brains of quicksilver and collapsing theatre stars forcing smiles at debutantes who fluttered their kid lids. There were leavened bosoms on the rise, opera people with audible auras, and poets in trend-setting slap-dashery. Near the liquor, downing gimlets, were aesthetes out for blood, and beside them, in clusters, were anesthetized wives waiting out their husbands' obligations.

The rooms were shoulder-to-shoulder of the best shoulders the nation could muster. Truly it was mostly top-brass military and top-flight mon-eymen trying to keep up with their aggressive, younger counterparts, who were legging up-and-up on a daily basis. But women too sipped, sniffed, and quipped. Our Invisible Man weaved in and out of the conversations, unobserved by the murmuring, cackling, whispering, shouting, side-hugging, side-eyeing, conferring, confabbing, hobnobbing, cobb gobbling, and laughing luxuriant luminaries.

"Five hundred dollars says Mary doesn't even show up tonight."

"Francis has metallic bowels now. Top of the line."

"I told my brat that I didn't pay three hundred dollars to get him out of the Army so he could play billiards with his rowing buddies. 'Practice rowing!' I said. That's what's important."

"Have you seen the art at Kingsley's new gallery? These artists, their work is so fresh, so pre-modern."

"No, no. I'm off snuff. I do opium now."

"I heard they finally excavated writings by Socrates himself. It's the first time Socrates' own thoughts are available in his own words, and he de-nounces Plato and Aristophanes, denying all the thought they attributed to him."

"Yeah, and I heard they burned that right away. They're saying it wasn't real. You know how many copies of Plato are sold each year?"

"There's an after-party at Kingsley's. He hired musicians that do some-thing new called a *hambone*."

"I never talk about race because I know I'll say the wrong thing, or use an outdated term, and I couldn't bear looking ever so behind the times, whatever they might be at the moment. So I never talk or think about race. Because I don't want to hurt anyone with the wrong words, you see. So, no, I'll be abstaining from voting on the 13th amendment."

"One good rule can't work in all cases. One of our blocks of gold won't save the man in the desert, no matter how much we know ourselves to want it. If we aren't capable of seeing he wants water . . . we're fucked."

"Shut the hell up, Kingsley."

"Not everything is about race."

"I'm so glad you feel you can think so."

"My agent said he'd handle it, but he hasn't. So, I can't wait to fire him in front of my lawyer, because I need my manager to know that I mean business."

"I'll see you at Kingsley's, right? I need to run something by you about having a servant killed. It's turned into a nightmare for me. I'll tell you about it at Kingsley's."

"Is there a place on Earth that isn't political?"

"People are saying that art will get bad on purpose or something unbelievable like that. I'd suggest to keep buying Ingres and Constable."

"I have daughters, so, no. I don't have offspring."

"Shoes are terrible after the first wear. And their smell in the fire is even worse."

"Can you believe he declared *she* was beautiful?"

"To describe how something IS is so offensive."

"Right? Who is he to say how she IS for everyone? One must say that 'X *seems* to be Y to oneself, but it could very well be Z to thee.'"

"I assumed that was always implied in speech."

"Fuck off, Kingsley."

"They said the natural world was amoral, and I asked if they'd ever seen a mama critter lick her young. That closed that discussion."

"I say if *our* class isn't setting the example, then the under-classes won't know with what upon which to strive. Dreams are dependent on imagination. The American Dream is no different. If one lacks ambition, the root cause is a lack of imagination. Success is a creative act, to be sure. And for those lacking in creativity, *we* shall be the model."

"We paid an artist and his writer colleagues to come to my salon to explain 'life in the time of war,' but all they discussed was cunnilingus. It's chic, I suppose. But what happens when we all cycle out of this trend, and some of us have gotten stuck on it? I say don't even start."

"Last time I was at Kingsley's, he surprised me with the Speaker of the House, and we have our history, so I had to make my wife fake a fainting spell. And I blamed it on her little opium craving. And now the town thinks she's a hophead, and she is, so that's a big problem. Fucking Kingsley, that cad."

"I disagree. We can't fix things by denying how things are. There *are* ugly people. And acting like we're all not interested in beautiful people will not make ugly peoples equally loved. What? That's not horrible. It's the truth. I love ugly people, Baby, I'm married to one."

"But seriously, how does a pluralistic democracy come up with a unified, universal code of ethics that is impervious to individual interpretation?"

"Yes, how do we define the universal when everyone in the country insists they're so damn unique?"

"Maybe first imagine yourself in the worst of all cases, and then design the government you'd want around that?"

"Horseshit. Your heart is as soft as horseshit."

"The English sailor says he found apes on Galapagos that are his relatives. Apes! I gotta read this insane book."

"Fat is fat. And she's gotta eat to get fat."

"It can't be evil to simply not care about every single thing. I don't have the time to care about every single person. I'm sure a kid is being tortured as we speak. Many. How could I possibly stop that? The trick is to accept the things I cannot change, have courage to change the things I can, and find the wisdom to know the difference. So, I just don't worry about kids in cages, because what can I do about it?"

"You can't make a man love a meal. But you can make it seem cool to acquire the taste . . ."

"Two words: Corn King."

"Corn?"

"Trust me. In the future . . . reality will be made of corn."

"There's DuPont."

"Speak of the devil and he shall do business."

"You want the devil? Look inward, angel."

"Actually, I did want to run a patent by him."

"Mary's in black with literally thousands of white carnations on her."

"So much for 'styled by psychics.'"

"Great taste is only *better* taste than that which is about to become obviously good."

"McClelland is running. Pick a ship, because the waters are about to get choppy."

"Most deals with the devil are unconsciously signed. One need only look at the Irishman for evidence."

"I want to see this new George Washington, then it's off to Kingsley's."

Grant would not drink in front of these people. What did they think of him? A raider? Why not? A butcher? Sure. A hero? You bet your ass. A drunken bum? Well, I don't quite know what you mean.

"There's the man of the hour!" Halleck was on him with avuncular intimacy, clamping his shoulders and soaking him with a displayed ownership.

"*My* General. Nice work in Chattanooga. *I* told these guys you were the man for that!" Then he whispered "I'm the one who loves you," giving Grant a wink and a lasting pat before saying, "ah, Ulysses . . . meet Abraham Lincoln."

Grant took in the face that launched a thousand shits. To him, Mr. Lincoln was about the most average-looking countryman he'd ever seen, only tall, thin, and gently jovial. Lincoln was circled by unnameable asteroids belting out demands—professional party boys and old-world power men—tumbling 'round the space of anyone occupying the sun spot of presidency.

Stooping down, Lincoln smiled his eyes at Ulysses and said "The people here couldn't make you out without your 'bruised helmet and bended sword,' huh?"

"I guess not, Sir."

"Halleck, if you are buried alive, the first movement upwards is the hardest, and it only gets you slightly less buried alive. But you still do it, don't you, Grant? Bit by bit, it gets easier, even if you still feel dead. You did those first hard digs out, General. For all of us."

"I suppose so."

Halleck interrupted, saying "And I believe you have met Stanton."

Darkened, still, and intense, there was Stanton in "full Dracul," counting Grant's heart rate from across the carpet.

Halleck, again with the social grease, said "Does anybody need a drink? Grant, you need a whiskey?"

"Nope."

"No? They have Old Tub. Still no? Okay. Odd. But I get it."

Lincoln took over with the intros.

"General Grant, I want you to meet some smart men worth hearing out. Meet our august whale-oil baron."

Grant slowly shook this warm smooth hand.

Lincoln continued: "Here we have the wizened old coal baron. Fine sage, there. And always good to be under such auspice as our fine friend, the steel baron, here. Grant, there you go. Shake, shake, yep, yep. And . . . these sainted souls right here are the lumber baron, land baron, and beef baron. Better . . . better give them a shake, there, yep, there you go. And of course, over here we have our fur baron: Astor, next to Rand of, well, Rand Corp., and Tyrell of Tyrell Corp., and here's Cornelius Vanderbilt with John W. Garrett. Evening, gents!"

"Richies in the cockpit?" Grant whispered to himself.

Lincoln squeezed Grant's shoulder harder than would be expected and said "They give us railroads and boats and actual, practical nation-building advice. They're vital people."

Vanderbilt raised a brow and split his lips: "Mr. Grant. Can you do what needs doing?"

"I can lick Lee. I don't care what it takes, how many men, or how many years."

Stanton swiftly interjected, "Mr. Lincoln is looking to get reelected this year, General. We chose you for swift victories, *like Chattanooga*. If Lincoln gets victories, he gets reelected. He gets reelected, he gets slavery outlawed in the Constitution through Congress. That's the plan. With or without Lee."

Garrett added "No more Shilohs! Made me lose half my stock portfolio. And make sure to use that Sherman, too."

"Oo, cheese!" Lincoln took Grant by the arm and led him away.

"Anti-rich-ite, huh?" he asked, once they were out from earshot of the capital cadre.

"What? Is that even a thing, Mr. President?"

"I believe you're making a good case for it, Son. Keeping these types close, it is the IS of it. The way of the world. When tending crops, it's better to *know* there's shit in the soil so at least you wash your hands."

Grant scrunched his face a teense. Lincoln continued.

"The South thinks slavery is an extension of their freedom. They imagine we'd want the same unrestricted freedom to choose to enslave or not, even if we won't. The Golden Rule isn't complete, is it? A Platinum Rule might allow others the freedom to define their own desires apart from our own, and irrespective of our imaginations of what it's like to be them."

"Is this a sympathy/empathy thing? Because I could never get that straight."

"Excuse me. You're right, Grant: I know you from afar. I've assumed I know you close. But that's the me talking, isn't it?"

"It was you talking, Sir, but it is loud in here. I can understand the confusion."

Lincoln looked over the cheeses while he spoke.

"Now, let me ask you point-blank: Is this about licking Lee? Or is it about bringing on a More Perfect Union? I heard you were anti-slavery; I heard your father was a progressive. That *that* was why you fought. Or am I thinking of Sherman?"

"No, no. That's me, Sir. But the *way* we stop the war—and to roll into that new More Perfect Union—is for me to beat Lee. It's the only way. It's a win-win. And I'm ready to die for it."

"Okay. Bag your boogeyman. I think you and I have the same ultimate goals. I'm not worried about you. But I sometimes think ol' Halleck is more dangerous than a diary. But he's as funny as a bunny dick, so I keep him around. What do you think?"

"Well, bunny dicks are a hoot, Sir."

"Damn right they are. You've taken his job, you have. Usually does something bad to a man when they've been pushed out of a top slot. But *Old Brains* over there won't admit it was even a competition. He'll twist up a fresh perspective to reframe the situation to fit his needs. Tomorrow he'll warp his new job into heretofore-unknown importance. You know the man. He'll make it out to be essential for humankind; but really, he'll just be puttering about as my Chief of Staff, where I can keep an eye on him, and he me, I suppose. Anyway, that ain't you, is it?"

"No, Sir."

"Good talk. Okay. Grant, get it done. Plan it with Sherman. Get me reelected for the greater good. If you fall, fall forward, as you've done."

"Aye, aye, Captain."

There is the chance that none of our imagined moments are correct. That none of our empathetic inhabitations of others, past or present, are accurate. That none of us nobodies can understand the problems of the somebodies. And perhaps once you're a somebody, maybe never again can you inhabit the nobodies, meaning you can't know again what it's like to be lower than your present station. Perhaps our imaginings of our "betters" are obviously resentful and silly when seen by them. Perhaps when they look down upon our daydreams of how we think it was, or how it is to be them . . . perhaps they're embarrassed for us. And perhaps they find it entertaining. Perhaps even William's superiors simply allowed him to depict a dumbed-down court within which groundlings could grasp with awful awe at something that safely could never ever be how it actually ever was. Perhaps and maybes are all I have. So, I'll say *You and I* are nailing it.

Toward the end of the night, after their toxins were imbibed and their breath ruined with cheese, the crowd attached Grant's face to his story, and before most had moved on to Kingsley's party, the "best people in the nation" heaved Our New (littler) Washington upon a red velvet couch so that they could get a look at him together, at once.

The accolades piled up about his Olympian temples, stacking there in laurels, garlands, and wreaths. About his shoulders hung flung sashes and flags. And at his glossy, booted feet, there between the couch cushions and rose stems, was what looked to him to be a used condom.

Chapter 18

Bull v. Goat

APR.–JUN. 1864

AGE 42

IMAGINE IT FROM ABOVE, FROM THE EYES OF ATHENA AS SHE surmises this most dangerous conglomeration of professional life-enders. Put your sight up there in hers; train it upon this thick parade of blue moving into the vast green gardened hem of Virginia.

Hear the noises of telegraph poles getting erections, of communication cables slithering as never-ending pythons wrapping about the earth. Feel the carts' wheels spinning up the soft, newly made roads loaded with death tools and pain gainers.

Do float through our line with Athena and count our men to one million Blue Boys supplied to the teeth. At their ready see drummers, fifers, pickers, grinners, piano men, rocket men, and tethered eagles upon golden roosts. Come, witness a thousand lumbermen, even more road engineers, and several pachyderms as they cut roads on the world and make things of trees as bees do honey from flower sex. See the war machines, the horses, the trailers with munitions piled high. See the artillerymen and their masculine cannons coming through. Note the painted, toothy, flat mouth wrapped across the front of that war wagon there, which says to its foes "Ye shall be eaten."

You must, Dearest Reader, note how close D.C. was to this bleeding heart of the war, how vulnerable our capital had been this whole time under the ineffectual guard of gutless Generals. But not anymore . . .

Armored in the clothes of Ahab, Ulysses S. Caesar lorded over the largest land Army the world had ever known, and it was bigger than the last few times this same thing was said. He was a real man in the way that kids think of men, in that door-darkening way: he ate life, shat hamburger, and yelled with his whole body. This man didn't write letters back home. He hadn't seen his family in years, and he was so focused he didn't care. Love maketh men vulnerable, so his heart was as calloused as his hands. He was close to killing his lifelong goal. After that, he could look around and see what else might need him in his life. His only drive now was to prove to the world that he was the alpha ape of the Earth. Gripping and smelling the wind with his setae, he was a hypertensive ape that was a wolf, which was a Bull that would kill anything so that everyone could finally eat in peace. In short, he was a man truly made in God's image.

Many before him had tried to trap the white Goat of Virginia, and many had become cartoon steaks on a plate for Lee. A good portion of the Union saw the Bull as equal to the Goat. But most thought Grant was outclassed. It was said Lee was so big he'd have scars on his shoulders from simply moving through life if it wasn't for life getting out of his way. Diabolical R.E.L. had already brought the war dangerously close to the nation's capital and had almost captured the flag a few times. He had not ever been beaten at anything. Never been made to feel wrong. And one thing harkening back to West Point haunted Grant: Lee was demerit-less. Who would overcome whom? Which was the overdog: the Overbull or the Overgoat?

The Union HQ of The Eastern Theater cringed just outside the Virginian Wilderness. Sherman already waited for Ulysses and Rawlins inside the usual pine office, sitting cross-legged, eating a strawberry donut. Rows of lesser-named B-team back-up boys waited, ridged, not confident enough to take part in what the Craft Service Corps had set up. Cump took note of the others.

Young Philip Sheridan was there, full of eager spirit, which he downplayed, clearly having read the fresh wiki on Grant. This rookie could flat-out ride a horse. He could score twenty at the half, pop a couple of Confeds with one bullet while riding backwards, and he'd smile while doing it. The stud drew press. He was an asset. Everyone knew it, and the oldies sucked in their guts around him. Sheridan had the new generation's style, he used newly minted words, gestures, and he'd risen up the ranks the right way, too: poor kid, kill school, infantry, cavalry—all before his thirties. Of Irish descent, his orange bristles and skin-spritzing made Sherman do a double-take. The new wave was here, and it looked like him and Grant from a lifetime ago.

G.G. Meade was the exact opposite: a slow old tide. Meade was old-fashioned, proper, and controlled. His sensitive emotions—not banished by his outsized logical mind—were painfully one thin membrane away from rupturing, so people often witnessed the man dropping his water, emotionally. Some said G.G. had defeated Lee at Gettysburg, and for that he was a starter on this Dream Team. But he himself classified Gettysburg a draw, citing Lee's current rating and freedom. Meade had grown up with silver and wooden spoons in his mouth, having been raised by a father who traded with Spain during turbulent times. But he carried himself like a richie due to his encyclopedic education. The man was as wonderful a re-source as our rotting and dormant public libraries.

Stanton had put together quite a team for Grant during the winter break. But Sherman knew Meade would have a hard time with his old friend. G.G. was a formal Eastern type, much in the West Point model of high-class aristocracy. He was the kind of guy who couldn't fall asleep if his nails weren't sanded. Seriously, he was always asking about tea times and checking pocket watches. This guy could ride up in a top hat on a giant snail and no one would blink.

Late on that sparkling April morning, Ulysses floated into the office with shades on and Rawlins in tow. Grant did the handshakes, smiling around a cigar. After introductions, still controlling the floor, Ulysses let a long silence stagnate while he stuffed a muffin and doctored his coffee. They had to watch as the boss smacked and readied himself.

"Cump, go."

Sherman was now radicalized. He launched into his belief that the South needed a baptism by fire. Lately he'd been cleaning everything with fire, was off water entirely, and intended to help burn Lee's wicked Wilder-ness down to its roots.

Meade tried to keep his eyes lidded.

Grant swallowed cruller crumbs, and said "I'm deploying Sherman against Johnston in Atlanta."

The heads turned to Sherman, who seemed to dry out entirely in one exponential second upon a long-drawn wheeze through the crackling brush of his nose thickets.

"And in the morning," Grant continued, unfazed, while dunking, "I'll be taking the fight to Lee with these two and the rest. In a month the war will be over, and Lincoln will be reelected."

Meade smacked.

"What?"

And with that dubious invitation, Meade and Sheridan, each in their own way, jumped to voice their trepidations of attacking Lee on his turf.

"I'd advise—"

"I'd advocate—"

"*I'd* fire both your asses if Stanton hadn't put you here," Grant said, as he whipped his sunglasses against the wall. "We're taking our massive force . . . and we're pushing it up Lee's ass. And the devil take the hindmost."

Sheridan shook his head and went for a fritter.

Meade clarified. "Lee is unlike anything you've encountered. You may know him in the broad sense. But I know from firsthand data, and . . ." Meade's face trembled, "well, they say the devil's in the details."

"Yes, but I say they are in their disregard," said Grant.

"But . . . isn't that what the original saying means?" asked Meade.

"No. Yes, but no. See, people think the details themselves are devilish," Grant said.

"I don't," added Sheridan, cutting Meade off mid-purse, before giving a "my bad" gesture to his senior. But Grant waved them back.

"You know what I'm trying to—people think that the saying means that the details themselves are harmful, the devilishness gets transferred to the details, but it's not the details' fault. The trouble is in our having not re-garded the details with care, you see?" Grant was ready to talk this through until someone told him he was right.

Sheridan tried to change tactics with a little light teasing: "Boy howdy, what would good ol' George Washington think about two redheaded, freckled Ohio Boys running the whole of the Army?"

Sherman uncrossed his legs. "Thought experiment: Which side of this Civil War would the Founding Fathers be on?"

Sheridan backed away and showed the palms of his yellow buccaneer gloves. "I see what you mean, there, Man. Go easy."

But Sherman was ignited. "Fuck what Washington would have thought. He enslaved people. Game over. Fuck him in his wooden teeth."

Meade tried not to cry.

Sherman yelled to anyone, "This is not a joke. Have you heard that Bedford Forrest just massacred six hundred black soldiers after they had surrendered? Look it up. It'll be in history. And it will be our future too if we don't get *mean*. This war isn't cosplay, Boys. We're fighting off a possible evil *future* where inequality is American law, as it *was* when your precious Washington and his shitty pals wrote up the Constitution. The old ways should burn."

We're reminded to mitigate when outdone in extremes. Grant did so.

"Generals, please. Okay, okay. Great start. Great start. We got that behind us. Sherman, I get it. We all get it. Jesus. But we don't want to throw the baby out with the bathwater."

"Baby's bad, Jack."

"Yes, but . . . say, what if the bad guys have some scientists that know how to build rockets that will get us to the moon? Huh? We should make use of them, even if those scientists were once working for evil, right? We shouldn't set fire to those scientists. Same's true with the Founding Fathers and Framers. It's like how we gotta sift the good stuff from the badness in the classics."

"No. Burn it. Read no classics. Burn those. Evil travels like a virus on the droplets of their breath."

Rawlins shared his Tums with Meade. Grant made a conciliatory gesture and addressed the room.

"Okay. Okay. Marketplace of ideas. Sherman, Godspeed. Everybody else, listen up . . . tomorrow—it's my birthday, no biggie—*tomorrow*, we cross over *our* Rubicon: The Rapidan, into Lee's territory. And we give Lee my birthday present that he won't much like. Maybe after he surrenders, we'll have a forced horse-riding competition between him and me for *Horse Lord Magazine*. You get in there, too, Sheridan. See what you can do against us. Eh?"

Cump smacked his hat down over his frill and dumped his coffee into a to-go cup. In the bright light of the door's rectangle, he turned and said "Kill Lee in public, Grant. It's not enough for the devil to die; evil kings have evil princes."

"Got it. We'll see. We'll see."

Grant had three goals: Defeat Lee (and maybe kill him in public), capture Castle Black Skull at Richmond, and deliver to Lincoln the South's king: "President" Jefferson Prime. Yet, he had no way of knowing where Lee and his sharking Army currently were in this sea of trees. So, the next morning, he chummed.

The huge blue procession lurched into Virginia's depths to begin seeking in plain sight. The woods were thicker here than any that Grant had ever worked. They had the heat of Panama's jungle, and the awe of the Pacific groves, but it was a motley hot tangle with much underbrush, thickets, and younglings tangled about the old growth and fallen deadwood. The disquieting insect song was a solid sonic field alluding to its friend the heat and vice versa. Compasses spun. Maps erased themselves. Horses reacted to baleful nothingness. Ghosts? Gremlins? Ley lines? Hanging from its rope, Grant's inner plumb bob stuck straight out and moved in different directions. His surveyor's vestibular sense was discombobulated.

"Is this a valley or a peak? I can't detect slope. My inner ear is deranged."

Days grew indistinguishable in the shaded, humid march. Men drenched themselves in their own brine. Sleep was a challenge due to the heat, the eeriness, and the hand-sized mosquitoes plunging into men's hides. Wild dogs and pigs were found and eaten. Doo-doo came out bad. A woman was revealed in the Wilderness. When asked how long she'd been living in the woods as an animal, she said "One thousand two hundred and sixty days." Sheridan took her on as a horse brusher and had her fed. But before nightfall she'd folded back into the ethereal wild, and no one—not even I—could recall her well.

On May 5, it happened in a moment, as everything does. Before anyone could sense it, before the scouts could detect the slightest sound, Lee's rebels were yelling the air apart. The Battle of the Wilderness had begun in the Union camp, right there in morning's broad daylight.

Grant awoke to the ingredients for ice-blood. A man in gray with weapons and murder-face skidded into his tent but ran out in a delirium. Ulysses looked over at Rawlins, who was petrified in mid-shave.

Outside was the Garden of Dastardly Delights. One's eyes only filled with men locked in brutal hand-to-hand blurs. Knives and bayonets glinted. Every head had the teeth going doggie-style, the features of man pulled back to allow the beast inside the better part of the face.

Drum and horn went wild like big and little animals getting crushed together.

Grant stuttered with the unwanted gift of bafflement. He yelled to hold, to not run, but no one could hear. His cursed voice bounced off them like an egg off the street.

Lee's men were nimble, horrible, ruthless gymnasts.

Ghastly gunfire rained in from foliage.

Beyond a few yards, there was zero visibility in this wild forest, and eyes were given heavy helpings of smoke.

Grant's men shot each other on accident a lot, over and over.

When Ulysses sought officers, he found Meade on his horse, behind a bush, looking at the bush, thinking "Bush, bush, bush."

The first-round draft pick, Sheridan proved adept, and Grant had to give the rook some respect as he watched the lad and his horse-boys gallop like regal slayers toward a large concentration of the conflict.

"Okay, he's got heart."

Opponents conked and gouged at heads, breaking backwards kneejerked fingers, before competent contact could be connected.

Opponents cradled each other cruelly, vigorously forcing one another into their stories' endings. The slow blades penetrated the shields of folding arms.

A white horse went like an out-of-place zebra behind the trees in the low sun's beacon. "There! Didst thou see?"

Drum and horn.

Ulysses sought the power in himself but found only fear, like finding a bunch of hockers instead of Silly Putty in the plastic red egg. Where was his specialness now?

A group of tussling men were thrown into the air after the leafy hill under them revealed itself to be the hip of a slumbering jolly green giant.

The "future-bound" and the "maybe-nots" punched each other's wicked tickets to unknowable elsewhere via mesmerizing, kaleidoscopic violence.

A man on his belly was stomped upon with belligerence, the act looked upon with benevolence. "Damn good wrongdoing."

Lizard brains clicked into action, freezing some, but setting most a'skitter.

Two men performed judo without knowing it, earning belts and life-long bodily alteration.

"There! There! Flashing beyond those trunks: the white rider!"

Drum and horn.

Distant gloating bleated.

A napping, dappled carcass killed one more man that fell back on a well-augered blade. The carcass too would be killed once more before night.

A pro-slavery caterpillar leaped—legs spread-eagle in action—onto a Yankee eye in the midst of a vision-based attack, making the man's vulnerable second fatal.

Distant cousins continued to bicker whilst knifing.

Drum and horn.

Blare and boom.

Blow and bang.

Peel and pop.

Each rebel a bugbear, no yank a spanker.

A long-dead Mayan watched, wondering if his math had been wrong, and perhaps this day was the last.

Buzz. Cackle. Crackle. Whirr. Ack, ack, ack! Oh, mysterious Lord, how Satan works in obvious ways!

A rebel was already drinking champagne out of a buccaneer boot. Another desecrated the Yankee pennant.

Bloody Banana?

Shot in the bandage.

One frontal skull plate clapped onto its own back piece, a sloshy castanet.

The chatterbox animals went nowhere, watching from the trees like Romans in the Colosseum, cheeping for beheadings.

Cockles uncorked in this blood-letters' clearinghouse.

Death marked a volunteer bayoneted in the birthmark. Personal sunset number six hundred and sixty-six.

"My God, they know the guerrilla shit . . ."

Drum, horn.

Life to loam.

The fires ambitiously took to the dense trees, leaping like a weightless circus. Men who fought too close to the flames had their belts explode due to the ammunition they dutifully carried. The smell of cooking flesh and hair was unavoidably up snout, on tongue.

Lee's men were happily dying for their cause, yelling and yelling in the Rebel language as they died smiling like the cult members they were.

Sheridan returned to Grant after taking one by the team. "The rebels really don't have solid lines," he said, "and Lee was spotted pulling his men back."

"He was *here*?" Ulysses asked in shock. "Lee is commanding from the field?"

The Goat had sent a message: he wasn't scared, and Grant was vulnerable on his turf. Our Man tried not to blink, as he looked about the finalizing battle scene. Mostly only dead men in reddened blue remained. The gray faded. But the forest stayed around them, limiting vision to fifty feet, save for a section of old growth where the trunks were fat, and their bottommost limbs started higher up. There was a football field's distance between Grant's eyes and the sun-drenched clearing beyond this old grove. And there in the clearing beyond, rearing back on his horse's tapping backers . . . was that white rider, Capricorn. It was Lee tearing up a devilish, fishtailing donut in the lot behind the trunks before trotting off, top speed, through the thicket, without one leaf touching him as he stood straight up in his saddle, arms crossed, boots: third position.

"Baphomet . . ." Grant whispered, as his eyes fluttered in disbelief. He'd now seen inhuman acumen, godhood goods.

That night, men held their wounds, clutching their apocalypse goodie bags.

At the nighttime recap meeting, Meade demanded a retreat in front of everyone.

"Well, you've had a taste. I think we should return back over the

Rapidan and rethink. God does not want us in Virginia. He let us know this today. Let's listen."

With undeniable body lingo, the room seemed to agree. Grant looked at Sheridan, who replied "Good's good. And that was bad."

Our Man stood among the sitters, looking in disbelief at the down-cast heads of these hangdog men. So he took to his tent, where he secretly pushed the overreaching nerve-endings back into his skin with the sooth-ing curve of a warmed spoon's backside. The pressure to come through and prove that he was a hero hung heavy on him like that albatross-shaped nov-elty anvil I once saw at an anchor-maker's forge next door to the hospital that housed my sick kid when I went looking for any open store to find a gift for her, but there was only a blacksmith's forge nearby, and not even a gift shop in the hospital because it had closed due to a customer's sick kid choking on a loose whatever that had come off a twenty-dollar Wheel of Fortune plushy. For a second, Grant and I looked at that albatross anvil and wondered: "Maybe I'm *supposed* to have that."

Rawlins examined his master's face for the slightest information. Ul-ysses looked up at the moon, that skeleton planet, that prophetic picture of our future-Earth after we out-mass the dirt with bones.

The agonizing silence was finally broken when Grant spoke.

"Why is God famous, Rawlins? Because he kicked the asses of the other gods."

And Rawlins probably knew what this meant.

The sun appeared again despite a majority of prayers to the contrary. Grant arose and ordered "tents up." He called for his black steed, Dar-zoth-o-kag-a-thuuz. Once mounted, Grant rode slowly through the main lane of camp with his officers behind him. He gave no speech. Made no gestures. The word was his body, and it went forward deeper into the Wilderness, into the fight. The men, finding pride, blinked away the retreat in their hearts. Their bodies responded to his. The huzzahs began to grow and grow until the whole of the gigantic force could be heard across these accursed states. The message was clear: we fuck back.

Grant engaged Lee, skirmish after skirmish, passing through woodsy towns well-worn by war, finding only the xylophone bones rising up from the bodies of the left-behind dead. They fought in the once-thriving rustic townships long since gutted. They battled in Wilderness villages where usefulness had been indefinitely borrowed. The homes of evacuated families had been fortified, fought over, and abandoned many times over. More than most surfaces were stained with blood or tears. And surprisingly more than one sun-ruined piano got an off-tune tinkle by the fingers of marching men. Rotting, splitting, molding, and warping instruments leaned in what were left of unlivable living rooms, and they often got a few harrowing plucks from pluckers who invariably frowned at the sounds from dead pleasant times.

On May 8, U.S.G. again suffered major blood-loss at the minor vampire habitat of Spotsylvania. Lee's movements were dazzling. Slippery. He seemed to be toying with the cumbersome, flat-footed forces of Ulysses. The press painted the matchup as "Lee, the Artist in Prime" against "Grant, the Minotaur on Robitussin Lost in Another's Maze." The casualties were high; the press ate it up.

"The Bum Butcher is Back," said the *Times* (all of them).

"It's Best if Lee Puts Grant in the Rot Box," ran the headline of a very progressive abolitionist paper.

Lincoln was nervous about the upcoming election. McClelland had indeed announced his bid for the 1864 presidential race as a Democrat, which was then the party opposite of Lincoln and goodness. McClelland ran on a promise to end the war immediately. He said he'd allow the South to continue as a slavery nation. The white voting world was fed up with snuff journalism, and they wanted the war over at any cost but death. McClelland was a genuine political threat to humanity, not to mention to Lincoln's second term. This rich son-of-a-bitch also had the gall to run as a "current military man," rather than the disgraced, procrastinating former General that he was in the eyes of anyone with a sense of time.

Meanwhile, the men under Grant, as in a fairy tale, were hunting a monster in this arboreal otherworld, but none could find a moral to the story anymore. They marched in circles, coming across familiar glades and creeks from which some drank and after felt forever changed, mostly for the worse. They discovered caves and found it hard to resist the sexual giggles echoing down deep in them. That satanic-headed genius Lee took Grant's pieces at the edges of the board, then he drove down the middle when Ulysses was distracted. Behind the columns of Union Forces came an Army of carrion, turkey vultures, possums, and rats that waited to chow down on this dished-up glut of death.

Ulysses fought off dreams of bum faces becoming his face, or bum faces revealing that his face was the cause of all bum faces. So he drank himself up a pair of blinkers for his thinker. He'd fall asleep clinching himself around the pearl of Lee in his mind. He'd not listen to anyone, nor would he take suggestions.

"I'm the one who got us here by my gut! So shut up, you by-the-book, craven, checklist critics!"

But in truth he felt he needed the quiet to hold the drifting special parts of himself together. He'd given up writing home. It was too complicated. The last he'd said to Julia wasn't good, and he knew it: "How am I supposed to know what you're feeling if you don't tell me?" She'd stopped writing after that, and he did know what that meant. He had a lot to fix there, but he didn't have the bandwidth. His mother's letters reached him, and it seemed his dad might be gravely ill. Rawlins read the letters aloud.

"She says his feet are cold as stone."

"I haven't got time for this!"

Little losses.

Little battles.

Little battles.

Little losses.

No wins. Only blood-soaked baby steps going 'round and 'round. The number of dead on both sides caused national outcries. Lee was drawing the process out. He knew that the more the death piled up, the more likely Grant would be replaced by someone else. He knew that popular opinion wanted the war over. If Lee could keep this up, perhaps McClelland could win the presidency and Dixie could become its own nation.

Grant tried to hold it together. The Goat Man had lured him anywhere he wanted here in his Backyard Wilderness for way more than forty days and forty nights. Across Virginia were hidden rebel bunkers and trenches and big bad fuck-offs, which Lee exploited in a series of deathly pranks. Men got lost forever, Blair Witch style. Soldiers became puddings, mashed up into hot potted red-brown pastes. Came and went memorable dogs. Cats. Horses. Birds. Bugs. "Don't kill that fox! It's a changeling!" Memories were made, stored, and released by bullets. There was death by berry. Cuts by nuts. And some caught rot from sex stores in weary wild towns. Others were crowned with virus and had to march fever-faced with clattering somnambulant souls. Grant questioned Sheridan about that horse-brushing woman who had appeared at the beginning of the quest.

"Was she green? Was she glowing?"

"Of course not."

"See, George Washington, during a trying moment of the Revolutionary War—you know that story?"

"Uh, nope."

"Well, Washington had wandered into the woods away from the men, and he had an encounter with this Glowing Green Woman who told him how to win the war. So, he did. And I thought, maybe because you're redheaded and horse-connected that maybe this same green lady mistook you for me and, look, don't, don't—hey, you want a drink?"

And on June 1, 1864, Grant did the third of the three worst things of this book.

See, Lee had cozied back into a defensive haven, bedded down beyond the tree lines of a wide clearing near what was left of a landlocked town weirdly called Cold Harbor.

This had to end. Sherman had started his siege of Atlanta, and it was only a matter of time before he could proclaim victory. Now, Grant needed to win without Sherman, and he certainly had to win before Sherman could win without Grant. Ulysses had to birth this breech-baby, had to just push a victory out of this painful bottleneck. He needed this win to prove that he was the best. It had to be he, and not that perfect Sherman, to help Lincoln win the election. And Lee was just right there on the distant side of the field, snickering in the acidic morning. Grant's forces were still enormous; yet he could not get around to the back of Lee's position due to cliffs and rivers and Lee's amazing strategy. Anyone who tried to cross that expanse of sunlight would become more lead than man. Rawlins listened to Grant as he laid out his plan.

"I'm going to send a bunch of men across that field."

"That . . . that may actually be criminal," Rawlins said as gingerly as he could. "Sir, I don't want to see your career end with you tried for war crimes by a jury of your peers."

"Such a jury could never be assembled. For I am peerless. Send the orders, Rawly!"

And so, row after row of humanity marched and fell. Marched and fell, marched and fell. Lee's guns in the trees liberally sprayed them down into a melted layer cake of men, angels, men, devils, men, hopes, men, The Dream, and more men. Grant piled his bodies there to ruin in the howling waste of a Wilderness. Sure, he tried to send medics to fetch the wounded, but invisible snipers sniped. And it was full-on summer, Man. The wounded did what wounded do, but they were also doing it while baking.

In the night, the screaming grew more intense, and the healthy men safe in their tents cried like bats driven mad by the echo-located scene of brotherly hell.

Ulysses didn't sleep. He tried to think. But something, no, someone was keeping his mind stopped still in a timeless grip. Someone was in his brain-maze, dropping an itchy line of breaded thread behind each step . . .

Morning! The power came back on slowly to the squinting sentries, but relatively fast for the deer in the black-and-white world of dew-drenched breakfast. The embedded reporters had already filed pieces overnight. The nation recoiled. War was for once on Earth given a bad name. Even country boys were appalled and stopped playing guns for a minute.

Grant sent Lee a letter requesting a cessation of hostilities—just for a minute—so that the wounded of both forces could be tended to. Rebel delegates came back, smirking with tidings for false amelioration wherein Lee replied that he would only accept an "unconditional surrender" from "Unconditional Surrender Grant."

A Union *surrender*? Grant's first ever? That would destroy Lincoln's hopes of reelection and would cast Grant backwards into a gutter from which he couldn't re-stand.

"There is, beyond the sun there, in the dark of the wild, that behemoth who rolls in the cockpit mud of my mind. I must dig him out!"

He sent more men. More rows of human beings went forward and down, forward and down, forward and down. The potential change-makers and laugh-starters and sweethearts went out like mountaintop candles. Bodies, bodies, bodies with souls, souls, souls.

In his tent, Grant dropped to his knees, head in hands, both Hamlet and Yorick. He whisper-yelled "God! Come down here and fight like a man! Anywhere! Anywhere! Anywhere else but here. Anywhere in time. In life. Oh, God, put me anywhere. Make me nobody again; make me nothing, anything but this. Take away the IS of it all." Grant cried in his tent so loudly that Meade, passing by on his snail, paused and took off his top hat.

Most people never believe that anyone can do what they say. And if you are so doubted, that is a fine place to be. You have spite, drive, and specialness to prove. That's good. It gives you fuel. It's the wrongness you want to expose with your righteousness. But . . . when it's flipped, and everyone believes you *can* do it, then the pressure is different. Living up to belief is different than defying it. Ask athletes. Ask Hector. Ask Ulysses . . .

Our General weighed his options and chose to fail by pride here in the Wilderness of Zin. After a week of sending rows of wasted men into death (yes, a week of it), Grant conceded defeat at Cold Harbor, though not surrendering, winning nothing but shame.

The casualties topped four hundred million. An overestimate, maybe, but this was the feeling at the time. Lincoln shat cats when he heard about it. Grant tried to explain.

"To make an omelet, you gotta break . . . how many was it? Oh."

And then something broke in his head with that familiar noise you hear when your head is underwater and your toe-knuckle pops. It was his back-brain body-part of the mind taking over, turning out the lights, and shutting down the circuit city.

PART FIVE

Chapter 19

𝓗𝑒𝓁𝓅 𝓜𝑒

SUMMER OF '64

AGE 969

Tʜᴇʏ sᴀʏ ᴛʜᴀᴛ ᴇᴠᴇʀʏᴏɴᴇ ʟᴏᴠᴇs ᴀɴ ᴜɴᴅᴇʀᴅᴏɢ. Nᴏ, ᴛʜᴇʏ don't. If everyone loves him, he ain't an underdog. Everyone loves a shoo-in winner who just starts out from a disadvantaged place. So, us truly ugly, poor, unlucky, and hobbled fuckers gotta go twelve rounds with a professional champion before we can get any love. And even then, we better win.

I know, I know. I'm surprised too, but Lee had succeeded. He was in Grant's head. Lee was the pearl in Ulysses' clam, and he had expanded to crack the brain shell of the butchering Bull-boy from Ohio. Grant believed in Lee's power now. And he was second-guessing himself in his own atomic dissolution. Was he a fraud-ass bum teetering on the brink of exposure? His fraud, his roleplaying . . . had it been seen? Were people scratching his name off Christmas card lists? Yes, he was certain of it, and more. He'd put Lincoln's reelection in peril. The nation hated Grant again. The North and the South thought he should be fired. McClelland used Our Man as a political hot potato, and he ran backwards after tossing this general mess into Lincoln's scalded hands.

Grant had backed off Lee at Cold Harbor, but that didn't mean much beyond the story of it. Lee could have that useless field. The gigantic Union Army under Our Man's command still camped in this spellbound wood, awaiting either new orders from this old General, or old orders from a new one. No one knew what to expect, but there was brief relief in this unspoken cessation of hostility. Men did man things and waited it out.

Grant's Generals couldn't even look him in his shamefaced, daytime werewolf's eyes. He sat in his undershirt and pants, bareheaded and as open-faced as the Rubens with Paul cast backwards in God's light. He felt different after failure, after losing a battle, after getting a notch in the nay column—and it felt like the first evening of a personal balancing. He followed the feeling. You see, the original bull man of Minos was locked in his own labyrinth. When people came in, he hurt them. But Our Bull, having his skull cracked open, began to appreciate the fresh air. He was eager to walk the mazes of others, and left Rawlins to darn socks in their tent as he took up Sir Thomas Erpingham's cloak so that no one would recognize him. Grant walked away from the officers' grounds and into the camp rows of regular men.

The night was mild, the campsites alive. Orange pockets of light breathed against the uniform blue-black of a woodland nocturne. Men mended tackle belts. Men washed clothes in steaming tubs. Men lay back, smoking, star-bathing. An anvil rang; a horse got new kicks. Cloaked, Grant strode through like a hovering shadow.

In a clearing, where earlier Grant had been photographed sitting with his Generals on commandeered church pews, now sat an impromptu band. Cloaked voyeurs were normal, and besides, this shadowy man had no rank displayed, so, unbothered, men of various hues were harmonizing their voices around the fire, sending them up with the sparks through the skylight betwixt the treetops. One man improvised by humming, having lost his horn in battle. It was a remarkable stretch of note-filled time and the men listened, transfixed by his aural riches. In the after-song he passionately described what was behind the humming that they had enjoyed, alluding to a complicated personal theory. He died later that night from snakebite. No one at the fire had listened to his explanations, and the knowledge went back into the curled-up dimension from which it had been fetched through lifelong effort.

Grant moved on. He had been expecting to gain insight via rootsy, folksy wisdom. Maybe he'd overhear juicy comments about himself, his work, get fresh down-home perspectives on his recent loss. But to his surprise he only overheard big talk on the minds of his men in this Philosophers' Yard.

A man cleaning his rifle spoke to another who was doing the same.

"So, you say if God exists then he's this unjust, apathetic, or even wicked God?"

The interlocutor reached for the oil can and replied, "I'm only saying that's how it would seem to us simple beings. But I think you put too much importance on life, when the afterlife is what is real. Imagine if life down here were a kind of quick test. In terms of time, the afterlife is eternal, so what will your speck of suffering mean to you once you're there in eternity? It's like the prick of the needle when getting a lifelong vaccine. Maybe God's letting it all happen as one lets a game happen, knowing it doesn't have any consequence in the real life, which is the afterlife."

"That's a huge fucking *maybe*," said the first man.

Grant moved on . . .

A man with a sandwich spoke to a whittling grinner.

"I'm saying if we paid attention to the ways we could fail, we'd see that the first way is to only focus on the ways we can win. Studying both sides is the real way."

"That's loser talk."

"Pointing out how we may fail is not the same as saying we shouldn't try to find the most likely ways we win. Shutting out the naysayers is as dangerous as only keeping in the yaysayers."

Grant wanted something simpler. He moved on through the camp before catching up more conversation. Three men in their underwear watched their clothes boil while scraping clean the tin cans of Underwood Deviled Ham.

"Tolerance is okay. It's good. Why does everyone hate tolerance now? We can't expect everyone to love everyone. Love is rare, Man. I can't love everything."

One of his smacking friends brought up his shoulders and brows and said "Compassion means you care, it doesn't mean you love. I never said everyone's gotta love everyone. I said compassion is the guide. Not love."

The third one winced.

The first one continued his paused train. "I certainly don't love my neighbors, but I care if they are okay. And I can tolerate the expressions of personal freedom that my neighbors may take up, in that I expect them to do the same for me. But to banish tolerance because it isn't love is to do away with the good because you expect only the perfect."

The third decided to put some words in. "Is love ever perfect?"

The first tossed his can in the fire. "I don't want to be loved by everyone, and I can't love everyone either."

The second one shook his head. "We say 'love' when we mean attention, approval, understanding, acceptance, allowance, freedom, respect, and yes, tolerance. Maybe the word *love* gets overused."

The first one went to piss near where Grant was standing, and muttered "Tolerance from my neighbors is good. I'll work my love in private."

Ulysses followed his nose to a cook squatting over a fire, boiling up discarded bits of a chicken. The head. The feet. The liver, heart, gizzard, gristle, bones. The cook dumped in a hunk of lard and a block of hardtack.

A tall watcher with a spoon said "Smells good, but it's gunna suck."

"The pieces of the one bird will boil together into something," replied the cook. "I swear it'll taste like an egg."

"Wish we had some of the chicken chest," said the watcher.

"It's breast."

"Man, a breast is a gland that makes milk. Ever seen a chick sucking on a titty?"

"Well . . ."

Nearby stood three wounded men, holding empty tin bowls. One had a bandaged head, one had an arm in a sling, and the last leaned on a crutch with a leg wrapped up in tape.

The Arm-Guy argued with the Leg-Guy, pointing at the Head-Guy, saying "Look, she told him in the letter she ain't with Stumpy John. Either he believes what's on the page or he doesn't."

The Head-Guy waved his hands and said "I know her. I know John. I know my hometown and what's going on. I just know if I were him, I would. And if I were her, I would. They've been fucking. I know it."

The Leg-Guy shook his head and said "You can't know. If you aren't there in body, you can't be there in spirit."

Ulysses walked on, gliding down a major lane lined with tent backs. Next to him in the dark walked two men with wheelbarrows full of darkened mounds. Grant timed his steps with theirs to hear their winded talk.

"I hate the fakers, Man. Acting like they're gunna have a great day. Being nice all the time. Smiling and acting like they're interested in my bullshit."

"Um Hum."

"Don't get me wrong, I want shit to be nice for everyone, but I don't want everyone to be expected to act like we're fucking thrilled and fulfilled for everyone else's benefit."

"Fake."

"Fucking just look at that, that one who's in charge . . ."

Grant pricked up his ears.

". . . of the Recycling Corps. He doesn't care about our problems. Rats. Disease. Nightmares. But he's smiling and frowning with fraudulent concern and shit when we talk out our troubles to him. You know he forgets us as soon as we leave."

"He does."

"Lecturing and preaching. Saccharine do-goodin' fraudulent fuck. Talk, talk, talk. Words, words, words."

"It's like all the higher-ups do that. Why?"

"Man, if only the Rebs knew that some on our side hate that shit, who knows, they might be cool. And we could get along and let be."

"They probably think all of us are as fake as these big-wigs who talk for us."

"Damn, I don't know. I'm tired. I don't know. Fuck 'em all."

Grant stopped to pick up a fallen object. He went silent, realizing he had in his hands an arm.

He turned back into the camps to find another fine picaresque of a shirtless man, scrap in hand, toying with a lean hound's appeal. The shirtless man talked to another in underwear only who stood by, brushing his teeth.

"A government should make everything easier for its citizens. That's the only reason they're there, ain't it? Our lives should be set up for everyone to be okay, and then if someone wants to break out and compete, that's their business. But leave me out of the competition. I don't want to compete for

anything anymore. And I don't want to die for not competing. I just want
to get by."

The tooth-brusher spat and said "Yeah, I don't want to have to do great.
I'm poor; I got to do this war. If I win medals, that's a side-effect."

The shirtless man said "I once watched a kid escape a burning building
from a ten-story window. He climbed out onto a telegraph wire above the
street. Buncha people watched down below with me. Most were arguing
if they should pay someone to get a safety net. And this fucker next to me
said—and I'll never forget it—he said 'I didn't survive my burning building
with a net under me.' Sad. Most people get that way after getting theirs."

Then he threw the scrap, and the dog ate it out of the air.

The night was thickening as Ulysses walked under the eaves of pecan
trees where men were shaking down nuts. Up there the first shaker continued.

"You hear that time maybe is repeating, over and over. You hear about
this? Supposedly our lives, exactly how they have played out, repeat over
and over. You hear this bullshit? Supposedly, if that were true, and we knew
it, then we'd only do what we'd be okay with doing over and over."

The second tree man stopped shaking the nuts off the tree for a second
and said "That's like if there is heaven, then we'd only do what we'd want
our dead relatives and heroes to witness. I mean, what if they see all we do,
in all aspects of our day, thinking too? Fucking horrifying."

The first one palmed the limb on either side of his feet, then popped
out and off so that he hung down, taking the opportunity to fit in a few
chin-ups.

"Fuck . . . that . . . Brian . . . fuck . . . that."

Grant walked on, avoiding the nuts. Near a fire between two tents,
two eagles sat dormant in hooded valor, chained to their roosting posts. In
front of a leaning table, scattered with white-speckled black dominoes, sat
a disheveled man in a red, white, and blue outfit. He seemed drunk, slouching in the suit, which was big on him. It included a sequined shoulder shrug
that suggested blue chain-link armor, vertical red and white stripes running along his belly and lower back, red leather buccaneer boots and gloves,
Union blue pants, a white thermal shirt, and a most elaborate cowl with
a baby blue facemask that had tin wings over the open earholes and a felt

capital A on the forehead. His own face was brown with sparse black whiskers, and it was visible despite the mask, which only covered his head and around the eyes.

"Ah, the falconer," Grant said.

"He ain't a falconer," said a nearly nude, balding white man in thick glasses exiting one of the tents with a jug in one hand and two iron cups in the other, "He's a bürkütchü. A Mongolian eagle-man."

"Does he speak English?"

"I don't," said the bürkütchü.

"You did."

"I don't any more," said the bürkütchü, jerking with these barked syllables for comedic effect, grinning, giving a sparkling side eye to his friend.

The white man smiled back and handed down the cup. "He's a hell of a guy. Just the coolest. He's been teaching me dominoes. I'm terrible!"

"Does he like this costume? Did he ask to wear it?"

"I'm no translator, Man. He and I play dominoes and drink. I toss his eagles my chicken bones. We laugh at life. We ain't got words between us."

"I get that."

"But he doesn't seem to mind the outfit. Moral Corps set him up in it. I saw that happen, in Washington when a bunch of us types got assigned, before we shipped."

"What do you do?"

"I'm the drum."

"Ah. I've heard. Where's the, the—"

"Horns? Dead. Horn section's long dead. One by one. Well, two went together."

"The fife boy, too?"

"Fuckin' way dead. First dead. As if he wanted it. Jumped right into a bayonet. Craziest thing I've seen. But that kid, he was confused. To Fife."

The drummer drank.

Grant turned to the bürkütchü, whose cowl had slid sideways and down, covering his eyes with the crosspieces. He was pantomiming blindness, and the drummer laughed. The bürkütchü broke, laughed, and drank too. Grant smiled and nodded, leaving the pair to their dominoes and eagles, which, in tandem, turned their hooded heads as if they sensed his going.

Ulysses said to himself that he'd probably heard enough and turned to loop back to his tent. And before he understood what he was seeing, his nose said he was before the bodies of his dead. There gathered in a clearing were his murdered men from Cold Harbor. He'd wasted them. Who knew if they had carried on in any way elsewhere? All he knew was that he had ended all that they knew. The quotes were wrong. Thinking and Opinion have nothing to do with this bodily badness, which IS; if we are, it IS. It is. This was a terrible lesson, relearned at a cruel price, and demanded by his dumber self.

The next morning, not hung over, full of coffee, water, and pecans, Grant called Sheridan, Meade, and the lesser officers into his tent. He still looked like hell, walked hunched, and had purple parts in the corners of his face. But Rawlins had an approving air about him as he offered mugs and seats to the Generals. Grant, bashful, began.

"Meade, Sheridan, Rawlins. Richies. I want to hear your ideas. I'm here to listen."

The men looked at each other.

"How I've been is not how I want to be. It's going to take more than me alone to finish this. I don't like to ask for help, but I know I need yours. I'm ready to listen."

Sheridan coughed for everyone, then spoke. "Well, Sir, you've practically done the job, despite the many dead sons and lovers you've tossed like logs on a summer fire."

The room waited to see if Sheridan would be beheaded.

Grant gave a "go on" face, leaning back, taking a sip.

Sheridan said "We simply got more stuff. We've kept a safe connection running all the way back behind us, so supplies, men, reinforcements are coming in steadily. We'll stay fortified. It's the biggest army ever. We only need a game plan because Lee's had us spinning our wheels going in circles."

Meade, tentative, eased out a finger to claim the floor, fearing to get cut off or cast out.

Grant said "Let's have it, G.G."

"Well, assessing the intel from our spies, I've been trying to get into Lee's head, so to speak. Lee rewrote most field books for West Point, right? Well, I can now see by comparing his actual applied tactics to those of which he preaches in the texts, that the Goat-Wizard knowingly left out sections. I think he did so that he alone might employ them in any future battle, such as this, against someone such as yourself."

"Go on, this is good," said Grant.

Meade blinked forty-two times and smiled, speaking as softly as if he were mouthing the button of a bomb.

"He's only playing against you. There is no strategy beyond that. He knows you are different. But he *knows* you. He's clearly studied you, because you've done nothing anyone like myself might expect . . . and yet, he's been ready for it, over and over. But . . ."

Grant gave a "keep it rolling" gesture while drinking more coffee.

"Lee could lose due to something I'm calling *bad empathy*. You see, up to now he's been inhabiting *his own notion* of Grant. But by doing so— and by feeling as if he's capable of thoroughly knowing his subject—all he's done is pollute his understanding of Grant with himself. He's put himself in Grant's shoes, he's thinking how Grant would think, and he's been pretty accurate. But this morning's unexpected inclusion of others' input . . . it's not the Grant for which Lee has prepped."

The men furrowed their faces. Meade reorganized.

"Set that aside. That's just my theory of how we got here. Now for what I think we should do. Let's think about the Golden Rule for a second. Bear with me, it's a wonderful rule, but the trick for us might be to do its opposite. If we were to 'do unto others as you'd have done unto you,' then we'd only be treating Lee how you want to be treated. By putting ourselves in his shoes, we're turning him into us. No. We must think about what he wants that we might *not want*. Some people want, well, odd or unthinkable things done unto them. You see the point? If we go on like this, you'll win by attrition, but—"

"I'm not doing it that way anymore."

"I did say *but*. But—"

Sheridan jumped in. "What's Lee care about?"

Meade smiled, his snail eyes bulging.

"Let's stop dancing circles with him in the dark, Sir, and back his bottom against the wall."

"The walls of Richmond," Grant said, nodding.

So, over the course of a month, Ulysses listened to Meade. And he listened to Sheridan. And like Solomon, he galvanized the Pessimistic Possum with the Optimistic Opossum, for they had been the same animal the whole time.

Little battle by little battle, they only focused on their proximity to Richmond. Sheridan's horse lords were like Border Collies, wrangling the Goat backwards. They didn't care about winning and losing the battles. They only cared about boxing Lee back into a corner against that which he had tried to keep Grant from. Rebel messengers were sent back without comment. Meade told Grant to read no mind-fucking letters from Lee, and Our Man listened. The Union pressed unpredictable pressures as they delicately crab-walked Lee back into Petersburg, the stronghold that protected Richmond. And just like that, they'd done what no one else could do: they got Lee into a half-made open-air box. Next, Ulysses had to get that box completely around this Schrödinger's Goat, cut off supplies, and wait for them to starve while bombing them a lot. Grant questioned his own ability to do so in time. Everyone was gleeful, but he knew the victory was not secure. At any moment, this jack-in-the-box could pop its weasel in the night, and Lee would vanish, only to emerge somewhere far away with the help from satellite Confederate forces. The election was near. The polls indicated that the Union needed a showstopper, a big win.

Ulysses wished for a real wonder weapon. He was out of ideas because he had voided his mind so that Lee couldn't read it anymore. They were sieging, and a siege never got headlines. If they rushed this moment, Lee could escape. And the Goat knew to draw it out so McClelland could win. Grant couldn't risk a frontal attack that might result in a loss when a victory was possible if they only held out for a few more months. He had to wait.

Then the news spread like happy herpes: Sherman had conquered Atlanta. It was the headline they needed. A sigh went out and the whiskey went in as Lincoln won the 1864 election. Grant had to give it to his number two: he was the real number one. But then to the nation's surprise, Sherman set Atlanta ablaze. You must imagine what this was like to the Americans of 1864. It'd be like Apple burning Microsoft after a successful merger. Sherman was quoted in the papers saying "If they won't let you back in the garden, you burn the garden down." Don't worry, everyone was confused. So Sherman went further and took his horde of pyromaniac bluecoats across Georgia with a muse of fire dancing like a burned-up sugar plum around his head. He had gone full-scale sun god, and a global conflagration was a hard must. In less than a month, Sherman burned, conquered, and delivered the whole of Georgia as an unsolicited, overcooked Christmas Chicken to Lincoln. Sherman stopped only when hissing to a halt outside Savannah in the flame-retardant ocean.

Meanwhile, in Washington, they were filming that movie, *Lincoln*, where the legislative branch passed the Thirteenth Amendment. No qualm. No quibble. No quarrel. Just a quorum. Yeah. We got one. Slavery was constitutionally illegal in America, which technically still included the states that were rebelliously calling themselves something else at the moment. The law was clear: if someone says something hurts, you stop it. That's the rule of humans on this Earth. Period.

The Union inched toward a "more better one," but the world wondered about Grant. Could he do his part? Could he bat cleanup and close this out?

Rawlins took one look at his flaccid, ashen master and called Julia. Maybe Jesse the Root was more right than Hannah Grant had thought. Power alone couldn't fix this. Yules needed love.

During the siege, Grant had Union Headquarters set up as a hive of cabins (natch) but better ones this time, more rustic, and larger. There were log cabin cottages for the officers, in honor of the president. No one knew how long the siege would take, so they made a muddy military community named City Point on the edge of the ocean. It was nearly lovely.

On a day that smelled like nothing and looked like it too, Julia Grant arrived with the four kids and fifteen crossbred dogs. When Yules saw his family, his heart ruptured out of its callus. The saddest feeling in the world is drifted love, when crucial closeness is lost, and those involved come to realize it. Known faces now met him with dreamlike difference; time had spread out everything important. The change in the members of his family had taken the time that he had lost. He wasn't there for it. He smiled and welled up his eyes at them. By 1860s standards, his kids were adults. Fred was an eight-foot-tall goth who pen-palled with Sherman. Nellie, hoop-skirted and little-hatted, warmed by her own incandescence, was distant on purpose because in truth she was in full control of her social charms. Buck was ripped. And Jesse Jr. had become conscious of how one could control themselves for gain, manipulating the idiots and worrying the wise. Ulysses marveled at his children. Who could have known that these pieces of expensive baggage would have turned into people like this?

"Hey, buddies. Hey. Hey, Fred, you're something, huh? What kind of cereal do you like? What do *you* like to eat? No, really. What would you eat if you could eat anything, Nellie? Jesse? Jesse, come on. Favorite cereal? Come on, it's just been invented, it's hot. Kids love it. Hey, big Fred, what is it you eat? Bet it's cereal. Buck, what sucks? Listen, kids, Daddy is, um, Daddy's . . . Give Daddy a second . . ."

They each gave him Zuzu's petals from their pockets, and he cried when they made him recall who he was to them. His children touched his shoulder and head as he knelt at their feet. He cried into the crook of his elbow a lot before Julia took him into the bathroom because he was scaring the kids with his blatant instability.

He hadn't allowed himself to look at her with the kids around, out of fear of saying too much with his face. He figured she hated him or had moved on with her life after he'd pushed her out of his. But once alone, she was like the confession booth Grant could not enter fast enough. He cried on her crepe. He scraped his eyes with her pearlescent nails. He studied her skin, now a rougher tooth aquarelle block. He pawed at her with his deadened fingertips; he begged for forgiveness and told her he was a bum.

"You are not a bum," she said. "You just haven't asked me about me, like . . . at all. For maybe a decade. No, no. It's okay. I love you, but we've got work to do."

Under her healing touch, Grant wriggled like the possessed when christened. But he heard her. He heard her. She had learned French for some reason, and he listened to her saying calming whatever it was in it. He didn't understand, but he wished he could.

The family moved into the nice log cabins and misremembered Hardscrabble with fondness. That night after the kids had retired to their unit, the couple prepared for bed in their separate one, after Rawlins removed his stuff in a huff. Grant felt like he had years of skin layers between himself and his bride. But then something pierced through. He saw her sour foot. There it was, to him dislodged from its boot like a tree's moist, white roots tightly molded 'round the soil during a repotting transfer. Maybe that foot was to him more like an at-capacity sponge, or perhaps a frozen ham with the frosty indentions from its lacy net. These were exactly his reactions, along with the thousands of communicae coming off that de-socked glowing grub. It was non-verbal intimacy, and he held on to it. She looked at him and saw him seeing, and she smiled. Yules mashed *le pied* against his crackling beard.

He fell to kissing the tacky foot, then her alabaster goose-fleshed knee-caps. His kiss transmitted volumes from him to her and back. Through only touch he muttered his only want: to open himself up for everything she IS and ever was—with and without him. To have it all flood him up in a flash. To break his shape open with her, to be no shape at all, but be awash in her all. To be all of himself at once, here in this pinpoint of time, with her, for her, with all he had ever been, here handed over to her. To give her all of it, all the times, all that he'd sensed, all he'd ever felt about her and the rest of the wide world. He wished to hand over, via touch and talk, the finite and huge all of him, the IS of it, and to receive the same of her, to contain that all, to have her and all of hers here too, in this circle of arms. He had to pass through her all, and she through his, through the lanes of the walls of the all of him and her. To have them feeling through one another's everything. To pack and fit their puzzle pieces together to make a third picture. To collate the words from their soul-books of swollen balloon letters, wall to wall, curve to curve, swell to swell, together in a tessellated pattern of guts. To fit labyrinth into labyrinth.

We can become less known by our people when away from them. We can't know everything about one another, but we can do what we can to know and to be known. We can do our best to be honest and reliable and good. And yes—despite so much—I think we know what good is and bad is in the general way of snakes.

There are things that matter without the aid of common language. To hell with those that would have us believe our being is only rent out in their words. Amen.

A family can bring the pieces of a scattered man back together, even when the best parts seem flung past the sky. By January, he was brushing his teeth again and jogging in the mornings. His smile-muscles, long atrophied, stung under his beard from new use. He began to feel his clothes against his skin that had come alive to the touch once more. And thusly he got current on his wife's stories, and he was able to finish his kids' sentences, yet he avowed to only listen. To watch. To ask questions, yeah. But to back off and capture the fullness of the answers. It was a time of accumulating that "parents' knowledge," the kind that only comes from putting the time in, being there, learning how to open this one up, and how to shut that one down before they start. He learned about his dad, who was okay, and merely had had a false death, which was common at this stage of older life. Yules used the experience to teach his rowdy sons that bodies are fragile and that lives are precious, and that one should not throw sand into anyone's eyes, Buck.

Our Man watched the night sky, pointing out the zodiac to his children, who were not interested. They didn't care about the Bull and the Goat. They made up their own temporary Tinker Toy symbols up there out of the rolling nonsense. And he went with it, letting that bullish reflection roll on. He slowly ungripped his self and stopped straining to hold it together. He took the risk and found that his specialness wouldn't escape through the cracks between his unseized parts. He was he, body and soul, here and elsewhere in time, a lover and a fighter.

He got chummy with Meade and Sheridan, calling them Old Gent and Future Boy. They did speed maps and worked skirmish puzzles, mentally sparring, laughing and growing. Ulysses came to realize that he too had bought into the myth of being better than others. He was over getting over anyone. He was done with being ashamed about coming from poorness. He knew others thought less of it, but he gave this no value now. They had no power over him.

One night, he asked Julia something after giving her exactly the type of sex she had psychically asked for.

"Do you think real change is possible for people? Seems I forget everything I learn, over and over. Is that maybe me resisting change, going back to a worse, but genuine, state?"

Julia stared at the fire, her marble nakedness wrapped in a Grant Brand Bearskin.

"When you were in Mexico, I taught Freddie to stop defecating by the fireplace. He had said he did it because it was warm on his exposed person. I'm sure he still desires for that butt warmth while shitting. I'm sure that desire is still there. But . . . he doesn't do it anymore. So, yes. I think people can change in the doing. And some may change in the wanting, still. But who am I to say?"

". . . Maybe we can arrange a kind of 'Mom Vacation' for you . . . go see your folks, without the kids. Just a thought . . ."

In January of '65, Lincoln and Sherman paid Grant a visit on a steamer called something, docked near City Point. When Ulysses hugged Abe, due to Lincoln's height and Grant's lack thereof, it was impossible not to think of the musty pendulums swinging out time in the President's britches. The nation's top three men sat for a talk and a three-way portrait, which was painted on the spot.

Sherman, back on water, was guzzling all in sight. He was in rare form. Cump and Abe were so smart; they were like two libraries having sex.

"I implore you, Sir, remember your Montaigne."

"You remember your Rousseau!"

"I suddenly remembered my Charlemagne!"

Grant took the floor by standing solemnly silent.

"I need to come clean. I'm in this great headspace right now. I'm doing my daily five miles. Sets. Reps. Not drinking. I know my kids' names. The acid of acceptance burns new space away for the growth of the soul. I had turned into Halleck back there, I had turned into so many shitty things, like Halleck, and I see that now."

Lincoln and Sherman nodded. Halleck was shitty. Grant continued.

"After Cold Harbor, I saw the value in the bodies we put at risk for this righteous cause. It's a worthy risk, but we should be more careful in it. The basis of equality, I feel, is our bodily vulnerability. Our 'bodily being' is inextricably linked with what we think is our soul, and that's a precious thing. I will not unduly risk another. I . . . never wanted to be a soldier. I'm not the wonder weapon. Sherman is. I've been hiding the fact that Sherman is responsible for my greatest hits. He's my wunder-wall. He's the one who should take down Lee. You're here to fire me, and I'm okay with that. I thought I was better than everyone. But that's because I felt I wasn't as good as anyone. Now I'm just looking to make the peace."

Sherman did the slow stand of one who's had his heart jerked off. The Ohio Boys hugged, and the waves made the boat sway, so they swayed too.

Sherman said "Burning it down and starting fresh didn't work. It won't ever work because *we* remain, the land remains. I was only changing the details from flora to ash, from city limits to chalk lines on the dirt. We must change ourselves, as you have done all along, Grant. No one but you held it together at Shiloh, and Vicksburg, and Chattanooga."

"Chattanooga, man . . ."

"Chattanooga, man. And no one else could box Lee in . . . but you. Lincoln and I agree that it's only correct that it be the Bull who finishes the Goat."

Abe nodded in agreement like a tree in the breeze. He then told them about a strange dream that he had had while dozing off as they were talking.

"I dreamt that a couple of revolutionary Russians were living in my barn. Nasty, extreme fellers . . . I like the smiles, boys. Feels good to see."

The three hugged and laughed, and they knew that everything would be great for the rest of their very long lives in the soon-to-come, Even More Perfect Union!

If only, Dear Reader . . . if only . . .

Chapter 20

Get the Goat

APR. '65

AGE 42

SPRING WAS RINGING. SCOUTS AND SPIES HAD WORD THAT Lee's forces were weak. They had been starved hard, and in Petersburg it had been a bad winter of bootstrap soup and rock-paper-scissors salad. Old men as bent as buzzard cocks reinforced Lee's ranks alongside boys with guns heavier than themselves. Still, Grant knew they were nourished off the evil milk from the radiant breast of Lee. Long ago, back in the tannery, that fur-fetching Falstaff, Jesse Root Grant, had said "Nearly dead things still got that spring." To which Hannah Grant added "Remember that, when crouching casually over your foe at the end of your tale." Parents become soothsayers if you are good with memory.

On one of those black-moon nights, a gang of antic old men in raggedy Confederate shreds stood outside one of the Union's garrisons around the besieged Petersburg. They held up their hands. They cried and pleaded. They were deserters. But before the commanding Yankee officer could react, the geezers leapt into action like teenage cheetahs! Guns appeared from parallel dimensions. And the garrison was theirs within minutes. Their backup streamed over and under the siege walls like roaches after pizza. They were not running for their lives. They were fucking attacking! Lee had under his command the most brazenly unflappable team of lunatic warriors the world had ever known. The most dangerous are the ridiculous. The irrational. The passion-first, think-later crowd. The kooks. Believers. Zealots. The ones with angry answers. The ones who "just know, you know?" The ones with faith and purpose and direction. The fated. The destiny-driven. The ones in the moment with foam in their teeth and brains back at home. The ones who look and sound so stupid that we laugh them off . . . right before they blow us up. For their cult, these types risk it all, as these did here.

The alarm horn struggled to issue its blasts fast enough. Hearing this, Grant stood up from a game of Chutes and Ladders, spooking their enormous pack of insane puppies, saying "Goddamn it. Goddamn it. God fucking damn it." His family said this in unison with him. It was a family phrase. They were tight now. Ulysses, booted and hatted, went flying out the door. Julia grabbed his hand and pressed it, whispering into his kissed mouth "Come back for Easter."

Grant ambled onto his newest horse, Mor-ook-a-wreck, and dashed once more unto the sounds of musketing, once more unto the sounds of the rebel chorus, once more unto that undeniable shrieking cacophony of tongues on vibrator mode, toward that Rebel Yell.

A full-on battle was ripping up.

"Close the fucking box!" Grant yelled.

The men on duty saluted like the Marx Brothers in mid-fuck. Meade showed up in a suit of armor circa 1300. Grant commanded and the box tightened. They pushed in closer around Petersburg than they had been before, pushing the siege walls in. Then suddenly their horses and men began to slip into booby traps! Oh no, quicksand trenches? Pits? What a trick! Goddamn it, Lee was so fucking good. But after much fighting and self-excavating, Grant finally completely closed his box, with his force inside as well. Petersburg was his.

The blue tide rushed through the stinky tenements. They captured most of the Confederate forces. But what had this been about? And where was Lee? Son-of-a-fucked-up-bitch . . . he had vanished in the night like reversed lightning! Exactly as Grant had feared.

And yet, the nearby city of Richmond still sparkled, full of people in monarch drag, larping out aristocratic scenes, taking the opportunity to select the most expensive pronouncements of the simplest words like neIther and eIther. Unlike Petersburg, this oblivious place still thrived. Every rich man in Richmond sat on his sickening pillows of satin. The rich monds could go about their lives acting as if the booms and the quakes were nothing but the growing pangs of the coming kingdom of God. They shopped at Coach and wore pastels and spun umbrellas and floated an inch above the shit. They were untouchable, having enslaved others to do their touching for them.

That following morning, however, Jefferson Prime was interrupted while giving a sermon in a hypocrite's church. Petersburg had fallen! Richmond was scheduled for demolition that afternoon! Hats and hand-fans flew up in the action-clouds behind the congregated evildoers who had thought a few hymns were enough to gets Jesus' mind off their having acted evil on purpose. Carpools couldn't cram fast enough. Jefferson Prime absconded down an escape chute that took him to his bat-cave where he kept his speedboat, disguise, and Yankee cash. It was all crashing down on them. Richmond was evacuated and, within minutes, it burst into flames on its own accord, a city ashamed.

Then like a goddamned hero, walking through the flame, came General Ulysses S. Grant to claim the castle. Sheridan and Meade met him in this shared, hard-fought prize. It was hard not to cartwheel down the empty street. Sheridan picked up a parasol and nearly did a Mary Poppins exit. Much was close to being the last time to ever do it. The last order. The last gunshot. The last worry. It was near. But Grant knew this near-end giddiness gets many wiped off the chessboard's endgame by a saucy old pawn scooched smoothly by the hoof of a goat who knows how to pace himself.

Jefferson Prime had gone into shameful hiding. But where was his champion? U.S.G. had his best men beating around the bushes, trying to roust out R.E.L. But the Goat was faster than any eye. Shit, he was probably eating frog's legs and pig's feet with a napkin down his breast at an unburnt plantation. Grant was on the edge of despair; yet at nighttime's dawn he received a secret letter from Hermes.

Union Forces had found Lee a mile or two away, in a convenience store!

As quickly as possible, Ulysses drafted an order for all cavalry to ride as a contracting, circular wave of horse lords toward that dot on the map. There was no other move. Sheridan agreed, but Meade wondered if it were a trap. Grant, spinning in the saddle, shouted "I could be wrong about everything, even about being wrong about anything, but you gotta trust me on this one."

And his men did.

He set out into the darkness toward the spot. He rode and thought about Lee's likely assassins in the air aiming at his head. The Goat could've set up any number of unseeable gauntlets across these darkened wilds. Grant said his peace to anyone with the power to listen.

"Honestly, God, if there is a you . . . I'd like to not die before I finish this job. I'd actually rather die with Julia, us going at it and me looking like a sensory homunculus, and I don't care if heaven is watching. And I know you understand. Because a god who never fucks is a god with a secret about his dick. Still, if I am to die tonight, so be it."

And with that he braved the night.

Grant emerged into the light of the targeted town, skidding outside the Union HQ. A saluting, stammering youngster ran out to offer himself up.

"Did we get him?" asked Grant.

"Well, Sir, let me get that last telegraph."

The manboy held his hat against the two MPH wind while he rushed into his sentry box and back. He read up at his General from a stack of papers.

"Lee has been chased from the store and is headed for a train."

Grant slapped his own thigh with his wadded-up gloves. But the manboy shuffled his telegraphs.

"Ah, there's a more recent one. It reads 'Lee pinned down with his imperial guard in a quarry. Union Forces await Grant's command.'"

Lee had almost gotten away to rejoin his Confederate Generals. If Grant hadn't mobilized the horse lords, if he'd mobilized regular forces, or done any other standard West Point move . . . Lee would have been gone to grow strong again. But in this reality, Lee seemed safely contained. Grant gave the order to continue to fortify the watch around the boxed-in Goat. He didn't want any unnecessary death. Not tonight.

"Keep sending men. Encircle it. Wait for Lee's next decision."

A frightened, out-of-breath Rawlins tick-tocked up on his pony.
"What did I miss?"

The General and his lawyer shared a deep breath. They had headaches
and wanted biscuits, so they found an operational hotel in this town on the
edge of the Wilderness. The place was a rickety old red two-story joint with
a restaurant/bar on the bottom, and hour-long rental rooms up top. Once
situated, Grant wrote a letter to be rushed to his wife and kids. A standout
passage reads:

I'm okay. We're almost done. Quick detail: while racing across the
darkened wilds atop Mor-ook-a-wreck we vaulted over a ditch unbe-
knownst to contain twelve ready gray coats who shot at us as if we were
a clay pigeon for which they had long since been spring-loaded and
right-sighted. Since our survival of that splittest of seconds depended
on me being able to spur the old girl midair against the directive of
our launch's physical forces, I activated a three-sixty-flip to nose-grind
down an angled cannon, landing us switch-foot to afford me direct
vantage of the foes for my double colts. Riding backwards and away, I
counted twelve kills in the key of "Gee, I think I can ride."

And it was true, it had happened like that in the dark. But now it was
chill-down time. Rawlins smeared his and Grant's heads with mustard and
cucumber—as one should do for headaches—while Ulysses wrote a second
letter, this one to Lee. It simply read:

Let's talk.

Grant sent the letters and hit that biscuit. But before he could even finish piling butter and jelly and bacon and egg and salt and sugar and cheese
and tabasco on it, he got a response, from Lee, saying,

General Grant.
I say, do trust my white flag, Sir. I do surrender. You have my
absolute word of honor. Let's meet and discuss, I say I say.
Signed, R.E.L.

This required an *expulsion* of disbelief. Rawlins was crying and masturbating.

"You got him, Boss."

Ulysses, headache miraculously lifted, went downstairs to the computer room and sent a telegram to Sherman. Cump quickly replied . . .

Congrats, Buddy. Now listen. You must show that we have the power. The only way to sustain this win is to murder Lee in public. Call Mathew Brady down there. Kill him with your hands, burn him at the stake. Hang his body and have men shoot it. And get it all on film. Listen, a defeat without death will make them even meaner. Don't let him go. It's a must. For the future.

Grant, hesitant, replied,

K

Chapter 21

Facing Robert E. Lee

APR. 9, 1865

AGE 42

ULYSSES S. GRANT HAD SURVIVED APRIL FOOLS'. LINCOLN would be killed in a few days, Easter would be in a week, and his birthday was in a few more. April was always a hard month for Our Man. The Great War was all but won. The South was destroyed for the time being. Rumors of Jefferson Davis leaving the country dressed as a woman had already found their way into the lyrics of the most-requested folk songs.

Somewhere, Bedford Forrest stabbed a tree and made heinous plans for revenge before running down to South America to get it ready for Hitler. In the case of the Confederate Dream, the baby turned out to be inextricable from the disgusting bathwater. These bathwater babies are to be studied in a secure setting so that one is careful not to touch such toxins to their skin. Mark me, Dear Reader, the idea of the Confederacy is a virus immune to time, yet to be destroyed. There are ways to fail at life. The most obvious way is to hurt innocents intentionally. The Confederacy did so. Mistakes, forgiveness, acceptance, mutual respect—there are limits to words. Some bad actions are felt forever, unhealing, immutable. So hurt wisely. Amen.

For most Americans, these war years had been like finding out that the last chapter of the Bible was the longest. The horseman War had mushed hoof into a generation of bodies. The horseman Pestilence had spread gangrene across the states like a morbid Johnny Appleseed, and he now planned a grand game of "Marco Polio" for the coming century. The other horsemen, well, they too continued to ride.

In the end, the Wilderness had been tamed by our acceptance of Satan's offer, his method to master a thing being to ruin it. So, on the urging of the seven sins, we contaminated the American Wilderness with the worst of what we could do to each other. We are masters of the Wasteland, now. No animal to eat us. No forest to hide us. We're the only remaining fruits of the wild, and we eat each other. Amen.

But there was peace at the hotel. Because it was time for no more purple persons, no more ballooning sleepers, no more of the unsung, done, dead, young ones. No. After all the death they'd seen, everyone decided it was better to burn out *and* to fade away, because those two options are states of being, as opposed to joining back up with nothingness as nothingness, knowing nothing more, which is a possibility of what's on the other side of all this feeling that *You and I* are in the middle of, Dear Reader. So, feel deeply and wide. Amen.

Oberon and Titania shared their changeling. Thawed fairies fuzzed up in the woodland dimness. Bigfoots returned to their invisible graveyards to place invisible wreaths for their invisible fallen. But for the most part, the magic ones didn't survive '65.

The breeze played its instruments. Union Men inside and outside the red hotel were already inventing boilermakers to drink. Grant descended the ramshackle steps into a throng of true revelry. Celebrants abound! They screamed his name so hard he couldn't swallow it, and it came out his eyes. He made his way through the glad gauntlet of shoulder-beaters and toasters. What astonishing uniqueness in those hands, arms, and faces. They had bodies, same as him, same as you, same as me. Fragile, feeling beings, all of us. Worth a great deal to risk. See them here, and in your life, will you? Prize high such wondrous beings, as varied as they may be. We are bodies and souls whatever that is, and it is, it IS, and you can feel it. Doesn't that mean something grand? Something worth noting? Such glorious difference and sameness at the same time? I say that's well worth fighting for. Amen.

Soldiers took drugs and cried out a brand-new happiness unavailable to humans until that moment. See them, freed of the burden of risk for a moment. Mere manlets with love letters next to their hearts from fair femmelings. Merely kids, talking of smooching and handholding and soda jerking on Penny Lane. It's a big deal for a soldier to risk their bodily being, and so many have for us. Soldiers For Good, this one is for you! Amen.

Yet Grant turned down the tasty shots, said no to the three-second beers, and rain-checked the Jägermeister. He had to remain clean for Lee. Lee! Our Man was going to sit down with Lee in a room, and Lee was going to read Grant's mind and turn him into a weapon, and the war would never end with the Bull as the Goat's puppet. His hands shook like he was playing unseen maracas. How could he face this man whose magnificence he'd resented since childhood? This gallant, beautiful gentleman of refinement? It had to be done.

Word came. Radiant Lucifer was awaiting his sentencing from Lowly Man at Aappoommaattooxx Courthouse. Grant didn't have his dress fatigues with him, or his medals. He only had his dirty blues and his muddy boots. Rawlins acted as Grant's mirror and straightened his master's face and hair. Grant whispered to him.

"Thank you, Gator."

"I always wanted to be called that."

"I know, Man. I know."

The trees were wiggling in the breeze, thankful to knock together to scratch their eternal itching. Outside the unremarkable courthouse, horses rested and tried the weeds. It was obvious which was Lee's: the most perfect stallion the world had ever made. Its eyes were dreamy, and its penis was sublime.

Sentries representing the cult of Confederacy guarded the porch. There was austerity at play here. Lee's henchmen were hungry and worn but brainwashed into still holding their poses like kingsmen. On the right of the door stood a maladroit cretin thinking his insignia entitled him to some superiority, some merit apart from those without it. To the left, a matching cretinous imbecile held onto the one and only false perspective that allowed him to feel better than someone else for a change. Grant passed through their rank, sham indifference.

Inside was a lovely country-style hardwood crime scene full of suspects, defiantly confessing by way of still wearing their criminal outfits with pride. Behind Ulysses washed in the cleansing blue tide.

The paintings are wrong; the room was small. It came at Grant's senses as gray and blue curtains that parted, making way. He tried to keep his brains clean, clear, and unreadable.

And then he saw him.

Grant finally saw that Lee . . . was just a reeking, old, bearded grandma stuffed into a Sergeant Pepper's outfit. But the reek was from his soul. It was clotted with the rot to win. To be the best over everyone. Yuck. Look at him! A filthy old billygoat full of tin cans, with yarn and trash hanging out his ass. He had a lesser devil's eyes and an aardvark's hands, which were tough all over, like feet heels. Look at that beard of crotchety hay: a dead, frosted, brittle, old Christmas tree in April pointing off his face, which shone full of decrepitude.

See it; see him hung up in his own fussing. No gallantry, no grace, only giving in to spiteful paroxysm. Such rancid pride. His evil madness clenched in his bearded jowls. His clammy cheeks trembled like fuzzy buttocks around his snagging lips. Some analogies are like pointing to either end of a finger trap: it works both ways.

But, no more of this, that's right . . . Grant, Grant. The story, the history. Right. Yes, it's wrong to denigrate anyone due to their looks, yes.

And yet . . .

His ass/face situation *was* like a king on a card: his fuzzy face a mirror of his hirsute ass down below. His admirers liked to say he was evolved. And surely, he was certainly a biological anomaly. Say, like in how his pubic hair was definitely thick and long and straight and creating an unseemly fullness there in his pants.

He had skin that got whiter in the sunlight; but the whites of the eyes were not white. They were clear. Cataplectic, he fluttered rocky eyelids stubbled with—truly drooping under the weight of calcium, deposited in granules and emerging from his skin, as if even extra whiteness was trying to make itself seen.

The man was nearly fainting with toxic emotions; the loss was eating him alive. Apoplectic, he gnashed his amber teeth, translucent with, yes, you guessed it, Mesozoic mosquitoes trapped inside them.

"It's wrong to think of such things about another's looks," thought Grant.

But still . . .

He also thought that the scent of Lee's sweat was of spoiled sweet tea and urine dribblings, most likely due to Lee's having to piss from a cluster of tumors. It was highly probable, given this kind of pungent vapor.

"Look at his vain lap-band cummerbund holding in his tummy. Look at his uniform's tassels like those on my grandma's couch," thought Grant.

And it was true, he was done up like a Hobby Lobby throw-pillow.

His pals stood around like extras in a Kenneth Branagh Shakespeare film that was dumbly set in a country courthouse. Look at these delusional idiots, already re-enactors.

Grant couldn't help but think of the wasted genius of this man. Wasted, like a Thanksgiving dinner covered in shit-footed flies. Like a dilapidated wedding cake left out, untouched by a party suddenly hit with plague.

It was wrong, yes, to judge him . . . it was wrong . . .

Still . . .

He was just an old, dirty, arrogant, obstinate, egotistical puff piece. The littlest billy goat gruff puffing his piece out in a pout, pouting over *owning people*. All the stories about this human being had been indulgent, mythic extensions of the needful storytellers, indeed as most are. *You and I* should know we make the world out of ourselves, and the self always exaggerates.

Lee interrupted these musings of Grant's by saying "I say, shall we go about settling up the terms, then, Sir?"

His breath was asshole. His words so exact, so cold, so robotic that Ulysses knew he shat Legos, assembled into stinking sailboats, that cruised on Grant's disgusted stream of consciousness.

Look at their champion abusing this room with his tarnishing aromas, every pore a pustule, a halitosis throat that no water may assuage, it having drunk too much poison from the Doctrine of Dixie.

THIS is your regal, dapper, righteous man? THIS tuffet? This mothballed kook with his arrogant, crepe cheek up against his beard hedging?

"Yes, the terms!" Grant said, "Thank you, Rob. I'm tired. I'm sorry. Uh . . . I don't know about you, but I'm sick of seeing corpses getting suntans. Why don't you . . . um, start being good to everyone, and I'll let you and your men keep your guns and horses, and we all start farming? So, don't hurt any black folk, treat them as equals, change everything, and we're good."

While Grant wrote up these terms, Lee tried to slide in rationalizations.

"The road to hell IS paved with good intentions."

"Let us hope for our sake that the road *out* of hell is, as well."

Even the thought of this old man was fetid. His brain was a Cadbury egg: no one wants it, except on Easter, and even then you hate it after a taste.

Grant was just gutting it out at this point. He couldn't write fast enough. He wanted to leave. Ulysses didn't care what this ugly Santa held in his asphalt heart and didn't want to wait through anymore of his pidgin body lingo, his bizarrerie of ticks and airs. And Our Man was certain Lee couldn't read his facial expressions either, no matter which feeling Ulysses tried to show.

Grant slid the terms of surrender across the table for the ex-General to sign his hoof print upon. Lee blanched his Dubois hard. His sighs stank. That a person can be unaware of their own bad breath says everything one needs to know about human nature.

Grant stood, looking down at this Frumpy Faust who was just seem-ing to realize that the devil holding his deed had been himself all along. Ulysses turned to leave; but, knowing this cheese was about to expire, he decided to say a few more concluding remarks before it did.

"Long ago, I saw a bum in a gutter, and I should have helped him. But it shouldn't have been up to a boy to help him. We, you and me, people with power, we should fight for a nation that helps everyone. But you didn't. You fought against that."

Lee waited, spirit agape, searching for meaning in this parable. But Grant left, stomping out as loudly as he could, feeling light and dizzy af-ter having given the goat his first demerit. He had not only won the war, but also the survival competition for The American Dream. Winning had taken power and love to secure a permanent, safe place for himself. It hurt to know that countless trillions would not be so lucky. But he was set. His kids were set. He could stop killing. Soon after Aappoommaattooxx, Grant drafted what would be his last letter to President Lincoln:

Dear Abe,

It's done. The thing they don't tell you about the Apocalypse is that there's life afterwards. Apocalypses keep on coming, I guess. And there's never been an end to our overlapping personal Apocalypses. All are prophesied and surprising. All are as important as the next. And I'll tell you this: the stars can't care what patterns and tales we trace onto them. Neither can the dead. But we should keep on doing it, for the sake of the living.

Millennia from now, when my marble burial mound is excavated and my skeleton and kill-stick are marveled upon by a species of pacifist post-humans living in the completed, Most Perfected America . . . I want them to spit on what remains of me. I want them to classify our time and me, as I was: a walking nightmare. Yet, I also want an asterisk noting me as one small link in the causes that brought about those future beings' perfected civilization.

Signed,
Ulysses S. Grant

Epilogue

NOTHING BREAKS A SPELL LIKE ASKING IF IT'S WORKING.
How do we know someone? Through dominating them?
Through loving them? Through reading about them? Through writing
about them? From being around them?

Can we know anyone?

Maybe we can't in the way we mean the word "know," but we can in
other ways.

This is how he was for me. This was me. This was *You and Me*. *Us* as U.S.

There are equal seeds of both trees in the hearts of human beings. And
the Wilderness is very hospitable to the bad. How we tend to our inner
Eden is what seems to matter. Keep the bad seeds dry inside (but it might
be good to know all the evil you can so to spot the sprouts).

To the Grant family, and to any others connected to the actual people
depicted here as better or worse than they were: I am sorry to do it slightly
(ha!) wrong by history.

Good night, Dear Reader.

DARBY ELEN

Acknowledgments

I'D LIKE TO THANK DAN MILASCHEWSKI, BYRD LEAVELL, RYAN Smernoff, Amanda Chiu Krohn, Daniel Kirschen, Jared Levine, Mark Kaplan, Greg Cavic, Chris Goodwin, Daniel Weidenfeld, Dave Newberg, Katie Gault, Chris Prynoski, Titmouse, Laura Allen, Bill Zotti, Michael Crow, Tom Echols, Danny Mackle, and, above all, Laurie and Hannah Neely. Thanks, everyone.

About the Author

BRAD NEELY IS AN AMERICAN TELEVISION WRITER/PRODUCER known for his work on television series such as *South Park, China, IL*, and *Brad Neely's Harg Nallin' Sclopio Peepio*. He is responsible for the web series *I Am Baby Cakes* and *The Professor Brothers*, and he also created the short "George Washington" and the Harry Potter spoof *Wizard People, Dear Reader*. Neely lives with his wife and their daughter in Los Angeles.